# RUNNING STEEL

## JOHN STEEL BOOK 6

### STUART FIELD

*This book is dedicated to all the writers, both veterans and new. Thank you for inspiring me on my writing journey, and may you continue to inspire others in theirs.*

*Thank you.*

# ACKNOWLEDGMENTS

I would like to thank:
My darling wife, who had to endure being dragged on so much research while I wrote this.
And to Miika and the Next Chapter Team for all their hard work.

# CHAPTER ONE

CHARLES KING WAS FREE, WHICH DIDN'T SIT WELL WITH John Steel.

Steel was a British detective on loan from Scotland Yard, or at least that had been his cover story for the past year that he had worked with the NYPD.

The truth was Steel was a member of MI8, the British Secret Service. He had been sent to New York to hunt down a secret criminal organization. They specialized in arms deals, assassination, corruption, and blackmail, known as SANTINI —an organization responsible for the murder of Steel's entire family.

The investigation into SANTINI had led MI8 to believe that the organization had something planned in New York. So, of course, this meant Steel had to go undercover and work alongside the 11<sup>th</sup> Precinct. The cover story had been arranged, but a case involving a serial killer changed all that. But for Steel, it was the perfect way to integrate himself into the team because this case had SANTINI written all over it.

He had hoped to be on the first plane home once the case

was done. But unfortunately, Whitehall and Washington had thought it a good idea if he stuck around, just in case the SANTINI reared their heads again.

But the organization had gone quiet. So now, he was left hunting down arseholes like Charles King when he should be in London doing what he was paid for.


Steel's interest in King had started when MI8 had contacted him and told him to investigate several buildings demolished courtesy of explosives. Something to be expected in an ever-changing city.

However, these buildings were not due to be demolished; the explosives used had been military-grade and not for civilian contractor use. Explosives that the SANTINI organization had been known to sell. This news had gotten London's interest.

Was the bomber working for, or had dealings with, SANTINI?

Steel had used his NYPD cover to carry out the investigation, and it all led to one man: Charles King.

King was the son of a billionaire construction tycoon. A man who had come up from nothing and built and owned half the city.

However, Charles King preferred to destroy rather than create. He had been arrested for destroying old buildings around the city using explosives. Even though the buildings had been empty didn't change the fact he had used explosives and had endangered life. Luckily, no one had been killed. However, four people had ended up in the hospital after Charles King's last job.

In Steel's eyes, the man was a menace to society, someone who had been caught and arrested and should spend the rest of his smug ass life in prison. But Steel had learned that people with money and power sometimes slipped through the net on technicalities. That was why, when Steel put this case together, it was watertight ... or so he believed.

But somehow, the months of work, investigating, and gathering evidence was for nothing. Charles King sat with a broad grin as twelve lawyers surrounded him. Of course, he did. Charles was Edward King's son, the billionaire construction tycoon, a top dog in the city.

What should have been a slam dunk turned out to be a waste of time. Evidence had somehow been tainted, witnesses had changed their testimony or had just disappeared, and the lawyer from the DA's office seemed to be off her game.

The case had fallen apart.

The judge had torn the assistant district attorney apart for his lack of hard evidence and inadequate preparation. The case was lost, and King walked free.

Steel stood at the back of the courtroom, watching everything slowly crumble apart. But, as the judge told King, he was a free man. Steel clenched his fists. Hoping the act would help him run down to King and smash his face through the table in front of the judge. As the bailiff told everyone to rise, King turned to look at the door, almost hoping to see Steel's face, but found only a gap in the crowd. A roar of mumbles and mutters flowed as members of the crowd conversed over what had happened.

The lawyers ushered King and his father out the doors, and the inevitable media circus awaited. White blinding flashes from cameras lit faces as the media took picture after picture. Then, finally, Edward King spoke, thanking the jury's decision and condemning the police for trying to lock up an innocent man while the actual bomber was still out there.

Steel watched from afar, away from the crowds, blending into the shadowy backdrop of the courthouse. Steel knew King would do it again – it was inevitable. All Steel had to do was wait and catch the bastard in the act.

————

Two months had passed with no new incidents concerning Charles King. It was September, with longer days and soaring temperatures. Steel sat outside the King building, a massive monstrosity on West 42nd Street, waiting. Disguised as a homeless person, Steel peered from his perch. It was a decent enough costume that had fooled most. But Steel only needed to deceive one person, and by the look on King's face as he looked straight at him, Steel had done just that.

He first noticed how distant King looked, as though his mind were somewhere else. Steel smiled to himself as King waved down a cab and hurried inside. Steel got up from his perch and waved down another cab by standing in front of it to stop it.

'You crazy, man?' yelled the cabby.

'Look, I'm a cop; follow that cab,' Steel said, showing his shield and pulling off the fake beard.

'For real?' the cabby said with a curious look on his weathered face.

'Yes ... for real,' Steel replied, watching in desperation as King's cab disappeared into the traffic flow.

'This isn't a TV show?' asked the cabby, suddenly excited.

'On a TV show, would they drag you out of your cab and beat you half to death for wasting time?' Steel snarled.

The man sat silently as a sudden sense of panic washed over him.

'Look, catch him, and you get this,' Steel said, pulling a hundred-dollar bill from his wallet.

The cabby smiled, faced the steering wheel, put the shift

into drive, and put his foot hard on the gas. Steel was pushed back into his seat as the man sped after the other cab.

The cabby talked all the way—about how he'd seen so many cop shows and never thought a detective would actually say 'follow that car' to him for real. The man was ecstatic, but Steel's thoughts were elsewhere; for one, where the hell was King going?

The cabby drove for around twenty minutes; all the while, Steel got more nervous the deeper they carried down 11$^{th}$ Avenue.

'Where the hell are you going, King?' Steel said to himself, but loud enough for the cabby to overhear.

'Maybe he's going to a mall ... to get his ... wife a present?' the cabby suggested with a skip in his voice.

A sudden shiver ran down Steel's back. The mall—he's heading for the mall.

Steel pulled out his cell and tried phoning Samantha McCall, his partner, but there was no reply. Steel hung up and tried Captain Brant. The phone rang a couple of times before an angry voice came down the speaker.

'Where the hell you at Steel? Please don't tell me you're tracking, King?' Brant yelled angrily down the phone.

'He's heading for the new mall at Brookfield Place. I need backup,' Steel said. His brain had already calculated that he had to do this by the book, or King would walk again.

'He's probably going for a present or something. Look, Steel, I get it. He won, we lost ... just leave it alone and get your ass back to work,' Brant growled.

Steel said nothing. He just hung up and put away the cell phone. King was off to do something stupid, and Steel couldn't let that happen.

King's cab stopped, got out, and slipped into one of the entrances.

Steel told the cabby to stop behind the other cab, passed over the promised cash, and then jumped out and followed King. He was close behind but far enough away to be unnoticed by King.

Even for a Tuesday, the place was heaving with shoppers. The mall was bright and modern, with an arched glass roof, brown marble floor, and white stone pillars. The top-level held fancy fast-food restaurants and shops for people with expensive tastes below.

Steel walked in and looked around quickly, hoping to catch a glimpse of King, but found no trace. So he headed amongst the shoppers, hoping his luck hadn't run out. From what Steel had seen, Charles King was nervous about something that couldn't be good.

Steel made his way to the next floor, which had most of the various food courts. The smell of Chinese, Italian, and another he couldn't quite place, filled his nostrils, causing his stomach to rumble. Steel could feel people's eyes on him, but then he remembered that he was still disguised as a homeless person.

A sea of people waiting for food made sighting King virtually impossible, but Steel couldn't give up. Something was off, and King was volatile.

As Steel stood near the top of the elevators, something caught the corner of Steel's eye. He turned to see what had caught his interest, just in time to see security guards on the ground level rushing towards him. Steel cursed his disguise choice and went to head off the guards so they could catch up to him and give him a chance to explain.

Then Steel saw King.

King was frozen to the spot. In his hand was a large black canvas bag. A bag that he'd not had before when he had entered the mall. King stood between Steel and the approaching guards. His terrified eyes were glued to them.

'How did they know?' King thought to himself.

Steel went to call out for them to stop, but it was too late.

King had ripped open the bag to reveal an explosive device, then took something from the bag and held it high in the air. 'Get back, I'm warning you, get back,' King screamed. His voice filled with panic.

Steel didn't have a good visual of what King was holding, but he knew it was a kill switch from the guard's expression.

Slowly, the guards backed off, their weapons still drawn and held in aim. People rushed about in a panic, tripping over one another to get to one of the many exits. Steel backed off and crouched so King wouldn't see him. King was spooked enough without Steel adding to it. The four security guards remained while others tried to calm people's hysteria and get them out safely.

Steel needed a plan of action that didn't involve being blown to pieces. As he watched, the floor he was on was slowly being cleared. 'Good,' Steel thought, his gaze slowly moving back to King.

Outside, the police arrived to begin cordoning off the area and setting up a Forward Command Post. Soon the bomb squad would be there along with fire and ambulance crews. Not forgetting the wave of press that would undoubtedly make things a thousand times worse with media coverage.

———

'It's OK, sir. We can work this out. Nobody needs to get hurt,' said one of the guards.

'Get back ... stay back ... I'm warning you,' King screamed, waving the kill switch about so the guards could see it, his thumb tightly on the button.

Steel remained crouched and watched everything. King's

demeanour was all wrong. He was panicked, out of control ... frightened. Perhaps because he had been caught, it made sense. People like him derived power from anonymity and the fear of others. Now that was over, he was cornered and out of options. But what was he doing in the mall with the bomb? It wasn't his MO.

'Drop your guns and kick them over here,' King ordered.

The guards complied, their hands raised above their heads, looks of fear covering their faces. King looked around to see the mall was emptying. A glimpse of realisation came over his face; he was losing hostages.

'Everybody on the ground, *now*,' King yelled, grabbing a gun from the ground and firing two shots into the ceiling.

Glass fragments fell from the shattered ceiling, smashing on the ground below; it stopped a group of people who had ventured too close to Charles King. They screamed in terror and lay on the tiled floor, trying to make themselves less of a target.

'You ... get over here and join them,' King said, waving his gun towards the guards in front of him as if directing the twenty-five unlucky souls who didn't make it out in time where he wanted them. The people got up from the floor and quickly obeyed, running to the guards. Their eyes were wide with fear, women and children crying, thinking this would be the last day they would ever see.

'Now, everyone ... get your asses on the ground ... spread out so I can see you all,' King directed, wiping the sweat from his brow.

The weeping crowd of hostages complied. Then, sitting cross-legged on the cold marble floor, eyes fixed on King and that wireless kill switch in his left hand.

Steel moved around the upper floor, ensuring he was out of sight. The hostage situation made Steel's plan fall apart, but he had somehow expected it. King was smart, a survivor. Unfortunately, the whole situation went against everything that King was. Steel could understand taking a hostage at gunpoint, but using a large bomb to level a small building? It went against his character.

'You,' King yelled at one of the security guards, 'How do you lock this place down?' The guard went to mumble something but was stopped by another guard.

'He doesn't know; he's just started,' said an older guard.

'But *you* do, I bet?'

The man nodded.

'Then what are you waiting for? Lock it down, now,' King ordered.

'I can only do it from the security room,' lied the guard.

'Well ... you better hurry. You have five minutes; if you're not back by then, I'll start shooting people,' King said, pointing the gun at different people, making them flinch in terror.

The guard quickly rose to his feet and ran towards the escalators.

Steel watched the display—King was getting bolder, more organized. He felt a sense of power, and once it was locked down, he would be damn right dangerous. Once those security gates came down, the police would have little chance of getting in without alerting King due to the alarm system.

Steel had to find a way of defusing the situation and get that trigger away from King. One mistake would put innocent lives at risk.

———

Outside, the media were already telling the story of how the recently acquitted Charles King had a bomb and several hostages. The media circus was filling up by the second, along with people with cameras and cell phones. Police cars and vans from the Hostage Rescue Unit created a boundary so the cameras couldn't catch any Command Post—or CP—footage. For now, the police were in charge. But soon, the Feds would arrive in their blacked-out vehicles, taking control, playing the whole *domestic terrorism playbook* thing. But in the meantime, snipers, spotters, and entry teams were put into place, awaiting orders. Everyone was looking for a peaceful solution. The press waiting for a story.

Steel noticed more and more people who weren't quick enough to get out moving around the top floor. More lives hung in the balance. Steel showed his shield and told them to get close to the other side of the mall and get out through any exit possible. Telling them to take others that they found with them. But Steel didn't have time to play shepherd to stray people—he had to get to the security room and talk to the guard.

———

Steel found his way to the security office. The guard was busy closing the shutters but ensuring he left the parking lot until last. A security monitor showed people still herding through the exit, the guard giving them time to escape.

'Nice job,' Steel said, causing the man to turn.

'Who the hell are you?' asked the guard, spinning around in his seat and looking for the crazy guy from downstairs.

'I'm NYPD,' Steel replied.

'But your British?' said the guard with a look of distrust.

'I'm on loan from Scotland Yard.'

'You got ID?' asked the guard.

Steel scowled at the man. 'Seriously, we are doing this dance while an arsehole is a downstairs, trying to hold everyone hostage with a bomb?' he growled. His accent was British, but his voice was neutral. It is a product of being in the Army, where all accents are made neutral after a time, sometimes making it hard to tell if someone was from Scotland or England.

'Look, I'm here to try and get everyone out,' Steel said.

'Thank God,' replied the guard, looking at the ceiling and making a prayer gesture.

'Oh, don't do that just yet ... it's just me,' Steel said with a shrug.

'Wait ...' The guard suddenly realized something. 'You're the bum we were told to toss out.'

Steel shrugged again. 'Guess it's lucky you didn't,' Steel said with a smile.

'How's that?' The guard had a confused look on his face.

'Because I'm going to get everyone out of this alive,' Steel said sternly.

He watched as Steel grabbed the first-aid box and began sorting through the bandages.

'Is someone hurt?'

Steel took one bandage and unrolled it with a smile. 'No ... this is for ... something else.' He rushed over to the monitors. 'How long do you have?' Steel asked.

The guard looked at his watch. 'Two minutes.'

'You better go and try not to let it slip you saw me. I don't want to get him any more agitated.'

The guard nodded in agreement and took off. Steel looked at the monitor just in time to see the final escape route close. He knew he had to get this right, for everyone's sake. Steel headed back to the overwatch and onto the ground floor. He needed a distraction to catch King off guard, something subtle ... but then, Steel never really did subtle.

He pressed redial on the cell phone's display, taking out his cell; he needed to talk to Brant quickly. Steel knew the police would want to take a shot at King the first chance they got, but they didn't know that King had a kill switch.

The phone rang for a minute before Brant answered with an excited voice. 'Please tell me you're *not* in there,' Brant said, his voice trembling as though expecting bad news.

'Would it make you feel better?' Steel replied calmly.

'Not really. What we lookin' at?' Brant was unsurprised by the answer.

'Well, King has around twenty-five hostages, a big black bag with a device of some kind in it and ... oh, did I mention the wireless kill switch?' Steel said in an amused tone as if trying to lighten the mood of the bad news ... but Brant wasn't laughing.

'A friggin' kill switch?' Brant asked, hoping he had heard it wrong.

'Look, captain, I have a plan, but I need a distraction.'

'What kind of distraction?' Brant asked, rolling his eyes, almost fearful of the answer.

'Fire alarm and sprinklers would be good,' Steel replied.

'I can't authorize that?' Brant declared, knowing full well someone would, but the city would get the bill for damages.

'Sorry, Alan ... I missed that ... it's rather loud here.' Steel spoke as if they had a bad connection.

'I can hear .... no...wait. Steel?' Brant yelled, but it was too late.

Steel pressed the fire alarm button and ran back over to the glass wall of the balcony. There was a sudden burst of an alarm; the noise was deafening. Orange strobe lights began to blink, and all the emergency lighting came on, showing the nearest exits.

King looked confused; then he gazed up as water began to cascade from the sprinkler system. He glanced at the people on the ground. None of them had moved. He then thought about the security guard, but he had returned just as it had started—

so, who had set off the alarm? Then he heard a noise from above. He turned and looked just in time to see a homeless guy landing on top of him.

Steel rolled and was up on his feet in a flash.

King was dazed from the impact as if he'd been hit by a truck. Slowly, he forced himself to get to his feet. But Steel was waiting for him, watching the man rock back and forth like a drunk. Then, just as King was almost standing straight, Steel hit him—with a powerful clenched fist to the nose.

Everyone watched as King was ripped off his feet and landed hard on the tiled floor, making a dull, sickening thud. Before King could recover, Steel grabbed King's hand and started to wrap the bandage around it. Steel made sure the bandage was tight, fastening King's grip onto the kill switch, locking the thumb into place, making it impossible for King to release the trigger.

'Handcuffs,' Steel said to the security guards. The men tossed over their cuffs so Steel could secure King to a bench leg.

'Don't go anywhere,' Steel said to King.

King bared his teeth in contempt, his eyes red with anger. Steel looked over at the security guard who had activated the lockdown and nodded to him. It was a silent command. As though a prearranged signal had been given. 'All clear.' The man doubled back to the security room to release the security doors, giving the police and Special Reaction Team—or SRT—an entrance.

Steel smiled as he saw the guard disappear, and the other guards ushered the hostages back towards the nearest exit. No one was risking sticking around just in case King got free.

Steel looked down at King. He seemed small, no longer the big confident man he had been earlier. King lay there, his arms cuffed to the sides so he couldn't tear off the bandage. Steel had thought about breaking the fingers of his left hand, but some might class that as excessive force. So, Steel went for another option and knocked him out instead. It was another mighty fist to face, but from the side this time, it had the same desired effect of knocking King's head backwards with such force that he smashed his head on the wall behind him. Lights out.

Steel looked around; the guards were doing a good job getting people out. Soon, the cops and the bomb squad would be there. King was subdued, and the weapon would soon be disarmed; all was right with the world.

Steel walked over to the glass frontage and looked out across the bay. The sun was bright, and the sky a cloudless blue. A tiny sound like a stone hitting a windscreen was followed by a massive burst of energy from behind Steel, heaving him forwards through the window. Everything went black.

———

Brant looked at the cell phone in his huge bear-sized hands. Had Steel just hung up? He rushed to the command wagon; he needed to speak to the agent who had just arrived on the scene to take charge.

'My guy inside said King has a kill-switch and a big-ass bomb, so no snipers,' Brant said, moving in between the other people from the agencies.

Inside the command vehicle, a man sat at a communications desk and relayed the information to the teams.

The agent, who had identified himself as Headley, said nothing. He just sat there and looked at Brant with a cold expression and Ray-Ban sunglasses concealing his eyes.

The noise from the fire alarm made everyone look over to the mall.

'Um, that's my guy's distraction. He's going to try something,' Brant admitted.

The agent gave Brant the stare again before getting up and walking away to make a call. Brant closed his eyes and looked up to the heavens, praying it all went as Steel had planned.

The explosion rocked the mall and shattered the windows of nearby cars and buildings. Brant looked over in horror as a colossal fireball rose from the shopping centre. Fire trucks and ambulances raced over, as well as the police teams. No one thought of personal safety, only getting the people out. Brant followed, his heart in his mouth. Something had gone wrong. Had Steel missed his mark and paid for it with his life and the others?

Fire crews got to work to contain the fires while the HRT teams breached the building, searching for survivors and possible accomplices. Alan Brant moved around the front of the building where the blast had originated. If Steel had gotten out, he would be there, possibly sitting by the water's edge, waiting for a chewing out. Brant stopped suddenly at the sight of a homeless man's body lying amongst broken glass and burning debris. Brant yelled for help before rushing over. Brant rolled him over to find Steel in disguise.

Glass shards were embedded in the suit, and he had cuts to his face and hands. Steel was breathing but unconscious.

'Medic, I need a medic over here,' Brant yelled, then he looked at the burning wreckage of the mall. Bodies were mangled by the blast, and a crater where the device had once been. Brant looked at Steel and shook his head.

'What the hell did you do, Steel?'

# CHAPTER TWO

Two months had passed since the mall incident, and life had gone on as it always did. People went to work, school, and college. Tourists came and went. People went about without a plan, just their daily routine, except for the shadowy figure that held the woman in its gaze.

The Sentinel had been observing the woman for some time. Alison Kline, forty-two years old. A single, career woman, a lawyer. It was a dull day, with grey clouds looming overhead with a promise of cold winds and possible showers.

———

It was late November, and most of the trees had shed their golden foliage; winter was not far away, and bone-chilling winds and snow showers would come with it.

But today, it was a fresh twelve degrees with a slight easterly breeze.

Alison moved with the busy New York Street. Her brown Burberry coat wrapped around her tightly to keep away the chill. It was 12:22. Alison made her way to the coffee shop across the firm's road, her favourite place at this time of day. Inside, Alison ordered a caramel cappuccino with cream and a chicken wrap to go.

Alison didn't know she was being watched or had been for a week.

But The Sentinel saw everything she did. The way Alison ran her fingers through her long brown hair. How she wore the skirt suits to every meeting; today, it was grey with a sky-blue blouse and a pair of black Christian Louboutin platform shoes. And how Alison had slipped into that Victoria's Secret black lace number she'd gotten two days ago.

The Sentinel took note of everything Alison did. How she dressed, how she went to work, how she made love to all those men. Her life had been catalogued and studied like an experiment. But she was more than that to The Sentinel: she was a name on a list.

Alison took her lunch and left the coffee shop, heading back to her office across the street. The traffic that day was maddening as everyone rushed to get somewhere.

Alison used a crowded pedestrian crossing, holding on to her lunch as if it were made from gelignite. Avoiding the oncoming traffic of people by swerving and dodging the hordes of pedestrians.

Alison made it safely to her building with an exhalation of relief and headed inside. She said hello to the two security guards at the desk and used the elevator to get to the third floor. It was another quiet day at Alison Kline's office, the top attorney at a reputable law firm.

Alison placed her lunch and moved the mouse on her desk to reactivate her computer from the power-save mode. The screen returned, showing a calendar of appointments she had throughout the week. Today was Saturday, not much on, but

Tuesday was full. Including preparation for a big case on Friday. This meant lots of working late at home during the night. Alison noted plenty of wine and takeout food from Tuesday onwards on the jotter next to her keyboard.

The Sentinel moved a small laptop around for a better view. The picture on the screen was Alison at work; the feed was from a camera hidden in one of her office's strip lights. The Sentinel zoomed in on the computer screen and then the jotter. Finally, The Sentinel took a screenshot of what was written on the yellow legal pad.

The final phase of a plan was coming together.

The Sentinel had cameras everywhere: Alison's work, home, and even her car. The Sentinel paid close attention to Alison and her lifestyle. *Very* close attention. After all, reconnaissance was crucial, especially if you were going to get rid of someone in public without ever being there.

---

Dark clouds loomed over the Manhattan skyline, and flashes of lightning flickered in the distance. The clouds appeared heavy, but not a drop of rain fell. Instead, the streets were full of midday travellers, tourists, and workers searching for that diner or fast-food stand to grab a quick snack. Long silver mobile dressing rooms and sound studios lined East 40th Street, setting up another big production, hoping the weather wouldn't break.

People walked past with interest, hoping to catch a glimpse of a movie star or at least find out what was about to be filmed.

The Sentinel was clad in a long black hooded trench with black cargo trousers and military-style boots. Black leather gloves met with black leather gauntlets. It had been quite a look in some places in Europe in the 1800s or even now.

The figure moved fluidly through the streets, almost as if

they were made from the mist. The Sentinel didn't rush or push past other pedestrians but moved lithely and blended in with the masses.

The crowd walked past an alleyway, and the figure ducked in unseen as if it had never been there. The Sentinel moved through the alley, then got on to the next street before heading back up the street to a hotel. Looking around, The Sentinel ensured no one was following before ducking through the hotel entrance.

The inside was gloomy, but streaks of light from the windows revealed dust particles in the air. It was an old hotel, a pay-by-the-hour and no-questions-asked kind of place. Perfect for what The Sentinel needed. The figure moved to room 213. Faded, peeling wallpaper from the eighties barely hung on the walls, and what used to be red carpet was dark, stained, and walked flat. Despite all this, it was a place for low-rent people. Some people had made arrangements with the owner and had a lease. It was a steady, cheap income, so the guy didn't mind.

The Sentinel opened the door to room 213 and went in. Inside was a short hallway leading to the bathroom on the right. Down past, this was a big room equipped with a small kitchenette comprising a small sink, a tiny workspace that held a coffee machine, and a single electric cooking plate. This was next to a built-in wardrobe on the back wall of the bathroom. Directly in front was a long, dirty glass window with orange and white patterned curtains.

To the left: a desk and a small cheap flat-screen television. A double bed with a dated orange bedspread sat against the right-hand wall. The bed had two bedside cabinets; each had a snaking aluminium lamp that came through the side of the bedhead. It was clean but required updating. The wallpaper was from the late seventies, brown with orange cut-out triangles, and the carpet used to be cream but was now a greyish colour. It wasn't the Ritz, but it was all that was required.

The Sentinel moved towards a desk facing one of the back walls. On the workspace were a computer and printer. On the wall next to the workspace was a large board. Several photographs of Alison Kline, a map of the locations she frequented, timings at each site, and distance from one place to another. Alison was the perfect target. She stuck to a routine to the second. Her compulsive nature was part of her reputation; it would also be her undoing.

The Sentinel took a memory card from a camera and placed it into the computer. There was a gentle hum. It started to download Alison's surveillance photos taken throughout the day. Some included photos from the night before and the grey-haired man in her bedroom. With a mouse click, the printer started to spew out photographs.

The Sentinel stood, walked to the kitchenette, opened the refrigerator, and pulled out a carton of orange juice. Taking several mouthfuls, The Sentinel then placed the container back. Next, The Sentinel plugged the camera into a power socket and headed for the bed, moving back to the table.

It would be a while until Alison would venture out again. So, The Sentinel decided to get some sleep. And if Alison did make an unscheduled visit somewhere, The Sentinel had Alison's phone tracked so she would find her or at least learn where she had been. The gentle whir from the printer was soothing to The Sentinel, almost like those ocean machines to help someone sleep. But The Sentinel didn't have any problems sleeping; it was the nightmares that The Sentinel feared.

# CHAPTER THREE

It was several months later. After the incident in the New York shopping mall, London ordered Steel to take extended sick leave. This was to rest his injuries and give him space from the NYPD.

In his report to the head of MI8, a man known only as CO, Steel insisted that his time in New York was over with no further signs of SANTINI. Steel suggested that he should return to Britain for reassignment.

CO had agreed that his time was best spent doing his job with the Secret Service, not playing detective and eating doughnuts. London was satisfied with what had occurred, but they were still puzzled about how the bomb had detonated.

Steel had thought there might have been a second person involved, someone with an electronic detonator, just in case something went wrong. However, London had dismissed this theory and thought it more plausible that the device had a fault.

The skies above Barcelona were watercolour splashes of red and purple on a cloudless canvas. Barcelona's streets were filling with people, commuters heading about their business, and flocks of tourists who wanted an early start.

Freshly fallen leaves danced along clean pavements, and the fountain display roundabouts lay dormant and unlit until later that evening.

The city streets were filled with a mix of modern and turn-of-the-century style buildings—breath-taking architecture. Christmas lights hung from lamppost to lamppost across the streets, dressing up the roads and making fantastic photo opportunities during the dark of the evening. The cries of seagulls mixed with traffic sound as they swooped and danced in the perfect blue heavens.

Even though it was November, it felt like a British spring morning. It was nine degrees at seven in the morning, with the promise of high teens later in the day. So, the heat would be warm but not uncomfortable.

Steel had been up for hours; the truth was, he had hardly slept at all. His flight had gotten in around eight o'clock the evening before. After a fantastic meal in a local restaurant, he'd headed off to the casino to try his luck.

The modern casino had been loud, more Las Vagas than a quiet room, with people in tuxedos. Steel had played a couple of hands at the poker table and won around two grand, then lost a couple of hundred on craps. He was there to unwind and blow off some steam. His last case had been tough, and he needed some time alone.

He had left without warning. No goodbyes or news of where he was going; he'd just disappeared two months ago after being sent on sick leave. Steel had used the time to sort out his father's company back in Britain and recuperate from the shrapnel they had taken out of him. The costume he had been wearing was padded on the upper body, so he had taken several shards to the legs and arms. Just more scars and bad memories to add to his collection.

Steel could hear Captain Brant of the 11th Precinct yelling and cursing. But Steel didn't care.

At that moment, he felt nothing apart from the warmth of the sun and a fresh, subtle easterly breeze on his skin. Steel smiled as he walked off, the stiffness caused by the long flight and the lack of sleep from the night before.

Steel was dressed in black, the suit and shirt he had bought at a local store, which still blended in during the day without looking like he'd spent the night in it. He took off his jacket and slung it over his shoulder. Steel decided to take the route near the beach. It was over a half-hour walk, so he thought he'd make the most of it. The sea breeze continued to feel good against his skin, and the sound of the ocean was like soothing music to his ears.

The sidewalks near the seafront were almost clear at that time in the morning, less for joggers, dog walkers, and the occasional person who wanted to watch the sunrise. As he casually walked towards his hotel, Steel could feel the wondering gazes of women on him as they headed to their places of work. He had to admit that he did look good for a guy who had only had two hours of sleep on the plane. Steel put it down to the suit, tanned skin, and the twelve o'clock shadow he had going. He had left his cell phone and unique sunglasses back at the hotel but wore contact lenses to hide his green eyes.

Here he was, just Steel on vacation. He didn't even feel much of a British Lord. Let alone an NYPD Detective. *Lord Steel*. The title made him laugh every time he heard it. But, of course, he wasn't Lord Steel; his father had had that honour. As far as he was concerned, that died with him that fateful day. But Steel was, if anything, an honourable man. A man who believed in everything that people didn't want to get involved in, such as duty, code of honour, and keeping up tradition. For that reason, he kept the title he'd inherited and carried on the family business. So not only did the multi-billion dollar company give him a little extra capital but gave him access to some exciting toys.

Steel had to admit that the title did have some perks, such as the best hotel rooms and not waiting in line in busy restaurants, and of course, it proved a massive hit with the ladies. But as much as it was a blessing, it was a burden. His whole job was to blend in and disappear when required. He was trained to be a ghost, and someone shouting out his name and trying to photograph him could blow that whole thing out of the water. So, he kept to himself and indulged in the press a few photographs when he was back in Britain, dealing with the family business. But all that seemed irrelevant at that moment. Steel was hungry and tired. All he needed was coffee and a good breakfast.

Steel made his way past the harbour that housed expensive yachts and catamarans and headed for a footbridge that connected the main footpath with a sea view mall to his left. The building was a multi-level glass, concrete, and Steel construction, with wooden decking flooring up to the main entrance. Steel glanced at it and moved towards a towering statue of Columbus, which stood on a decorative column of stone and weathered bronze.

Steel was enjoying his first holiday. Sure, he had time off in the Army, but he had always spent that time with his dear wife, Helen. So, now, he was alone except for the people watching him. At first, he had thought it was MI8 keeping tabs on him. But these were different; these were company people. Steel figured CIA.

Steel hadn't done anything about them. Why should he? So far, all they had done was follow him. He kept checking his room for cameras or listening devices but always came up empty. So, were they there for him or someone else? Or was it a mere coincidence?

But Steel didn't like coincidences. He believed in them, but it didn't make them less tiresome.

Following the street, he passed several government buildings. Structures that, despite their unkempt state, still held a grand elegance. He was heading left, following the natural curvature of the sidewalk, past the World Trade Centre to a curved pale stone building near the water's edge: Steel's hotel.

About twenty feet behind him, a man in a blue tracksuit and black hair, pretending to jog, followed Steel all the way.

As he entered the lobby, he felt an invisible pull, as if his bed were summoning him. The lobby's ample open space was full of people checking in and out. Still, three people positioned on a long sofa caught his eye: two bulky men and a tall woman. One of the men wore a grey suit and had a serious look.

At first, Steel thought nothing of it. He was too tired to care. Besides, they would be there for someone else if they were suits from an agency. So, Steel put them down as private security for one of the many rich people staying at the hotel.

They couldn't be there for him because nobody knew he was there. Steel hadn't even known he would be there until he boarded the flight the day before. It was a last-minute decision, one he was enjoying.

Steel waited for the elevator while ensuring he kept the three in his line of sight using various reflective surfaces. They just sat there and looked ready to pounce at the first sign of trouble.

'Nice way to blend in, lads,' Steel said, joking.

The suite was lavish and modern, with a wooden floor stretching throughout the open plan. A small lounge area was doglegged to the right of the sleeping area. Directly in front of the bed was a balcony and a panoramic view from a huge arched window.

For Steel, it was more about the view than the price, something his mother had always taught him and something he still aspired to do. He tossed his jacket on the bed in the hotel suite before collapsing next to it. His eyes felt heavy, the bed soft ... and the next thing was inevitable ... as Steel fell into a deeply troubled sleep.

———

Three hours had passed when Steel woke to the sound of housekeeping entering his room. The woman was in her late twenties and quite attractive from what Steel had seen through blurry eyes. She had long raven-coloured hair, straight and unstyled. Her white uniform hugged her athletic figure.

'Oh, sorry, I didn't think anyone was in here,' the maid gasped. 'I'll come back later.'

'It's fine,' Steel said, heaving himself off the bed. 'You go ahead and clean. I am off to take a shower anyway.' He stepped into the large bathroom.

The woman thanked him and watched. Her eyes widened as he took off his shirt, revealing an athletic, muscular frame. But her gaze was fixed on the six-round scars on his back. Three formed an odd V-shape from his shoulders to his lower back. Three more were at the centre of his back in a curious design, almost like the number one. The door closed, and she shuddered to think what he had been through; then she smiled, considering that tight muscular back and wondering what the rest of him would look like naked.

———

Steel turned on the water, took off the rest of his clothes, folded them neatly, and placed them on the toilet seat. He looked in the mirror as it started to fog up due to the steam from the scalding hot water, noting how tired he looked, with bloodshot eyes and a day-old beard. Steel gazed into his soulless dark-green eyes, hoping to make the memory of the last case go away. Wishing he would wake up and find it was seven months earlier ... that London hadn't given him that case.

Steel closed his eyes tight and then opened them again slowly, gazing back into those lifeless eyes. From the other side of the door, he could hear the cleaner hoovering and a couple of knocking sounds which he put down to the woman hitting the furniture. He climbed into the shower and stood under the cascading water. Letting it hammer his tight muscular frame.

# CHAPTER FOUR

AFTER THIRTY MINUTES, STEEL EMERGED FROM THE bathroom. The room smelt of cleaning sprays, and a fresh breeze blew through the open window.

He didn't have much planned for the day, possibly a pleasant walk around the sites or a stroll along the beach. After all, he was on vacation. So, why should he have a schedule or plan?

That was until he looked over at his computer and saw the maid had left a brochure for the Montserrat Monastery. Steel picked up the thin folded brochure and opened it. A message was written in thick black ink: **15.00 today at the restaurant with a lower-level view**.

Steel screwed it up and tossed it into the wastebasket as he headed out the door. Before the door had time to lock, Steel returned and retrieved the paper ball and placed it in his pocket.

'I knew this trip was going too bloody well,' Steel cursed, heading back out the door. Walking down the corridor, he saw a maid cleaning a room four down from his.

'*Hola, bon dia*,' Steel said.

The woman turned around and responded with a smile, but it wasn't the woman from earlier. Steel smiled and made his way to the elevator. He didn't know who had sent her but was glad they had. It was nearly one o'clock, and there was a long way to go.

———

Because of his lack of time and local knowledge, Steel had to take a taxi to Placa de Espanya station, northwest of his hotel. The driver was initially from Nigeria but had settled here twelve years before. The man was chatty and friendly, pointing out local features and explaining which train to take to the Monastery.

They got to a massive roundabout with an ancient statue in the centre. To the left were two immense red-brick towers which came to a pinnacle, and beyond this, on a hill, was the MNAC, a grand-looking building reminiscent of a castle.

The underground station was bright and clean, with plenty of ticket machines; a woman in a red shirt darted from person to person, helping them get the correct ticket. After buying his round-trip ticket, Steel headed for the platform, towards the Aeri de Montserrat. The journey by rail and then the cable car to the top would take just over an hour, giving Steel time to catch up on the unread messages on his phone. He wasn't surprised that he hadn't any from the precinct. If anything, there would have been one from Brant telling him he was fired, but not even Brant actually had that power.

Steel had been assigned to the 11<sup>th</sup> Precinct. He wasn't even a cop as. He was something else, something the others didn't know about, nor could they.

After an hour, he looked up at a sign for his station. From

there, it was a minute's walk through an underpass to the cable car station. Steel made his way out of the station and towards the platform. The view before him was breathtaking; the grey mountain range loomed over a small village. A distant main road passed alongside the river that separated them.

The sun was at its highest point, and the heat was bearable thanks to a constant cooling breeze. Steel showed his ticket and climbed aboard the small yellow cable car.

Inside was like being in a greenhouse. The glass from the windows reflected the sun onto travellers. However, the magnificent view made them forget the heat, and cameras and cell phones took picture after picture. Steel just stood and held onto the rail. It was a remarkable sight, but his mind was elsewhere. Who was he going to meet, and what was the mission? The car swayed with the momentum of travel. The sound of metal-on-metal as the gears and winches pulled them along. Despite this, the ride up the mountain was tranquil. The chatter was minimal, less for the inevitable oohing and aahing.

Steel smiled as he thought back to the maid and hoped he would see her again, this time over dinner and drinks. Unfortunately, her poorly fitting uniform and the lobby suites made him suspect she wasn't a real maid. Steel wondered which agency she belonged to. He had sent a photo of her to a friend in Whitehall. He had taken with his specialised sunglasses when he spoke to her. He loved gadgets, but sometimes he missed the times when he relied on his own intellect, cunning, and ingenuity.

If she was CIA or FBI, he would soon know. He'd considered she was simply meant to go in, leave the brochure, and possibly go through his stuff.

Steel looked over as the car began to slow and creak, as brakes and gears worked to bring the vehicle to a halt. The passengers moved out of the small yellow box, stopping at the large opening of the station to take in the view.

Tiled steps led to the exit from the station house and onto a long winding pathway that led downwards to a long winding path; it ended on the main road leading to the Monastery.

Steel took a path that led upwards, around the side of the cable car house. The view on his left provided a fantastic view of the world below. To the front, surrounding the monastery, was a towering mountainside. These were reminiscent of looming mythological gods, giving Steel a strange and uncomfortable feeling.

At the top was the main street. This held another station for the monorail that led to the very top of the mountain. There was a restaurant with a gift shop, but neither was what Steel was after. The card had said *the restaurant with the view*, but this one was back against the mountainside with no real view.

Next to the road was a billboard map that revealed the location of a second restaurant. It was further up, on the mountain's edge, giving the customers a clear view of a vast landscape below.

The Monastery was a set of modern and ancient buildings that created a dramatic, awe-inspiring image. Steel stood and looked out across the vast, green expanse of Catalonia. The landscape was beautiful, but he didn't have time to stop and take it in; he had a rendezvous with someone. Who? He could only guess.

Steel followed the signs for the restaurant as he waded past tourists taking photographs and movies on their cell phones. But Steel was invisible to them, a blur in the corners of their eyes, which suited him just fine.

The restaurant was big enough to accommodate large groups. The place was modern with a tiled marble floor and brown compressed wood furniture on stainless-Steel legs. On first impression, it could have been a self-service restaurant anywhere in the world, but one with a view. Above was an outdoor seating option, but Steel thought this might be a little crowded for the sort of meeting that had been arranged.

He found a table with its back against a wall, facing the only door; he preferred to see what or who was coming while he enjoyed a cappuccino.

Steel watched people as they went here and there, some in large groups and others on holiday. But none stood out as being alone, only him.

'Is this seat taken?' asked a familiar voice.

Steel looked up to see the woman who had pretended to clean his room. He smiled and stood, beckoning her to sit.

'Thank you, kind sir,' she said with a smile.

She looked very different in black cargo trousers and leather-strapped boots, which came to the bottom of her knee. Her top was a thin cotton blouse with a crossover opening and long sleeves, and her black hair was tied in a ponytail.

'I take it the maid's job didn't agree with you,' Steel joked as he took a sip of coffee.

'I don't know; it had some perks,' she said, returning his smile.

'So, who sent you and why?' he asked with a curious smile.

'Straight to the point. He said you didn't mess around, well with words anyway,' she joked. 'Stanton sent me.' The smile and playful gaze became severe. 'There is a problem back home. After your little meltdown in New York a couple of months back, he wanted me to see if you were OK to do the job.'

'And am I in my right mind for the job?' Steel almost hoped she would say no.

'Mr Steel ... John ... if you weren't, you wouldn't be on holiday.'

'You say that like holidays are unusual.'

'For you, yes, very. Apparently, you've never been on one,' the woman said, wearing a look as though she had many questions.

'I went to Malta,' Steel shrugged and took a sip.

'Yes, I read the report. If that is your idea of a vacation, then it's lucky I'm taking you away from here,' she laughed.

Steel looked down at his coffee, then back at the woman. 'Forgive me. Can I get you a coffee? It appears to be all self-service here.' He hoped to change the subject and her mind ... and let him stay there to do nothing but enjoy himself.

She smiled. 'Coffee Americano, please.' She watched as Steel went to get the drinks, all the while wondering if he would use the opportunity to run off. But she could see he was curious because if he wasn't, why was he here?

Steel soon returned and placed her coffee in front of her before retaking his seat. They smiled at each other once more, wondering who would start first.

The woman started to say, 'I'm—'

'Kitty West, Virginia office, transferred from Boston two months ago. You grew up in Brooklyn in a foster home after your birth parents were killed in a car accident. You were only seven months old,' Steel said matter-of-factly, sitting back and rechecking the room for anyone who looked out of place.

'I see you did your homework. Thanks for proving my point,' Kitty smiled, covering up her shock and amazement upon hearing his quick background check. She glanced at her watch, then at him.

'I take it I'm leaving tonight then?' Steel asked.

'In two hours, actually. We've already packed for you, don't worry,' Kitty smiled cockily.

'How do you know you haven't missed anything? I may

have something hidden away in a secret compartment?' Steel asked calmly, trying to draw her in.

'Then you can come back and get it when the jobs are completed, and you continue your vacation,' Kitty grinned.

'Oh, something tells me this place is the last place I'd come. A tropical island with no cell reception would be better,' Steel joked but meant every word.

One thing began to bother him as he finished off his coffee. Why had she insisted he meet her here? She could have just as easily met him at the hotel. And why was there another team there to back her up?

Steel had noted the couple to his left at eleven o'clock, a red-haired woman and dark-haired man both in dark suits, she with lots of jewellery. Another group, a team of four pretending to be part of some football team he'd never heard of, to his eight o'clock. At twelve o'clock were three nuns wearing traditional habits. One had forgotten to change her shoes, as he sighted sneakers when she walked.

'Looks like I have no choice,' Steel said with a weary smile.

Kitty smiled and nodded curtly to confirm his assessment of the situation.

'Shall we?' Steel stood and dropped a twenty euro note on the table next to his coffee cup.

'What's your rush? You didn't finish your coffee?' Kitty said smugly.

'Oh, it's fine. I think I've had enough drugs in my system with all this caffeine,' Steel said as he walked to Kitty's chair to pull it out for her.

'Always the gentlemen,' Kitty said with a surprised look.

'Oh, not always.' Steel tipped the chair forwards when she was halfway up, causing her to fall onto the table, spilling the hot drink.

Kitty yelped as the scolding liquid fell onto her trousers and arms. She spun around to call the others but found the other teams had already reacted and rushed over.

Steel was quick on his feet, dodging grasping hands. He vaulted over one table, and an agent went to follow. But as he lunged, Steel kicked the table, hitting the man in the gut and winding him.

Steel spun around and rushed for the door, but his gut told him to expect more agents to be ready for his exit. So, he took the second exit to the rooftop. When he reached the roof, he headed for the end of the building.

Agents ran after him, but Steel had already jumped from the roof and was heading down the street.

The nun with the sneakers was hot on his trail and nearly within reach as they raced down a long street. As she grabbed his jacket, Steel stopped suddenly and sidestepped, causing her to crash into a group of priests.

Steel smiled childishly and ran towards the cable car station.

He noted the time; a car should be ready to leave. All he had to do was be on it. As he made his way to it, he began to second-guess his getaway plan. He knew a team would be waiting at the cable car station, ready to grab him when he got off.

Steel knew this because it was what he would have done, but he also knew he had to get off the mountain and away from Kitty and her colleagues ... and the only way might just be that cable car.

Steel ran into the small building, with Kitty's team only a few seconds behind.

As she entered the building, she saw the car had already left, full of people. She smiled as she watched it depart.

'Don't worry, Kitty, the team at the bottom will catch him,' said a tall agent standing next to her.

Kitty looked over at Agent Martin Brena, the guy in charge, a cool-looking customer with brown, styled hair and a charcoal-grey suit. A career agent whose arrogance made his decisions for him. Kitty looked back at the car and nodded.

'I'm sure they will,' she said, smiling as she walked away.

Brena looked down at the car and smiled confidently. 'We got you now, Major Steel; we got you now.'

———

The obvious choice would be to make it down the mountain using the train that hugged the mountainside, a safe way of travelling for those with height issues. Steel had gone through the cable car station, then jumped onto the rocks below before heading for the walkway that curved its way to the bottom.

Steel knew the team would be small, eight- to ten men strong, if that. A compact team did not stick out, but it was too small to cover everything.

The cable car and train were the better choices; they were perfect for a quick escape. However, Steel preferred things slow and structured—it was paramount to know where your enemy was, making them think they had you. That was just pure entertainment, and this was no different. Steel had doubled back and climbed to the parking area near a circular overwatch. Steel needed a vehicle to get down from the mountain; to do so by foot would take too long, especially for what he had in mind.

Steel smiled as a man on a Can-Am Spyder RT stopped to drop off something at a store. Moments later, the man came out laughing and whistling and made his way to where he had left his machine. He stopped and looked around as if puzzled. He was confused at the disappearance of his ride and tried to figure out what could have happened. Then he remembered he'd left the motor running while he made his delivery. In a rage, he tossed his helmet and cursed his stupidity ... just as two nuns walked past. The man blushed and apologised as the two young, wide-eyed sisters hurried away.

———

Below, on the winding road, Steel opened up the machine. His hair was brushed back by the open air. He knew it wouldn't be long before the police stopped him for not having a helmet, or more likely because the man had reported his machine stolen. But Steel only needed the vehicle to get him as far to the bottom as possible ... to the next town would be perfect. Either way, Steel had left Stanton's dogs barking, which felt good.

He had no idea why they were after him because he hadn't done any missions since the thing in New York had gone south —or maybe that was why?

Had the Charles King case come back to haunt him? But what had happened hadn't been his fault; it had been the system he had believed in that let them down. However, one thing was for sure. Steel had to speak with Stanton. Find out if Stanton had put these dogs on his tail, and if so, why?

This woman Kitty had tried to convince Steel he was coming in on a mission for Stanton. If that were the case, why had a snatch team been recruited? But the more Steel thought about it, it made sense. Stanton was a great one for giving as little information as possible. He made an agent do their home-work. Was the target friend or foe? How much was necessary?

Looking back, Steel had no idea why he ran. After all, they were just taking him back to the States to meet Stanton. But there was something off about the whole thing. And who was the joker in the grey suit? He had tried to blend in but stuck out like an arsehole? He was a company man, probably in charge of the whole damn thing. Thinking about it, Stanton was a bastard, a good man, but a bastard nevertheless.

Steel remembered being given many missions with very little data to go on. 'Go and pick up this man.' Steel wouldn't know if the person was a friend, foe, or random person. Stanton was a trickster for his amusement but a hell of an agent.

Steel smiled to himself.

That was why the team was there.

They knew nothing about Steel apart from what was in the files, which wasn't much. Steel had read it once and had to admit it had been watered down. He thought about the guy in charge of the OP; he didn't understand the parameters or had a hard-on for Steel, and he wanted to prove a point. Either way, he had failed.

He had considered giving himself up, but where would the fun be in that?

No, if they wanted him, he would make them work for it. This wasn't arrogance on Steel's part. It was payback for trashing his holiday.

———

Steel followed the road down, ensuring he kept close to groups of bikers or coaches he could hide behind. He was good at blending in. After all, it had been the company that had taught him. Steel found a parking area with a scenic view and stopped, checking the back storage bin, hoping for a spare helmet. Instead, he found a couple of new Harleys in the parking lot, possibly rentals. Their owners had wandered off to see the sights, leaving their helmets strapped to the handlebars.

Steel rechecked the bins for a toolkit and found what he needed. Quickly he quickly removed the plates from the Can-Am, swapped them with one of the motorcycles, and took one of the helmets. Then, pulling on the helmet, he started up the three-wheeled machine. Then, he was gone with a rev of the throttle and a spit of gravel. At least the plates and helmet would buy him some time.

Steel figured returning to the hotel in Barcelona was out of the question. Besides, they would have his luggage by now, and the room would have been wiped clean.

# CHAPTER FIVE

AGENT MARTIN BRENA WAS MORE THAN ANGRY. THIS MAN he had been sent to bring in had fled, and no one knew where he was. The ground units had reported Steel hadn't come their way. The train and the cable car had both been cleared.

It was as if the guy had just vanished.

Brena was on a deadline; he had one hour, and then he went home empty-handed. The only thing they did have was Steel's luggage from the hotel. Brena had people looking through the guy's things to try and get an angle on him. Brena knew next to nothing about Steel. Sure, he'd read the file, ex-military, did some work with the agency, and then joined the NYPD. Apart from that, this man's life was nothing but a half-empty file.

Stanton had said to bring him in alive and unharmed by any means necessary but didn't say why and Brena's mistake was that he hadn't asked.

It had been hard to find the guy the first time, and from what Brena could see, Steel wasn't trying to hide. He felt that if Steel didn't want to be found, you wouldn't find him.

Brena scowled. Who the hell was John Steel? And why did Stanton want him?

———

Kitty West sat in a taxi heading for the airport. Brena had sent her to secure the plane and take Steel's belongings with her. She had changed at the hotel, dying her hair back to its original raven black, and slipped into a black trouser suit with heeled ankle boots. Kitty preferred the look she'd had at the Monastery, but these were work clothes, nothing more.

She looked through the window, watching the world whiz by as the taxi drove hurriedly to the airport. She caught her reflection in the window; a sad face gazed back at her. Kitty wondered about this guy John Steel. She had seen his file. They all had. But they had no idea what Stanton wanted him for. Sure, the briefing was to tell Steel he was needed on an urgent mission, but she had no idea why. What could Steel do that they couldn't?

Then she thought back to the café. This Steel guy was fast, quicker than anything she had ever seen. Kitty smiled as she thought back to Brena's face after he had learned Steel had escaped. Seeing the veins in his temple throb was delightful. Brena was her boss, but he was an ass ... or rather, a kiss-ass.

Brena had sent her away because he blamed her, but at the end of the day, he had dropped the ball, but she had no doubt it would say otherwise in his report. Kitty looked at the approaching airport sign, and her heart sank. She was leaving Barcelona empty-handed, and she hadn't fully seen the city, but then it was work, not a vacation. Well, that was what Brena kept telling her anyway. This was odd because he always found time to slip away and do recon. It had been his idea that she poses as a maid, possibly his way of telling her that was all she was worth. Never mind, she had gotten the job done, more than what he had done.

The taxi pulled up to the tarmac and headed for the Gulfstream jet, the company's first-class ride.

The taxi stopped, and she got out. The driver popped the truck and helped her with the bags. Kitty smiled and tipped him after he placed down the last suitcase. Not only was she transporting Steel's items, but those of the whole team. Kitty looked at all of the bags and sighed. There were at least twenty bags and suitcases, four belonging to Brena.

'Don't worry, Señora, I will take care of the bags for you.'

Kitty smiled and thanked the man wearing grey coveralls and a white baseball cap that covered his face. Kitty climbed onto the jet and took a seat. She could hear bumps and bangs as the luggage was stowed in the compartment at the rear.

With a content smile, she closed her eyes for a second, relaxing in the comfortable leather swivel chair, unaware of the door closing and the engines starting. Kitty began to dream as the aircraft taxied onto the runway. As she slipped into blissful sleep, the Gulfstream headed skywards.

There was a screech of tires outside on the tarmac as company cars skidded to a halt. Brena got out and watched the aircraft disappear into the endless blue sky.

'What the hell just happened?' Brena screamed, tossing his sunglasses to the ground. 'That dumb bitch just left us behind.' He turned when one of his colleagues coughed as if trying to get his attention.

'That's not all she left,' said the woman wearing the nun's outfit earlier.

Brena looked over at the bags and suitcases and screamed again as he kicked the side of the SUV.

'It's OK, Brena,' shouted another man checking out the luggage. 'She only left yours.'

The others turned, hiding giggles, while Brena screamed under his breath and took his phone out of his pocket. He needed to reach the pilot or inform Langley to get another flight. Brena was bloody mad, and he would make her pay for this.

# CHAPTER SIX

A QUICK JUDDER OF THE PLANE WOKE KITTY FROM HER slumber. She looked around with sleepy eyes, half expecting Brena's disapproving look, but found Steel seated across from her with a glass of whiskey. Kitty sat up and looked around at the empty seats.

'Where are the others? Where am I ...?' Kitty grasped the arms of her chair and looked around. She turned back to Steel with a confused look on her face. 'Why are you here?'

'I killed the rest and shoved them out of the door,' Steel said calmly, leaning forward and staring at her through his sunglasses.

Kitty felt a shiver run down her spine. Had he really done that? Had he killed the whole team? Then she saw the side of his mouth arch as he broke into a smile.

'OK, so where are they?' Kitty asked angrily.

'Back at the airport and mad as hell, I suppose,' Steel said, taking a sip.

'What changed your mind?'

'The way you asked so nicely,' Steel said with a shrug and a smile.

'Really?' Kitty said, surprised.

'Nah, I figured if Stanton sent you, he only gave you part of the information. He does that to everyone. That bloke is a complete arse when it comes down to his sick sense of humour." He watched her expression change as she began to calm down.

'Why did you leave the others and only take me?' Kitty asked, suddenly feeling uncomfortable again.

'Because you show promise, the others just follow. You use your head. You were the only one who worked out that I never took the car down. I'm just wondering why you didn't tell Brena?' Steel poured a glass of eighteen-year-old whiskey for Kitty and handed it to her.

Kitty held it to her nose and smelt the mixed odour of wood, herbs, and something she couldn't put her finger on. 'Like you said, he's an ass.'

'I left the others because this Brena seems to be a real dick, and the others ... well, no reason apart from that it seemed like the thing to do at the time.' Steel grinned and raised his glass.

Kitty said nothing; she just shot him an angry look and peered out the window.

'So, what's next?' Kitty asked after several seconds of tense silence. 'When we land, I mean.'

Steel thought for a moment and stared into the dark liquid in the glass. 'We go see Stanton, find out what that fruit bat wants.'

'Fruit-bat?' Kitty asked, puzzled.

Steel shook his head, feeling it wasn't worth trying to explain, and went back to looking out the window.

———

The midday sun was high in the sky but a fraction of the warmth of what it had been. Pedestrians moved about like colonies of ants while the built-up traffic moved slowly. The Sentinel had gathered more photographs and data on the next target. Alison Kline would be next, but she wouldn't be the last. The Sentinel had a list of names and their crimes. Each would be observed, documented, researched and eventually taken out. Each would know the same terror the people had felt when faced with a simple device.

The television in the corner of the room was showing the news.

A reporter was talking about a bombing in a shopping mall that had happened months before. The man responsible had been killed instantly. It had been someone the police had suspected in previous bombings. Charles King had been the son of a multi-conglomerate billionaire, Edward King, a man with enough juice to make things disappear. But only one man had stood up and tried to do what was right, which cost him. In other words, the cop was 'on administrative leave' ... gone, probably a mall cop.

The Sentinel had created a mission board. It was filled with maps, timings, and locations. The rest of the intel would come later. The Sentinel had time.

The reporter spoke about the bombing, showing footage she had dug up from last week's broadcasts. People sat crying in the streets, covered in blood and dust. Emergency services lined the streets, helicopters from TV stations landing to offer their services to help carry the wounded—for a price, of course. Others, because it was the right thing to do.

Slowly The Sentinel eased into the chair. Unblinking eyes stared at the screen as footage showed bodies being carried out. There was no fire. The blast had been massive and destructive, with plenty of shrapnel.

The bomber hadn't intended to be in there with the device. Instead, the idea was to be somewhere away from the blast but within the line of sight, watching it all happen.

But the cop had intervened. He was trying to disarm the situation. But something had gone wrong; the cop had stopped the bomber, but the device went off anyway, according to the witnesses who made it out at the last moment. Thirty had died, thirty people, and the cop didn't have time to save. But The Sentinel knew it wasn't a timer that had run out; the kill switch in Charles King's hand set it off.

The Sentinel found it interesting there was no television footage of the cop, almost as if they wanted him to completely disappear. But The Sentinel knew who the cop was and what he could do.

So, The Sentinel picked up a postcard from the desk and started to write. Finally, The Sentinel wrote the name and address: Detective John Steel, 11th Precinct Police Department, New York City.

# CHAPTER SEVEN

The Gulfstream landed at Ronald Reagan National Airport. The ride had been smooth but somewhat quiet. Kitty had spent most of the flight gazing out of the window, looking more like a kid who had just been grounded.

The plane taxied into a private hangar, where two GMC Yukon SUVs were waiting. The aircraft powered down, and the door hinged downwards, creating steps.

Steel let Kitty go first, giving the illusion the rest of the team wasn't too far behind. However, the welcoming party looked confused as Steel stepped onto the concrete.

'Who the hell is this?' asked a tall, broad-shouldered agent. 'And where are the others?'

'Nice to see you too, Stan,' Kitty said flatly.

Stan Norris was a veteran agent. Six-two with a military-style haircut. The brown was slowly greying at the sides. His features were rugged, a look he had gotten from his time in the Marines, that long stare from seeing too much action.

'So, what's the story?' Stan asked, confused at the situation.

Kitty looked over at Steel, who stood stone-faced and

unwelcoming. 'Never mind, it's a long story. This is John Steel. Section Chief Stanton sent us to get him.' Kitty pointed to the moody statue dressed in black.

'This is *him*?' asked the agent, with a fascinated look on his face.

'Yes, we can do autographs later. But, in the meantime, can we go? I've got some questions for Stanton,' Steel said and strolled to the first Yukon and climbed into the back seat.

An electronic whir caused Kitty to look over at the plane as the cargo hold began to open.

'Well, at least you didn't forget their luggage,' laughed one of the other agents in the second vehicle.

Kitty scowled at Steel, who just sat calmly and looked out of the window.

———

The drive to Langley was long, but this gave Steel time to wonder what Stanton wanted.

The two men in the front of the car were no help; they were simply there to pick up the team from the airport. Steel had tried to make conversation, but it seemed they were told not to talk to him, or perhaps they preferred not to engage him.

Steel had found his luggage when he had loaded the team's bags onto the plane, disguised as the baggage handler. Now, he was wearing his unique sunglasses, which had built-in HUDs in one of the lenses and his smartwatch. Steel pressed an icon on his cell phone and waited as the watch, cell phone, and glasses were synced and ready to go.

He checked for missed calls and messages on his cell phone. There weren't any. Steel felt a little disappointed. Even his partner at the NYPD, Samantha McCall, hadn't tried to call. But maybe that was for the best. After all, they had let him down, not the other way around.

Steel slipped the phone back into his pocket and closed his eyes. There was still over an hour to go. So, he decided to sleep. That was if the nightmares would let him.

Kitty sat in the other car with the tall agent, who questioned her about what had happened. Possibly more out of interest than a debriefing.

'He stole the plane didn't he?' the agent asked with wide, excited eyes.

'Kind of. I must have fallen asleep. When I woke up, he was there, and the others were– well, you get the idea, Frank,' Kitty said, her voice full of shame.

'Don't feel bad, Kitty. I wouldn't have expected less from reading his file. One thing does surprise me, though,' Agent Frank Dorson said.

'What's that?'

'Why did he wait until you were on board? By the sounds of things, he could have taken off ages ago, but he waited for you. Why?' Dorson asked, giving Kitty the once-over.

Sure, Kitty was pretty, but not stunning. She was shorter than the others, around five eight if that. But there was something about her. Kitty was tenacious when she had to be. Also, Kitty had a problem with authority, meaning she was a perfect match for Steel.

Kitty had lost her parents in a major accident: wrong place, wrong time. Yet, despite all this, she was a good agent with a bright future. If she could get from under Brena's grasp, that was. That guy was a career killer at best. Brena would use new agents to make himself look good and toss them under the bus if they made him look bad. If he messed up, great; he'd just say it was their fault.

But Steel had seen that somehow, which meant he'd known

the team had been there at the restaurant. So Steel had just waited for them to make their move.

Dorson smiled to himself as his theory unwound in his head. 'I think I know why Steel picked you,' he said with an enlightened look on his face.

'What do you mean 'picked' me? Steel had no idea we were there ... did he?' Kitty asked, looking dazed. Had he known all along? She shook her head, unable to accept that Steel could have known that there was a team watching him all that time.

'Did you find anything in his room?' Dorson asked.

'Nothing ... well, nothing of interest. There were no messages on his cell or laptop. Looks like he really was on vacation,' Kitty said. 'I heard stories about him, but you know the gossip, how things get blown out of proportion.'

'Don't worry. This guy is beyond anything you can imagine. That's why Stanton wants him on this one,' Dorson stated.

'On what? We haven't been briefed on anything new.' A sudden shiver ran down her spine like Spidey-Sense. Something was wrong, especially if they were bringing this guy back. They knew nothing about this Mr John Steel; his file was as mysterious as he was.

'Don't tell me. Above my pay grade, I take it?' Kitty turned to Dorson, who just shrugged.

'Both our pay grades, actually. I'm as much in the dark as you are on this one, but if they bring him in, it's bad,' Dorson admitted.

Kitty shot him a curious look and leaned forwards. 'Who is he? Why doesn't he exist?'

'His file is thin. I mean *paper-thin*. Probably because the work he did never happened. If you get what I mean,' Dorson explained. 'This guy worked black OPs back in the day. I had to pull some favours to get that much. Steel was in the British SAS and then the US Navy SEALs. After that, he falls off the map until he joins the agency as an asset. After that, it went cold until a few years ago when he joined the NYPD.'

He paused, then frowned. 'Believe me when I say this guy is badass. Apparently, he was shot six times or something. Nobody knows where or when, or even how the bastard survived.'

'His scars, right? I couldn't believe them when I saw ... never mind,' Kitty said, stopping herself before she said more.

Dorson smiled and nodded. 'Yeah, the scars. One old Japanese guy said they were the mark of the Phoenix, rebirth or some bull like that. Steel is as badass as they come when he's in the zone; don't be near him. A buddy of mine in NYPD SWAT did a job with him, some bust on a ship or something. Anyway, this guy took on a whole Army of bad guys and sunk the friggin' ship.'

Kitty noticed how excited Dorson was, like a movie-star crush. But Kitty couldn't see it. This guy Steel couldn't be that good; no one could be unless they were in a book or movie.

She put the stories down to just what they were: stories. Steel had probably done some fantastic things, which had been blown out of proportion; it happens. Chinese whispers. Information to boost an ego or relate dangerous things—especially to people who counted on them being accurate when it counted.


The men regarded the sleeping Steel in the other SUV. Watching every hand movement and foot kick. Stanton had warned them about Steel's nightmares; no one knew what they were about, only that he woke up disorientated and angry. So, each of the men sat sweating and armed with a taser, hoping it would be enough if he snapped.

Steel was curled up on the seat, snoring happily. But he wasn't sleeping; he was reading the data on the small drop screen in his glasses. The information he had received was a copy of a case the CIA had just gotten.

A serial killer was targeting random people; there had been two so far. The latest one had been a lawyer in a prestigious law firm, a woman called Alison Kline.

# CHAPTER EIGHT

A STORM BROUGHT IN A NEW DAY. BLACK CLOUDS LOOMED
as torrential rains washed over the city. Forks of purple lightning streaked across the sky, and booms of thunder shook
windows and set off car alarms. The lengthy warm weather had
changed suddenly, bringing weather of Biblical proportions.

Water filled the streets, and storm drains choked on the
water overflow. Traffic was at a minimum. It was a Sunday, so
most people stayed home. Most people, but not Alison Kline.
Alison had a case coming up, and she needed to be prepared
for it.

She had left the house after the power to her house had
gone down. A tree had fallen and taken out the power lines to
that street. An accident, an act of God, most called it. But
most hadn't seen the man with the detonation cord in the
early morning. It was a string-like explosive used by a
specialist for doing precise work–such as cutting trees or poles
in half.

The rolling thunder and massive booms covered the explosion. Some kid had caught it on his cell phone and posted it on

the internet. Over a thousand clicks of approval made him happy, unaware he had just shared evidence.

Alison, in her frustration, decided to get a cab to city hall to finish off her work. It was a long way to go from Upper East Side, but necessary. The taxi took twenty minutes to arrive, which topped her bad mood, but as she stepped into the bombardment of heavy raindrops, she felt she'd better not complain. Alison knew all too well one wrong word and he would refuse to take her. She bit her tongue and hoped they would get there in one piece.

The cabby drove slowly, but Alison was impressed he could see at all. From where she sat, all she could see was water. Alison could have believed they were on a boat on rough seas if she didn't know better. They headed south on Park Avenue and headed for Union Square. From there, they would take Broadway. Typically, it would be an hour's ride, but today, she would be lucky if it took only two.

Alison looked at the man's ID, pinned to the dash next to a Lego minion figure. The cabby's name was unpronounceable, for her anyway. She guessed he was from the Balkans or someplace like that, but he had a kind face from what she had seen in the photograph. Alison tried speaking to him through the gap in the safety window, but he gave no response. The man wore a thick jacket and a grey hood; leather gloves covered his hands.

Suddenly, Alison got a bad feeling. She had seen this movie before. She tried the door, but the deadbolt stopped her from leaving. She began to panic and banged at the window, but the streets were empty, and the car's window was streamed up. Her fear grew as the driver began to speed up, despite the lack of visibility. Her fists slammed against the glass so hard her hands hurt.

The more she screamed, the faster he went. Alison pulled out her cell phone and began to dial the police, but she had no signal. She felt herself cower into the fake leather seat and await what was to come. Closing her eyes, she began to pray, something she hadn't done since she was a kid. That was when the cab stopped.

Alison listened as the taxi driver got out and walked around to her door, her eyes clenched shut, fearful of seeing her end coming near. Then her door opened, and she heard a voice yelling at her in a tongue she didn't understand. Alison felt a pull on her arm, and she resisted. The driver pulled harder, and she resisted further. Then another voice spoke a woman's voice. Alison looked up and saw they were outside Cornell Medical Centre. The cab driver was speaking to a nurse.

Confused and shaken, Alison got out of the car and looked around. 'Why am I here? I asked for city hall?'

The nurse spoke with the driver in broken Croatian.

'He said that this was where he was told to take you. He was told that you were sick, and when you started to cry out, he was worried about you. So, he rushed here as soon as fast he could,' explained the nurse.

The taxi driver nodded and gave a thumbs-up as if in approval of his actions.

Alison went to speak, but she was lost for words and began to laugh instead at the whole incident.

'Why would I want to go to the hospital? I'm not sick. There's nothing wrong with me,' Still laughing, Alison headed for a concrete wastebasket holder to have a cigarette.

———

As Alison neared the wastebasket, there was a massive flash and a roar of an explosion. The container exploded, sending dagger-like shards of concrete into Alison's body.

As she was launched across the ground, the nurse ran over

but stopped abruptly upon seeing Alison's angry wounds. Especially the long spear-like shards that had punctured Alison's eyes.

Other hospital staff ran out carrying trauma packs, and two others pushed a gurney. Two doctors looked down at the fresh blood flowing from the deep wounds and being washed away by the pouring rain ... along with any evidence.

Screams from passers-by dulled the sound of the rumbling thunder.

———

A figure stood on East 68th Street, next to the sign for the Rockefeller University. Clad all in black, with a long black coat and a black hood. The stranger did nothing; they just watched the scene unfold. The assassin had waited for such a night; sure, there had been plenty of other contingency ideas, but this one felt right.

A bus pulled past, followed by flashes of blue from the police cars behind it. When the bus drove away, the figure had gone.

# CHAPTER NINE

THE YUKON SUVs STOPPED, AND THE AGENTS GOT OUT ALL at once. Steel joined them and stretched off as if he had been sleeping, taking time to bask in the warmth of the sun before following Dorson and Kitty into the CIA building at Langley.

Steel felt eyes on the other end of the many surveillance cameras watching him, like beady hawk eyes assessing prey. Steel smiled and waved to let the person know they were there.

As they passed through a metal detector, an agent stopped Steel and placed a small grey plastic basket on a counter next to him. 'All metal and electronic devices must be put into here, sir,' said the agent.

Steel smiled at the medium-built man and placed his wallet, phone, watch and everything, less for his glasses, into the basket.

'Your sunglasses as well, please, sir,' insisted the agent.

Steel stared at the man. 'Oh ... I think it's best if I keep them on.'

'Glasses in the basket *now*, please, sir!' The agent attempted to assert authority.

Dorson stopped. Curious about what would happen next, Kitty stopped and looked at Dorson.

'What are you doing?' she asked. 'Leave him. Steel will be okay or arrested, or maybe we'll get lucky, and they'll shoot him.' She laughed.

'I just want to see what happens next, see if the rumours are true,' Dorson said eagerly.

Kitty looked at him, confused.

As they watched, Steel took off his glasses, his face down as though he was looking at the tray. Slowly, Steel brought up his head, so their eyes were level, but his eyes were closed. Then, slowly, Steel opened his eyes and gazed at the agent.

Frightened, the security agent stared into the cold, soulless green eyes. He wanted to look away but couldn't.

Steel smiled and closed his eyes again. He was feeling a little childish pleasure at the man's discomfort.

The agent backed off and insisted he put his glasses back on, but Steel had already done so.

'Thanks very much.' Steel's words rang with satisfaction.

Dorson grinned as if he'd just won a bet. His calculated eyes fixed on Steel as he walked through the metal detector and began putting items back into his pockets.

Steel looked over at Dorson, feeling the man's gaze on him. As if Dorson were studying him. Watching to see what Steel did next, like a scientist observing a rat in a maze. He ignored Dorson and walked on. It had been a while since he had been in the building, but it felt like yesterday. Despite a few minor changes and upgrades, it was the same as he'd remembered.

Kitty caught up with Steel and walked next to him. She said nothing at first. Steel had the idea she just wanted to get away from Dorson, which was understandable. The man creeped out even Steel, which was saying something.

Dorson walked past them both as if he were showing them the

way. They took the elevator to the third floor, then followed the corridors to the west wing and Stanton's office. Steel smiled as they headed towards a large wooden door with a brass plaque. Nothing had changed: the same office, the same door, the same secretary.

'Hello Brenda, good to see you again.' Steel leaned down to give the woman a peck on the cheek. Brenda Woods had been Stanton's secretary back in the day; she had been a sexy thirty-something then and was now an elegant forty-something. Luckily, she abandoned the skimpy clothes and revealing tops, swapping them for more attractive skirt suits. But, of course, she was still a beauty, and the years had been kind, which was more than could be said for Stanton.

Steel remembered Stanton as a bear of a man, a brown flat-top with razored sides, broad shoulders, square jaw, and a quarterback body. Now, his double chins had double chins and a gut held in by a buttoned jacket. The flat top remained, but now it was grey and didn't suit him. Steel could see success had bitten him in the rear. 'If it's not broken, why change it,' Stanton used to say when an agent was too good at his job. It was a polite way of saying, 'You're good at what you do, and we can't be bothered to train someone to take your place.'

Stanton and Steel exchanged nods. Each man seemed to hold a distance they felt comfortable with as if this were enough for them instead of hugs and handshakes.

It was an odd display to the others, but they knew Stanton wasn't the hugging type and Steel, well, they figured he was the same.

'Glad you could make my boy,' Stanton said in a gritty southern accent.

'Oh, just seeing you made it worthwhile,' Steel said sarcastically.

Next to Stanton stood another man, director Frank Headly.

The man was at least six-three, with broad shoulders and a crewcut greying on the sides.

'Steel, you remember the director?' Stanton motioned. He waited for the two men to shake hands and exchange pleasantries.

'Last time we saw each other, you were section chief, sir; congratulations,' Steel said. He had known Headly for a time and had a lot of respect for the man.

'Thanks; well, I'm glad they convinced you to come along; we're in a real jam with this, and it couldn't come at the worst time.' Headly pointed to a flat screen in the corner.

'How do you mean?' Steel asked, and a look of sudden concern crossed his face.

'The Vice President is talking about running for President; the guy is an idiot and a pain in the ass for us, *all* of us,' Headly explained.

'Shall we?' Stanton asked before making his way down the corridor.

Steel and Headly shook hands once more and said their farewells; then Steel lagged behind.

The group followed Stanton down another corridor and a row of glass-walled offices. Each had spartan amounts of furnishings, a desk computer, filing cabinets, and an office chair. But all were empty and had been for some time from what Steel could tell.

'Budget cuts, can you believe it? They want us to catch bad guys but won't pay the agents to do it. Too busy spending the cash on promoting themselves in elections or pointless crap nobody wants,' Stanton complained as he pointed to the row of empty offices.

Steel followed, still not sure why he was there—apart from the fact he was cheap labour as far as Stanton was concerned.

They stopped in front of a large conference room; the doors were made of frosted glass and aluminium fittings.

'Steel, my boy, we have a problem. Actually, *you* have the problem,' Stanton said and smiled as he opened the door.

The room was large, around twenty-by-twenty, with white walls and a single window which probably didn't open. A long conference table with six chairs was in the centre of the room. Four of the seats were occupied by agents Steel didn't recognise. Judging by the half-empty water bottles in front of them, they'd been waiting a while for him.

'These are some of the other agents who will be on the case. Agents Karl Simms, Trish Edwards, Mark Dutton and Alex Brown,' Stanton said, indicating to each person as he introduced them.

Steel nodded a greeting to the group, then turned his attention to six murder boards that had been set up. Each had a map and photographs pinned to the board.

'Very impressive, so who's the lead agent?' Steel asked. Hoping desperately it was someone good and not Brena.

'You are,' Stanton replied bluntly as he took a seat at the conference table.

'I don't understand. What do you need me for?' Steel asked. Looking over each of the agents individually. 'Whoever put this room together seems to have things under control.'

'There have been two murders so far. The last one was last week. Before each killing, we were sent a postcard. That was the latest one we got,' Stanton said, pointing to the second board.

Steel walked over to an enormous whiteboard held on a wheeled frame. Steel took note of the collage of notes and photographs. Amongst them was a postcard in a small evidence bag. The picture was of the New York Superior Court.

Steel took the postcard from the board and turned it over.

On the back was writing, but someone had used a computer to type the script. *The small in German must pay a debt. When stormy weather comes, the sick will seek poison air and splinters of made stone will find them.*

'Thoughts?' Stanton asked. A smile crossed his face as he could see Steel in that place in his mind.

Kitty and Dorson watched, and Steel began to look at the rest of the board. The map, the pictures. The puzzle started to unfold in his mind.

Steel knew this was a test. Stanton was testing him to see if he could work out a murder that had already taken place. But he didn't care; it was exhilarating. He didn't want to play a game but felt compelled to participate.

In truth, Steel wanted to be back on the beach in Barcelona; he wanted to wake up late and go to bed even later. He didn't want to have another case that ended like that one.

'The killer is playful, intelligent, patient,' Steel stated.

'Patient?' Dorson asked, puzzled.

'The killer says when it's going to happen, a stormy day, which means a plan has been in play for a long time. They just required the right element, a storm perhaps,' Steel answered, his focus never leaving the board.

'The name of the victim?' Stanton leaned back in the chair and waited for the mind step to kick in.

'It speaks of a small German, so we are looking for a tourist, right?' Dorson spoke up as if he'd solved the whole thing.

Steel shook his head, his hands moving across the board as if he were looking for something specific. 'No, it said "a small in German" and not "a small German",' Steel said, pondering the board. Suddenly, he stopped and eyed the picture on the postcard. The picture of the courthouse. 'We are looking for a lawyer, a good lawyer.'

'A German lawyer?' Dorson asked, surprised.

Steel turned to Dorson with raised eyebrows as if surprised by the stupidity of the answer.

'How do you know it's a lawyer?' Stanton asked.

'The picture of the courthouse, and not just any courthouse, it's Superior Court,' Kitty said, taking the postcard from Steel.

Steel smiled. At last, he got a playmate.

'We are looking for someone called Klein or Kline,' Steel added.

Dorson went to ask a question, but Steel stopped him with a shake of his head. 'Klein is small in German, so it—'

'Would be Klien or Kline, right?' Stanton said with a smile.

Dorson shot Steel a confused look as if what Steel had said made no sense. Yes, the name and the postcard made sense, but the *profile* of the killer? Dorson didn't buy it.

'Our killer doesn't so much stalk his victims as he observes them. So, it wouldn't surprise me if there was a dossier on the victims,' Steel stated solemnly. 'Favourite restaurants, how they get to where they are going, be it taxi, car or subway.'

He turned back to the board; the map was held by six-round magnets. A red arrow showed the location of Alison's home; a blue one was her place of work. There was another marker, a white one, next to a hospital.

Steel turned to Stanton and looked at the man as he sat in the chair. 'When was she killed?' Steel asked.

'Last weekend. We only got the case because of the—'

'Bomb. They blew up something concrete, something that would splinter,' Steel finished for him, looking at the words on the postcard again.

Dorson's mouth fell open as he watched Steel pull everything together.

'It was a wastebasket container; a cab had taken her to the hospital after Dispatch gave the wrong address to go to. She went for a smoke, then boom,' Stanton said, making grand arm gestures.

'Small device, shape charge, I take it?' Steel returned his gaze to the board.

Stanton nodded but said nothing. He didn't want to disturb Steel's train of thought.

Steel stood transfixed by the clues on the board. But the more he looked, the more he felt something was missing, almost as if Stanton had left something out on purpose. Steel's eyes followed the lines of every street, noted every notation on the board, the black line of the timeline, and space for a time or date to be filled in. It was almost as if the board had been set up purposely with as little information as possible. As if the murder hadn't taken place yet. But it had. That meant Stanton was holding back.

'Are you testing me, Stanton?' Steel asked.

'Perhaps,' Stanton answered calmly.

'So, where's the real murder board?'

Stanton laughed out loud and clapped his hands. 'Oh, my boy, you never disappoint.' He heaved himself out of his chair and walked over to the board, and turned it around to reveal the completed murder board. With crime scene photos, reports, and diagrams, the timeline at the bottom had been filed out, ending at one o'clock in the afternoon, the time of death.

Steel looked at the new evidence with great care, like a curator took in the beauty of an old piece of art.

Dorson remained seated and looked around the room like a kid at a birthday party he didn't want to be attending. He had read up on Steel. Even managed to get the redacted copies of his file. The man was a legend to him, but this man before him was lost and broken. The man before him was nothing more than a profiler, not the John Steel he had heard about.

Steel turned to face Dorson, busy looking into nothing in the corner.

'You seem disappointed at something,' Steel said calmly, already knowing the answer.

'You ... you're ....'

'Not the man you expected me to be,' Steel smiled and looked back at the murder board. 'That's the problem with stories; they get blown out of proportion, make you into something you are not ... judge me by my actions, not what you have heard.'

Dorson thought for a moment and stood up and walked towards the board. 'So, what have you found?' he asked, finally taking notice.

Steel pointed out the wastebin; the front was missing, but only partially, and a large round hole sat in the centre of the concrete mass. However, the rest of the container was intact.

'This was the work of a professional, possibly police or military, an engineer or bomb squad,' Steel said.

'Why serving personnel? Why not retired or injured?' asked a voice behind them. Everyone turned to see Brena walking in. His mood was surprisingly sombre.

'I see you made it back OK,' Steel said sarcastically.

'No thanks to you,' Brena said, giving both Steel and Kitty an unpleasant look.

'Don't blame the girl; she was unconscious all the way, a little something in the water to help her through a difficult flight,' Steel said, covering for Kitty. Steel felt it was the least he could do, considering it was his fault, after all. And he felt he needed to take her out of Brena's sights for a while.

Steel figured Brena was a vindictive man, someone who would throw you under the bus if it meant making his life more comfortable or better. Steel had seen his sort before, driven with no regard for others.

As Brena approached the board, Steel offered a handshake. Brena didn't even look at the offer; he just strolled past and looked at the board.

Steel smiled and shrugged before walking to the long table, grabbing a water bottle from the centre, cracking it open, and drinking.

Kitty raised an eyebrow at the macho display, which didn't seem to faze Steel one bit. If anything, Steel found it amusing. But Stanton didn't, his face went red at the display, but he held in his anger.

'So, Agent Brena, your thoughts?' Steel asked, watching the man make a display by rubbing his hands and rolling his neck.

'I think our killer is ex-forces, someone who feels the system has let them down somehow, a person who is trying to put right a wrong. Maybe the guy got blown up in Afghanistan and is looking for compensation. But, unfortunately, our lawyer got it tossed out,' Brena said confidently.

Steel nodded as if agreeing with Brena, who smiled when Steel smiled to confirm his assessment.

'Good, so you agree, Mr Steel?' Brena asked.

'Oh, only what the others are thinking, Brenda,' Steel said, standing up and heading for the door.

'It's *Brena*, wise-ass limey, and where the hell do you think you are going?' Brena shouted as if he were in charge.

'Well, *Brenda*, I'm off to find a decent hotel. Settle down for the morning. Have some breakfast.' Steel turned to Stanton and smiled. 'Avery, any chance you can send over the files of the two murders to my hotel? I'll let you know where as soon as I find a place. Thanks.' Steel waited for Stanton to respond.

He nodded. 'Agent West, copy all the files and take them to whatever address Mr Steel gives to us,' Stanton said.

'Yes, sir,' Kitty said.

Stanton left the room, leaving Brena, Dorson, Kitty, and the rest of Brena's team.

'So, what's the plan?' asked Agent Karl Simms.

'We don't need this Steel guy; we can solve this ourselves,' Brena said confidently.

Dorson shook his head in disagreement. Sure, Steel had pissed him off before, but something told him once Steel was out there, he would see what all the stories had been about.

'You disagree, Dorson, so what's your plan? Join up with your hero and sit around?' Brena laughed.

'I hear he didn't just give you the slip off a mountain, but he also stole your ride home. So, yeah, I think teaming up with Steel is the best bet. At least he does his research and doesn't just rush into a situation,' Dorson scoffed.

Brena scowled, unable to reply.

Kitty headed for the door; she'd had enough of this testosterone fight.

'Where are you going?' Brena asked harshly.

'Off to get copies of the files, like the chief asked,' Kitty replied.

Brena's eyes squinted with distrust. 'Make sure I get a copy also,' he ordered and waved his hand like a headmaster dismissing a pupil.

Kitty walked away. As she turned the corner, she stopped and hugged it, listening to Brena as he briefed the team.

# CHAPTER TEN

AGENT KARL SIMMS WAS CHOSEN BY BRENA TO WATCH Steel. Simms didn't mind, but he got the feeling Brena was just trying to keep him out of the way. Simms was the first black guy from his street in Detroit to join the CIA. His dad wanted him to be a basketball player, but his knee injury at college changed that. Nevertheless, Simms was a bright guy with a real future. He'd studied law at Yale, then worked in the Philidelphia office, which was where the Bureau had poached him, or more accurately, Stanton had.

Karl Simms was six-one with a slender build. Even though he didn't look like much, he could chase down a cheetah. He knew if Brena had taken him along to the meeting instead of having him watch the cable car station, they would have caught Steel before he'd had a chance to bolt. But that was Brena all over.

Simms didn't know much about Steel, only what Brena had on file. Still, as Dorson had pointed out, Brena didn't research unless necessary. Even then, he'd get someone else to do it, someone like Kitty.

Simms had followed Steel to McLean, a small town of around fifty thousand, most of which were politicians, diplomats, and government officials. It had bars, restaurants, coffee shops, supermarkets, and everything a regular town had.

Karl Simms watched as Steel's taxi pulled up outside a hotel. Quickly, Simms pulled the Dodge Challenger into the parking lot and waited. He recognised the place alright. It was about the only place in town to get a room. They mostly did suites, but they were comfortable enough.

Simms put the Challenger into park and took his to-go cup out of the cupholder. He blew on the small opening, then sipped fresh coffee.

Kitty said she would bring him something to eat when she dropped the files to Steel. She was one of the good ones, maybe too green and shy for the moment, but she was eager. Simms looked at his watch. It was a German military brand with luminous dials and a picture of an eagle just below the hands. It was now ten in the morning, and his stomach told him so.

Karl Simms figured Steel had phoned Stanton with the location, and Kitty was on the way. The trip would take around an hour, plus time to get something for him at the cantina or a fast-food joint. Two hours at the most. Simms' stomach growled again. He feared that it would be too late.

# CHAPTER ELEVEN

STEEL WAS CHECKED IN BY A SMALL WOMAN IN HER LATE twenties. She had black hair and huge blue eyes. She wore a black skirt and a white blouse that barely held her oversized chest. The woman, or Irene as the name shield on her shirt stated, was charming and helpful.

'Sorry, all the rooms are booked apart from the main suite,' Irene informed Steel.

'That's fine,' Steel assured her.

Irene filled out the booking on the computer and then looked for the key card. 'You're lucky; with this conference happening, all the rooms have just about gone.' She smiled and passed the key card to Steel.

Steel thanked her and headed for the elevator, leaving Irene to lean on the counter and watch him walk away. Her eyes were captivated by what they saw, and her thoughts roamed elsewhere.

Steel unlocked the door to the suite and entered. It was spacious with a sitting area, kitchenette, and a bedroom with an en-suite bathroom. The whole place was a tasteful mix of black and white. The fully stocked kitchenette had all the necessary appliances: a coffee machine, microwave, double refrigerator, and freezer. It was a tiny home away from home, and he hoped the coffee was decent for what it was costing.

Steel explored the rooms, making sure the suite was to his liking, but then he would have been comfortable with a wooden cabin in the middle of nowhere. He tossed his suitcase on the bed and hoped the team had gotten everything from the room when they packed for him. But then, he never took that much with him when he left for his little getaway.

Steel went to a small writing desk. In the corner was a folder with information on the hotel and the surrounding area. But all he needed was a good dinner and a proper breakfast. He had noticed a Chinese restaurant just over the road, as well as a steak house and a coffee shop. The options were there. The thought of a good steak and a bottle of Châteauneuf-du- Pape with the evening meal made him feel all the more hungry.

He opened the suitcase and looked through the pile of clothes, and closed the lid angrily. His expensive clothes had been shoved into the case as if they were a laundry hamper. He picked up the phone and dialled 1 for reception.

Irene answered in a chirpy voice, possibly because she'd noticed the room number that came up on display. Steel asked about dry cleaning and good restaurants. She explained about their one-day laundry system and gave a list of decent places to eat, and also offered to take him to one of them if he wasn't busy that evening.

Steel thanked her and asked for a rain check, knowing full well he would never take her up on it. Probably. Still angry about his clothes, Steel decided to shower and go to the coffee shop for a snack. Kitty wouldn't be there for ages, giving him time to freshen up.

———

Kitty was outside Simms car in forty minutes. The weather was bright and sunny, with cloudless blue skies. A perfect day for driving. Of course, getting as far away from Brena as possible. And as quickly as possible, it had nothing to do with it.

She had brought Simms a double-cheeseburger menu and a diet Coke. His eyes had lit up like a kid at Christmas when he saw it, which made it all the more worthwhile.

'Is he still in there?' Kitty asked, looking at the hotel.

Simms nodded as he took another bite of the burger.

'Enjoy your breakfast Karl,' Kitty said, patting him on the shoulder.

Simms just nodded the best he could with a mouth full of food and ketchup dripping from his mouth and along his chin.

Kitty walked into the lobby and headed for the elevator. Irene gave her a quick glance and thought nothing more of it, guessing Kitty was a guest. Steel had already given the room number in case of emergencies, so Kitty knew where he would be. The room was on the top floor with the other grand suites.

Kitty knocked and waited. She tried again but to no avail. Luckily, a woman from housekeeping walked past, and Kitty hatched a plan. 'I'm sorry, I appear to have locked myself out. I went to get something from the desk, and I forgot my key, but my husband is in the shower,' Kitty explained. Putting on the best performance of her life.

The maid opened the door, heard the shower running in the background, and let Kitty in. Kitty thanked the woman and gave her a ten-dollar note for her trouble. She snuck in and headed for the desk where she would leave the files. A simple in and out. Steel wouldn't even know she had been there.

Suddenly she froze as she heard someone cough behind her. Kitty turned slowly to find Steel standing with just a towel wrapped tightly around him. She blushed as she found herself in a familiar position.

'You know, I'm beginning to think you like seeing me in a towel,' Steel joked, pulling on a bathrobe he grabbed from the wardrobe next to him.

'I-I brought you the files. Sorry, didn't want to disturb your shower. In fact, when you didn't answer, I thought you were sleeping,' Kitty stumbled on her words, unable to look him in the eye—or rather, the sunglasses he'd put on earlier.

'Oh, so you wanted to catch me in bed this time,' Steel joked, causing her to blush even more.

'I have to go. Lots to do back in the office,' Kitty started to back towards the door.

'No problem. Can I get the files first, though?'

Kitty looked at him, puzzled for a second, before realising she still held the files. Quickly, she placed them on the coffee table in front of the couch and rushed off.

'Would you care to join me for lunch?' Steel called behind, tightening the belt on his bathrobe.

'I don't know ... I should get back,' Kitty said, stopping at the door and trying to avoid looking at him.

'What? To Brenda? He probably doesn't even know you're not there. Come on, have lunch ... you can let Simms know he's invited as well,' Steel said, heading into the bedroom and closing the door behind him.

Kitty looked at the door in wonderment. How the hell did he know Simms was here?

She went downstairs to give Simms the bad news; he was blown. Somehow, Steel had made him. But it didn't matter now.

Steel came down and handed Irene a bag with all his suits and other clothes that needed dry cleaning. As he left the hotel, the warmth of the day surprised him. Steel stood for a moment and enjoyed the sunshine and then headed towards Simms's car. He had already gotten out of the car and leaned against it with Kitty standing next to him.

'So, what's up, doc?' Simms joked.

'First breakfast, then we talk,' Steel said with a grin.

Kitty gazed at Simms, looking at her for the same response. They both shrugged and followed as Steel headed for the deli on the other side of the street.

The deli was a five-minute walk away from the hotel. A quaint-looking place with red and white striped overhangs and umbrellas for outdoor seating. Steel preferred to walk, knowing how much one missed such things when one drove—taking note of where the nearest store or decent-looking restaurant was. Kit and Simms had caught up but remained silent.

The three walked in and waited to be taken to a table. A server called Joan, a small woman with bleached-blonde hair and too much lipstick, showed them to a corner booth.

Steel took the chair facing the doorway while the others made do with their backs to the open walkway. Joan passed out their menus and took drink orders. Two coffees and a cup of English breakfast tea.

The squeak of white plimsolls on a vinyl floor signalled Joan's return.

Kit and Simms had the coffee, both black with no sugar. Steel took out the teabag before it spoilt and dropped in a bit of honey instead of milk or sugar.

Joan didn't ask for order straight away; she'd gotten the idea they needed more time the way the young woman was scanning the card and then looking at the food in front of people, so she left them alone. Hopefully, they'd find something before the end of the shift that night.

There was silence while each chose their orders. To Steel, everything looked good. Kitty spent more time observing what everyone else had, possibly to get an idea of portion size. Simms had known what he wanted before he'd left the car.

'So, Brenda sent you to watch me?' Steel asked Simms, breaking the silence.

'Brenda—oh, you mean ... yeah. He doesn't trust you,' Simms said, laughing at Steel's play with Brena's name. 'You're not gonna tell him about this, are you?'

'Your secret is safe with me,' Steel smiled as he called Joan over from the end of the counter. Making Kitty look up as she saw Joan's approach.

'Why did you do that? I haven't found anything yet?'

'Well, I'm hungry, so is Karl, and I bet he even had an idea of what he wanted before he'd stepped out of the car,' Steel said.

'How did you know that?' Simms asked, a look of surprise on his face.

'Because even though you were looking at the menu, you were just being polite. You looked at each page for three seconds,' Steel said with a shrug.

Simms laughed, unaware Steel was already profiling him.

'So, what will it be, folks?' Joan asked in a bubbly voice.

Simms got pancakes and bacon, Kitty requested the BLT, and so did Steel, but he'd asked for turkey bacon.

He watched Joan walk back to the counter to place the order. Her shoes still squeaked as she went. 'So, two murders you guys didn't even know about? Who was in charge of the cases?' Steel asked as he blew on his tea.

'You have the files. All the information is there,' Kitty said, feeling slightly bitter at having been the errand girl.

'OK, no Cliff Notes, fine. But why were you guys sent to get me like a criminal?'

'That was Brena's idea. He was told to bring you in. He had heard some of the stories and decided to use the heavy approach if you caused problems,' Simms replied, feeling embarrassed.

'What is his deal anyway? Daddy didn't get him a pony when he was a little girl or what?' Steel asked, his eyes searching the room for anything out of the ordinary.

'Brena is ... well, Brena. For some reason, he wants to prove himself, stand out, be the man,' Simms said, taking a sip of coffee.

'So, in other words, he wants to solve this case, even though it has nothing to do with him. Stanton brought me in on this.' Steel said.

'The way Brena sees it, the moment he was sent to get you, he was on the case,' Kitty said, waving to get Joan's attention.

'So, what's the plan, Mr Steel?' Simms asked, his eyes lighting up at the approach of Joan and his breakfast. The conversation stopped as she placed the plates down and got Kitty's order for orange juice.

'Well, I was going to have this, then head off to the market over the road and get some items for the suite. Then, go back to my room and look at the files. But, unfortunately, you'll have to sit in the car. And Kitty will have to drive back and listen to Brena and his foolish ideas,' Steel said as soon as Joan had gotten out of hearing range.

He noted the sombre expressions of the two agents.

'Or, we could all got to the market, stock up on food and drink, then work on this together in my suite,' Steel suggested with a shrug.

'You got cable in the room?' Simms asked, his eyes squinting as if he was going to be disappointed.

'Is there a ball game on?' Steel asked.

Simms smiled and shrugged, then took a bite of his bacon.

'My place it is then,' Steel said with a smile.

# CHAPTER TWELVE

STANTON SAT IN HIS OFFICE. THE MEETING HADN'T GONE well, primarily due to that arrogant son-of-a-bitch Brena. Stanton knew it had been a mistake bringing him in on it, but then Brena would have found a way anyway. But Stanton felt more at ease now Steel was there. Sure Steel was an immense pain in the ass, but he got results.

Stanton looked over to a picture he had hung on his wall; it was a group photograph of him and several others, including Steel. Stanton cracked a smile as he thought back to those good old days. He remembered back to when he had pulled Steel out of the SEALs to work for them, a job that proved to be beneficial to both of them. Stanton remembered the day Steel's team was ambushed and how Steel blamed himself for letting his guard down.

The funny thing was Steel hadn't been on the operation; he had another mission to take care of. Steel was working for MI8 at the time. A mission that would later get him brought into the fold of the British Secret Service.

Stanton had to admit he'd never seen anything like Steel

and had never seen the like since. Most people are driven by money, power, love, or lust. Steel was motivated by one thing; the problem was Stanton still didn't know what it was, or he could have used it to his advantage. A knock at his door made Stanton look up. In the doorway stood a stone-faced Brena.

'What can I do for you, Martin?' Stanton said, seeing Brena.

'Sir, I would like to know what the hell is going on: why did you send us to get Steel, and why is he on this case?'

Brena's words rang with composure, but Stanton knew he was ready to burst out of his skin.

'Sit down, Martin,' Stanton ordered, pointing to the chairs facing his desk. Black leather swivel chairs that felt as uncomfortable as they looked.

Brena sat down; his bottom lip pulled up so far he could have swallowed himself whole. 'I won't lie to you; I brought Steel in because he is the best I've ever seen. The man is a machine and definitely not to be fucked with, but he is also expendable if things go wrong. Believe me, Martin, this is one case you do not want. Hell, I didn't want it, but we got it. Besides, I had to bring him in,' Stanton admitted, his voice almost choked by the secret.

'Why, what's wrong, sir?' Brena asked, almost *not* wanting to know the answer from the look on Stanton's face.

Stanton pulled a postcard from out of his drawer; it was in an evidence bag. The picture was of Berlin. Brena took the postcard and scrutinised it before turning it over. The colour drained from his face as he read what was on the back: Detective John Steel, 11$^{th}$ Precinct Police Department, New York City.

———

Steel, Kitty and Simms had gone back to start their investigation.

Simms sat on the bed and grabbed the remote while Steel began to prep the coffee machine. There was a blare of noise when Simms switched on the TV, not knowing the last tenant liked his television loud and had left it on the news channel.

'Oh great, this guy,' Simms moaned, pointing at the television with the remote.

'Who, the Vice President?' Kitty asked, confused at Simms's issue with the man.

'Senator James Freeman. Now there is one mother who has a silver spoon up his ass,' Simms groaned before changing the channel to sports.

'Not a fan, I take it?' Steel smirked, emptying the grocery bag onto the table and spilling the items onto the table.

Simms said nothing, just shot Steel a look that spoke a thousand words.

While they were out getting breakfast, Steel had arranged for three whiteboards to be brought up from the hotel's conference room to be set up in his suite. He also got other items, including minicams, markers, sticky tape, maps, and Post-it Notes from the local store.

Simms had made the coffee and found a ballgame while Steel arranged the boards, so they stood against an empty wall near the bathroom, then suggested using their files to create two murder boards.

He took Alison Kline, and Kitty was working on Mark Trent. Mark Trent had been the first murderer. He had been a security officer at the Manhattan Mall. Trent had died when his computer screen blew up, and he took glass shards to the face and throat.

Kitty and Steel's boards were almost similar in an arrangement. With a map showing where the victims lived and worked and Post-its with information stuck onto relevant points, only Steel's had a timeline.

Trent was killed at home on his day off, where Kline was on her way to City Hall.

Steel stood back and compared the two, hoping for a link, a possible connection between them, but he had nothing.

Trent worked for a security firm, so he moved around, working in different locations. On the other hand, Alison Kline was a high-powered lawyer. She dealt with everything from movie stars stealing jewellery to Daddy's little son getting off a hit-and-run while under the influence. In Steel's eyes, they couldn't be any more different if they came from different planets.

'Got anything?' Steel asked, hoping for her fresh eyes to have spotted something.

'No, not really, just the need for more coffee,' Kitty joked as she headed for the kitchenette.

Steel followed and noticed Simms engrossed in the game and eating a bag of popcorn.

'When did you get popcorn?' Steel asked. Impressed at the man's lax attitude toward Brena's orders.

'Never mind that; Brena wants us back at the office,' Kitty said, showing a text she had just gotten.

Simms stood up, grumbling under his breath at having to miss the rest of the game.

'You coming, Steel?' Simms asked.

Steel shook his head. 'I don't think that I'm meant to be there. Don't forget, you're not supposed to be here. You're watching me from your car,' Steel explained.

Simms nodded in agreement; it would look strange if Steel turned up with them. They all turned as Steel's cell phone when began to vibrate loudly across the small breakfast bar of the kitchenette.

'Who is it?' Steel asked as Kitty picked up the device to check the caller ID.

'It's Stanton.' She tossed the phone over.

Steel swiped the answer icon on the glass screen and held the device to his ear. 'Avery, to what do I owe this honour?'

He listened to what his old boss had to say. 'I'll be there as soon as I can.' Steel disconnected and picked up his jacket from the couch. 'OK, I guess I will take that ride after all.' He pulled on his jacket.

————

Brena had left Stanton's office and headed back to his. He had plans to make. He knew now where the killer's next target would be; he just didn't know who. For Brena, it was a race against time, not just to save this latest victim but to beat Steel to the punch.

As Brena left the office, Stanton began to have reservations about Brena's motives. This case had the makings of an international incident, especially if the killer was going abroad — that was INTERPOL's backyard, and Stanton didn't need that sort of heat. Straton rocked in his office chair, pondering what to do next. Forcing Steel and Brena to work together was a bad idea. Steel was a lone wolf, always had been, and Brena was a glory hound. Their working together would create more problems than it would solve. If he ordered Brena off the case, he would find a way to get back onto it. No, there was only one solution to the problem, and he didn't like it. They would both work the case, but Brena would be under the impression Steel was out.

Stanton didn't like the plan because that made Steel leave last time.

———

Steel sat in the back of the Challenger, his thoughts elsewhere. Simms had the game on the radio. By the sound of things, it would be a close one. Steel never really understood the game; for him, it was like a game he had played as a child back in Britain. Simms was rooting for the Tigers; Steel guessed it was his local team from Detroit. Steel hadn't caught the other team's name. To him, at that moment, it was just noise. A sound that faded into the backdrop and became a hiss, like white noise, as he began to process things in his mind. Not just about the cases, but about Brena and Stanton, about Kitty and Simms. To Steel, something was off, and he didn't know what it was. Then the memory of his last case started flooding back, filling him with anger.

Simms let out a loud 'yes', punched the air, and briefly swerved the car into the other lane.

The noise brought Steel back to earth with a start, and he was slightly disoriented by it all. 'What happened?' Steel asked, looking around.

'His team won,' Kitty explained, holding on to her seat belt out of fear of Simms's driving.

'Do you always celebrate by trying to kill people?' Steel joked.

Kitty smiled at Simms, who said nothing, just drove with a broad smile on his face.

———

After showing their IDs at the gate, Simms parked, and they all got out. Their cover story for Brena was simple: Steel had found them in the hotel parking lot and asked them for a lift.

So, there was no need to mention the breakfast or them all in Steel's hotel room.

They entered the lobby and passed through a security checkpoint, bag checks, and metal detectors. Steel caught up with Simms and Kitty, and they took the elevator up to the third floor. The ride up was quiet, so quiet Steel felt the need to start whistling just to break the silence but fought the urge. Finally, the doors slid open, and they got out. Steel headed left and the others right. Each said nothing to the other, almost as if the past few hours hadn't happened.

Steel headed towards Stanton's office, where Brenda was waiting for him with a huge smile.

'Go straight in, John; the old man is expecting you.' Her words were soft and seemed to float on air.

Steel thanked her and knocked before entering.

'Come in, Steel, my boy, come in,' Stanton said while pouring two glasses of whiskey.

'A bit early for that, don't you think?' Steel smiled, accepting the glass.

'Son, I've seen you are drinking much worse in Bosnia, a lot earlier than this,' Stanton laughed.

The two men clinked glasses and took a seat.

'So, what's up, Avery? You pulling me from the case?' Steel saw the look of awkwardness on the old man's face as if he were trying to find the right words for the bad news.

'I am sending you to Berlin; see if your hunch was right. Brena will remain here and look at another angel,' Stanton started to explain.

Steel felt that he was being sent away for another reason.

'Look, Steel, I didn't bring you in on this. But, unfortunately, he did,' Stanton growled, pulling the postcard from his desk drawer and handing it to Steel. 'The killer wants you on this, and I'll be damned if I know why, but it doesn't matter.

You and Brena are working on it, together or apart.' Stanton downed his whiskey and moved to pour another.

Steel looked at the postcard, the picture of the Brandenburg Gate, and the writing on the back. Nothing more than Steel's name, no clues to the next victim.

'The next clue is in Berlin; why does he want me in Germany?' Steel asked, downing the contents of the glass.

'Your flight leaves in an hour. So, don't be late,' Stanton took a sip from his fresh drink. 'And Steel?'

Steel stopped as he started to leave and turned to face Stanton, his face expressionless.

'Be careful and watch your back with Brena,' Stanton warned him.

Steel nodded. 'I hope you gave him the same advice about me.'

'Something like that, yeah.' Stanton shrugged. 'Now, get your ass outta here; find this son-of-a-bitch before he kills someone else.'

As Steel left, Stanton looked out his office window and sighed deeply.

# CHAPTER THIRTEEN

STEEL MADE THE HOTEL RESERVATIONS HIMSELF, JUST IN case Brena checked. But, as far as anyone was concerned, Steel was in Berlin attending a trade conference as spokesperson of his family's company.

The long flight allowed him to catch up and ask for some equipment to be dropped off at his hotel. For Steel, the Regent Hotel seemed a perfect choice. Sure it was a little over the top, but he was working undercover.

Steel had booked one of the suites, hoping it would draw attention, knowing Brena would be all over Steel's movements. Still, more than that, he was hoping the killer would also be watching. After all, that was what he was good at what he was doing.

The killer wanted Steel in Berlin. Why? Nobody knows? Perhaps Steel was next, and it was a trap, something Brena would love, but Steel had the feeling there was more to it. Apart from the first killing, the killer had sent a postcard giving a clue. Steel paused to think for a moment. Why hadn't the killer sent a card for the first murder? Was this person relevant? Or maybe a test run to see if they could get away with it?

Steel looked at his watch; they still had another eight hours to go. Finally, he put away his notebooks and settled down for the night. After several complimentary drinks and a meal, Steel closed his eyes and hoped the nightmares didn't return. Not tonight, not ever.

———

Brena sat in his office looking at the files Kitty had brought him earlier, a large, cat-like smirk on his face as he remembered the news; Steel had been sent to Berlin to follow a lead. Of course, Brena had one of his minions track Steel's whereabouts, but regardless, the case was his. He'd asked Stanton for the postcard. After all, it was evidence.

Stanton had sent it down to Brena an hour later, and now it was on the board with a collection of Post-its and scribbles.

'So, where are we with this postcard?' Brena shouted, hoping for some lightning-fast answer that would solve the case.

'The lab found no fingerprints. The ink is regular black Biro, the person is a righty, and it was hand-delivered,' Simms answered with a steaming cup of coffee in one hand and his phone in the other.

'So, what is he trying to tell us? What is it he wants us to see?' Brena walked up to the near to empty board and stared at the picture on the postcard.

'Maybe the next clue is in Berlin; perhaps it's a game, a see-how-smart-you-are sort of thing,' Kitty added.

Brena shook his head, dismissing the idea, probably because she had spotted it.

'No, the other killings had taken place in New York. So, there must be something there to do with Germany or Berlin,' Brena said, trying to hide his disappointment in himself.

'Maybe it's to do with a piece of the Berlin Wall that was brought back?' put forth Trish Edwards.

Trish was wearing jeans and a white blouse instead of a nun's habit.

Brena's eyes lit up. 'Good, find out how many pieces were shipped to the States and where they are now,' Brena ordered excitedly.

There was a hurried sound of typing as the agents got busy with their searches—all but Simms and Kitty, who knew this was a wild goose chase.

Kitty had found Steel and raised an eyebrow when she saw where he was staying. She cracked a smile, knowing he'd had the same thought as she'd had. It was a pity Brena was too full of himself to see the truth.

'Got it,' Trish cried out like a schoolgirl, making Simms roll his eyes.

'There are several pieces all over the US, but there are five in New York. Madison Avenue, Kowsky Plaza, The Intrepid Museum, Ripley's, and the last is at the UN building.'

'Right people, grab your gear! We're off to New York,' Brena yelled like a drill sergeant.

Everyone stood up and grabbed their IDs and guns from their desk drawers. Brena went to walk away when his phone rang; it was Stanton. Brena rolled his eyes at the old man's timing and answered it.

'Yes, sir,' Brena said, hoping the call would take too long.

'Brena, I need Simms and West in my office, special assignment,' Stanton ordered.

'Yes, sir, no problem,' Brena said with a grin. Suddenly, his day was getting better, he had a lead, and he was getting rid of two of his worst agents.

'Simms, West, the boss wants you upstairs now,' Brena said with a smirk. The words 'special assignment' was usually coded for an outstation in Siberia. Simms and Kitty watched as their team left, each member wearing a grin of satisfaction.

'You two,' said a voice from behind.

Surprised, Kitty and Simms spun around quickly to see Stanton standing with a grin of his own.

'Grab your gear; you're going on assignment,' Stanton said with a mischievous grin.

'But sir, we are on this case,' Simms started to argue, suddenly feeling like he'd been kicked in the balls.

'Sorry, you two, something has come up. It looks like a British businessman also happens to be part of the aristocracy. He requires *two* bodyguards, it seems,' Stanton smiled and tossed two brown document envelopes onto Kitty's desk, then turned and walked away.

Both of them stood for a moment, mouths gaping open like carp. Disgruntled, Kitty began to read her orders. Suddenly, the frown was replaced by a huge smile.

'How's your German, Karl?' Kitty said, watching Simms read his.

'*Sehr gut,*' Simms laughed.

Steel's flight landed around two in the morning the next day. The eleven-hour flight had only been disturbed by the transfer flight in France. He'd gotten about two hours of sleep, which was enough to recharge his batteries.

As he walked through the airport to the exit, he couldn't help feeling a little disappointed. He had been in the Army in the nineties, and he'd never managed to see Berlin as it once was. Many of Steel's Army colleagues had visited the city for a long weekend. Others had been stationed there on a tour of duty. But for Steel, this was his first time.

Steel collected his bag from the baggage carousel and headed through the exit. As he made it through the automatic doors, he saw a man in a black suit holding a large sign with Steel's name on it.

Steel walked over to the driver, who was in his late twenties. The man was tall and slender, and his tar-black hair was styled with a military cut. Steel figured he was an ex-marine or other special operations unit. The man definitely wasn't in the forces now, despite having that military look about him.

'I'm John Steel,' Steel said with a mix of suspicion and curiosity.

'I am Daniel Jones. I'm here to take you to the hotel, sir,' said the man with an American accent.

'I never ordered a car,' Steel said, eyeing him closely.

'The managing director sent me, along with your lost luggage,' smiled Daniel.

Steel nodded and beckoned the man to lead the way. He loved the way the Secret Service used aliases for their people. For example, in the MI8, CO was called Managing Director, and the quartermaster was known as Boots and Socks.

All the way to the limo, the conversation was mute at best. Neither of them felt the need to speak, meaning no awkward silence.

The car was a blacked-out Mercedes-Benz Rolls-Royce Edition limousine. Steel looked at the seventeen-foot monster and shook his head in disbelief.

'What's wrong? Couldn't find anything bigger?' Steel joked.

'Sorry, the USS Ronald Regan was on manoeuvres,' the driver laughed. He opened the rear passenger door for Steel, who looked inside and shook his head before getting in.

———

Even at two in the morning, the traffic was pretty heavy. Finally, they pulled up outside the hotel, where the doorman was waiting to open the car door for Steel. The driver got out and started taking the bags from the trunk just as a porter came with a brass luggage trolley. Steel got out and inhaled lungs full of city air.

'*Guten Morgen, mein Herr,*' greeted the doorman.

Steel guessed the man must have been six-six at most, with slim features and short sable hair. His white-gloved hands were the size of shovels.

Steel followed the porter inside while the driver hurriedly got back into the car and disappeared into the traffic. The inside of the hotel lobby was filled with red marble and luxurious fittings. As Steel looked around, he felt he was in another time. This was a five-star hotel, earning them all from what he could see.

Steel made his way to the reception desk and pulled out his passport, ready for the check-in. Behind the desk were two women, a blonde and a brunette. Each was attractive and wore little in the way of makeup.

They were dressed in hotel uniforms: an onyx-black blazer with a skirt and egg-white blouse. Steel took the time to study the lobby as he waited for one of the women to be free to check him in. Steel noticed the cue for the brunette move, and an angry German couple stood next to be served. Finally, a spot became free at the blonde receptionist, and Steel hurried into the spot before the place was taken.

'Hi, John Steel. I believe you have a reservation for me?' Steel said, placing his passport on the desk.

She smiled and took the passport, then checked for Steel's name on the computer.

'Ah, yes. Herr John Steel. We have you down for the superior suite.' Her eyes widened, and the smile broadened as she passed Steel the slip of paper with the check-in details.

Steel thanked her, took the key card, and headed for the elevators.

———

The suite was spacious with a sitting room, two bedrooms, and a bathroom most could only dream of having in their homes. Double windows in the sitting area showed a spectacular view of the city; its lights twinkled like embers of a fading fire. Steel stood for a moment, looking across the magnificent view while the porter unloaded the bags from the trolley.

'Will that be all?' asked the man.

Steel turned to see the man waiting at the door. He smiled and reached into his pocket to find the ten euro note he'd been keeping for such an occasion.

'*Danke*,' Steel said, shaking the man's hand while discreetly palming the cash.

The man bowed slightly as a thank you and left the room. Steel turned back to regard the city and sighed. How he wished he had brought his wife, Helen, here—before that fateful day when everything had changed. Steel glanced at the two black pieces of luggage. One was an armoured suitcase for all your international spying needs and the other a canvas suit carrier.

Steel picked up the suit carrier and was shocked at the weight of the thing and took it to the wardrobe to hang it. He figured there were new suits in there. By the heft of it, he thought there must be at least ten. As he opened the zipper, Steel gasped with surprise. Inside were four new black suits. Five shirts: three black, a dark blue, and deep burgundy. And a special Kevlar-and-titanium vest that was as thin as one of the shirts but had the strength of armour plating. Steel smiled and turned to the suitcase, wondering what possible toys lay within after seeing what was in the suit carrier.

---

Kitty West and Karl Simms searched for their seats in economy class.

She found her seat between two large, sweaty men and Simms was seated next to an attractive woman and an empty seat.

Simms shrugged and smiled sympathetically at Kitty before taking his seat. Kitty looked at her place and hoped the guy with the aisle seat would move and let her in. But the man just smiled at her and waited for her to squeeze past.

*Oh great, this is going to be a very long flight.* Kitty sighed and stuck her bag into the hold above the man's head, with him still not moving, letting her brush up against him.

'Miss West?' asked a male flight attendant.

'Yes?' Kitty replied with a pissed-off look.

'You and your colleague have been upgraded to first-class,' he informed her.

Kitty looked over at Simms, laughing and joking with the woman.

'You can ask him, but I'm pretty sure he won't want to go,' Kitty said, taking her bag down, making sure her CIA badge showed to the man below her. As their eyes met, she smiled. 'Don't worry, it's not like we know where you live,' she joked, hoping the man pissed himself.

The flight was long, for Simms anyway, as he had ended up meeting the woman's husband, a trainee quarterback for the

Chicago Bears. While he sat in silence, Kitty was enjoying the comforts of first class. She didn't know who had paid for the seats, but she was glad they had. In fact, only a complete idiot would give it up—and he was sat in coach with a huge monster of a guy and his hot wife that Simms dared not look at.

# CHAPTER FOURTEEN

STEEL HAD UNPACKED. HE HAD A DISAPPOINTED LOOK ON his face as the suitcase contained only clothes and toiletries. He decided to get some sleep before breakfast, as there was nothing he could do until the daytime. He'd asked for a morning call at seven o'clock and ordered room service and a map of the city.

At seven sharp, there was a knock at the door, and a woman informed him it was room service. Steel yawned and stretched off, almost unwilling to leave the comforts of the bed. He walked over and opened the door. Before him stood a man dressed in a hotel uniform with a service trolley—and, most importantly, breakfast.

He let the man in and tipped him on the way out. The cart was packed: a silver coffee pot and china cup and saucer, mixed fruits, bread, jams, and under a stainless-steel domed canopy were two eggs on toast with bacon.

By eight o'clock, he had eaten, showered, and changed into one of the new suits. The weather outside was warm and inviting, but he feared he wouldn't have much time to see the sights. So, he took the elevator down and decided to hit the streets.

Steel's first port of call was the Brandenburg Gate. He thought it was too obvious a clue to send a postcard with a picture of where the clue actually was, but Steel feared the clues would get more challenging. Whoever the killer was, he wanted them to work for the answers.

Steel stood outside the hotel; he had memorised the street names he needed. Along Charlottenstrasse and then left onto Bundesstrasse 2. Which was a fifteen-minute walk at most.

Steel turned left and followed the street, his mind switching into the zone. He was on the hunt for a killer who was *very* focused. One that had the patience of a sniper and the skill of an EOD tech. Steel was used to track maniacs and terrorists, but this was something new and deadly. But Steel didn't know what scared him more: facing this killer or the fact he was beginning to like the game.

———

Steel arrived at the Gate, a vast sandstone construction with an almost pantheon feel. Twelve towering pillars topped by a decorative hood of copper and stone, crowned by a statue of a woman riding a chariot. Once a symbol of peace and then one of victory.

He walked around the majestic gateway. Looking for a clue or even a hint of why he was sent there. There were plenty of tourists and people going about their business. But nothing out of the ordinary. Steel looked at his watch. It was nearly nine o'clock. He peered around again, ensuring he hadn't missed something. Nothing.

Steel took out the copy of the postcard and examined it again. It was a night-time scene of the Gate in full illumination. He turned the card over. The only thing written on it was Steel's name and the address. There was something about it all that didn't fit, and if he was meant to be there to get the next clue, where was it?

Feeling slightly annoyed and somewhat deflated, Steel headed for the nearest coffee shop. He found a nice restaurant not too far from the Gate and decided to take a seat with a clear view of it, just in case he had arrived too early.

A waiter came and took his order. Small cappuccino. People came and went. Still nothing unusual. Steel pulled out his cell phone and checked his messages, taking advantage of the restaurant's free WI-FI.

He had plenty of missed messages but none from the 11th Precinct. One was from Stanton informing him of Simms and Kitty's departure. Before he'd caught his flight, Steel had phoned Stanton, suggesting that Simms and Kitty would be useful in the investigation. Stanton had agreed and sent them to meet him using a later flight. He'd then gotten back to Steel, giving him the flight number, just in case he wanted to meet them when they arrived. Playfully Steel had upgraded them from coach to first-class; he guessed he did it to rub Brena's face in it. Two of his staff flying first-class would sting, or at least he hoped it would. Steel was surprised that Brena hadn't tried to stop it, or at least tried to send one of his lackeys as well. But then, he didn't like Simms too much, and he most certainly had no love for Kitty.

Their plane would be in around four in the evening. A fifteen-hour flight with one stop-off. Naturally, they'd stay in Steel's suite; after all, they were his security on the trip, or that's what their cover was. A simple ruse enabled them to show their IDs in public without raising suspicion. Steel found it amusing that their jobs would be their cover story, but not half as funny as when they found out he was an actual Lord.

The rest of the messages were spam or people he had no interest in talking to at that moment. The last text message was from his man in his father's company—the man who had sent the new clothes. Steel just referred to him as The Tailor, something that someone had once called the man, and it just stuck.

Steel looked up as the waiter returned with the coffee. Steel thanked him and paid straight away. He figured five euros was enough for the drink and a tip. He sat and watched the stone gate and sipped. It was half nine, and he had nothing. The thing Steel didn't like about this game: he didn't know the rules.

Steel looked at the postcard one more time. Something about it bothered him, but he couldn't put his finger on it. The CSU Department had done every test to ensure there were no hidden messages. Used everything from blacklight to testing with lemon juice but found nothing. Steel figured the message was less complicated than expected, possibly so simple overthinking would draw a person past it.

Steel picked up his cell phone and dialled Stanton's number, figuring that Stanton would be spending a lot of time at the office because of the case, and he'd told Steel his in-laws were over for a visit. The phone rang several times before a groggy-sounding Stanton picked up.

'Hi Steel, any news?' Stanton asked moodily.

'No, I didn't find any messages. So, maybe it's all a big ruse to get us out of the country,' Steel said, disappointed.

'Maybe, but keep on it. Brena is checking out New York; he figures that the Berlin postcard could refer to a piece of wall that had been brought back Stateside.'

'It's possible, doubtful, but possible. I'm going to check out a few more ideas before I pick up my security detail,' Steel laughed.

'OK, watch yourself, Steel; if the killer is there, he's dangerous and smart,' Stanton said.

'Oh, Avery, before I forget, how did the 11<sup>th</sup> Precinct know to send the card to you?' Steel asked quickly before Stanton had time to hang up.

'They didn't. It was hand-delivered.' Stanton's voice trembled with confusion.

'It was hand-delivered to Langley, but it had my New York address on it?' Steel didn't wait for an answer. He ended the call and placed the phone back in his pocket.

Once again, he looked at the postcard and realised *that it* was the missing piece. He was too early. The message said Brandenburg Gate at eleven that evening. Steel smiled smugly, finished his coffee, and stood to leave. He had solved the puzzle. The question now was, where would the next one be, and could he solve its mystery in time?

————

Stanton slammed the receiver onto its cradle. He hated when Steel did that. Having thoughts and not sharing. Stanton finished the glass of Scotch that sat on his desk. He had meant to finish it earlier, but the wait was exhausting, and he'd dozed off on the couch in his office. The dash across the room to his phone had woken him up slightly, but not that much. He couldn't slip back into the dream he was having. A sixty-footer on a pale blue ocean and not a care in the world, and definitely *no* Steel.

Stanton forced himself back to the couch and settled himself for the rest of the night. The smell of Chinese takeaway filled the room with a musty aroma. But he didn't care. He was eating junk food and drinking eighteen-year-old Scotch, and there was no wife to get on his back or kids to argue with, and the most important thing, no in-laws to tell him how he was doing everything wrong. He worked for the CIA as a section chief, and what was his son doing? Twenty-five to life for armed robbery.

Stanton snuggled down, closed his eyes, and pulled the blanket over him. He was warm, fed, and comfortable. All he wanted now was a little time to himself.

Suddenly Stanton's eyes shot open, and he sat up.

'It was hand-delivered, so why did they address it?' Stanton said to himself as he stood up quickly and raced to the war room.

He had left his shoes in his office, but he didn't care, not right now. Stanton searched for the postcard amongst the mass of photographs and Post-its. His hand froze over the thin card. What if he was wrong? What if they both were? Stanton took the pictured card from the board and turned it over. $11^{th}$ Precinct.

'It's eleven o'clock at night, that's what it means, goddamn eleven at night,' Stanton muttered, exhaling the breath of air he'd been holding. Stanton reached for the phone on the conference table and dialled the switchboard.

'This is Section Chief Stanton. Get me Agent Brena in New York.' Stanton waited while the call was put through to the phone in the safe house Brena and the team was using. Stanton listened to endless rings. He wondered where they could be. There should be at least one person there to answer any calls.

Finally, there was a click and then a pause.

'Yes,' a woman's voice quietly answered.

'It's Stanton. Where's agent Brena?'

There was a pause again. Then the woman replied, 'Sorry, sir, Agent Brena isn't here. He's gone out for recon.' Her voice suggested uncertainty.

'Get him to call me as soon as he gets in,' Stanton ordered, looking at his watch. Where the hell was he at three in the morning? And a recon mission on a wall outside of a secure building? Something didn't feel right about the whole tale. If she had said he was out getting drunk or laid, possibly, but that story he didn't buy.

Stanton put down the receiver and headed back to his office. He needed time to think. Twelve hours was a long time to sit and wait but a perfect amount of time to think and plan.

———

Agent Trish Edwards smiled as she put down the phone. She knew where Brena had gone, but it had been their secret, all of them, and she wasn't about to be the one who told. Sure, it wasn't right. But the others had agreed to go along with it regardless. They trusted his judgment.

'Who was that?' Brown asked.

'Stanton. He wanted to talk with Brena. He's got to call the old man back as soon as he gets in before someone suspects anything,' Edwards said sternly.

Brown nodded as if taking in the order.

'Any word on Simms and West?' Trish asked.

'Not much. Heard they got a babysitting detail out of the country.'

'That'll make Brena happy if they're out of his hair,' Trish smiled.

'What will make me happy?' Brena asked as he walked into the room, tossing a long hooded black coat onto the couch.

Edwards's eyes shot over to the coat, one she had never seen him wear before.

'Simms and West have been reassigned, a babysitting gig,' explained Brown, and Brena smiled and nodded. 'Oh, Stanton called. He wants you to contact him ASAP.'

The smile on Brena's face fell away; this news was not so

good. 'When did he call?' he asked Brown, but his gaze fell onto Edwards, eyeing his coat.

'A couple of minutes ago.'

Brena said nothing. He stood there thinking, forming a plan.

'Get some rest; we'll start again in the morning,' he finally ordered. He walked over to the coat and bundled it into his arms, so it was unrecognisable. But Trish Edwards had seen it, and now she wondered not just about the coat but where Brena had been all night. He had told them he would see an old friend, a female friend, and he had some catching up to do.

Edwards had thought it unusual, not just the request for them to keep it quiet but the fact Brena had a friend. Brena was the most extraordinary agent. Straight down the line kind of guy. One that would do what was needed to get their man, but sneaking off and breaking protocol to see a woman? This wasn't the Brena she knew.

Edwards watched Brena disappear into his room. Maybe she was wrong; perhaps there was another side to him after all. Everyone should have love in their lives at least once. Trish had known at once. A great love, but that had gone, and all she had were memories and feelings deep in her heart.

# CHAPTER FIFTEEN

THE FLIGHT ARRIVED IN BERLIN ON TIME. KITTY WALKED onto the connecting gantry with a spring in her step. Simms looked tired and worn out and hoped that the hotel wasn't a dump full of crack addicts and hookers. After a trip from hell, he needed a long bath and a good night's sleep.

They waited at the carousel for their luggage. One suitcase each. Travelling light seemed to be the best option, just in case, there was trouble. In fact, Kitty was impressed with how Steel had moved. *Just buy what you need; everything else is expendable.*

They didn't have to wait long before the convoy of bags traversed their way along the snaking rubber belt. Kitty and Simms stood at either end, so if one missed them, the other had a chance to grab the cases.

Simms looked over with sleepy eyes to where Kitty had stood. He rubbed the tiredness from his eyes to wipe away his blurred vision. Then, as Simms opened them, he found she was gone. Suddenly, Simms was awake. Had someone taken her? Had she left already, thinking he had gone out? His heart began to race. Simms didn't know if it was the overload of coffee on the plane or the fact he'd hardly slept in fourteen hours.

'Karl, are you OK?' asked a familiar voice behind him. He turned to find Kitty with both bags at her side.

He let out a sigh of relief and nodded with a wavering smile.

'No more coffee for you,' Kitty stated, taking control of both bags and wheeling them out.

Simms was close behind, shaking his head and praying someone had sent a car for them.

Outside, the sky was bright but overcast. The odd beam of sunlight was warm as it broke through the clouds. As if playing peekaboo with the people below. Kitty stood for a moment and inhaled deeply. Taking in the scent of a new city. Simms just looked around for a place to light up a much-needed cigarette.

'You ever been here before?' Kitty asked Simms, who had spotted people walking around with cigarettes in no-smoking zones.

'No, you?' He shot back the question while sparking up and taking a long draw on the Marlborough. Simms closed his eye as he felt that sweet nicotine fill his lungs. So engrossed was he, in fact, he never registered her answer or the car that had pulled up to pick them up.

The extended black Mercedes Rolls-Royce Edition limousine glistened in the passing breaks of sunlight. Kitty smiled as a driver in a black suit and hat got out and opened the door for her.

'Simms, shake your ass. We're leaving,' Kitty shouted, making people turn to look.

Simms opened his eyes, and his mouth fell open at the sight of the expensive car. 'Oh, thank you, God,' Simms said, crossing himself twelve times before getting into the car.

There were gentle thumps behind them as the driver

loaded their suitcases. Then the driver's door opened, and their chauffeur slipped into the seat and buckled up.

'So, where are we going?' Simms asked, somewhat suspicious of this man.

The driver didn't answer. He put the car into drive and pulled out, and followed the signs for the Autobahn. Simms was about to ask again when the car phone next to the fully stocked bar rang. Kitty looked at Simms and then back to the phone.

'Do you think it's Stanton seeing if we landed OK?' Kitty asked.

Simms scowled at her and picked up the cordless receiver.

'Yes,' he said, not wanting to give his name away.

'Oh good, you got picked up alright. I'll see you both in about two hours,' Steel's voice boomed from the phone's speaker.

Simms looked at the receiver and shook his head as the line suddenly went dead.

'I'm starting to not like this guy,' Simms said, placing down the handset. He looked over to Kitty and saw she was already asleep. He smiled and decided to do the same. After all, they had plenty of time.

———

Steel sat in the sitting room of the suite. He looked up at the two murder boards and a third he had just constructed. The new board held as many details as he knew on the present case, which he had to admit were very few. The timeline was blank; there were no pictures, less for the postcard. Steel stared at all three while swishing the fifteen-year-old whiskey around in the crystal glass in his hand. If this were a serial killer, there would be a pattern. Someone this complex would have an end game. Steel took a sip of the Johnnie Walker Green.

To The Sentinel, this was a game he wanted Steel to play. This led Steel to believe that The Sentinel was a narcissist, playing a game of Catch Me if You Can.

Steel looked at the first board, the security guard. By all accounts, Mark Trent was an average guy who liked what he did. Trent lived alone. He had no pets or friends to speak of. Both parents had died years ago, leaving him the house he lived in.

Then the second board. Alison Kline. Single, lawyer, a good one at that. No record. Fancy place on 81$^{st}$ Street. No boyfriends, just brief acquaintances to scratch that itch. The two had no ties of any kind. He lived in Queens, and she Manhattan. He'd never done jury duty or been arrested. Steel's eyes drifted to the third board. A blank slate just waiting to be splashed with colour. Steel took another sip of his drink and looked at his watch. Simms and Kitty should have touched down by now, and the driver ready to bring them to the hotel. Steel took another sip of Johnnie Walker, and his gaze tracked back to the empty board.

If there was a pattern, he didn't see it ... not in time to save the next victim. That was the other thing: there was never any timescale given. Usually, it was a case of 'solve this in twelve hours or else.' But this time, there was nothing. It was five o'clock and six hours to go before the meet. Steel had several options to bide the time, but he had to wait for Simms and Kitty. He had no doubt they would each have one suitcase containing only one colour and no style whatsoever. Then, there was a ping on Steel's cell. It was the driver; they'd arrived.

———

Brena had eyes on the pieces of the wall outside the UN building, and Ripley's Believe it or Not, Ordertorium. There were three others, but given the killer's need for the elaborate, the parks and museums didn't seem right. The others had gone to get some shut-eye; he'd volunteered to take first watch. He was good, he'd got his sandwich from the deli, and there were two pots of coffee on the go. Brena prided himself on not sleeping during a stakeout; he'd let the others rest, but he'd stay awake. Brena had a fear of missing something if he closed his eyes.

Several monitors showed a feed from the UN and the Ordertorium. There were hidden cameras that picked up anyone who approached the walls. A good idea by all accounts. The great idea, however, was getting rid of Steel and sending those two idiots Simms and Kitty on babysitting duty. Brena smiled to himself.

Brena knew that Stanton hadn't gotten rid of his star quarterback. He would have been suspicious if he had. But it didn't matter, Steel was far away, and that was all that mattered. As for the other two, Brena's imagination conjured painful ideas of what they were doing while he solved the case of the century. Stanton had Simms and West watching some wealthy Brit who probably treated them like trash and made them sleep in the basement. As for Steel, he was likely stuck in Berlin, chasing false leads and stirring up trouble. Brena smiled again. Life was good.

---

The special edition limo stopped suddenly, giving the two a gentle jolt to wake them.

'Hey buddy, easy on the brakes,' Simms complained as if

trying to mask the fact he'd been sleeping. 'So, which shit-hole hotel have you brought us to?'

The door was opened by a tall man, but that was all either Simms and Kitty saw. The bright light and their sleepy eyes made everything blurry.

'Welcome to *der Regent Hotel*,' said the guy at the door.

As the two stepped out, they hid their eyes from the sun until they could refocus.

'You gotta be shittin' me,' Simms said, as he was the first to look around.

'Is it bad?' Kitty asked, more unwilling to look.

'Oh yeah, it's a real dump,' Simms laughed.

Kitty opened her eyes and looked up. Her mouth fell open.

'Oh yeah, a real dump.' She laughed as they both headed in through the main doors like a couple of teenagers on their first vacation. The lobby was vast, with red marble floors and antique-styled furnishings. Kitty thought it was a mistake or a practical joke made by Steel to get his own back for Barcelona.

'*Guten Tag*,' said a man behind the main desk. He was an older man in an ash-grey suit.

Simms started to say, 'Yes, we're here to see—'

'Ah, yes, the two Americans *für* Lord Steel,' the man said, beckoning them over. He produced two key cards, which they took, and put away in their pockets. 'I will see language is sent up to your room,'

'Room ... you mean rooms?' Kitty asked as a look of fear came over her face. She had seen how Simms lived, and he snored. There was no way they were sharing.

'Yes, you're all in the Presidential suite with Lord Steel, as per his request,' the man said, somewhat confused.

'Oh, yes, that's right, he did mention it. Sorry, long flight,' Simms said, backing away and heading for the elevator before there was a mistake or he woke up.

'Americans,' the man murmured, shaking his head and returning to what he was doing on the computer.

'Oh, my God,' was all that Simms said once they were in the suite.

Steel was amused the first time, but by the seventh time, it had worn thin. He tipped the man for bringing up the bags and waited until the man had left before talking.

'Oh, my—'

'Simms, I swear if you say that one more time, I'm sending you back to Brena,' Steel said, rolling his eyes behind his sunglasses.

Simms calmed down, and he and Kitty followed him around as he gave a tour of the suite. It was a vast multi-bedroomed suite with a dining area and a fireplace in the sitting room. Kitty could see this was meant for a family rather than a British cop pretending to be royalty and two CIA agents. Regardless, she was in heaven.

'OK, you've had a long flight, and we have time until twenty-three hundred.' Steel looked at his watch.

'What happens then?' Kitty asked, picking up her suitcase in preparation for finding the correct room.

'I'll explain everything during dinner,' Steel said as they passed the first bedroom. It was a big room with a king-sized bed and an ensuite bathroom.

'Damn, this room is bigger than my apartment,' Simms declared, checking out the complimentary toiletries in the bathroom. They moved out of that room and headed to the second. Kitty spotted the view as they entered the next bedroom and shouted, 'Dibs!' She tossed her suitcase onto the bed.

'You know I could call seniority over you?' Simms growled.

Kitty smiled and shut the door behind her. Simms looked at Steel for assistance but found him grinning and unhelpful.

'If you want to come between a woman and a view, be my

guest but remember, she's the one who's got your back,' Steel said, walking away.

Simms nodded, realising Steel had a point.

Steel picked up the house phone and spoke to the concierge, and asked if it was possible to make reservations for dinner at eight o'clock at the *Esszimmer*, a restaurant he had seen earlier that morning near the Brandenburg Gate. By all accounts, a great-looking place that appeared more turn-of-the-century than the twenty-first century. An excellent place to dress up rather than sporting jeans and a T-shirt over a cheeseburger.

Steel set down the receiver and looked over to Simms, who had left his bedroom door open, just in case he was needed urgently. Steel watched Simms, who was pulling a cheap black suit from his case.

'I take it you had to pack quickly?' Steel shouted from his chair all the way across the sitting room.

'No, why?' Simms shouted back.

'Because your suits are … disappointing,' Steel replied as he appeared behind Simms, causing Simms to jump.

'Jez, you scared the shit out of me.' Simms held his heart. 'What? Are you a ninja or a friggin vampire?' He laughed, hanging up a suit.

Steel felt the sleeves of the jackets, and a cringing look crossed his face.

'What's up with my threads, man?'

'Nothing for a field agent. But a bodyguard …well, that's a different matter,' Steel smiled. 'Kitty?'

'Yes, what?' she replied while walking out, holding a hand full of sexy underwear.

Steel raised an eyebrow and smiled at her innocent pose. 'Grab your coat; we're going shopping.'

Kitty smiled and disappeared back into the bedroom.

Simms just looked at his suit and stuck out his bottom lip. 'Ain't nothin' wrong with my suits, man. Dude's got a stick up his ass,' Simms mumbled under his breath.

———

At seven-forty-five, the three of them stood in front of the restaurant. Kitty wore a red satin dress with a slit on the left leg and a single strap on the right shoulder. Her Stuart Weitzman pumps glistened with the diamonds encrusted around the heels. Simms stroked the arms of his new Givenchy suit. The lights from the restaurant reflected against the material, giving it a satin sheen. His size-twelve feet were tucked nicely into a pair of Bally dress shoes.

Steel gazed at Simms, who had a smug look on his face. Simms felt Steel staring and turned to him, his hands dropping to his sides quickly as if he had done something wrong.

'OK, your suits are better, and mine are basically crap,' Simms admitted begrudgingly.

'*Were* crap,' Steel said with a smile and proceeded to walk in, followed by Kitty.

Simms froze where he stood for a moment, working over what Steel had just said. 'Were ... what do you mean, *were?*' Simms replied in a high-pitched, alarmed tone.

———

Trish couldn't sleep. It seemed like hours since Brena had sent them into the other room to get some rest. She knew everything was mission ready. They had teams all over, and surveillance cameras were watching and recording. Brena had everything under control; he liked it that way. He loved to be in charge. Trish thought back to Brena's trip off the reservation. It wasn't like him at all; he was a by-the-numbers guy, yet he had slipped away for a private rendezvous.

Her stomach gave a rumble. It was two in the afternoon, and nobody had eaten. Trish stood up and made her way out of the room.

Brena looked up as she sneaked out of the bedroom. 'Where are you going?' he asked as he watched her put her coat on.

'We need food to soak up the coffee, if anything,' she joked, but she just needed to be away from them, if only for a brief moment. She had worked with Brena on more than a few missions, but this time it was different. *He* was different.

'What you going for?' Brena asked, rubbing his stomach.

'What you want?' Trish asked, sounding like she cared.

'I saw a Chinese place down the way; grab some menus,' Brena suggested. Trish nodded and headed out the door. Brena's eyes squinted as the door closed, a look of distrust painted on his face. Brena could feel something was wrong. They had menus from all the local takeaways in a drawer; she knew that. He closed his eyes and shook his head as the sound of loud snoring emanated from the room she had just left.

'Yup, now I get ya, kid,' Brena said with a smile, shaking his head at the volume of Brown's snoring.

# CHAPTER SIXTEEN

DINNER HAD FINISHED WITH COFFEE. THE WAITER HAD insisted they should try the brandy, but Steel had to decline, to his disappointment. The night sky was clear, and the cloudless heavens displayed a vast sky with a blanket of stars and a full moon, which painted everything with a blue tint. The three left the restaurant and headed for the Gate.

'A beautiful night for a stroll, isn't it?' Steel asked as they stepped out into the chilly night air. He looked over at Kitty, who was beginning to shiver. He took off his jacket and placed it on her shoulders.

Kitty looked at Steel and smiled gently.

'Nice night, my ass,' Simms complained. 'I'm freezing my butt off.'

Steel smiled and looked at the heavens. The north star seemed exceptionally bright, as its sparkle seemed to wink at him.

'All I ask is a tall ship and a star to steer her by,' Steel stated.

'That's beautiful. Who said that?' Kitty was impressed at Steel's love for the classics.

'Captain Kirk,' Simms said proudly as he walked past them.

Steel smiled and shook his head in disbelief.

Kitty rolled her eyes and followed behind.

It was a two-minute walk to the Gate. Steel didn't want to rush or seem eager. He knew if the next clue was there; it had been dropped a while ago, possibly before they left the hotel. Kitty had made sure there were cameras nearby to catch a glimpse of the person making the drop—hopefully. Steel knew that whoever it was, they were there just for show. In fact, they probably didn't even know what they were bringing to the Gate. The sound of nearby traffic hung in the air like the sound of the ocean.

The plaza near the Gate was empty, less for the odd couple out for a walk or taking the dog for exercise.

'We stick together, no matter what,' Steel affirmed, looking at the structure.

Simms looked over at Steel with a frown. 'Really, you think something is gonna happen to us here?' He laughed with disappointment. 'You disappoint me, Steel; I figured you were good. Now, I find that you're just paranoid.' Simms shook his head and headed for the carved stone edifice.

But Steel had the feeling something was off. Almost as if someone was watching them.

'You're right,' Steel shouted to Simms, hoping to make the man stop and turn around.

'About what?' Simms asked, toying with Steel, knowing what Steel was apologizing for.

'About me. I do get a little like that sometimes, you understand?'

Simms stopped and looked at Steel, a look of amazement on his face. 'So, what you are saying is I'm—'

Simms never got to finish the sentence. Black SUVs pulled up, and men in black tactical gear leapt out. There was a scream for help as the team dragged a man away. The men screamed orders for him to shut up and piled him into the back of a black transit van before it sped away.

Simms stood open-mouthed.

'Anyway, you were saying I was what?' Steel asked smugly as he walked up to one of the columns.

Simms and Kitty followed, wondering who the men had been and what they wanted.

'Who was that?' Kitty asked, looking about, just in case, there were more hidden in the shadows.

'Lady and Gent, you just witnessed INTERPOL at their finest.' Steel searched the left wall of the centre archway. The walls were smooth to the touch, possibly due to a cosmetic touch-up after the wall had fallen. There was nothing to be seen, such as a hiding place to contain the next clue. Steel ran around, checking the other walls, but found nothing. He sauntered back to Simms and Kitty, waiting at the first wall.

A look of confusion was on his face. 'I could have sworn it would be here ... so that's what the message meant, I'm sure of it,' Steel said, puzzled.

'Are you sure that's what the message said?' asked Kitty, resting a consoling hand on his shoulder.

'What do you mean?' Steel asked, glancing at where the man had been snatched.

'Aren't you a little curious that INTERPOL turned up at just that moment we should have been there?'

Steel thought for a moment and then nodded in agreement. Their being there simultaneously was too much of a coincidence.

'What's the plan now?' Simms asked, hugging himself as he attempted to keep warm.

'Go back to the hotel, get some rest, and start fresh tomorrow.' Steel's words were hard, almost angry.

The walk back to the hotel was silent. Simms and Kitty dared not speak, especially to Steel, who had the look of a man ready to do damage.

———

Trish lay awake, her eyes mapping out the marks on the ceiling as if they were some filthy constellation. She couldn't sleep. It was in the middle of the day, and she didn't want to confuse her body's clock. Besides, something was eating at her. Where had Brena been the night before, and where had the coat come from? She wondered about Simms and Kitty. Trish had passed on the message that made Brena extremely happy; they were on babysitting duty for some Lord. On the other hand, something inside her felt sad, almost disappointed, jealous even. They were on a job that could lead to other things, Whitehouse things.

Working on this case was a golden opportunity for Brena. She knew, first chance, his name would be all over the report, possibly his face in the paper, whereas the rest of the team would be lucky if they were a footnote. Brena was an excellent agent, but he looked after only one person: himself. Trish had seen him ruin careers because of anything or anyone that might make him look bad—and lucky her, she was the guy's replacement.

Trish sat up and reached for the bottle of water that sat on the floor next to her bed. The ice-cold condensation on the bottle tickled the skin of her hand as the droplets rolled over her fingers. Finally, Trish cracked the top and took a mouthful.

The room's air conditioner was busted, so the humid air was thick and warm. Outside, it was in the high twenties. Inside, the room felt like a South American jungle, except the jungle probably had fewer bugs.

Trish got up and headed for the bathroom. White-tiled walls and floor made the whole place look like a butcher's work area. Pockets of a black mould formed in the corners, and the mirror were made from polished metal instead of glass.

It wasn't the Ritz, but it was the only place close enough for the teams to be near the UN building. Trish ran the water until the colour resembled something clear, then splashed water on her face.

Trish looked up at her reflection in the metal; she hoped this all worked out. She hoped they find the killer. But most of all, Trish hoped Simms and Kitty were having a really shitty time.

———

Simms and Kitty went back to the suite while Steel headed for the bar. It had been a long and fruitless day, and he needed a drink. A martini, two shots of Blue Sapphire gin and a lime wedge. He had acquired the taste for a simple drink. Tonight wasn't a night for whiskey. He needed something with a bit more kick.

Steel ordered the drink and waited while the server mixed the concoction. She was a young blonde with long legs and a happy smile. Her uniform fitted her well, unlike some places where they expected the waitress to serve wearing high heels and scanty clothes that barely fit them.

'Is it your first time in Germany?' she asked, sliding over the drink.

'No, I was here a long time ago, with the Army.' Steel smiled as if a fond memory had just crept into his mind.

'So, you're here on holiday?' she asked, checking his fingers for a ring.

Steel smiled. The attention was a welcome distraction.

'Something like that, and have you worked here long?' he asked, observing her eye movements and gestures with her eyebrows, mouth, and hands. This was a definite come-on; he just didn't know why. Possibly for better tips, places did that, but then she was dressed wrong for that. The attraction couldn't be ruled out, be he had just come in.

Steel paid for the drink using small change and gave her a tip with more change. She thanked him and stayed to talk while she polished her glasses. Steel looked up at the mirror behind the bar to see two other men walk in and sit down at the far side of the bar, and two others sat in the chairs to his far left, near a window. All four men were big and looked like they could handle themselves. Steel sipped his drink. Not wanting to risk getting poisoned. Not on the first night, anyway.

The server, whose name tag said *Brigit*, walked over to the two men at the bar and began to talk in German. Steel could tell the small talk was as fake as the covers. Steel re-checked the mirror. The two men sat, pretending to look at bar menus. Steel began to have that feeling again. He knew this setup. Hell, he had shown it to her. The question was, where was Agent Sabine Boese of INTERPOL?

Brigit came back, wearing her wide white smile. They probably chose her because of her bubbly personality and good looks, hoping to lure Steel into a deadly nightcap.

'So, where are you from?' Brigit asked, picking up a glass and cleaning it with a cotton cloth.

'The UK ... just here on a spot of business and to see the sights,' Steel answered with a charming smile.

'Oh, I love London,' she said with a dreamy look on her face.

'So, you've been to London?' Steel asked, waiting for some sort of brief but made-up account.

'No, I've never left Germany,' Brigit responded with a smile and a shrug.

'Oh, that's a shame. You should ask your boss if you could go.' Steel sat back on the barstool.

'What, Herr Franks?' Brigit asked, looking over at a small, white-haired man on the other side of the bar, checking menus.

'No, Agent Sabine Boese,' Steel said.

The smile dropped from her face, and the men stood up to surround him. Steel just sat and enjoyed his drink, waiting for her to arrive.

———

A woman stepped into the bar and stopped at the entrance. She was in her late thirties, with long legs and an hourglass figure. She had short-cut hair with no particular style, her skin was smooth, and her blue eyes sparkled like the jewels in the chandeliers. Sabine was of African-American-German descent. Her father had been an American MP stationed in Berlin. Her mother had worked in a bakery down the road from the barracks.

Steel had almost forgotten how stunning she was, with a smile that could put a rainbow to shame for its natural beauty.

Sabine spotted Steel and smiled. She knew he was watching in the mirror. 'Old habits die hard,' she thought as she sat down on the empty seat beside Steel.

'Good to see you again, John.' Her words were like silk, soft but with a hint of strength.

'And you are looking as fantastic as ever, may I say,' Steel replied, spinning on his chair to take a better look at her.

'As do you, John; I see you've bulked up a bit since last we met ... still training like a madman, I see,' Sabine joked, giving Steel the once-over. 'What are you doing in Berlin?'

'That's what I've always loved about you, Sabine, always straight to the point, no foreplay. I'm on vacation, just thought I'd pop over to see the city I kept meaning to get to but never found the time for,' Steel replied before taking another sip of the poorly made drink.

'And the agents, why are they here?' Sabine asked.

'Bodyguards,' Steel said with a flippant tone.

'Bodyguards, Including the girl?' Her face was screwed up in anger.

'Yes, you never know when I may get attacked. But, unfortunately, it does happen,' Steel shrugged.

'John, of all the people I know, you are the last person who needs a bodyguard. And the only person who may attack you is me,' Sabine growled.

'Interesting, but you're going to have to buy me dinner first,' Steel said with a grin.

Sabine looked away, trying to force a smile from her face before she turned back. Her hands gripped the bar before she found them around his throat.

'You still like Italian, right?' Steel placed a hand on hers.

Sabine looked at him; her eyes were wide and glassy, a mixed look of happiness and anger swirled in the pale blue pools. 'You can't turn back time Steel; what happened, happened, and you can't change that,' Sabine said flatly, pulling her hand away and standing up. 'Be on the next flight home; your trip is over,' she ordered.

'I can't do that, Sabine; I'm sorry.' Steel stood and looked at his watch. It was more early than late.

'Why are you here, John?' she asked again, her tone harder.

'Speak to Stanton. He'll explain. In the meantime, I'm tired. It's been a long day.' Steel leaned forwards and gave Sabine a small peck on her cheek.

Sabine closed her eyes at the warmth of his breath and the

smell of his skin and cologne. All the memories came back to her, and not only did he look as good as ever, but he smelled even better as well. Sabine felt her knees buckle slightly as he whispered something into her ear.

Steel stepped back and smiled. 'We really must do lunch or something, perhaps dinner, tonight?'

Before she could answer, Steel had turned away and left, leaving her standing at the bar. All her emotions tangled in a knot.

'What do you want us to do?' asked one of the men at the bar.

'Keep tabs on them. I want to know every move they make,' Sabine ordered as she turned and picked up Steel's drink and downed it in one gulp. Her face cringed with discomfort. She slammed the glass on the bar. 'Jez, Steel, have you got any liver left?' She winced at the taste of the drink.

The men hurried out of the bar, with Brigit close behind. Sabine pulled out her cell phone and dialled a number on her speed dial.

The phone rang for a short while before a voice answered on the other end. 'Stanton here.'

'Avery, it's Sabine Boese.'

'Sabine, it's been a long time. What can I do for you?' Stanton replied with a joyful tone.

'You can tell me why John Steel is in Berlin.' Sabine's voice almost purred; she was hoping he was there for one purpose. The postcard killer who called himself The Sentinel.

## CHAPTER SEVENTEEN

STANTON LOOKED OUT OF HIS OFFICE WINDOW. BLACK, foreboding clouds had brought the rain that came down in sheets. He rested a massive sprayed hand on the cold glass as he stared out onto the car park and the flashes of light from the heavens. Stanton didn't know if it was a bad omen that the weather had changed just after Sabine had hung up. He didn't believe in such things, but the irony of the situation was only brought out in movies. As far as Stanton was concerned, the woman was trouble. In fact, she was a female version of Brena. Stanton smiled at the thought of those two getting together.

Steel had known her for a long time, but the last time they met, it didn't end well, not for Steel anyway, nor for Stanton. Sure, she was a good agent, but she was also a massive pain in the ass and someone he could do without. Stanton had told her why Steel was there; she seemed happy to hear about it and was probably ordering a new suit for the press conference.

Stanton turned to his desk as his phone began to ring. The caller ID said it was an unknown number. Cautiously, he picked up the receiver and answered with a simple, 'Yes?'

'It's Steel. I ditched my phone, and I got the others to do the same. I'll have new numbers for you by morning,' Steel explained, but Stanton didn't answer. 'Why is she on this case, Stanton? What aren't you telling me?' Steel asked from the public phone.

'She said she got a tip, a postcard which was identical to the one we have,' Stanton explained, hoping Steel wouldn't bail because of her. 'I told her we have a point. So far, there has only been an incident on US soil, so she doesn't have jurisdiction.'

'I don't want her on this, Stanton; she better stay out of my way,' Steel growled, making the man at the next booth turn away, scared by Steel's tone.

'I know Steel, but that is out of my hands. Just try and stay out of her way, solve this and come home,' Stanton said calmly.

There was a click to signal Steel had put down the phone, but Stanton stood still, frozen.

'I hope to God she stays out of this one, for all our sakes,' Stanton said, falling into his office chair, the receiver still in his hand.

———

Steel walked back to the room from the street. He had used a payphone he had found in a nearby restaurant. He was lucky; he thought things had all gone due to cell phones, but he had faith in people's needs to stay in touch. Steel knew it wouldn't be long before Sabine had tracked down the phone and traced it back to Stanton, but that didn't matter. He had passed on the message. That was good enough for now.

Steel had another problem. If the killer was going to drop off another clue, her little stunt hours before might have spooked him, and now he was in the wind, or worse, The

Sentinel thought Steel had brought her in. As Steel neared the hotel, a man in a long hooded coat bumped into Steel.

'*Entschuldigen Sie*,' a gruff male voice said before continuing on his way.

Steel quickly patted himself down. Good, everything was there. Steel felt something in his coat pocket. Slowly, he placed his hand in and pulled out a piece of a card. Steel's eyebrows raised, and he tucked the card back into his pocket. He looked back down the street, but the person was gone. Turning, he headed inside the hotel. He had much to tell the others about Sabine Boese and the card the killer had just slipped into his pocket.

'That was quick,' Simms said, looking at his watch. 'Thought you Brits liked to drink?' he joked.

But Steel didn't laugh. His face was expressionless and cold. Steel looked around the suite. 'Where's Kitty?' he asked, expecting her to be lounging on the couch or at least in bed, catching up on her sleep.

'She just went to a local garage to get a drink. Apparently, the mini bar has bugger all, and I was being polite compared to what she had said,' Simms laughed.

Steel remained stone-faced and unamused, but it was more due to the situation than Simms's attempt at humour. There was an electronic beep and a click as the suite card was used. The door opened, and Kitty stood at her door, holding a carrier bag full of bottled water and chips. She saw something was wrong. Something had changed.

'What is it?' Kitty asked, stepping out into the sitting area and placing the bag on the carpet next to her seat.

'I met with INTERPOL, or rather they tracked me to the bar downstairs. I spoke with the lead agent, Sabine Boese,' Steel began as he crossed the floor to the drinks cabinet and poured a

Treble whiskey neat. 'It appears they are also on the case because the killer also sent them the same card as what we have.'

Kitty and Simms gave Steel a look of shock and puzzlement.

'So, our killer has a sense of drama or weird humour, his making us fight for the right to catch him, pitting us against INTERPOL?' Simms snarled.

'What happens now?' Kitty asked, sitting down on the couch and picking up a water bottle from the plastic carrier.

'I've spoken with Stanton. He wants us to carry on. So far, INTERPOL has no case. The killings have only happened Stateside,' Steel explained, his face cold and unfeeling.

'I mean about the next clue; this Sabine chick probably scared off the killer with that circus earlier this evening,'

Steel smiled grimly and shook his head.'I think the first postcard was a test to see who would do what,' he said, sitting opposite Kitty.

'So, who won?' Simms asked, hoping this Sabine Boese had dropped the ball.

Steel smiled and pulled out the card using the tips of his index and middle finger. 'Don't pack your bags. The game is still on,' he said with a wicked smile.

———

The following day was cloudy with a stiff breeze. People filled the streets, going to that job they had to endure to pay the bills, or tourists escaping the life they'd left behind, if only for a little while. All of them were stuck in that rut, oblivious to the killer who watched them from afar. But none of them were The Sentinel's targets. Instead, his foes hung on several whiteboards and were shown on monitors. Their lives are mapped out and on display.

The Sentinel sat at a special workbench full of bits of metal, fine adjustment tools, and watchmakers' magnifying glasses fixed to the bench. Boxes of wires and solder sat next to a precision soldering iron.

As The Sentinel worked on a small circuit board, 'We Have All the Time in the World' played in the background from a CD player. The haunting voice of Louis Armstrong echoed throughout the apartment.

A clap of thunder was followed by a low rumble, signalling the storm had arrived. The woman on TV had predicted it days ago. A low front from the south was meeting up with a high from the east. It was bound to have happened at some point; they'd had days of sweltering heat, and now it was about to break.

Another clap of thunder followed by a brilliant flash filled the room. The noise was like an explosion. The Sentinel rocked in the chair and watched, finding the storm calming as the rumbles grew louder.

———

Steel had made a photocopy of the postcard and shipped the original back to Stanton in Virginia. Steel suspected Sabine wouldn't get another card; she hadn't played nice, after all. However, he understood this was a game and, like most games, there were rules. The problem was no one knew what these rules were. Steel pinned the copy onto the board and stood back.

'So, what does it mean?' Simms asked as he stared at the photocopies of the front and back of the card. The front picture was of an eagle with the Manhattan skyline in the background.

'To detective, John Steel 425 Precinct' was written on the back in bold letters and had no characteristic handwriting pattern.

'Well, in all of these, the killer has used a thick pen and not printed them, meaning he is mobile or he's smart enough to know each printer can be traced. The pen has been held straight up, like how a child uses a pen; this means it will be hard to say if we have a lefty or righty here. We now know that the address means time, but it's the picture that is always the puzzle,' Steel said, staring at the pictures.

'Well, it seems to me like he's sending us back Stateside,' Simms said.

Steel shook his head. 'Then why bring us all the way here? No, there is more to it than that?' Steel's face was filled with a strange excitement.

'Maybe we should look at this as if there are two pictures, not one,' Kitty said, holding a copy of the postcard.

Steel looked over at her and smiled.

'How do you mean?' Simms asked, holding the A4 copy up to the light.

'What if each piece in the picture was a clue in itself, like the eagle and the New York backdrop, two completely different clues?' Steel suggested.

'Exactly, we just got to figure out what they mean before four-twenty-five tomorrow afternoon,' Kitty shrugged.

'OK, it's midnight. I want everyone to get some rest, with fresh eyes tomorrow,' Steel ordered.

Simms and Kitty nodded and said their goodnights. As Steel watched their doors close, he knew there was no chance he was sleeping, not with the clock ticking on a person's life.

He phoned down to room service and ordered a fresh pot of coffee, and told them to put it into a Thermos jug. It was going to be a long night, but his adrenaline was pumping. Steel opened his laptop and got to work. He had to find who was known as The Eagle or the *Der Adler*. The picture of Manhattan was also part of the clue. The question was, how?

The coffee arrived ten minutes later, along with a turkey-bacon sandwich to tide him over. Steel was hoping that Stanton was on the same wave of thinking; if not, the note Steel had included in the overnight delivery would give him a push.

Steel poured himself a cup of coffee and picked up half the sandwich. His mind sifted through streams of data and possibilities. They were in Berlin for a reason; a person would be chosen, given the killer's MO. They knew that The Sentinel found public places to assassinate people. Given that they had travelled halfway across the world, the idea of a random killing was out.

Steel looked at his laptop, hoping to get more than ornithologist sites and pictures of birds. The Sentinel wanted him to search for someone called The Eagle. That was the clue. He was sure of it. The internet was a bust. Steel had inspected birdwatchers and *Wikipedia* information sites that came up in the search. Steel tried *Der Alder* and got the same but in German.

Steel's fingers danced on the keyboard with just the right amount of pressure to make a sound but not enough to enter a letter. He was missing something. A bit of information stuck in the back of his mind. Steel finished the coffee and then poured another one before using the search engine to look for the type of bird of prey in the picture, hoping that was the big break. Unfortunately, the search revealed nothing more than a thousand pages of birds of prey.

Steel downed the rest of the coffee and placed the cup by the side of the computer. Steel didn't know if it was frustration or tiredness, but he found it hard to concentrate. It had been a long day, and a little sleep would help him think clearly. He closed the laptop and headed for his room. There was nothing more he could do for now. Fresh eyes, a fresh start in the morning.

As Steel shut off the lights and closed his door, a figure crept out of one of the bedrooms. It moved quickly but quietly across the floor and out of the suite.

———

It had gotten dark early in New York. The blackened clouds remained, but the storm had passed over hours ago, leaving lakes on the streets and roads. Brena looked at his watch: seven o'clock. They had been sitting in the safe house for hours, watching the footage but with no results. Brena could feel the veins in his forehead twitch and his blood boil. He had been made to look a fool, but the worst thing was that it was his own doing, but he couldn't take the blame. Brena looked over at Trish and the other team members with a look of callous intent. He needed one of them to botch the mission so they could all go home.

Brena looked back at the monitors and hatched a plan; the question was, who was getting thrown under the bus?

Trish caught Brena's reflection in the window; she saw the look of cold calculation. He was plotting something, and it involved them. She carried on working, checking the computer for any updates on the bombing in New York, but the tests would take time.

Trish changed her search for information on the first victim, Mark Trent, the security guard. The guy had no web history; he didn't even come up on Google. For all purposes, he was a nobody. So, why kill someone like that with such vicious intent? By all accounts, the two victims had no history together, nothing. Trish looked at the window again and caught Brena's reflection once more. Now, he looked smug, almost as if he had found a solution. But she feared who the plan was for: the killer or them?

———

Steel had woken early and was already pounding out an eight-mile run. Outside was dark with a bitter chill. But that didn't concern him; if anything, the cold air against his skin was refreshing and stimulating. He had let the other two sleep. They'd had a long day, and today would probably prove to be just as challenging.

He headed for the Brandenburg Gate with the hope that seeing it again with fresh eyes might jog something in his mind. Steel thought back to the stranger who had passed the message to him. He had been shorter than Steel, had a long black hooded coat, and ... a scent. The man had smelt of something that Steel recognized but couldn't quite place.

The sound of Steel's footsteps echoed in the plaza. The sound of his heart was in his ears, mixed with every steady breath. Why had the message been passed that way? A possible signal to say 'I can get close to you or even a warning to confirm he is being watched?

Steel stopped at the Gate and looked up at the grand structure. Why had he been brought here? Of all the landmarks in Berlin, this was the most prominent, yes. But surely others, such as the Cathedral or Checkpoint Charley, would have done just as well?

The chatter of birds grew louder, as did the sound of traffic as it began to build. Steel hoped that Stanton had come up with something on the name Adler or Eagle, but he wasn't confident that would have happened. He walked along the stone walls of the massive gateway, his fingers brushing the cold smoothness as his mind wandered and calculated.

The picture was almost certainly that of an eagle. The background was undoubtedly New York, so what did they both mean? Steel checked his phone; there were no new messages. He tucked the cell into his pocket and ran back to the hotel. Time was running out, and he had nothing to work on.

By the time he got back, the sky was light purple. It was going to be a beautiful day, but they wouldn't have a chance to enjoy it. Steel headed up to the suite and stretched off in the empty elevator. What he needed now was a shower, a cup of coffee, a good breakfast, and a lead on who they were searching for.

On the fifteenth floor, an old married couple shuffled into the elevator. Steel smiled and nodded a greeting. The couple returned the gesture and waited for the doors to close. Steel said nothing. He just looked into space and listened to the old couple's conversation. Steel figured they were from the south, possibly the Munich region, given their accent. Most of the chatter came from the old woman, complaining about the flight they had taken and about the customs officer who had pulled them over for a baggage check.

'As if I could smuggle anything in those old suitcases of ours,' she complained, her husband nodding without interest, just to keep her amused.

Steel smiled to himself, not just because of the old couple's conversation but because she had just given him a clue to the identity of the person they were looking for.

———

Steel burst through the suite door to find Simms and Kitty enjoying breakfast. Kitty looked over to Steel with half a croissant sticking out of her mouth; Simms had a cappuccino moustache.

'The man we are looking for is called The Buzzard, not Eagle or Adler,' Steel said eagerly.

'How do you know?' Simms asked, wiping the foam from his top lip.

'A while back, we uncovered a weapons smuggling operation in New York—'

'The ship in the harbour?' Kitty interrupted.

'Yes, the ship in the harbour. Anyway, we discovered most of the people involved, and the name The Buzzard came up; I believe that's who we are looking for,' Steel explained.

'What makes you think he's here?' Simms asked, unconvinced.

'Because his name is Karl Falkner, and he lives in Berlin,' Steel replied with a smile. 'The only problem is, that information is *years* old, and we don't know where he is now,' he admitted, the smile falling from his face.

'So, how do you know he's still here? He could have moved. He's probably in Frankfurt or bloody Australia by now,' Simms exploded.

Steel nodded. He had to admit that was a possibility. 'True, but you're forgetting one thing.' Steel walked over to the boards. 'The Sentinel sent us here,' Steel said, tapping the first postcard.

'So, how do we find him?' Kitty asked before shoving in another mouthful of the croissant.

'We could cross-reference all known criminals with travel arrangements, get onto the German authorities, and see if they have a possible location,' Simms put forth excitedly.

Steel poured a coffee and picked up the phone, and waited for the front desk to answer.

'We could check the FBI, CIA and Homeland database to check for last known locations or alias,' Kitty added, her heart racing at the sudden thrill of the chase.

'We could do all that, I suppose ...' Steel paused and raised a hand as the front desk picked up the phone, 'Good morning, Lord Steel here. I wonder, do you have a phone book I could borrow?' Steel requested smugly.

Kitty looked over to Simms and shrugged, 'Or we could do that, I suppose,' she said with an awkward grin.

# CHAPTER EIGHTEEN

It was ten to six when Trish made it to the piece of the Berlin Wall at the UN building. She didn't know what she was there to do; they already had cameras on the place in the hope of catching a picture of the killer. But Brena had sent her anyway. An agent called Mark Dutton had gone to Ripley's to do the same. Dutton was a new agent fresh from the farm. He was a tall, thin-looking guy in his mid-twenties. A crew cut shaped his soot-black hair. He was green but a quick learner and capable, from what Stanton had seen.

Their orders were simple: observe and report. A simple task for sure, but if anything stupid was done, if this killer were that smart, he would be able to spot an agent a mile off. That's when it hit her; they were there to mess things up. It all made sense now. The operation had been a bust from the start, but Brena didn't have the balls to admit it had gone under—too much of a spotlight for him to fail, so he had to send someone who could be blamed if it went sideways.

Trish sat in an old beat-up Ford transit van, which smelt of greasy food, BO, and cheap air fresheners. Another agent had driven the van. Ensuring that it was parked away from any street lamps on East 45<sup>th</sup> Street at the beginning of the operation.

It was just a guy parking his van, a great disguise, she had to admit to the casual observer. The side-panel windows were blacked-out, allowing enough room for the monitoring cameras to get full shots. Trish was glad she had gotten the UN building; less chance of things going sideways. Ripleys was too confined and had nowhere to hide out. But still, she had to be on her guard even though this was an 'observe only' task, one slip-up and Brena would say it was her fault and scrub the mission.

Trish took out her tablet and opened it. The images were broken down into six smaller screens, each live stream. Placing the tablet onto its angle rest, she cracked open one of the bottles of water she had brought in her away bag and began to take small sips while she watched.

Outside the van, it was quiet and dark. The section of wall was on the grounds behind the UN building, making a line of sight impossible from the road. The UN security was on standby to apprehend anyone as soon as she gave the word. The other observation team had gone, leaving her with the next eight hours. Trish just loved shift work, especially in the back of a cramped van. She wasn't surprised to see she was on this by herself, even though regulations stipulated there should be more than one at any given time. Trish knew why she was alone, but she didn't mind. In fact, she welcomed it. If perchance, she did catch the killer, it would be her alone who had done it.

Trish took another sip of water. Her gaze switched between those on the tablet and the ones on the monitors. She smiled as she watched the images on her tablet. Black and white pictures of a man in a bedroom, working on his laptop.

———

Steel had showered and changed before feasting on a hearty breakfast. He was on his second cup of coffee when he contacted a friend in an agency, asking if they had or could get Falkner's location. The phone book idea would have been a good one. However, Steel hadn't counted on so many Karl Falkners in Berlin.

Kitty West decided to shower while they waited. She knew as soon as they had a lead, Steel would be out of the door in seconds. Karl Simms decided to wait it out and finish his breakfast while he did something on his tablet.

Steel watched Simms as he flicked through images on his device, images from what appeared to be security cameras. Steel's sunglasses hid his eyes, ensuring his gaze was unnoticed, making a perfect cover to catch a look at the tablet as he walked over to the boards. However, idle curiosity and Steel's trust issues played a significant role in his actions. He decided to stroll past Simms.

Simms watched Steel walk his way, pulled his tablet close to his chest, and waited for Steel to be at a safe distance before continuing his work.

This made Steel smile at the man's evasive actions. He stood in front of the whiteboards and checked the copies of the postcards. Looking to see if there were any similarities in how they were set out.

Two of them had pictures of New York, each with different times of day, whereas the new one was of Berlin at night. Each address gave a different precinct number that didn't exist, which they had worked out to be a particular time. The killer was playing a game, leaving clues, breadcrumbs, that others had failed to see. If they had, the other people wouldn't have been killed.

Steel crossed his arms in contemplation as he stared hard at the boards. Something about the first two seemed different, as if something was missing. Then, feeling that someone was behind him, Steel turned and found Kitty close by. She wore a bathrobe with a towel wrapped around the top of her head.

'Found anything yet?' Kitty asked, looking hopeful at the prospect.

'No, not yet,' Steel replied, shaking his head, his eyes fixed on the problem. 'Did we get copies of everything?' Steel finally realised what was bothering him.

'Yes ... I mean, I think so. Why?' Kitty asked with a confused look.

'Something was bothering me about the boards, a nagging feeling something was missing.' He pointed to the three boards.

Simms put down his tablet and moved over to join them.

'What's missing from the other boards?' Steel asked while a smile cracked the side of his mouth.

'Well, there are postcards, each one different; there is a map,' Simms said, his eyes failing to see Steel's noticed problem.

'Before each of the previous murders, the killer sent a single postcard, but this time he sent two. Each postcard had hidden within it a location and time. But the latest has a time and a name.' Steel pointed to the most recent card on the board.

'So?' Simms asked, failing to see the point.

'My point is, why didn't he do it the other times, and if he did, where are the other postcards?'

Simms' eyes widened. If Steel was correct, there should be more somewhere. If so, that could help break the code that could help find the victim and hopefully locate the killer!

Karl Simms picked up his cell phone and pressed the speed dial for Stanton's office.

Steel and Kitty looked on as Simms waited for someone on the other end to answer.

It would be about four in the morning in the States, but Simms knew Stanton would be at the office to see this through.

'Sir, it's Simms. Yes, everything is fine, apart from we don't seem to have all the copies of the postcards from the previous murders,' Simms said, looking at Steel, who was still staring hard at the boards.

'Yes, sir, I understand. I'll let him know,' Simms acknowledged Stanton and hung up the call.

'He told you we had everything, didn't he?' Steel asked, still taking in the information before him.

'Yes, how did you know?' Simms asked, amazed.

'I don't think there were any more. In fact, I believe our friend here didn't start sending second clues until I was brought in,' Steel said, taking the new postcard from the board.

'So, this is about you?' Simms asked, a tone of anger in his voice. 'That's a bit self-aggrandizing, don't you think?' He took a seat next to Kitty.

'Possibly, but looking at this whole thing, I believe he wants us to find these people first,' Steel explained as he put the card back on the board.

'People?' Kitty asked, almost scared at what Steel would say next.

'This killer studies his victims. Knows their schedules, routines, their lives inside and out. For someone to do that, they don't usually do this once or twice,' Steel explained. 'We are looking at a serial killer, and he won't stop until we figure out his game and stop him.' He picked up his cup and downed the last of the cold coffee.

There was a low buzz as Steel's cell vibrated in his pocket. He took the phone and opened the new message: one hour, the café on Friedrichstrasse.

Steel smiled at the text and tucked his cell back into his pocket.

'What's our next step?' asked Kitty, her eyes wide with both fear and excitement.

'We try and find Karl Falkner, and fast,' Steel stated as he placed down his coffee cup and headed for the door, grabbing his coat from the back of an armchair in the sitting room.

'Where are we going?' Kitty stood quickly, ready for action.

'I'm off to see ...a friend. You two stay here and try and figure out what Falkner was doing in New York recently,' Steel ordered.

'What makes you think Falkner was in New York?' Simms asked, angry at being left behind.

'The postcard shows a bird and the Manhattan skyline; he was there, and something happened when he was,' Steel said, pulling on his coat and pulling open the door. 'There is more to these postcards than just the name of the victim. I can feel it.' Steel looked at the two and smiled gently. 'You can do this.'

And with that, he was out of the door and heading for the elevators. Simms looked over at Kitty, who wore the same concerned look he did.

'Do you think he's right?' Simms asked.

Kitty nodded. A serious look crossed her face. 'Yes, and that's what scares me. What terrifies me more is Steel's involvement in all this.'

'What? You think Steel is part of this?'

'No, I believe he's the last one on the killer's list,' Kitty said with glassy eyes and a tremor in her voice.

———

Stepping out of the hotel, Steel was greeted by the warmth of the morning sunshine. White clouds sailed past a light-blue backdrop. High above, the vapour trails from aeroplanes left their marks. The street was busy with townsfolk and tourists.

Taxis shuttled their fares, and the odd police vehicle drifted by as they made their patrols. It was a warm day with no signs of turning.

He stood for a moment to get his bearings, taking note of places anyone could watch from or possible snipers nest. Steel knew that vans were a favourite for reconnaissance vehicles, so he looked for transit vans, especially those that appeared like they had been there a while. Steel knew he was being watched, but by whom was a different matter. If he were a betting man, he'd say it was INTERPOL, but he couldn't be sure.

Closing up his coat, Steel took a right and headed north towards the local stores. He could feel eyes on him, but he didn't care. After all, they weren't after him. Steel walked a few more blocks, ensuring he made as many turns down side streets and went inside as many stores as he could. If there was a tail, he wanted it to be as tedious as possible for them.

As he passed a parked car, Steel noticed the person following him in the vehicle's windscreen, which was as good as a mirror.

The man was an average-looking guy with brown hair and sunglasses. He wore blue jeans and a white T-shirt, almost covered by a blue fleecy bomber jacket. The man tried to look as ordinary as possible—no earbud cable hanging down or talking into his wrist while pretending to cough. No, this guy blended in OK, apart from his stature, which screamed ex-Army, the stiff posture, and the way he tried not to swing his arms in time with each step. It had taken Steel years to lose that look, but he knew it crept back from time to time.

Steel headed into a clothes store with tailored suits and overpriced shoes from Italy. A bell's chime alerted the store-keeper to Steel's presence, forcing a tall senior man out of the back room.

'*Guten Morgen*,' the tailor greeted Steel with a warm smile.

He wore pressed grey trousers and a white shirt with pink stripes; a yellow tape measure hung loosely from his neck. Gold-rimmed glasses sat perched on a Roman nose, his wavy grey hair styled with a side parting.

'*Guten Morgen*,' Steel responded with a nod and smile.

'*Engländer?*' asked the gentleman with a hopeful expression.

'Yes, sir, on holiday,' Steel replied.

'Ah, very good. Is there anything special you are looking for?'

'No, just looking for the moment. *Danke*,' Steel said.

He smiled and left Steel to his own devices. Outside, the man stood for a while, pretending to check a paper map and orientate himself to the location. Steel smiled and checked out some of the London suits on display. He picked out several outfits and headed for the changing rooms at the back of the store.

The older man followed Steel with an interested gaze. It was a good sale at nearly a thousand euros per suit if they were all to go.

The man following Steel looked inside the store, hoping to maintain his observation. Suddenly, a look of panic crossed his face; Steel had gone! Quickly, he entered the store and rushed towards the changing rooms, hoping Steel was there and hadn't slipped past him.

The tailor spoke to the man but was dismissed with a quick show of the man's INTERPOL badge. He backed away and left the agent to his search.

As he drew back each curtain, he found only an empty cabin. Reaching the last one, the man held his breath, hopeful of finding Steel trying on something. Quickly, he jerked back the curtain and cursed as he saw an empty changing booth, less for the six suits that hung neatly on the hanger and a note: I'll take all these. Please charge them to my account, ask the poorly dressed man who I am and where to find me.

The INTERPOL agent cursed and turned to find the older gent immediately behind him; he smiled.

'*Bitte,*' he said with a broad grin and passed him a pen and paper.

———

As the agent had made his way to the back rooms, Steel had hastened past a row of suits on high racks, which hid his escape. He headed out the door.

He was counting on the man's sudden panic to blind him from what was happening, a risk that paid off. Steel made his way back the way he came, all the while alert to the possibility there was a second or third agent waiting to take over just in case the first man failed to keep track of their target. It was, of course, an old trick that he had used himself many times. He was alone, but he wasn't about to risk it as far as he could tell.

Steel winded through the busy streets, keeping the same evading tactics, following no particular route. But with one final destination in mind, a café, where he hoped a contact would be waiting.

———

Simms had showered and put on fresh clothes. At the same time, Kitty searched for Falkner's recent movements, particularly those to the US. Steel had a theory, and they were enabling his hunch while he went off to do something secretive. Simms played along for the simple reason Steel had once worked for the agency and had gotten a reputation for getting the job done. But now, he was a hidden asset. Simms could imagine Steel behind double plate glass with a sign saying, 'Smash glass if you're in the shit and there's no other option.'

So far, Simms hadn't been impressed by what he'd seen of Steel; sure, he pulled off the whole badass look with those all-black suits and mask-like sunglasses, but work-wise, he hadn't seen anything that compared with the stories.

He poured himself and Kitty another coffee, then joined her in the sitting room.

'Anything?' Simms asked, handing Kitty the cup of fresh coffee, white with two sugars.

'He's made a lot of trips, especially to Miami, but six months ago, he visited Philly,' she said with a grin.

'But nothing to New York?' Simms asked, hoping Steel's theory had paid off.

'He flew into Philly but bought a train ticket to Grand Central two days later; he was trying to cover his tracks, but he used a credit card that popped. Steel was right; the bastard was in the city. The question is, why?' Kitty took a sip from the cool coffee.

'And what the hell is the killer's beef with the guy?'

They both stared at the board and the colourful picture of the sun-kissed Manhattan skyline with the eagle head looking to the side majestically.

———

Steel had entered *Café Braun* after going through side streets and even a market. He was confident he hadn't been followed, but then Steel was always wary of the fact the opposition was intelligent and had contingency plans in place. Steel walked into the busy café and sat down next to a blonde woman in an ebony skirt suit.

The woman was in her late forties, with a perfect

complexion and tortoise-shell wide-brimmed sunglasses. Her golden locks hung naturally over her shoulders and across her back. Red lipstick glistened on a full set of lips. Long talon-like nails sparkled with red nail varnish. She was a looker for sure and most certainly a panther in the sack, but that was her forte. Most called her Killer Cougar, a slightly distasteful name for such a passionate creature, but that's what she was. Nastassia Petrov was the best at what she did, and that was to kill using sex, or rather the build-up to it. Nastassia could make it look like an accident or—as some clients preferred to say—messy.

Steel and Nastassia had been friends for a long time—ever since she had tried to kill him in Cuba.

Steel had spared her life, feeling she was only doing her job and it wasn't anything personal. And, after a lobster dinner with a bottle of Dom Perignon '75, they ended up together that entire weekend.

'Nastassia, you're looking as fantastic as ever,' Steel cooed.

'Steel, you are looking ... well, the same, actually ... perhaps a little bigger,' Nastassia smiled.

'Well, lots of time to hit the gym recently.' Steel replied with a smile.

'So I heard, but not what I meant.' Nastassia displayed an almost cat-like grin.

Steel felt himself become warm under the collar and quickly called the waitress over to distract himself from the enchantress next to him and ordered two glasses of the *Sekt*.

'I got your message.' Nastassia spoke with the tone of an angel.

'And, where is he?' Steel asked, curiosity ringing in his voice.

'Not so fast. What's your hurry?' Natassia purred.

'Someone wants to kill him, and soon,' Steel explained.

'Let them; the little shit sells death to children.' Her tone had soured; the smile was now venomous.

'Unfortunately, he may have the answers I need to catch a serial killer who is killing innocent people. After that, the killer can have him,' Steel said to oppose her need to see Falkner strung up. But he needed answers and fast.

'You'll find him at this address,' she said, handing Steel a folded note. Steel went to take it, but she held the other side tightly.

'And the price?' Steel asked with a flirtatious smile.

'Dinner and dancing,' Nastassia replied with the same feline smile as before.

'Monte Carlo?' Steel suggested.

Nastassia purred and kissed him on the cheek. 'You know me so well. Who knows, maybe the hotel will have a whirlpool?' She grinned wildly.

Steel looked up to see the waitress standing with a small round tray with two champagne flutes and a blushing face.

He took the filled glasses from the young waitress and handed one to Nastassia. They clinked, and she toasted.

'Here's to the future. May Falkner fail to have one!'

Steel raised an eyebrow and took a sip of the German sparkling wine and found it had a bitter, somewhat hard taste to it. He took another sip, hoping it would be better the second time. No luck.

'Interesting toast. Almost sounds personal,' Steel said, placing the flute aside with a frown.

Nastassia just smiled and took a sip. 'So, who is the little one with you?' she asked.

'Agent Kitty West?' Steel replied curiously.

'West,' Nastassia said with a curious tone. 'I do not know the name, but her face seems familiar somehow.' She shrugged as if to dispel the thought and smiled. 'I guess she just has one of those faces.' She raised her glass again and laughed. 'We are lucky in that way, John. Nobody ever forgets us.'

'To dinner, dancing and whirlpools,' Steel toasted to lighten the mood.

Nastassia laughed again and clinked her glass against his before finishing the drink. Then, she stood. 'I'll let you know when I'm free, John, and do me a favour. Don't get yourself killed on this one,' she said with a wink and a kiss blown from her palm.

Steel had stood with her and watched her leave. As the door closed behind her, Steel waited before heading to the waitress to pay the bill. Something Nastassia had said was nagging at him. Did she know more than she was letting on, and if so, what?

Steel paid the bill and left a decent tip before heading out of the café. Outside, he reached into his pocket and pulled out the note.

'He's behind you in the corner,' it read.

Steel turned and gazed back into the café. He saw a man sitting alone in a grey suit with cola-brown hair and a moustache. He was drinking coffee and reading the local newspaper.

Steel opened the cell phone and pressed Simms's preinstalled number. It took two rings before he answered.

'Yes, Steel?'

'Simms, grab Kitty and get yourselves to *Café Braun* as quick as you can. We've found Falkner,' Steel said calmly, with his gaze firmly fixed on him.

The search was over. Now all they had to do was to keep him alive.

# CHAPTER NINETEEN

IT WAS TEN IN THE EVENING WHEN THEY GOT THE CALL TO shut down the operation. Trish was just happy to be out of the cramped van and sucking in clean air once more. She knew that Brena would be pissed, so she took her time getting back to the safe house.

Trish didn't know what had caused the enviable close-down. However, she suspected it was a call from Langley, possibly Stanton himself. Whatever it was, she was grateful.

———

'You're an hour late. Why?' Brana asked Trish as she walked through the front door of the safe house.

'Nice to see you too,' she responded, hoping her comeback would choke him.

'We are wanted back in Langley. There have been ... developments in Berlin,' Brena said with unease as if the very words were made of broken glass.

'Did they find the next target?' asked Dutton with enthusiasm, making Brena twitch with awkwardness.

'We will be briefed when we get back. But, in the meantime, don't speculate on anything,' Brena warned. 'It's probably nothing.'

Trish smiled to herself at the thought of Brena's skin crawling because of Steel making progress. She didn't show it, but she had admired Steel for a while. She had read all about his exploits, most off the record. Steel was a man of right and wrong, regardless of the rules. MI8 had trained to think outside the box and get the job done. Something he had tried to do once before and got stung for it. A trail of thoughts that Steel had been told to ignore months ago, despite knowing the serial bomber would walk from the courthouse and kill again.

'We leave in one hour, so pack up your shit,' Brena ordered, then began to walk towards one of the bedrooms he'd claimed as his own to pack.

Trish gave a sarcastic salute behind Brena's back, then sat on the couch and checked her messages on her phone. Luckily, she'd packed before she left for the UN building, just in case this situation arose.

Brena was more of a pain than usual, which brought the worst out of Trish. She had joined at the same time as Brena, but he was the golden boy for some reason. She was as good an agent as he was, if not better.

Her mailbox was full of missed messages, most of which were of no concern, apart from one. It was a message from a friend abroad: 'Package delivered, another team is in play. Be careful.'

Trish deleted the message and looked around, ensuring no one had seen her. The side of her mouth raised slightly as she gave herself a secret smile. All was going to plan.

———

Steel went back inside the café and bought two coffees, one American and the other with two sugars. He'd purchased them at the counter and carried them over to Falkner's table. Falkner was busy reading *The Berlin Post*, a sizeable cumbersome paper attached to a long wooden pole.

'Coffee, two sugars,' Steel said, placing the coffee cup down in front of Falkner.

'NATO standard, as you Tommies would say,' Falkner said with a surprised smile before beckoning Steel to sit in the chair opposite. 'It's been a while,' he said, placing the paper down on the chair next to him.

'Not that we actually met, but yes, perhaps too long,' Steel replied.

'And what can I do for the NYPD? Or is it still British Intelligence?' Falkner asked with a curious expression on his face.

'I'm here for you.'

Falkner raised an eyebrow and laughed out loud at Steel's statement. 'A little out of your jurisdiction, are we not?' Falkner said with a wide smile.

'It's not like that, Falkner. I'm here with the agency, someone wants you dead, and it's happening today. I'm here to take you to a safe house.' Steel wished it wasn't a safe house but a prison he was dragging Falkner to. But Falkner was a target, not a criminal this time.

'People have tried before,' Falkener said smugly.

'This one is different; you're not the only one who has been targeted, and I don't think you're the last,' Steel admitted.

Falkner saw the look on Steel's face and knew something was gravely wrong. If Steel was lying, why would they send him, of all people? Why not a regular agent?

'Do I have time to grab some personal items?' Falkner asked.

'We need to hurry ... wheels up in an hour,' came a voice behind Steel.

Falkner looked up to see a tall black guy with an expensive suit and a bad attitude.

'Falkner, Simms. Simms, Falkner,' Steel said, introducing the two men. 'OK, now that's over, shall we?' He groaned, wanting nothing more than to get Falkner to safety and then interrogate him.

'I need my laptop and some items from my apartment,' Falkner said with an urgent expression.

'Don't worry, we have an agent at your place. Just let us know what you need, and she'll get it,' Simms said, pulling out his phone, ready to send the text.

Steel turned and shot Simms a disapproving look through his sunglasses.

'Some things I need are ... well, are personal,' Falkner admitted quietly.

'There is no way we are letting you out of our sight now we've found you; if you want something, my agent will get it,' Simms growled.

Falkner nodded with a look of defeat. 'My laptop is the most important thing, and my passport, which is in the top drawer of my desk.' Falkner's words sounded frail, as if he had lost everything or a dirty secret had been learned.

Simms texted the information to Kitty, who sent a simple reply: 'Roger that.'

Falkner was piled into the back of a blacked-out G wagon that Simms had rented using the company's credit card. Simms sat in the back with Falkner while Steel drove.

Half an hour later, Kitty sent a quick text saying that she was already at Falkner's place. The lock had taken her less than a minute to pick, and the alarm system took even less time. And Falkner's apartment was spacious with plenty of books and works of art, from paintings to sculptures.

Simms replied, 'Be careful.'

Kitty texted that she wondered about taking sneak peeks into drawers and a large wardrobe. Not looking for anything in particular; just interested in how an arms dealer like Falkner lived.

Simms replied, 'Get the stuff and get out; no time for snooping.'

Kitty responded with a sad-face emoji and a 'LOL.'

A little while later, she texted she had found the desk with the passport and an eighteen-inch laptop. She messaged that the computer was new and the box lay open, almost as if it had just been purchased.

Then she sent another quick text to Simms, asking if the new laptop was the correct one to bring.

'Is it the new computer, or do you have another one?' Simms asked.

'No, it's the new one,' Falkner nodded and looked glumly out the window at the streets as they whizzed past as if he knew he would never see home again.

A sudden thought caused Steel to shoot a desperate look at Simms and then Falkner.

'When did you get a *new* laptop?' Steel asked, a bad feeling running through his body.

'This morning, mine broke, so I sent off for a new one. I was surprised how quickly it came,' Falkner said with surprise.

'Simms, get hold of Kitty! Tell her to drop the laptop and get the hell out of there!' Steel growled as he pressed down his foot on the accelerator.

'Way ahead of you, Steel,' Simms said, struggling to press the speed dial on his phone while being thrown about in the back seat. It began to ring, but there was no answer. Simms shot a look in the rearview mirror at Steel, showing signs of complete control.

Due to a massive traffic build-up, they took fifteen minutes to get to Falkner's apartment. Simms parked, and they all got out and gazed at the inferno that used to be Falkner's apartment. Rubble-covered cars and windows had been blown out in neighbouring buildings. Fire trucks cordoned off the building, and firefighters on cradles unleashed sprays of water to douse the flames.

Falkner just stood and watched as his home burning, and Simms kicked the tires on the car out of anger. Steel watched the flames and the black smoke bellow skywards.

'We have to go, now,' Steel snarled as he turned and grabbed Falkner and tossed him into the back of the rental.

Simms slid into the driver's side and started the engine. 'Where are we going?' Simms asked, still in shock at what had happened.

'To get as far away from here as possible,' Steel replied with venom.

He wondered what Kitty had done. Had she disobeyed Simms and gone to snoop around just in case she found something incriminating to use as leverage against Falkner? But that wasn't the plan. Get in, find the package, and get out. That's what it was supposed to be, but it was hard to tell with this team of Brena's.

Steel had seen that they were all loose cannons and had agendas, so why were they all still working with the agency?

Stanton used to pick his people well, so what went wrong with these? The only one who showed promise had been killed. Steel knew with an explosion like that, there would be little chance of finding a body, let alone signs there had been an apartment.

Everyone sat in silence as they drove to the hotel. Words had left them. Only anger remained. Falkner stayed quiet in fear of angering Steel further. Falkner had heard stories of Steel and his time in the SEALs, and that was enough to scare him into keeping his mouth shut.

Steel was in no mood to hear a word from either of them, so he didn't provoke a conversation. Instead, Steel pulled out his phone and pressed the speed dial for Stanton. Steel wanted to tell him about it before the press splashed it all over the media. It took a while before Stanton picked up.

'Yes,' Stanton answered, his voice sounding hoarse and tired.

'Stanton, it's Steel. We have Falkner, but there's been an incident,' Steel explained.

'How bad?'

'Bad. We lost Kitty,' Steel replied, anger and pain running through his voice.

After a short pause, Stanton asked, 'How?'

'Explosion at Falkner's place.'

'Accident?' Stanton asked.

'No, too much of a coincidence. It was more likely to be a trigger activation device. Kitty was getting Falkner's laptop when it blew,' Steel said, looking into the rearview mirror to catch Simms's reaction.

'When are you leaving?' Stanton asked.

'No. I'm going to get the hotel to forward the luggage back to the States. It's too dangerous to risk going back to the hotel right now. INTERPOL will be all over it,' Steel explained.

'Won't they be at the airport as well?'

'Most probably, but what choice do we have?' Steel looked back at the rearview mirror.

'We got another postcard,' Stanton told him as if trying to change the subject.

'Do we know where yet?' Steel asked, hoping for something to take his mind off Kitty.

'Someone recognised it as the Rijksmuseum in Amsterdam,' Stanton said.

'Good, that's our next location. Can you send the jet there, and we'll send Falkner to you from there?' Steel suggested, sneaking a quick look at Simms in the mirror. As he suspected, Simms was also looking over via the mirror.

'Will do. I'll get your bags sent there as well,' Stanton said.

'No, send them Stateside. Then, if INTERPOL checks, they'll think we've gone back home,' Steel stated firmly, knowing full well that Sabine Boese would be checking where their bags were going.

'Contact me when you've got to the airport,' Stanton ordered.

'Roger that.' Steel hung up the phone and tucked the cell into his pocket.

'What's the plan?' Simms asked.

Steel looked up and smiled at Simms's reflection in the mirror.

'How's your Dutch?'

Simms and Falkner both gave Steel a confused look.

———

It was around seven in the morning when Brena and his team arrived back at Langley, using a Delphine helicopter from JFK to save time. Two SUVs were waiting to take them the half mile to headquarters.

None of them had any idea what the rush was, but it had to be bad.

Brena was hoping Steel had messed up, and now he would be taking over the whole operation. Trish just wished they'd caught the bastard, and it was all over.

———

Stanton was waiting for them at the main entrance, a grim look on his face.

'I hope you're all rested because we got another one,' Stanton said, waving a copy of the latest postcard.

'Do we know where?' Brena asked, almost drooling over the prospect of taking his team abroad.

'Amsterdam. My secretary recognised the picture. It's a museum in the capital,' Stanton explained while he walked, the team following close behind.

'Any news from Steel?' Trish asked, prompting a vicious look from Brena.

'He got the target, a man called Falkner,' Stanton replied.

'The arms dealer?' Trish was surprised at the news.

'Yes, the arms dealer, but it wasn't without cost. We lost Agent West,' Stanton said solemnly. Everyone stopped, and mouths fell open at the news, all but Brena, who carried the same uninterested expression.

'What happened?' Dutton demanded.

'An explosion at Falkner's place. The Berlin office is sending me a report as soon as they get one,' Stanton said with sadness.

'So, we're going to Amsterdam while Steel heads back here?' Brena asked coldly.

'No, Agent Brena. You and your team are working on what Falkner was doing here six months ago and what he and the others have in common,' Stanton stated gruffly, shocked at the lack of compassion for his teammate.

'What's Steel and Simms doing ... don't tell me they're going to Amsterdam?' Brena cursed.

'You have your assignment, Agent Brena; I suggest you get on with it,' Stanton said, giving him a look that made him step back slightly.

As Stanton walked away, Brena watched the old man step into an elevator; he mumbled something under his breath at a sidewall of the lobby.

'We best get on it,' Trish said, hoping to break the tension that hung in the air.

'You two go up. I'll catch up with you. There's something I have to catch up on first,' Brena lied. He turned and walked into the brilliant morning sun.

'Come on, Dutton, let's find out what this Falkner guy has been up to,' Trish said, walking with the young agent to the elevators. 'Let's do it for Kitty and help catch this bastard.'

---

Fire crews fought hard and soon had the blaze under control. Falkner's apartment was destroyed, but somehow the surrounding ones were untouched, less for broken windows from the shockwave. Agent Sabine Boese stood with her hands buried in the pockets of her long, sandy-coloured overcoat and watched from a distance. She knew it was the killer they were calling The Sentinel, but she didn't know if the target was inside at the time.

The fire chief had said it would be a while before they could enter. Which would be pointless after all the water that had been sprayed and the fire crews that had trampled through the wreckage. All the evidence would be contaminated or washed away.

'The apartment belongs to one Karl Falkner, fifty-one-years

old, unmarried. He's an arms dealer for one of the major weapons companies,' said a tall, thin man.

The man was Sabine's second in command, a ghostly-looking man with a narrow face which showed too much bone structure. His salt-and-pepper hair looked like strands of thread that had been laid on in ungenerous layers.

Agent Gant had had the unfortunate nickname The Ghoul since he was a child. A name he'd had so long it didn't hurt anymore.

'Where are Steel and his two friends?' she asked.

'They're on their way back to the States; their luggage was delivered earlier to the agency's plane. I checked the flight plan; they're headed to Washington,' Gant said.

Sabine squinted disbelievingly as she watched the smoke rise from the apartment. 'That rental car, did it get back to the dealership?'

Sabine waited as Gant went on his tablet to check.

'Yes, it got picked up at the airport around the same time they boarded.'

Sabine nodded to acknowledge the information, but she didn't believe it. Sabine knew how tricky Steel was; it was his job to disappear and not leave a trace unless he wanted to be found.

'Check with the airport; ask them to let us know when the plane arrives and how many people are aboard,' Sabine ordered.

'You think they didn't make the flight?' Gant asked, wondering where her insight came from.

'If you knew Mr Steel as I do, you'd know he didn't make that flight. The question is, did he find his target, and is he with Steel or up there with the rubble?' Sabine nodded up towards the burnt wreckage. 'Also, see if there have been any car purchases at local garages. If he's not renting, he's bought a car.'

'He could have stolen one,' Gant said, shooting off an idea.

Sabine thought for a second before shaking her head. 'No, not this time. He wouldn't want to draw attention to himself,' she said with a smile, remembering something he'd done once on a mission for INTERPOL.

'We're done here. Get the local police to send us a copy of the report, and I want to know if there's a body in there,' Sabine said, then turned and walked down the street to a waiting white BMW sedan.

———

Simms understood why they gave the rental back, even why he had the luggage transferred onto the plane. What he didn't get was why they had bought an old beat-up BMW M3, clearly over-priced and for which Steel had paid cash and put in a bit extra for 'no questions asked.' They were flying under the radar with a man who was a target of a killer, not what Simms expected to be doing when he woke up that morning. Still, he didn't also count on losing his partner to the killer.

Simms felt terrible. After all, he had sent Kitty in there without backup, even though he knew there was a killer planning on taking out Falkner that day.

Steel was still keeping conversation to a minimum, and Falkner wasn't talking at all. According to the navigation device, it would take just over eight hours to drive there. It would be a long and painful drive without any of them speaking.

Simms put on the radio and hoped there was constant music instead of lots of talking because he didn't understand the language. Sure, he was fluent in Italian, Japanese, and a little Russian, but not Dutch.

The navigation system Steel had bought from a local gas

station indicated they had another six-and-a-half hours to go. Luckily, most of that was on the Autobahn, which meant no speed restrictions for most of the way until the Dutch border.

Simms looked back at Steel, doing something on his cell phone and frowned. He felt shut out, and he didn't like it. They were meant to be a team on this, and Steel had left them in the dark ever since they'd arrived. But now, it was worse, as if Steel blamed him for Kitty's death. It wasn't enough Simms blaming himself without Steel laying it on.

Steel caught Simms's gaze in the rearview mirror and cracked a smile. The first one he'd given for a while.

'We need to get to Amsterdam airport as soon as possible; we will get our bags there, and we can get rid of Mr Happy here,' Steel said, pointing a thumb at Falkner.

Simms nodded and looked back at the road.

'In the meantime, Herr Falkner, why don't you tell me what you were doing in New York six months ago and why someone is trying to kill you?' Steel turned to Falkner and shot him an evil grin.

'I don't know what you are talking about, Mr Steel. I'm just a businessman; I travel, so what of it?' Falkner replied smugly.

'Oh, I'm sorry, I guess I got you mixed up with some other arms dealer called Falkner. My mistake. Simms, turn the car around. We're taking Mr Falkner home,' Steel announced with a devilish smile.

'No, no, wait,' Falkner yelped in panic. 'OK. What do you want to know?' he almost screamed, hoping to convince Simms from turning around and returning Falkner to what was left of his apartment.

Simms smiled, typed the airport into the satnav, paused for the device to calculate the route and distance, and then turned down the radio. Falkner started to explain his business trip to the States and why he was in New York. A lot of it was good to know, but not what they wanted. Then Simon Townsend came up, a low-life scumbag that Steel had the privilege of putting away six months before.

Simon Townsend was your average dirtbag's dirtbag. He was the sort of guy who would sell his mother for a profit and toss in his kids to sweeten the deal.

Simms made a mental note of the name and everything Falkner was saying. Knowing full well once Falkner was on that plane, they probably would never see him again.

'So, what did Townsend want?' Steel asked.

'Explosives and detonators mostly, but not your usual low-tech stuff. Instead, he wanted digital remotes that could be set off by a specific remote,' Falkner explained, almost as if he was telling a story in a bar. Falkner was cocky, possibly a coward when it came down to it, but at that moment of feeling secure, one self-righteous bastard.

Steel knew this guy would be back on the street selling again, but this time for Uncle Sam. It made sense in a twisted way; better the devil, you know, people in high places would say.

———

Steel traded places with Simms and took the wheel. There were three hours to go, and Steel had noticed the man was tired, not just from the long drive but because of everything that had happened. Kitty's death weighed heavily on all of them, but Simms most of all. He had, after all, sent her to the apartment alone, a decision he wouldn't make again.

Steel looked at the pair of weary men in the back seat. 'Good, they're sleeping,' Steel thought. *The second rule: get sleep when you can. You never know when you'll do it next.* More good advice the Army had taught him.

Steel looked at the clock on the dash and then at the satnav. They would get there at around seven o'clock. *Not good enough.* He pressed down the gas pedal. They needed to shave off at least an hour; more would be better. The sooner they were rid of Falkner, the better. He was now deadweight and would slow them down in their search for the next victim. Steel drove fast but steady, weaving in and out of traffic but not so erratically that the Autobahn Polizei would pull them over.

———

The night air seemed cold. Dark clouds travelled quickly over a stormy sky. The city's lights were bright and inviting, unlike the busy streets with their relentless flow of people. Earlier it had rained. A heavy shower had lasted most of the evening, but now the winds were pushing the weather northeast. It was eight o'clock, and the city was starting to get busy once more. Many had finished work hours before; most were just finishing. The noise melded the sounds of car horns, bicycle bells, and people marching home.

A man walked out of a library—by all accounts, an ordinary man with nothing much about him. Average height and build, an older man in his late fifties, grey hair neatly parted to the side. His brown suit looked new, but his shoes were old yet cared for. Dark-rimmed glasses framed his face, along with stubble from two days of growth. The man held himself upright and proud, but he was just another face in the crowd to everyone. However, to The Sentinel, he was next on the list.

The man walked down the street, completely unaware of his tail. A figure dressed all in black with a black hood. The disguise blended in perfectly with a crowd of delinquents and students, and people who hated their parents for being loving. The man walked on. His mind was a thousand miles away as he moved through the multitudes of people. It would have been easy to have killed him; simply move up behind him and a quick stab through the second and third rib at an upward angle. The tightly packed crowds would carry his body along for ages until they began to thin out, and then it would fall to the curb as if it had happened there. The police wouldn't have a chance of DNA, witnesses, hair samples, or anything. But The Sentinel had other plans, something more fitting.

The man moved inside a tall white building with 1930s architecture and a new paint job. The Sentinel entered the opposite building and used the elevator, taking it to the top floor. Stopping at the twelfth floor, The Sentinel got out and headed down a long corridor to room 520. The Sentinel reached into a pocket, pulled out a key and opened the door. Inside was a cosy, fully furnished apartment, but why wouldn't it be? The owner was away on a world cruise. The pad would be empty for months. More than enough time for The Sentinel. Most of the research had already been carried out. Now, it was a case of tying up a few loose ends and ironing out a couple of contingency plans in case something went wrong with the original plan.

The Sentinel moved to a desk with a computer and several monitors, two of which had split screens that showed different images inside the man's apartment. The Sentinel pulled out a digital camera and plugged in a USB connection to the computer.

A screen with images of buildings and tram stops, and junctions started to download onto the computer. Standing up, The Sentinel moved to a far wall and a large city map; bits of different coloured string marked out the different routes the man took each day. The man was also a creature of habit.

Something The Sentinel loved. It made things so much easier. The Sentinel took the other pin and stuck it into a large grey area with the name Alexanderplatz in bold letters.

The pale blue light of a street lamp illuminated the window The Sentinel was staring through. The street below was quiet. The odd car passed by, or a pedestrian on a late-night walk strolled without care. It was late. 'Some much to do and so little time,' were always words to live by. The Sentinel turned to the setup that sat on a table in the middle of the room. Four laptops showed views from different cameras, which showed the target's movements. A plan was forming. All The Sentinel needed was the perfect delivery system and the right time.

The images showed all the rooms in the man's apartment and office.

The man was in his mid-thirties with scruffy brown hair and thick-rimmed glasses that looked as if they belonged to a teacher or the late seventies. He moved about the room, pacing up and down as he spoke on his cell phone. The man held the appearance of someone who liked to be in control and had power over others through manipulation. The office was a twenty-by-twenty rental. Red fleur-de-lis on white background paper covered the walls. Expensive wooden furnishings sat upon a thick beige carpet.

Works of art hung under brass picture lights, and ornaments lay behind glass cases. This was the office of a man of distinction. A man who oozed euphoria. However, this was *not* the man in Berlin.

———

Trish sat at her computer. She was halfway through typing Falkner's name in the CIA's data search engine. Her fingers froze above the keys. Trish stared at the screen, unblinking. Kitty was gone, dead. She was killed by accident while she got some scumbag's things. It didn't seem fair to her that such a decent person should die and someone like Falkner should still be breathing.

Trish shook her head and got back to work. Her fingers regained movement and flew across the keys. The page she required was up in seconds. Karl Falkner: Movements and Associates. Using the information Steel had passed onto Stanton, Trish checked the dates Falkner was in the country six months ago. Where he had been and who he'd seen.

Kitty had been right. Falkner had indeed flown into Philadelphia and taken a train to New York using a card under the name of Edgar Raven. He had used the same card to rent a hotel suite at the Manhattan Hotel for six nights. After that, the trail ended until Falkner's return journey.

Tris widened the search to known associates, hoping he had met up with some. After around fifteen minutes and a lot of black coffee, the computer gave up a name: Simon Townsend.

Trish made a note of it and switched her search to Townsend.

His rap sheet was a mile long, and his favourite pastimes included underground fights and money laundering. But somehow, none of it ever stuck, so the police gave up arresting him. That was until Steel came along, and Townsend's luck ran out. Townsend had gotten twenty-five to life on a pitiful charge, but his priors caught up with him. *God bless the three-strikes rule.*

Even though the priors were before Townsend got smart, it still counted. Trish picked up her coffee mug without looking and went to take a sip. Her concentration waned from the screen when air met her lips as she tilted the cup back. She looked at the empty cup and cursed her taste buds for telling her there was one last mouthful.

She got up and headed for a long table on a far wall, which held three coffee machines, baskets with creamer in small sachets and sugar in paper sticks. There wasn't a break room; there was no need for one, as most just grabbed what they needed and then returned to their desks.

Trish filled the mug with a fresh brew and turned to head back to her desk just in time to see Brena reading what she had found on-screen and in notes. Trish froze, confused at Brena's approach to finding out what she had learned. She made her way back, hoping to remain unnoticed.

'I found your man; he got around a lot,' she said, walking up behind Brena, saying nothing or even giving an acknowledgement of her presence. 'Kitty and Steel were right. He was in New York on business.'

'With whom?' Brena asked coldly.

'A man called Townsend, a—"

'A piece of filth that should have been stamped on long ago.' Brena sneered at the very mention of the man's name.

'But Steel put the man away?'

'Far too late, far, far too late,' Brena said, walking away, 'Good work Trish; now go home and get some rest. It's been a long few days, and I need everyone rested.'

Trish watched Brena walk towards the elevators. He seemed different, calm even. She sat down with her coffee and looked at the screen. The name Townsend had sparked something in Brena—she wanted to know what it was.

———

The Sentinel sat in front of the desk full of monitors. The Moo Shu Pork and noodles takeaway meal from the local Chinese restaurant was almost gone. The Sentinel observed the next target, a middle-aged man in an expensive apartment. His concrete-grey suit was tailor-made, and the open-plan sitting area with the kitchen had an expansive panoramic set of windows.

The view from above failed to show the view from the window. But The Sentinel wasn't interested in that. Not yet, anyway.

The plan to get out Falkner had failed somehow, but it was no consequence. He was just a means to an end anyway. They all were. The Sentinel looked over at the time; it was almost four in the afternoon.

It would be time for stage two of the new target at eight o'clock. The new person that Steel was searching for.

All the pieces were in play. All that was needed was Steel to make the first move.

# CHAPTER TWENTY

EVER SINCE THEY'D CROSSED THE BORDER WITH GERMANY, Steel had noticed the change in weather. Black clouds covered the heavens and powerful winds pushed against the car, forcing Steel to counter-steer against it.

Steel had let the others sleep; no need for them to be awake and break the comfortable silence. He'd switched off the radio a while back, just after they'd fallen asleep, in fact. Steel needed quiet to think, and unnecessary noise would hinder that.

Langley had already found the next place: a museum in Amsterdam. This was a start.

Steel and Simms now knew how to break The Sentinel's code, pictures, and address. Knowing that would make things a thousand times quicker in tracking the victims. The problem would be if The Sentinel anticipated this and started to make the codes harder, or worse, lessened the time they had to do so.

Steel checked the satnav; the airport wasn't far now, fifteen minutes at most. Soon Falkner would be safe on the jet, and Simms would be going with him. Steel knew he had to do this alone. No more dead agents, not if he could prevent it. Simms was a good man and agent, but Steel worked best alone. No baggage, no worries, no bargaining chip. Steel saw the sign for the airport, took the turnoff, and followed the road. Steel followed the signs for the different terminals and headed for Departures. Finding a spot in the parking lot, Steel parked and turned off the engine.

The two men at the back were still sleeping, unaware they had stopped.

Steel pulled out his phone and sent a message to a number Stanton had given to him.

'We're here; where is the rendezvous?' Steel typed and then pressed Send.

The reply only took a few seconds. 'Terminal A13, a man in a black suit named Rodgers.' Steel closed the cell and tucked it away in his jacket pocket.

'Wake up,' he ordered, unbuckling his seatbelt.

Simms opened his bloodshot eyes and yawned.

Falkner woke up suddenly at Simms's movement and looked around blankly, unaware of his new surroundings.

'Time to go,' Steel said, getting out of the car.

Simms followed, stretching off the stiffness in his body, and Falkner opened the door and slowly placed one foot at a time onto the ground.

Suddenly, Falkner flinched at the stench of exhaust fumes, engine oil, and burnt rubber and placed a clean handkerchief to his nose and mouth.

'Let's go. They're waiting for us,' Steel said, locking the car and moving forward at a steady pace.

'*Who* is waiting for us?' Falkner asked, concerned with his fate.

'Apparently, a man in a black suit called Rodgers,' Steel answered with a happy skip in his tone.

Simms frowned as he searched his memory for a man called

Rodgers but drew a blank. He moved closer to Steel, hoping the distance between them and Falkner would add to them not being overheard. 'Steel, we don't have an agent Rodgers in our department,' Simms whispered, looking back to make sure Falkner was still behind them.

'No, he's with another section.'

'Do you know him?' Simms was surprised at Steel's knowledge of what was happening in the agency.

'No, but an old friend vouched for him,' Steel said with an almost nostalgic tone.

'What job was that?'

Steel said nothing in reply. Instead, he just smiled coldly and picked up the pace.

Simms knew what that meant; he had, after all, read all about Steel and his exploits or those they had filed, and that could only mean trouble.

Rodgers wasn't there to pick up Falkner to bring him in; he was there to finish what The Sentinel had started.

Simms imagined Falkner's flight would stop off somewhere remote, and there he would be killed or left to be killed. But, instead, Falkner was a loose end in someone's world now, which meant he was expendable.

Before leaving the parking lot, Steel had stopped and gazed at the massive airport. An enormous place with thousands of people rushing here and there. A perfect place for an unseen murder. An assassination without witnesses, a knife in the back or an unfortunate trip down the stairs. With the amount of armed police and security cameras, a sniper would be out of the question, which was at least one thing less to worry about.

Steel knew something was wrong the second the message said to meet inside, something that would never happen for the simple reasons of what was about to happen. It should have been an easy drive onto the tarmac and straight to the plane.

Simms stood next to Steel and looked at the mass of glass, concrete and, more worryingly, people.

'You know this is a trap, right?' Simms asked.

'Of course, it is. The question is, why?' Steel replied, knowing full well that as soon as they left the parking structure, the game was on. 'I need you to take Falkner to the meeting point.' His gaze was locked on the building, still assessing the possible threats inside.

'Where are you going to be?' Simms asked, staring at Steel worriedly.

'Here and there; all you have to do is follow my lead,' Steel said, pulling out his cell and attaching the headset to it. 'Keep your phone on,' he ordered as he saw his chance and walked forward quickly, disappearing from view in a large crowd of people passing by.

Simms looked over to Falkner, who was sweating bullets. In truth, he didn't know what to say to the man. Simms suspected Falkner had heard most of the conversation and was now wondering who would kill him first: The Sentinel or the agency?

'Come on, let's get you on that plane,' Simms said with an expressionless look.

Falkner nodded, then swallowed hard as Simms strolled out of the parking structure. Simms felt the sweat beading and crawling down his back. He was nervous, without a doubt, but he had to appear calm for Falkner's sake. If all the operations reports on Steel were to be believed, they were in good hands. All Falkner had to do was stay calm and follow Simms's lead, which in itself was a disaster waiting to happen.

Falkner was arrogant and self-absorbed, but he was a coward most of all. He'd probably been in too many situations where his end was nigh, or maybe he was just born that way.

Whatever the case, he could blow apart the whole plan in seconds and get them all killed.

————

Simms walked casually through the crowds with Falkner by his side, like two guys picking up someone from the airport. Simms was strong and confident. Falkner was not. His head spun around as if trying to spot a threat.

'Stop looking around and drawing attention to yourself,' Simms said just loud enough for Falkner to hear.

Falkner composed himself and started to walk alongside Simms, trying his best not to snap his head to the side at every sound or person walking towards him.

Simms looked over to a sign pointing towards A13.

'It's that way, come on,' Simms said, dragging Falkner down a long corridor towards the meeting point.

He started to feel nervous again, he hadn't heard anything from Steel for a while, but he knew better than to break the radio silence. Simms and Falkner picked up the pace by weaving through crowds like a pair of Formula One drivers. Then Simms saw their contact. A tall, well-built man with a blonde flat-top and a government-issued suit. Simms stopped Falkner with a flat palm to his chest and forced him to sit on one of the benches that had a perfect view of the man.

'What do we do now?' Falkner asked, his eyes wide with fear, wiping his damp palms on his handkerchief.

'We wait until Steel gives the all-clear,' Simms replied, his eyes fixed on the contact.

'And what if he doesn't? What if they got him first?' Falkner asked in a panic, forcing his voice to an almost whisper.

'You said that you'd heard of Steel, stories-around-campfire stuff. Do you think they got *him* first?' Simms raised an eyebrow, unsure of those stories, but he could imagine them.

'No, you're right, but what if ... ?' Falkner said in a low voice.

'Then we give him five minutes, and we split and find another way back,' Simms said reassuringly.


Steel moved quickly. He figured on a six-man team: one decoy, the contact, one spotter, most than likely in an elevated position, and four players. They would more than likely start at the four corners of the departure lounge and then converge. The spotter would use comms to give each man a movement order. He had to be the last to go. Any loss of communication and the teams would split. Steel saw the first target, a medium-sized man with a recognisable look about him. Even though he wore civilian clothes to blend in, he screamed Spec-Ops. Using a Special Operations crew for this was a smart move. They were trained to be invisible. Unfortunately for them, so was Steel.

The man wore black jeans, a striped shirt, and a dark-blue padded vest. His Hi-tec boots were also a giveaway—great boots but not the sort of thing you wore on a flight. He stood in the magazine section, pretending to read a magazine, the latest issue of *Guns Monthly*. How appropriate. Steel moved around him, keeping on his blindside.

There were too many people around to start a fight, so he had to be quick. Steel moved in carefully behind him and waited for the opportune moment. A distraction would have been perfect.

Steel picked up a magazine and rolled it tight, which formed a baton. A simple weapon, one that was effective in skilled hands. A quick blow to the back of the head where the spine met the skull would render the man unconscious for a while, enough time at least to find and dispose of the others. Steel didn't need to take them all out, just enough of them to cause enough confusion so he could get to his primary target: the contact.

Steel had picked his targets; the man in front of him and the small, stocky guy at the far end. Both lingered away from the exit, which was paramount if they had to get out quick.

Steel was counting on the over-watch to be focused on the contact and the surrounding area. Keeping constant contact with the other men would be all he needed to ensure no problems on the ground. That was fine if you were dealing with civilians, not if you were up against a former special-forces combatant.

Steel had joined the team to escape being chased by the SANTINI organisation, who had murdered his family; it seemed like the perfect hiding place. After all, he was supposed to be dead.

A friend and confidant had kept the family estate and business from going into liquidation, knowing Lord Steel would return when he was ready.

———

A drunken pair of men waiting for their flight provided a welcome distraction; their singing was quiet in tune but was enough to make everyone look in the wrong direction. Steel's blow was quick and laid out the man cold.

Steel slipped the magazine back onto the shelf and disappeared into the crowds. Soon, Steel was on the second target. The man stood away from the gathering crowd and leaned against a concrete post. As a security guard moved towards the confusion, a quick push to the man's head sent his domed skull crashing off the post.

'OK, Simms, move in slowly. See if you can move the contact away from that spot; use the café. It will be crowded enough,' Steel ordered.

'Roger that,' Simms replied, grabbing Falkner, who was wearing a look of disdain, and dragged him to his feet so the contact could see them.

'Stay close, and whatever happens, don't run off. The others will see you,' Simms warned Falkner, who mumbled his disapproval.

The contact spotted Simms and waved him over.

Simms stayed put and shook his head before gesturing the contact to follow them to the café, which stood on the opposite side near the main entrance.

'Just follow my lead,' Simms whispered to Falkner, who was getting tired of all the spy work.

Simms headed for the open café and found an empty table with four chairs. He and Falkner sat while they waited for the contact to join them. Across the way, the drama continued as screams for help sounded, signalling the unconscious bodies of the other men had been discovered.

'You Steel?' asked the bulky contact.

'No, the name's Simms; this is the package,' Simms said, nodding to the seated Falkner. 'What now?'

The man smiled and reached into his jacket pocket, and kept it there. Falkner's eyes widened, expecting the worst.

The noise from the crowds grew louder.

'He's got a gun,' a voice shouted. Everyone turned, including the contact, and watched as the armed security rushed towards the magazine outlet.

Rodgers face twisted into a look of annoyance as he figured out what was going on. Then, quickly, he turned back towards Simms, only to find the two men gone, and in Simms's chair sat Steel.

'Where are they?' asked Rodgers, pulling out his silenced 9mm and slipping it under the table.

'Tahiti probably, but then I hear that Croatia is nice this time of year,' Steel joked, leaning forwards as if to keep the conversation private.

'I won't ask again. Where are they?'

But Steel just smiled again and looked at his watch.

'Boarding a plane around now, if they got there, OK.'

Rodgers glared at Steel.

'What plane?' Rodgers demanded, his blood boiling, unaware of Steel loosely slipping a tie he'd taken from a stand during the commotion over the man's hands.

'Why, yours, of course.' Steel's smile faded as he grabbed the tie and pulled it towards himself with great force.

Rodger's face smashed against the hardwood table, knocking him out cold.

As people looked around to see what was happening, they saw Rodgers sitting alone with his head resting on the table's polished wood. His weapon was missing, but the tie remained over his hands and was tied to the table leg.

Steel walked out of the airport and headed for the multi-story parking lot. Even though things had gone well, he worried. Steel took out his phone and pressed the speed-dial icon for Simms's cell. It rang for a brief time before Simms picked up, his voice laboured as if he had been running.

'Are you at the plane?' Steel asked, hopeful.

'Yes, just about to load Falkner on now. I'll meet you at the car in about five minutes,' Simms yelled over the noise of the turbines.

'No, I want you on that plane with Falkner,' Steel said, slotting the tiny bit of card from the barrier into the paying terminal.

'But—'

'I need you to deliver Falkner to Stanton personally—no one else, not even Brena,' Steel ordered.

'You think whoever sent those clowns works for the agency?' Simms asked in realisation.

'I'd count on it. You and Stanton are the only ones I trust,' Steel said, paying for his exit from the structure. 'Oh, and Simms?'

'Yeah?' Simms kept an eye on Falkner as he boarded the Learjet.

'Watch your arse.'

———

The Sentinel sat at the desk. The light from the monitors was the only illumination in the darkened room. The only sound was whirring from the desktop computers' fans. So, The Sentinel just sat and observed the movements of the next victim. The man didn't seem like much, but his story was anything but.

Reaching forward, The Sentinel picked up the can of soda and took a mouthful before placing it back down and returning to the silent movie. The digital clock next to one of the monitors said it was nearly eight in the evening, but there had been no sign of Steel or the others.

Gloved fingers impatiently tapped the arm of the office chair. Was something wrong?

The tapping stopped as The Sentinel leant forwards. Eager eyes stared at a single monitor that showed a hotel front.

The Sentinel had predicted Steel would go for this particular hotel because it was the only hotel within walking distance of the museum. Not that Steel was easy to predict. However, this time the man wasn't trying to hide. On the contrary, it was as if he wanted to make it easy for The Sentinel to find him.

It was now a game between them, a puzzle. The Sentinel leant back in the chair and began to rock back and forth. Soon, The Sentinel would have to go; the next name on the list would need the same attention, but first, the next postcard would have to be sent to the CIA.

The Sentinel turned to the other monitors and carried on with research. This one would require a unique demise, fitting for someone as evil as this one. The Sentinel opened a giant sketch pad with several drawn blueprints for an exclusive device.

The Sentinel turned several pages until the perfect choice was found. It was a crude scribble that only The Sentinel understood. Finally, The Sentinel stood, walked over to a workbench, and got started.

————

The sun had set over Amsterdam, leaving cloudless, star-filled heavens. The wind had died down to a gentle chilly breeze. Steel had driven to the city of Amsterdam, happy in the knowledge both Simms and Falkner were safe.

Steel thought back on his decision to use that airport instead of Hannover. Steel knew that Sabine Boese would have had photos out to all airports and train stations in Germany. She was tenacious, for sure.

The last thing Steel needed was her interference, and that was precisely what it would have been. Steel knew, for her, it was about the job, not the victims. He also knew Sabine's only reason for being on the case was getting her name in the press and a foot closer to that top position.

It was apparent to Steel that she would figure out where he was, but it would be too late by that time. Simms and Falkner would be long gone.

The web search for a hotel revealed one within walking distance of the Rijksmuseum. A little pricey, but then why should he rough it? A beautiful place with rear hotel parking and comfortable rooms that looked as expensive as their listed rental prices.

Steel's cover was a rich guy on vacation, so this hotel ticked all the boxes.

He parked in the nearby lot and headed for the entrance. The colossal structure was a mix of old and new: the grandeur of a 1900s building and the modernistic glass framework of the ceiling. The furniture was black and chrome, giving the whole place a light and dark contrast that fitted the luxurious package.

Steel approached a long black reception desk; brass reception bells of different sizes sat in a glass display case in one corner. 'A nice touch,' Steel thought as he passed them and stood before a tall brunette with tanned skin, eyes like a tropical ocean, and short black hair with scarlet-red highlights.

The receptionist gave a glossy red smile, revealing pearly-white teeth.

'Good afternoon. I believe you have a reservation for John Steel?' he said, returning the woman's smile.

'*Einen Moment, bitte,*' she replied, forcing her gaze away from Steel and down to the computer. 'Yes, Mr Steel, we have you for five nights in the Penthouse Suite.' She raised an eyebrow as her gaze fell back onto his broad-shouldered frame.

Steel gave her his passport, which she photocopied and returned to him, along with his key card. She gave him directions to the lifts and explained meal timings and about the WI-FI. Steel took it in, along with mental measurements of the receptionist. She wore the raven-black uniform like a catwalk model and filled it in just the right places.

The suite was full of windows and the same styled black furniture as the lobby. Light-coloured wood covered the floors, and walls made of glass gave the place an open feel. Polished sandstone flooring and walls made the bathroom appear light and required little in the way of illumination during the day. The hotel was nothing short of magnificent, to be sure. Steel was sorry he wasn't there to enjoy it.

Steel wandered around the suite, checking the wardrobes and the texture of the bathrobes. As he made his way into the bathroom, his eye caught a longing glimpse of the shower. But he didn't have time. Realising he had no clothes apart from what he stood in, Steel knew he needed to go shopping.

Looking at his watch, Steel saw it was five o'clock, not much time before everything closed for the day; one hour to find new clothes. He smiled, picked up the house phone, and waited for someone to pick it up.

'Concierge, please.' Steel said after hearing the receptionist's dulcet voice.

———

Trish had gone back to her home in the small town of Vienna. It was a grey-tiled roof bungalow with bare-brick walls and white-painted timber. She'd parked her Cadillac SUV in the driveway and headed towards the glossy white door with a brass door knocker.

It was late, and she was tired. Trish had heard that Simms was bringing back Falkner on the Learjet. News that had somehow upset Brena.

Trish slid the door key into the slot and unlocked the triple-turn lock. Inside was dark, with a faint smell of lavender in the air. She slid her hand to the side and up the wall until she felt the light switch, and with a gentle click, the sitting room was illuminated.

It was a twenty-by-twenty beige-walled room with an open-plan kitchen. Varnished wood slats zigzagged along the floor and down the hallway. She would have preferred carpet, but her beloved black-and-white cat left clumps of unwanted fur all over anything.

Dragging her suitcase inside, Trish shut the door behind her and pulled on the door chain before putting the triple lock back on. It was a safe enough neighbourhood, and she was armed, but why invite trouble, she always thought.

What she wanted was a shower, a glass of red, and to sleep until Christmas. The past couple of days had been insane, and she still had no idea why Stanton had brought in this Steel guy. Sure, he'd been some hot shit back in the day, but what was he now? NYPD? Not exactly a step up by any means.

As she went, she ripped off her clothes as if they were covered in acid, letting them fall to the floor. Finally, she stood in her kitchen, wearing nothing but her underwear, and undid the screw cap on the wine. She took a clean wine glass from the dishwasher and filled it with cheap Merlot. She took a small mouthful and then headed to the bathroom.

The sound of her bare feet pattered on the wooden floor as she went. She was eager to feel the cleansing water on her skin. She took another sip from the glass as she turned on the water and let it run, allowing for the steam to build up.

Trish liked the feel of the heat on her skin.

Placing the wine glass next to the basin and toothbrush holder, she stripped her underwear and opened the hard plastic door to the cabinet, releasing a vaporous cloud of steam that filled the small bathroom. Trish felt the hard, scolding spray of water against her skin upon stepping inside. For her, it was soothing, therapeutic even. She took the bar of milky soap and rubbed it onto her body until it produced a creamy-white lather that covered her pink skin.

Trish tilted her head back, letting the water cascade over

her head and flow through her hair. She felt happy and content as the lather washed from her body.

Trish rested her back against the white-tiled wall and thought of nothing. Suddenly, her eyes opened, and she jumped out of the spray. Trish had that uneasy feeling that she wasn't alone. Someone was in the house with her. But she'd locked the door and put the chain on ... hadn't she?

Trish stepped out of the shower but kept the water running, hoping the noise would make the intruder think she was still in the shower.

Taking the fluffy pink bathrobe from the back of the door, she slipped it on and slowly moved out of the bathroom. She needed to get to her bedroom and the backup Glock 42 compact pistol. The hollow point rounds would make sure the perpetrator went down.

Trish moved silently across the floor, using a towel to cover the sound of her wet feet. Even though she could feel her heart slam against her chest, Trish was calm. All her training and years of fieldwork kept her in control.

At that moment, she didn't have time to feel scared. That would come later. Trish reached the bedroom; the door was partially open but not enough to see inside. Slowly, she nudged the door open with her foot, inching it open until she had a clear view inside.

Everything seemed as if she had left it. The furniture appeared to be untouched, and the covers lay undisturbed on the box-spring double bed.

Trish moved in slowly. She was making sure her back was to the wall, preventing anyone from coming up from behind. She could feel the veins in her neck start to pulse with every heartbeat.

Reaching the bedside drawer, she began to slide it open, only to find the weapon missing. Now, fear took hold of her.

Trish's only other gun was on the couch in the sitting room, and the other was in the hands of the intruder.

A sudden breeze rushed past her. Trish froze at the quick waft of air. The intruder had gotten in through a window and left it open, possibly for a quick exit, after doing whatever they were there to do.

She moved into the bedroom and shut the door before locking it behind her. Her only hope was to place a barricade between her and them, and the door would do just fine for now. Rushing over to the other side of the bed, Trish picked up the house phone. The lack of a dial tone meant the line had been cut.

She looked back towards the door, her eyes wide and expectant.

Trish cursed herself for being in such a rush to get undressed and leaving her clothes in the sitting room. Usually, everything would be folded and placed on the armchair in the bedroom corner. The first time she'd ever broken that routine, and it had bitten her in the ass.

A sound of squeaking metal caused Trish to look over at the door, just in time to see the door handle slowly turn back and forth as the intruder tried the door.

'Just so you know, I've called the police,' she bluffed, hoping to catch the intruder off guard and possibly scare him off. 'They'll be here soon.' Trish rolled her eyes at the attempt, realising whoever was there would know she'd had no phone to make that call. But she had to try something.

The door handle stopped moving. Trish moved slowly towards the door, hoping to catch the sound of footsteps walking away and down the corridor, but she heard nothing. Only the sound of her heartbeat in her ears.

Nervously, she stretched a sweaty palm towards the door handle. She didn't know if the intruder was gone, but she had to find out. She was a CIA agent, not some scared little girl. She'd fought off more significant threats.

Trish composed herself and took a deep breath before unlocking the door and slowly opening it. As the door cracked open, a great force swung it fully open. Trish's eyes widened as she saw the person in front of her.

A look crossed her face. It was a mix of terror and confusion.

'You? What are *you* doing here? I thought that you were—'

Trish's sentence was cut short by a forceful shove to the sternum. She fell back, and the bedroom door slammed shut behind them.

# CHAPTER TWENTY-ONE

STEEL FELT TIRED, EVEN AFTER HE'D GOTTEN AROUND three hours of sleep. But, of course, that was before the nightmares woke him. Still, the memories from the mall explosion continued to haunt him as if his consciousness were trying to tell him something. Steel almost missed his old nightmare. At least there, he could see his beloved Helen again.

Steel changed into the new onyx-black suit he had bought the night before; the old garments had gone to the laundry in the hope of removing the smell of Falkner's burning apartment. Steel sat down to breakfast at the dining table designed to seat eight. He took the breakfast items off the polished brass trolley and laid them out. He poured himself a cup of black coffee, placed down a file he had made on The Sentinel, and spread out the contents. Steel had work to do and not much time.

Stanton had sent Steel an image of the new postcard via a download to his cell phone. Two photographs: one of the front and one of the rear. The address was the same, less for the precinct. This time it was blank. Steel looked at it with a puzzled look.

Was The Sentinel stepping up the game and making the clues harder? Or was it a simple case of 'I get there when I get there?

Steel knew the next clue was at the museum, but the time was frustrating. He took out his phone and looked up the museum on an internet map search. Gauging by the entrance, Steel figured the picture was taken from the south of the building. He then checked at what time sunrise and sunset were. He smiled and sipped coffee.

Steel knew by looking at the postcard—judging by the shadows made by the lampposts and the people—it was possibly around noon.

It was half six in the morning. Five hours to do reconnaissance on the museum. Entrances, exits, where CCTV cameras were, nearest subway. Nearby parking and public transport. Steel needed to know every means of escape that The Sentinel could use.

After breakfast, Steel took his time getting to the museum, making the most of the bright sunshine that was just starting to give off warmth. People on bikes travelled here and there, and dog walkers went about their daily routine. The volume of pedestrian and road traffic was still low, but then it was seven in the morning, and the rush had not yet started. Steel imagined the town centre was chaos about now as people headed off to their jobs.

But Steel was too busy enjoying the calm of the morning to worry about the city. At that moment, he had time and a peaceful walk to allow him to think and plan.

———

Steel stood on Museumstraat, a busy walkway of zigzagged paving stones filled with tourists and cyclists. At the end of this stood the magnificent red-brick colossus—the Rijksmuseum. Built-in the 1800s and filled with treasures beyond belief ... and now the first clue to stopping a murder. Behind him were the electric whirs of trams as they hurried by, carrying commuters to and from the city. Steel looked around, pretending to be a tourist, which wasn't far from the truth. He used his cell phone to take pictures of nearby attractions and security cameras.

Steel moved around, acting like a tourist should, even to the point of making a quick stop at a nearby café and grabbing a coffee-to-go before heading for the museum entrance. He paid the entrance fee, finished the small coffee, and headed to the museum.

Inside, a spectacular glass roof of the atrium provided illumination, showing off the red brick of the walls and the white marble of the floor. A medley of old and new, coming together in a unity of splendour. Rooms filled with artwork from Rembrandt and Van Gogh hung on dark walls to make the vibrant colours stand out.

Steel checked the image of the postcard on his cell again. There didn't seem to be anything out of the ordinary about it. Not like the previous ones that screamed out, 'I'm here!' But there was something slightly off about it that Steel couldn't quite work out. Apart from being in black and white, while the others were in colour, nothing stood out.

As Steel moved further inside, he noticed a board with pictures and drawings of what the museum used to look like when it first opened.

He leant forwards with interest. And then he saw it, the same image as what he had viewed on his phone. It was a picture of the museum before the refurbishment. Steel looked around, excited. The first clue.

Steel spotted a tour guide speaking to her group and hurried towards her.

'Excuse me, I have a question,' Steel said, interrupting the woman halfway through her sentence.

The woman scowled at the interruption and turned towards Steel. Her eyes changed from thin slits to full gazes. Her brown eyes grew large, and her frown turned into a bite of the bottom lip.

'Sorry to bother you, but is there an old part of the building still intact?'

The guide put on her tortoiseshell-rimmed glasses and flicked her long brown hair. 'Oh, that's alright,' the woman said with an alluring smile while straightening her petrol-coloured skirt suit. 'How can I help?'

'During the refurbishment, did any of the original rooms remain as it was before?'

The guide thought for a moment and looked around as if searching for something. 'Possibly the Renaissance exhibit,' she finally said, turning back to face Steel with dreamy eyes. But he had gone.

Steel's quick thank you had been drowned out by the noise of the crowd. The woman looked around, trying to catch a glimpse of where he had gone. Her heart fluttered at the romantic-novel situation of it. Then, realising the tour group was staring at her, she coughed and straightened and resumed talking to her tourists.

Steel made his way through the crowds of people and groups of schoolchildren. He was hoping his hunch was correct, but even then, he had no idea what he was looking for.

The last time he had been lucky because they had received the postcard directly and not through the mail. Perhaps that was why there was no time on this one; The Sentinel had no idea when he or Steel would get there.

Either way, Steel was early.

He needed to know the layout of possible entry and exit points where the killer could come and go. Steel was there alone, just the way he liked it. Partners got in the way, a distraction, a tool the bad guy could use against you.

Steel made his way through the different exhibits laid out in chronological order. Works of art from centuries past hung in gold frames, and trinkets lay behind glass cases. Steel headed to the first floor and then the second. He needed to know what was on every level. How many stairwells and elevators, security cameras, and even toilets as there was a no better place to duck into and hide.

As Steel moved through, he heard one of the guides direct his group to a painting at the end of one room.

'And over here, we have *The Night Watch* by the master, Rembrandt.' The guide walked over to the enormous painting with the Civic Militia guard members. He wore a brown suit with a light-blue shirt and a red paisley bowtie. Steel noticed how passionately the man spoke about each subject, but Steel did not need history lessons; he'd had enough of those at Oxford.

Steel waited until the group moved away, and then he moved closer to the painting. There was something about the picture that intrigued Steel. *The Night Watch* was about striking back for justice and taking up arms to fight for what was right. And if Steel was correct, this was where he had to be at twelve.

It was now half-past nine; he had time to kill. He needed coffee and a place with good cell reception.

# CHAPTER TWENTY-TWO

THE SENTINEL SAT IN A DARKENED ROOM WITH ONLY THE desk lamp and computer monitors to illuminate the apartment. The Sentinel had to hold up the illusion nobody was there. The family would be away on vacation for at least another week.

The Sentinel had set up a smaller room with no view from the busy street below. This way, the rest of the house could remain with open curtains. Of course, the noise neighbour from across the road would spot anything amiss. But that was just one of the things The Sentinel had considered when doing recon on the apartment.

The monitors showed the apartment of the dark-haired man and his expensive lifestyle. He hadn't left his abode for hours.

The Sentinel picked up a bottle of water and took a mouthful. Staring at monitors for a length of time could dehydrate you ... as The Sentinel had learned a while back and paid dearly for due to massive headaches.

The dark-haired man sat at his computer, rocking back and forth, and he spoke on the house phone. The Sentinel thought the caller must have been a woman due to the man's body language. He was laughing and joking in between, taking mouthfuls of the whiskey in a crystal glass in his hand.

The Sentinel made a note on the A4 pad, circled it as if the detail was necessary, then took another mouthful of water and rocked happily in the office chair.

The man on the monitor went to take another drink, but something stopped him. He froze for a second before sitting bolt upright. He'd seen something on the television.

The Sentinel slowly sat up.

Something was wrong. Something had spooked the man.

Suddenly, The Sentinel leant forwards and began to check all the camera angles to see what the man was watching. Then, The Sentinel saw it in a reflection from a picture frame. The man had the local news on television. Hurriedly, The Sentinel searched the internet for the same broadcast. It had been a special report on the bombing in Berlin and how a man called Falkner was supposedly inside when it exploded.

A possible gas leak had been the initial story, but the counter-terrorist police unit that stood in the background advised otherwise.

The Sentinel leant back and looked on as the man began to panic.

Jotting something on the pad, The Sentinel underlined it several times.

Plan B.

———

Steel sat in the museum's café and sipped his cup of Coffee American. The open-air picnic ground was getting full, mostly with school kids on day trips. Steel looked at his watch. It was quarter-to-twelve. He'd spent the rest of the time walking around the museum, checking the escape routes the killer might take after dropping off the next clue. But he had to admit, choosing such an enclosed venue to stage the drop-off was ballsy ... or just plain psychotic.

The museum had minimal exit points, possibly to deter thieves. Because of this, the killer would have to get past security at the exit. He would also have to avoid all cameras and, most of all, avoid being seen by Steel.

Steel got up and made his way back to the painting. He wanted to get a good vantage point, away from the painting, to see who dropped the postcard. He found a good vantage point some ten feet away, near the entrance to the Rembrandt exhibit. It was a perfectly straight line of sight to the dropoff point. But, of course, that was only if Steel was correct about it all.

Steel was working on a hunch. He'd seen everything else in the museum, and this was the only piece of art that felt right, the painting called *The Night Watch*. Steel felt it was a fitting name for what he was seeking.

Groups of people came and went, including the several school tours he had seen. Steel had an idea in his head about what kind of person The Sentinel might be. Male, in his late thirties. A loner, but someone who would blend in. Average height and build, possibly dressed in black with something that covered the face, like a hat, hoody or sunglasses. Steel smiled as he realised he had just profiled himself. Then a shiver ran down his spine at the thought of the similarities.

Another group of school children went past with four teachers in tow to keep the eight-year-olds in check. Finally, one male teacher and three attractive colleagues herded the kids along, telling them not to touch anything.

Steel smiled at the group as they moved towards the colossal masterpiece at the end. His mischievous eyes checked out the teachers. The two blondes and long-haired brunette were in their twenties with that girl-next-door look about them.

Steel shook off his indecent thoughts and got back to looking for his mark. He glanced at his watch; it was dead on noon, and no sign of the killer. He convinced himself to wait another ten minutes, just in case. After all, no specific time had been given.

John Steel used the artwork as an excuse to move slowly down the isles. But he knew he had to keep moving, or he would look suspicious, not only to the other people but security. The last thing he needed was to get grabbed and questioned while the killer made his move.

'Ten more minutes, and then I'm out of here,' Steel promised himself, getting sick of the games this killer was playing.

———

The ten minutes had gone, and then some. It was nearly a quarter past when Steel decided to call it a day. As he turned to leave, he saw a man in a grey hoody and black leather jacket. Black sunglasses hid his eyes.

Suddenly, Steel got that gut feeling and turned to follow the man who fitted his profile of the killer. The man walked towards the picture and stopped. His hands slid into his pockets while he stood and looked at the masterpiece. Almost as if he was waiting for something ... or someone.

He waited for a moment on the off chance he wasn't who Steel thought he was. The man took out a cell phone from his pocket and checked a message before returning the device to the outside zippered pocket. Steel watched the man as he walked away. He moved as if he was disappointed by something.

Steel waited until the man had gone, then sauntered towards the painting as if he was just another tourist taking in art. As he walked up to the painting of *The Night Watch*, he noticed something on the ground in the alcove where the painting hung. So, he walked up and knelt down and found a postcard.

Steel took out a handkerchief from his pocket and picked it up. On the front was a picture of Fifth Avenue in New York. But all the flags had been changed to a red lion on a gold background. Steel turned it over and read what The Sentinel had written. 'Raindrops will consume the red lion, but the sins cannot be measured, but are seen through the eyes of false. John Steel 2330 Precinct.'

Steel's brow creased as he read it. Another riddle, another time set. He looked at his watch again. It was twelve-thirty, which gave him eleven hours to find the next victim.

Steel slid the postcard into a self-sealing plastic bag he'd brought with him, just in case it was required. But, first, he'd have to make a copy and send the original back to Langley via the American Embassy.

As he left the museum, Steel wondered when the killer had left the postcard.

———

The morning weather over Virginia was bright, with a few clouds drifting across a deep purple backdrop. A fresh westerly breeze had a chill to it. Still, the weathergirl had promised a beautiful day with temperatures into the high fifties.

Brena had gotten in early. He'd picked up a coffee and a Danish on the way. Breakfast on the go was all he could afford to have at this stage in the game. So, Brena had gotten home around one in the morning, slept very little, and was up at four.

Stanton had sent him a message that Steel had sent another postcard via the US Embassy in Amsterdam.

Brena was both angry and excited. Angry because he should have been sent to Amsterdam, not Steel. After all, Steel had gotten a member of his team killed. However, the thought of a new clue brought him down to a simmer, not a boil.

———

Brena swiped in at the security desk and passed through the metal detector. He was bored with the routine but was simultaneously glad to have it in place. Brena expected his team to be there already, working hard on cracking the new code. But he knew they would have gotten the same text at the same time he had. Brena was purposely a couple of minutes late; he loved walking into the room and saying, 'Right, what we got?' The feeling of power as he walked in was intoxicating to him.

Brena headed into the war room that held his team and the murder boards Stanton had shown to Steel. A fourth board was made up of a map of Amsterdam, the postcard, and at the bottom was a thick black line for the timeline.

The first timing was twelve o'clock when Steel had gotten the postcard; the last was twenty-three-thirty. The time The Sentinel had given.

'Right, what we got, people?' Brena asked with an authoritative voice.

Dorson turned around and shot Brena a distasteful look.

'You're late, twenty minutes late,' Dorson said, not knowing what was worse, working with Brena or him thinking he was section chief and he could saunter in and ask for updates like that.

'I was stuck in traffic, not that is your concern. Agent Dorson,' Brena said scornfully.

Dorson, like Trish, had gotten into Langley at the same time as Brena. For Dorson, Brena was just like the rest of them; the only difference was his mind. Sure, the old man put him in charge a few times, but Dorson was sure that was to shut him up.

'So, any ideas yet?' Brena barked, ignoring Dorson.

'Forensics got nothing, no surprise there. We know our boy is careful. The new picture is a puzzler, though. The flags on the postcard don't represent any country. However, we are still looking at other options,' said Agent Rachel Turner.

A fresh face was brought in to pick up Kitty's slack. She was an average-looking woman with short mousey hair, dull brown eyes, and a dull black suit.

'And Steel's location?' Brena asked with his hands on his hips; as if trying to show some sort of authority.

'He said he was going to check out a book from the library,' she replied and shrugged.

Dorson saw the confusion in Brena's eyes and smiled to himself.

Brena moved to the new board and began to glide his fingers across the map, mumbling to himself.

Dorson realised he was calculating Steel's next move instead of the killer's. This made Dorson nervous because Brena was making this personal, and he was coming undone. Their jobs were to help find the next victim and connect them. Steel was in the field alone while Simms had brought Falkner back on a stolen jet. No doubt a stunt that would go down in Steel's history files.

'I'm off to see the old man. Let me know when you have something,' Brena said with a nod. Brena headed out the door. He didn't need to be there for the footwork. That was their job.

As Brena left, Dorson looked around with a puzzled look on his face.

'What's wrong?' asked Rachel, who followed his gaze around the room.

'Brena is twenty minutes late, and Trish isn't here. He's never this late, and she never takes off, especially for cases like this.' Dorson did another check, just in case he was mistaken and Trish was sitting in a corner somewhere.

'Maybe she is on special assignment for Brena,' Rachel suggested, trying to reassure Dorson.

But Dorson could feel something was wrong, and he feared the worst for Trish.

Standing, he pulled his jacket from the back of his chair and slipped it on.

'Where are you going?' Rachel asked, surprised that he would abandon them.

'Need a quick smoke. Something tells me we won't get a break for a while,' Dorson lied. He made his way out the door and turned left, not right. He made his way to Brena's office, which he shared with Trish and Simms.

———

Brena placed the paper coffee cup down next to the Danish on his desk before easing himself down in his leather chair. He wore a broad grin, like a child who'd just won a bowl full of candy. Brena was pleased with himself; things were starting to happen, and they were all good. For him, anyway.

Brena picked up the pastry and took a bite. His perfect teeth sunk into the crusty outer shell and the soft centre. Brena rocked back and forth in his chair, contemplating his next move before taking a mouthful of hot coffee to wash down the Danish.

He picked up the receiver of his desk phone and dialled a number written down on a Post-it. Brena coughed as a flake of pastry clung to the back of his throat. He took another mouthful of coffee while the sound of ringing emitted from the handset.

Suddenly, a woman's voice answered with a simple, 'Yes?'

'It's Brena. I know where Steel is, and I know who he's after next.'

Dorson stood outside Brena's office, his back cemented to the wall, his ear close to the door. His mouth fell open in a gasp. Who was he speaking to, and had it anything to do with Trish ... or worse ... Kitty?

# CHAPTER TWENTY-THREE

An easterly wind brought dark, looming clouds and the chance for a downpour at one o'clock. People had already started rushing about in the streets, searching for a place to have lunch in the Dutch capital. Steel had grabbed a couple of Dutch frikandel and french fries, or *Pommes Frites*. He'd first experienced the strange-tasting sausage in Bosnia at Split North Port, a small base for soldiers to wait for their flights.

Steel headed for a web café. He needed a computer and fast. The hotel was too far away to head back to. Besides, he needed to be close to the city when he got a break. Sure, he had plenty of time. The Sentinel had said twenty-three-thirty.

Steel found a place next to a coffee shop and a fast-food place. Steel walked in and looked around for a free machine. He smiled as one became available but died as a spotty kid with strawberry-blonde hair and a face full of piercings took the slot. Steel said nothing. He just waited and hoped the next freed-up computer was close to him.

Steel looked at his watch impatiently and looked around for more empty seats. That's when he saw the kid who had taken the empty slot from him. The kid was talking to a girl who was on the next computer. However, the chair thief wasn't using the computer. He was just sitting there chatting with a girl who looked around nervously as if trying to catch someone's eye to help her. Steel walked up to the owner, paid for his time, and threw in a bit of extra.

'It's too much,' said the man behind the counter, waving the hundred euro bill.

'It's for any damages,' Steel replied, marching over to the kid, who was laughing and joking, trying to make a move on the girl. But he only succeeded in making her feel uncomfortable.

'Damages ... what damages?' the short man asked, standing and looking at the kid taking up the computer slot. 'Oh, dear.' He sat back down, hoping for not too much destruction.

'Excuse me, can I get to this machine? It's important,' Steel said calmly.

The kid spun around in the chair, gave Steel a once-over, sucked his teeth, and spun back around.

'Hey, kid, you're blocking the computer. Do you mind?' Steel asked, his voice slightly raised, the knuckles of his clenched fists white.

'I'm busy, fuck off, and drink some tea, English prick,' the kid laughed and produced a flick-blade.

Steel grabbed the kid's wrist and twisted it, then forced the kid backwards, so his head was on the desk. Next, Steel grabbed the knife and pinned the whelp to the desk. The blade dug deep through the kid's earlobe and into the compressed wood of the workspace, holding the kid down.

'If you move, it's going to hurt. So, be a good lad, stay still, and shut up,' Steel said calmly.

At first, people moved away but then started taking photos with their cell phones. Steel ignored the screams from the impaled youth and began to do web searches on the flag in the postcard. The owner brought over cups of coffee for Steel and the girl, who was in her mid-twenties. She smiled at the man and placed her attention on her knight in the black suit.

'Thank you,' she said in a sweet whisper of a voice. Her large blue eyes and small pouting mouth had that Betty Boop look. Long golden locks framed her blushing face and shoulders.

'You're welcome. Something tells me it's not the first time he has hit on you,' Steel said, blowing on the coffee and taking a sip.

'No, he's always in here. If it's not me, then it's another girl. But no one will touch him; he is a pig.'

Steel smiled and got back to his search. I hardly knew where to start at first.

'What a strange postcard,' the girl said with a curious tone.

'Yes, a friend sent it to me; he likes to send me pictures, and I have to figure them out,' Steel said, a tiny white lie.

'So, what does this one mean?' she asked, excited.

'I'm not sure; I just have to figure out what this flag is,' Steel admitted, shrugging as the search gave him lots of information, but none of which he was looking for.

'That is the crest for ours for ... what do you call them? Um ... counts, that is it. Like Dracula,' she said in broken English, grinning broadly.

Steel raised an eyebrow at the revelation.

'So, tell me ...?' Steel paused as if silently requesting her name.

'Anna, my name is Anna,' she said.

'So, tell me, Anna, what's Dutch for Count?' Steel asked curiously.

'It's *Graaf*. Why?' she said with a confused look on her face.

Steel leaned over, kissed the girl on the forehead, and thanked her before hurrying out.

Anna sat dazed. Suddenly, a huge smile came over her face, and she melted back into her seat.

Steel rushed along the street. Pulling his cell phone from his jacket pocket, he pressed the speed-dial for Stanton. He heard the rings that emitted from the device as he gazed at his watch; it would be around seven in the morning in the States. The rings continued. After a while, Steel stopped and looked around. He was alone in a strange city with no backup.

A smile crossed Steel's face. But that's how he preferred to be: alone. He placed the cell phone back in his pocket. Steel knew who he was after. A low-life smuggler called Thomas Graaf. He could arrange transport for anyone and anything— for a price, of course. The agency had used him once or twice, that was until they found out he was part of a human trafficking ring, especially kids to predators.

Steel had never met the man, nor did he particularly wish to, let alone save the man's life. But that was the game, and to find the answers, Steel had to play.


Stanton stepped out of the shower. A white towel straining at his waist and another he used to dry off his hair. He'd gone home to get something decent to eat and a much-needed shower to wash off the days of sleeping in his office. The ripe smell coming from his shirts had signalled the need for a quick break from the case. Besides, there was nothing he could do at the moment. There were good people on the case doing research, and Steel was in the field.

Stanton sat on the kingsize bed and took the towel from his head. The television was on the news channel. A report from Berlin was on. The reporter was coving the explosion at Falkner's apartment. There were still crowds of people taking photographs, using cameras and cell phones.

'Goddamn civis,' Stanton growled under his breath, cursing the people as they laughed and took selfies. As if the death of another human being was a joke. If it was up to him, he'd lock them all up.

The reporter, Emily Josh, couldn't give much information, less for the owner's name. She said that the investigation was ongoing and more details were to follow. This usually meant the cops had politely told them to fuck off. Stanton smiled to himself. It was precisely what he would have done if he'd been there.

Suddenly, ding-ding-ding from Stanton's cell let him know he had a missed call. He picked it up and swore out loud for his bad timing. The alert told him that Steel had tried to call several times, the last one being as he was walking out of the bathroom. Quickly, Stanton checked his messages and email, seeing if Steel had left anything. Nothing in either. Tapping the cell on his chin, Stanton thought hard. He knew Steel wouldn't contact Brena unless there was something Steel couldn't handle, which was unlikely to ever happen.

Steel's other option: go it alone and give a briefing later. Steel had done it before.

Stanton placed down the cell phone, then headed for the drinks cabinet to pour a generous two fingers of whiskey. As he tilted the mouth of the bottle over the glass, he stopped. Furious with himself, Stanton slammed down the bottle and screwed the cap back on.

'No, you dumb bastard, not now.' Cursing himself at his weakness. Too often, he had hit the bottle when things had gotten rough. And the past couple of years, they had been rough. His wife's battle with cancer had finally taken its toll, and he sought refuge in the bottle. Stanton's kids were both in their twenties and had left home years ago, but his demise drove them further away, and now the odd phone call had turned to silence. As he raised a shaking hand, Stanton knew things had to change. Stanton gritted his teeth and made a fist out of the trembling hand, gathering all of his strength and will.

———

Stanton changed into a slate-grey suit and shined his shoes. Of course, he had to bring his A-game. Steel was relying on it, on him. Simms was on the way back with Falkner, and it was up to Stanton to put the man in a room and get whatever information he could out of the man.

Stanton still had no idea why the backup team didn't make it back with Simms, but that could wait. For now, he had to get back to the office and do some work instead of sitting on his hands and letting Brena run the show. Stanton knew that everyone respected him, but the fear had gone. Years before he crawled into the bottle, people trembled at the very mention of his name. Now, it was just a curious *bossman* feeling. It was time the old Stanton returned.

———

The weather over Amsterdam had broken. Torrents of rain came down from angry black clouds that had been hurried along by a fierce easterly wind. Steel had made it inside an Irish bar not too far from the museum. A traditional-looking place with outside seating and an authentic Irish wood-and-stone bar inside. The place itself was actually owned by an Irishman called Patrick Callaghan. He was a bruiser of a man with fiery red hair.

He had made a few enemies back in his home country, which had forced him to relocate. Now, Callaghan was a respectable businessman and pub owner, or as respectable as the old fox could ever be. At least, that was what people thought. But, in fact, he was still doing deals of questionable legality on the side.

He had met the man some time ago when Steel was in the British Army stationed in Ireland on a six-month tour in Armar. Steel's company had arrested him doing gun-running for some less than savoury people. But, of course, money talked, and Patrick walked. Steel had kept track of Callaghan, just in case, he became useful. That was until 1996, when the cease-fire was called, and Callaghan became a liability to his once so-called friends.

Steel approached Callaghan via a colleague and offered him a new life in Europe. All he had to do was be prepared to be Steel's man in whichever region Callaghan settled. Now, it was time to collect.

Steel walked into the bar and looked around. The place was packed, even at two in the afternoon. He ambled up to the bar and found a gap next to a couple of Dutch bikers, possibly part of a chapter looking at doing some dealings. The two huge men, who wore denim and sleeveless biker jackets with their colours sewn onto the backs, turned and looked at Steel and grunted disapprovingly.

'We don't like your kind here,' said the bigger one with a shaven head and tattoos all over his arms and parts of his head.

'You mean devastatingly handsome with a full head of hair?' Steel joked sarcastically.

The man gave Steel an angry look and stood, making his friend react in kind.

'Oh, lads, I don't think you want to pick a fight with Mr Steel here,' said a familiar voice.

'Why's that? The man shouldn't be here,' said the biker.

'For two very good reasons. One, he is ex-SAS and Navy Seal, which makes him as nuts as anyone here and two, if it wasn't for this British gent here, I wouldn't be here now, tellin' you all this. So, leave the man alone and let me buy the bastard a drink,' Callaghan said with a yell, which was followed by the rest of the bar letting out a resounding roar.

'Oh, great,' Steel said, rolling his eyes behind his sunglasses. 'Drinking time.'

The giant Irishman placed down two whiskey glasses and half-filled them with Irish whiskey.

'Too old times and the hope they don't come back to bite you in the arse,' Callaghan toasted.

Steel raised his glass, and the two men downed their drinks in one gulp. Both men winced as the alcohol hit home. Callaghan roared with laughter, and the bar joined in. As Callaghan went to pour another, Steel placed a hand over the glass, startling Callaghan and the others.

'You refusing a drink from an old friend, are yeh?' Callaghan growled, the rest of the bar rising from their seats, ready to pounce.

'Not at all, it's just I want to share a drink with all my new friends as well. So, drinks are on me,' Steel declared loudly, taking the bottle from Callaghan and raising it up.

The bar roared once more, and the live band that had been getting ready to perform began to play.

Steel sat down and leant forward to speak to Callaghan. 'Want to pay that debt?'

Callaghan smiled and nodded, then disappeared behind the bar to serve the rest of the restless band of reprobates, bikers, thugs, and locals that liked spending time there.

Steel leant over the bar and grabbed a bottle of Johnnie Walker Red that he'd spotted near the rinsing sink. He poured himself two fingers worth and sat back as the bar exploded into joyful song and laughter.

Steel smiled. Now he had some new friends he could call

upon, and something deep down told him he might just be doing that.

————

'The police are still not saying what caused the blast in Berlin later today,' said the female news reporter.

The dark-haired woman sported a red jumper and grey skirt. The lettering at the bottom of the screen said Sarah Greenthorn, BBC News. The reporter gave precisely the same statement as all the other countries—that the police were still investigating and as soon as something official was received, they would let viewers know. This was universal language for the cops who have revealed jack, but it's something bad.

The Sentinel sat and studied the feed while setting up several laptops and monitors in a different room. The apartment was spacious, with signs of people with expensive taste. The furniture in the sitting room alone was worth over fifty grand. The thick velvet curtains were perfect for keeping the light in, the little light The Sentinel would emit via the computer screens.

After the final screen had been set up, The Sentinel sat back and studied the latest name on the list. This was a tall, thin man with a bad taste in clothing, mostly corduroy trousers and blazers with padding on the arms. The man had an air of a professor or wealthy landowner about him.

The Sentinel gazed longingly at the monitor, observing the man who had walked into a vast office and sat in a leather office chair. The office had the 1900s feel to it, complete with a drinks globe in the corner. The man had some bearing, but The Sentinel sensed this had been bought rather than bred into.

The Sentinel's gaze slipped back to the story on the news. Behind the reporter stood Sabine Boese. She had just received a phone call, one that made her excited enough to usher her colleagues back into the car and take off. She had received news of something.

The Sentinel stared at the screen as the vehicle took off, curious at what had made the INTERPOL agent leave like that.

The Sentinel stood up and moved to the partial set-up workbench. Several plans and roughly drawn blueprints of devices were pinned to a board next to it. The Sentinel looked through them and stopped at one, then tore it from the board. The Sentinel had the how; now, it was just a case of when and where.

# CHAPTER TWENTY-FOUR

STEEL HAD FOLLOWED CALLAGHAN INTO A BACKROOM office, which was a small but cosy place. It had a secondhand desk Callaghan had probably gotten from one of the antique places scattered about the city. Photographs of Callaghan and his adventures hung on the walls in cheap gold frames. Since settling down to a new life, Callaghan had married and had several kids.

'So, Johnnie boy, what do ya need?' Callaghan asked, pouring two cups of coffee from the machine next to a printer.

'I'm looking for someone who lives in Amsterdam. I need to find them quickly, and I know you have eyes and ears all over the city,' Steel said with an impressed smile on his face.

Callaghan gasped, his eyes wide with surprise.

'Oh, come on, you old sod, you're an old dog who knows too many old tricks to try and learn pointless new ones,' Steel said, taking the black coffee.

Callaghan laughed and nodded.

'That I am, Johnnie boy, that I am. So, who's the poor sod

ya lookin' for?' Callaghan asked before taking a mouthful of coffee.

'Thomas Graaf.' Steel moved just in time.

Callaghan sprayed the coffee where Steel had stood.

'What do you want with that piece of shit? To kill the bastard, I hope?' Callaghan boomed with an angry voice.

'To save his life, actually,' Steel said with a shrug.

'Now, what would ya want to do dat for? The man is evil, pure friggin evil.' Callaghan took another mouthful of coffee.

'I got questions; he's got answers. After that, the killer can have him.' Steel smiled and shrugged.

Callaghan looked over at the small portable TV on his desk; the news report was about the bombing in Berlin.

'Is it about that?' Callaghan nodded to the TV.

Steel nodded and took a sip of the lousy coffee. 'I believe he is next. I want to know why,' he said, his voice low and angry.

Callaghan frowned as he knew that look. 'You lose someone on this?'

Steel simply nodded. His expression said the rest.

'Consider the bastard found,' Callaghan said, standing from his ageing leather office chair. 'Where you stayin?' he asked, knowing it wouldn't be a YMCA.

Steel passed over a flyer he'd taken from the desk, just in case he needed to get a cab back to the hotel.

'Oh, roughing it, I see Johnnie boy,' Callaghan laughed.

The two men embraced like brothers, and Callaghan walked Steel to the door.

'Thanks, Pat, that's our square,' Steel said.

'No, this is on the house. Just catch the bastard that got ya partner, and if darlin' Graaf gets his on the way, well, that will be a nice bonus,' Pat said with a wink and a smile.

He saw Callaghan get on his phone as he turned to leave;

the search had already started. The question was: who would get there first? Steel looked at his watch. It was three in the afternoon. Eight hours to go. Steel hoped it would be enough time to find him.

———

When Stanton arrived back at the office, heads turned as he got off the elevator. Stanton was looking sharp and confident. *He was back.*

As he walked into the war room that Brena's team were using, heads shot around, and nods of approval made him feel good. But he kept the warm glow inside and maintained a stiff-upper-lip look.

'Where are we at, people?' he barked. The old gravelly voice had returned also.

'We are trying to ascertain what the flags represent,' said Rachel.

'It's the flag of a Dutch count or earl,' Dorson yelled out as the web page spat out the answer.

'So, we are looking for Dutch royalty, are you sure?' Stanton asked, unsure of the sudden outburst.

'Why is he targeting a Dutch count?' Dutton asked as he worked on Steel's location.

'Or earl?' Dorson added, walking over to where Stanton stood near Rachel's chair.

'OK, check any affiliations with Dutch royalty and New York, see who has been there recently and what they were doing there. If you are right, this could be something a whole lot bigger than just killing security guards and lawyers,' Stanton said, fearing the phone call he would have to make if they were right. Stanton hoped to God they weren't.

———

Steel headed back to his hotel. His hopes rested with Callaghan. Steel knew if anyone could find Graaf, it would be him. However, Steel was still slightly reserved about bringing Callaghan in on this. After all, he and Graaf had a falling out some time ago. One that Callaghan never forgot nor forgave. Steel just hoped that Callaghan would leave him alive long enough to get answers. After that, all bets were off.

Steel entered the immense lobby and checked at the front desk for messages. He didn't expect any, not so soon anyway, but he could also see if anyone had been looking for him as well. The shift change had denied Steel from seeing the blonde he had seen before. Instead, this time he spoke to a raven-haired beauty with eyes the colour of a Mediterranean sky and a body that fitted the uniform in just the right places. Steel noticed her name tag read Sarah Angel, causing him to smile.

'Sorry, sir, no messages.' Her voice was low and had a gravelly substance to it.

'Oh, that's quite alright, Sarah, but if you could send a bottle of Dom Perignon 2006 to my suite, that would be fantastic,' Steel said with a seductive smile.

'Will that be *two* glasses, sir?' she enquired. Her eyes sparkled as much as the ruby-red lipstick that covered her pouting lips.

'All depends on the company, but it's a shame to waste such a good vintage drinking alone, wouldn't you say?' Steel smiled and headed for the elevators.

Sarah's eyes followed him as she leaned on the front desk. Thoughts ran through her head, and none of them was decent. Sarah smiled and picked up the phone, and dialled for room service.

'Hi, this is Sarah at the main desk. A bottle of Dom 2006 to the Penthouse Suite.' She nodded. 'Yes, two glasses.'

———

Brena entered the war room and looked around as everyone was too busy to acknowledge he'd even walked into the room. 'What's going on?' he asked as he moved up to Rachel.

'We may have a lead with the next one. We're looking for a Dutch count, earl or royalty,' she replied without taking her eyes off the screen.

'We think this Sentinel is going after royalty now?'

Rachel said nothing. She just nodded and furthered her search into Dutch nobility and possible movements to New York or neighbouring places.

'Any word from Steel?' Brena asked quietly, looking around the room as if he didn't want to be overheard.

'Stanton had a missed call from him earlier. After that, nothing. Looks like he's gone to ground, or he's working on something,' Rachel explained as her fingers skipped over the keys of the keyboard.

Brena stood up straight and nodded to himself, self-reassurance that everything was under control and Steel was possibly in trouble.

'Let me know if anything comes up,' he instructed Rachel.

'Will do,' Rachel replied, her gaze still locked onto the computer screen.

Dorson watched Brena out of the corner of his eye. To him, Brena seemed nervous and edgy, but why he didn't know. He observed Brena slowly cross the floor and stare at the elevator, almost as if he was uneasy about going up to see the old man. Which in itself was strange. If Brena were kept out of the loop about something, he'd head straight up there.

However, this time it was different; he was different. It had started when they learned Simms was bringing Falkner back for questioning.

Brena checked his watch, spun on his heels and headed back the way he came. Dorson spun in his chair and watched as the man took the other elevator back down towards the lobby.

'I wonder where he's off to,' Dorson said softly.

Rachel looked up for a second, catching the numbers on the elevator display board, and shrugged. 'Who knows, who cares? All I do know is he's not here, breathing down my neck,' she said, shivering at the thought of Brena looming over her with his bad breath and cheap aftershave.

Dorson checked his watch. Trish still wasn't back, and it was getting late in the day. It wasn't like her to be late, not unless she had said she was going to be. Suddenly, Dorson had a bad feeling and stood up.

'Where you going?' Rachel asked, surprised at what seemed like a lack of commitment to finding the killer.

'Trish still isn't back. So, I'm just gonna check her place, make sure she's OK,' Dorson said, pulling on his jacket.

'Why don't you try calling first?' Rachel suggested.

'Tried that, went straight to voicemail,' Dorson explained.

Rachel thought for a second, then nodded. In truth, she had only noticed Trish's lack of appearance when Dorson had mentioned it. But then Dorson had always had a thing for Trish, but rules got in the way of him acting on those feelings. 'Go on, I'll cover for you; say you had to do some research elsewhere,' Rachel told him with a half-cocked smile.

Dorson smiled a thank you and hurried to the elevators. R

Rachel looked at her watch; it was ten in the morning. A smug smile broke over her face, like a child with a dirty secret.

———

Dorson drove the Challenger as if his life depended on it. All the government training with evasion driving technics kicked in as he weaved in and out of the morning traffic. Trish's house was a good twenty minutes away, and he needed to make it in fifteen at the very least. Dorson wished this wasn't an unmarked vehicle; he envied cops with their warning lights. Nothing screamed 'get the hell out of the way' like red-and-blue in your rearview.

Fourteen minutes and thirty seconds. An excellent time, but Dorson hoped it was soon enough as he pulled up outside Trish's place.

The street was quiet; school buses and busy parents had already gone to work. So now, there were only dog walkers and postal delivery trucks. A guy who lived over the road was on his lawn raking up leaves, but Dorson just reconned the guy was on a pension, and he loved to watch the world. The pure form of the nosey neighbour. No sitting next to the window and looking out from behind curtains for this guy.

Dorson paid the man another quick glance and thought nothing more of it. He knew the type. They saw everything but didn't want to share what they'd seen.

He made his way up the path. A biting easterly wind stung the side of his face, forcing him to close one eye for a second. After that, he moved steadily forwards, his hands by his sides so he could get to his Sig Sauer resting in a holster at the small of his back. From the outside, everything seemed normal. There were no lights on, and her car was in the driveway. He had the thought that she had slept in or her alarm had failed to go off. It happened. In fact, it had recently happened to him a couple of times.

Dorson tried the front door. Locked solid. He made a quick inspection of the door and the Yale lock. No scratches or signs of forced entry. Reluctantly, he moved around the side to the rear of the house. There was a small white gate under a rosebush archway. He clicked the latch and slowly pushed around. The grounds seemed quiet, too quiet.

Dorson slid his hand to his belt and back towards the polymer holster and the grip of the 9-mm.

Everything felt wrong. The car in the drive, the lack of movement inside, and the eerie silence of the backyard. Trish had once asked his advice on getting a dog, just something to come home to. He remembered telling her it would be cruel because of all the time away and late nights. She'd agreed and decided against it. Now, he wished she had gotten the damn mutt which would prove an excellent early warning system, letting you know if someone was there or something was wrong.

Dorson promised himself if he found her alive and well, he'd take her to the pound and buy her one himself.

Beads of sweat began to form on his forehead, and he could hear the sound of his racing heartbeat in his ears. Adrenaline was pumping through his veins, but his breathing was steady, his muscles tense yet ready for action.

The backyard was a thirty-by-thirty square with a patio and a couple of trees surrounding a grassy area hidden under a blanket of gold and brown leaves. A large bay window looked straight into the dining room, an office. Next to this was a long window and a door to the kitchen area. Dorson tried the door, but that, too, was solid. He stepped back and checked the windows, but nothing seemed out of place.

Finally, frustrated, Dorson headed back to the front of the house. He'd try the doorbell and hope she'd answer with messed-up hair and bleary eyes. He looked over at the neighbour, who was still working on leaf clearing and waved. The man quickly turned away as if doing so would make him somehow invisible. Dorson smiled to himself and shook his head. Then, raising his hand, Dorson extended a finger and pushed the bell. There was a faint sound of an electronic ding-dong and then silence. Dorson bounced on his heels while he waited. He'd give it two minutes before he tried again.

After the two, Dorson tried again. The same faint tone and then nothing. She was either in the shower or still sleeping if she was home. Dorson hammered on the door with his fist and yelled through the door. To no avail. Mixed feelings of fear and confusion poured over him. Something was definitely wrong.

Pulling out his cell, Dorson dialled Rachel's number. He needed to report this fast. As he listened to the ringing in the handset, he made his way around the house to try every window and door once more. He discovered all the curtains were open and doors and windows locked. Trish wasn't there, and her car was in the drive. Dorson could only come to one conclusion: Trish had been abducted.

'Did you find her?' asked Rachel's voice over the speaker.

'No, her place is empty, and her car is here in the driveway. Something is wrong; I think Trish has been taken,' Dorson admitted, nervousness sounding in his voice. 'We need to tell the old man.'

There was a pregnant pause, and then a new voice came over the speaker.

'Agent Dorson, why are you at Trish's place?'

A cold shiver ran down Dorson's back as he heard the angry tone in Brena's voice.

'Trish didn't come in today. I was worried. I believe some-thing has happened to her because her place is empty and—'

'Trish is taking some time off ... a personal matter. She phoned and asked me for the time off last night before she left work. Nothing to worry about, so you can get your ass back here and do your job before you don't have one.'

Dorson froze as the phone went dead.

Brena was mad. But Dorson wondered why. Was it because Dorson had slipped out, or was it something more sinister?

# CHAPTER TWENTY-FIVE

A KNOCK ON THE SUITE DOOR DISTURBED STEEL FROM HIS work at the murder board he had created. The magnetic white-board the concierge had arranged to bring up from a conference room was perfect for what Steel needed.

Steel answered the door with his shirt half undone and untucked. It was Sarah from the reception desk. She stood next to a brass waiter's trolley supporting two glasses, the bottle of Dom on ice in a champagne bucket, a big bowl of fresh strawberries and a small pitcher of cream.

'I didn't think it was coming,' Steel said with a raised eyebrow, noting the hungry look in her eyes.

'Sorry for the wait, sir; the timing wasn't right,' Sarah explained with a cheeky smile.

'For the champagne?'

'No, the end of the shift,' Sarah purred, pushing the trolley into the suite and closing the door behind them.

Two hours later, the ice had melted, and the champagne had lost its chill. Sarah lay curled up with a satisfied look on her face. This cat had definitely gotten her cream. Steel was up and about. He didn't have time to sleep. He hoped Pat would call with news of Graaf's location any minute. But so far, nothing.

Steel walked to the next room, where the whiteboard stood and picked up the blue marker. The name Thomas Graaf was circled four times. What did Graaf and all the others have in common? As far as he knew, nothing. Graaf and Falkner, he could understand, but the others?

Steel turned slightly as he heard a low moan from the bedroom. Sarah was dreaming. She had been a pleasant surprise and an exciting distraction. As well as exceedingly nimble.

Steel headed into the kitchenette and pressed the button on the coffee machine for black coffee. He needed a shower and to get the alcohol out of his system. Taking the coffee from the drip tray, Steel headed for the shower.

Steel hoped the noise from the running water would wake his guest, and she would scamper away like a thief in the night. He turned on the water and let it run for a while, allowing the water to reach the perfect temperature.

Stepping under, Steel closed his eyes and placed his hands against the back wall. The rainshower felt great, cascading water washing over his body. His mind was a million miles away, so he never heard the patter of naked feet on the bathroom floor or Sarah's naked body pulling up close behind him until the last second.

Steel turned and saw her fantastic figure standing before him.

No words were spoken or necessary. Steel pulled her in close, and they embraced; he pulled her up so her legs were wrapped around his muscular middle.

She groaned loudly as he pushed her against the wall, forcing her close to him. Her long fingers clawed at his back and ran through his hair. Sarah screamed as she felt him once more.

————

It was another hour before Sarah left. The timing was perfect.

As they said their farewells at the door, Steel saw Pat stepping off the elevator with a sad-looking man in a torn suit and a bloody lip and nose.

As Sarah moved past the two men, she looked back and wondered if this was the man whose name was on the board and what Steel was going to do with him. She had worked out that Steel was a cop or at least working for some agency. She had seen the whiteboard and realised he was in Amsterdam on an investigation. Then her thoughts on the bombing in Berlin. Was he there in search of the bomber? Was there a terrorist in Amsterdam? She looked back again to see the door closing, and all she could wonder was whether the man they had just brought in was the bomber himself.

————

As Steel closed the door to the Penthouse Suite, he noticed the look on Sarah's face and that cold chill he often got running down his spine. A tingling feeling that things were about to go sideways and fast.

'Why did you bring him here?' Steel asked, angry that the cover he was maintaining had just been blown.

'Well, that's thanks for ya,' Pat said, a tone of disappointment in his voice.

'I'm grateful you found him so quickly, but did you have to

bring him to my hotel? Couldn't you have phoned or some-thing?' Steel asked, pulling Graaf with him and heading for the bedroom to pack.

'So, you're the cop?' Graaf said, giving Steel a once-over.

'Did Pat explain why you're here?' Steel asked him.

'Someone wants to kill me, and you're here to save me. How noble,' Graaf snickered.

'Not quite, but close,' Steel smiled and gave a quick look around the room to make sure he hadn't hidden anything significant.

'Leaving so soon?' Pat said, watching Steel as he stuffed his clothes into a canvas travel bag.

'Did you see that woman in the hallway?' Steel said with a disappointed tone.

'Yeh, lucky bastard,' Pat grinned and nodded with approval.

'Well, she works here, and it wouldn't surprise me if she were phoning the cops as we speak.' Steel grabbed Graaf and the bag and headed for the room with the murder board.

'Where were you thinking of going?' Pat asked, suddenly feeling the situation that was about to unravel was his fault.

'For the moment, it's best if you didn't know. INTERPOL will undoubtedly be here soon once the police are informed.' Steel admitted that there was an agent hot on his trail in Berlin.

He decided to get passage on the Hook of Holland to Harwich ferry. He could hide Graaf back in Britain until it was ready to hand him over to the agency. The less Pat knew, the better it was for both of them. Steel knew that Sabine Boese would be on her way if she weren't already.

Steel thought about telling Stanton of his plan, but he decided against it. Instead, he would secure Graaf and then let MI8 handle it.

'Can you take Graaf to Hoek van Holland Ferry Port? I'll

meet you there,' Steel requested. A plan was forming in his head.

'You expecting trouble?' Pat asked with a hungry grin.

'You know me, Pat, I always expect it. That's why I'm still breathing. The trick is how to avoid it.' Steel smiled back and slapped his friend on the arm for good luck. 'Take him there and wait for me if I'm not there by,'—Steel checked the ferry information on his phone—'the next ferry is at nine.'

He calculated every eventuality. 'If I'm not there by half eight, get going and call this number.' Steel wrote down Stanton's number on a piece of paper and handed it to Pat. 'Only speak to a man called Stanton, *nobody else*.'

Pat looked at the bit of torn-off piece of paper and nodded.

'Right you are, boss,' Pat roared and gave Steel a big hug. 'Just make sure you're there.' He stuffed the piece of paper into his pocket and grabbed Graaf by the arm. 'Come on you. Looks like we're gonna spend some more time together,' Pat laughed.

Graaf said nothing. He just stared at Steel with an unamused look before being dragged towards the suite entrance.


Steel watched them leave, and a sudden feeling of relief came over him. INTERPOL and The Sentinel would be following him, not Pat. All Steel had to do was get to the ferry and return home. He had already secured two of the targets, but still, he had the feeling that The Sentinel didn't want them dead. If that were the case, they would have been killed without all of this drama.

No, The Sentinel wished to be found and wanted them to talk.

Steel grabbed the bag and made his way from the hotel suite, hoping that the device, or whatever The Sentinel had planned, would now be deactivated. But the target was out of play.

The Sentinel's MO was to scare the target. But if he was right, that didn't explain why Trent was killed at his apartment, then Alison in a quiet spot by a hospital, and Falkner's apartment was blown to pieces. Unless, of course, there was *someone else* who wanted to silence them.

This was no psychopath they were chasing. This was someone out for revenge. One of the purest reasons for what The Sentinel was doing. With Graaf gone, Steel had breathing room to work out what was going on. The deadline for Graaf was twenty-three hundred, or eleven, that evening.

Steel believed Graaf was now safe from the killer. That was the game: *find them or lose them.* Graaf had been found.

Steel had until eleven until the next card came in, but he would be at the ferry at nine. Five hours to find out as much as he could, then six hours on the ship sweating the truth out of Graaf.

Steel pulled the door shut and headed for the elevators. He had to disappear, but before he did, he'd have to speak to Sarah. If she had called the cops, they would have been asking them questions, and he didn't want her involved. He pressed the button and waited. Steel looked at the digital display, which showed the elevator was all the way down in the lobby. The numbers clicked off, unhindered. Steel knew the elevator would get to his floor in two minutes and eighteen seconds. He also knew he could make it down using the stairs in four and a half.

The display registered it was now on the floor below, and it had stopped. Steel scowled. That tingling in his spine told him there was trouble coming. Steel forced open the doors to the elevator and climbed in, using the side near the counterbalance to climb up. He'd wait until the elevator was on his floor and then climb on top of the metal box.

If he was right, even if Sarah had called the police, they wouldn't have gotten there or been able to form a tactical response team that fast. No, this was someone else, and he could imagine who. This was Sabine's doing, and there was a Special Armed Response Unit downstairs at the stairwell and another heading for his suite.

Steel hoped he was wrong. Hoping that it was just a guest going to their room down below. But that 'feeling' had never been wrong or let him down—well, not severely, at any rate. There was a clang of metal as the brakes on the elevator was released, then a whoosh as it flew upwards to the suite.

Steel carefully clambered onto the elevator roof and inched the emergency hatch open. Inside, several members of the Armed Response team were already out of the elevator and moving into position, waiting for the rest to form up.

The men wore protective body armour over civilian clothing and carried various weapons. Steel lost sight of them as they moved down the corridor. But one thing he was confident of: Sabine wasn't with them. She would be downstairs where it was safe. Besides, it wasn't her country, and she wouldn't have gotten authorisation to take over that quickly.

The standard protocol would be to seal off the area, restrict elevator usage, and cover all exits. That meant Steel's method of escape couldn't be through the front door as he'd planned. He smiled as he thought about all this. Wondering what story she had told the Dutch police to have gotten all this arranged.

Steel knew there would be hell to pay when they found out she had misled them. There was no way they would send an armed police team to arrest a British Lord on holiday or an NYPD detective; the scandal would be unthinkable.

They likely thought Falkner was with Steel and that Falkner was the bomber.

There was a gentle ping, and the elevators slid shut. Steel couldn't risk jumping inside; the security cameras would pick him up. Besides, why should he make it easy for them or her? Steel imagined Sabine biting those long painted talons she called nails. Nervous about the outcome.

What if it went wrong, and a twitchy cop shot Steel? The thought of it backfiring sounded more delicious to Steel.

The elevator moved down to the lobby. This time to pick up new guests. Steel climbed down while guests shoved their way in, then he used the elevator support structure to climb down to a safe location and waited for it to ascend.

Below would be a maintenance door. From there, Steel would have to feel his way around and eventually step out into the world. A clang of metal and the sound of air being released. The elevator flew up the shaft towards the second floor. Steel jumped down and looked around. He slowly opened the maintenance door, smiled, and hurried through. Now all he had to do was get out of the building.

————

Brena was pacing up and down in the men's room. He was nervous. Steel's investigation was moving too quickly, and now he looked bad. To make matters worse, the old man had found a new lease on life.

He needed a cigarette. He also required Steel out of the way or at least discredited or slowed down. Sure, he had called Sabine Boese and given Steel's location, he'd even lied and said that Falkner was with him and that Falkner was responsible for the explosion.

Also, Simms was a problem. It wouldn't be long until he

landed and walked in with Falkner. For the agency, it was a win; they had gotten one back alive, but it hadn't been Brena that had done it.

Brena stopped pacing; someone was coming. He could hear their shoes tapping on the tiled floor. As an agent burst through the door, he knew it was time to leave. The two men exchanged pleasantries, and Brena left. He could almost taste the nicotine in his mouth.

Brena headed out through the security check and the main doors. He moved around the side of the building and pulled out a pack of cigarettes, removing one with his teeth. As he lit the end with the electronic lighter, Brena inhaled and closed his eyes. Heaven.

Things were going wrong. The plan wasn't meant to move this quickly.

Brena had heard the whispers about Steel and brushed them off as a rumour, Chinese whispers, stories around the campfire. But now he knew the stories did this guy no justice. This John Steel was worse than what the stories had said. This guy was a nightmare incarnate.

# CHAPTER TWENTY-SIX

STEEL HAD MADE IT OUT OF THE BUILDING USING A tradesmen's entrance the cops had evidently forgotten about. He just strolled through the kitchen like he belonged there, and no one questioned him. Confidence was a significant part of blending. 'If you look like you don't fit in, chances are you don't,' he was always told by one of his teachers at the agency. Luckily, most of the waiter staff were wearing black, so Steel blended in nicely.

He walked into the prickly air. The temperature had dropped to around four degrees, causing his breath to turn to mist. His plans had soured but were not wholly ruined. 'Always have a Plan B,' his instructors used to say. So, Steel had learnt to have a Plan C and D, just in case B failed.

As he'd moved through the hotel, he'd spotted Sabine in the lobby; she was pacing about in a small area, concern on her face. Sabine had been weighing all the things that could go wrong while she was downstairs and out of the way. All the options he had thought of earlier, no doubt.

Steel smiled cunningly. Plan E just came into his head.

Sure, it was risky, but where was the fun in no risk? Besides, he would have an ally, not a hindrance, if it worked. Calmly, Steel entered the lobby and coolly walked up to Sabine, who was chewing on the nail of her left index finger.

'Well, this looks exciting. Looking for someone special?' Steel asked jokingly.

'Buzz off, pal, we're busy ...' Sabine stopped mid-sentence. Her eyes widened, and her mouth fell open.

'Really, Sabine, that's not a look for you,' Steel said, closing her mouth by gently pushing her chin up with two fingers.

'What are you ... you should be ...' Sabine fought to get out the words.

'Yes, I know. But what I need to know is who told you I was here?' Steel's smile changed to a look of anger, forcing her to step back slightly. 'Call off your dogs, Sabine. Let's talk about this before one of us gets hurt.'

'You're worried about yourself or your friend?' Sabine asked with an angry look and bitter tone.

'Actually, I was thinking about your career, and what friend? I'm here alone ... ah.' The penny had dropped. 'Brena?' he asked.

Sabine nodded, shocked at his deduction but not surprised. The head of the operation stood two feet away, talking to his men, requesting updates.

'The room is clear; he's not there, and no sign of anyone else was there—well, a male, someone that is. They did find a woman's panties, though,' said the commander to Sabine.

'Sorry, I would have cleaned up, but I wasn't expecting guests,' Steel joked.

The commander turned to face Steel. His eyes widened at the sight of the man they were hunting. The man's hand went for his gun and raised it. Sabine rolled her eyes as she knew what was coming.

In the blink of an eye, Steel had taken the weapon and then handed it back with the top slide removed from the lower body, the magazine in his other hand.

'Now, can we chat?' Steel growled.

The force commander's eyes were glued to the stripped weapon in Steel's hands.

'Buy you a drink?' Sabine asked, walking to the steps leading up to the fancy-looking bar.

'Thought you'd never ask,' said the commander.

Steel shook his head and followed them.

The commander called back his teams and closed down the operation. The guests that were hanging around, looking alarmed and confused, took pictures with their cell phones. As Steel couldn't help but think of the boosting the hotel's ratings would get. Who didn't like a little drama while on holiday? As the team dispersed, Steel stood at the top of the stairs.

'Ladies and gents, sorry for any distress, but what you just witnessed was a combined exercise by the brave police department and INTERPOL and the hotel. Displaying their willingness to always put your safety first,' Steel announced, prompting people to clap and applaud. Steel turned to the man behind the bar and called for glasses of champagne for everyone in the lobby.

The man began preparing while Steel wandered to where Sabine and the Commander sat.

'Nicely deflected,' Sabine said with a grin.

Steel handed the weapon parts back to the commander. 'No hard feelings.'

The commander was still confused about how Steel had gotten out of the building and taken the weapon so quickly.

'Don't worry, commander; it's his job to make people miserable,' Sabine said, noting the look on the man's face.

'Only yours, Sabine, and bad guys.' Steel said with a smile.

'Yes, talking about bad guys—'

'He flew back to Langley using the jet of the spooks the police picked up at the airport. I believe Brena's men,' Steel said, looking at the bar staff who were quickly distributing the complimentary champagne and waving one of them over.

'Steel, what the hell is going on?' Sabine asked.

'You know about the killings in the States?' Steel asked as the drinks arrived.

'The security guard and the lawyer?' Sabine nodded in reply as she took two glasses and handed one to the commander, sitting opposite.

'This postcard killer calls himself The Sentinel; you know this already because you got a card from him last time, correct?' Steel asked, to which Sabine reluctantly nodded.

'This guy has been bouncing me around, looking for his victims.' Steel admitted.

'Why? If you find them, doesn't that defeat the objective if he wants to kill them?' Sabine asked before taking a sip.

'I don't think he does; I think he wants them found. They all connect somehow. They all tell a story that The Sentinel wants to be told. I think the reason the others died was that somebody else was trying to shut them up. I think that is why The Sentinel brought me in on the case; he knew I'd do something before they were all gone,' Steel explained.

'That's a bit of a stretch, don't you think, and slightly self-aggrandizing?' Sabine asked, giving Steel a strange look.

'Okay, so just say that I'm right. That this killer is out for revenge ... one way or the other, we save them, and we find out the story. They die, and we investigate, but we don't find out the story. The Sentinel wants the truth to be found,' Steel said, calling the bartender over.

'What truth?'

'Exactly?' Steel said with a childish grin. 'You want a big

case, fine. Work with me on this, and you'll have it. CIA and INTERPOL working together.' Steel suggested.

'Don't tell me. All you want is to be left out of this at the end?' Sabine asked, a look of calculation on her face.

'I was never a part of it, merely a passer-by,' Steel said, raising his glass.

The commander did the same but had been lost in the conversation.

'Oh, one more thing.'

'Yes?' Sabine asked, rolling her eyes at the prospect of what was coming next.

'You may have to explain to the commander; I think we lost him about ten minutes ago.' Steel smiled and stood up just as the barman arrived with the bill. Steel billed it to the room and gave the man a twenty euro note for his trouble.

'Right then, things to do,' Steel said, hurrying back to the elevator.

'Like what?' Sabine called out.

'Find out what the killer wants us to find before eleven o'clock tonight,' Steel called back.

'Why? What happens at eleven?' Sabine asked, puzzled and a little afraid.

'That's when the new postcard should be delivered.'

The elevator doors closed.

———

Dorson returned to the office and was busy checking for anything The Sentinel's targets had in common. The good news was the more targets, the narrower the search. They'd still had no word from Steel, alive or otherwise, which Dorson felt was reassuring. But, of course, no news was good news where a man like Steel was concerned.

Upon his return, Dorson had shot Rachel the evil eye. He knew she had purposely informed Brena of what he was doing. And the fact Brena was there when he'd phoned Rachel spoke volumes. Rachel had always been one to seek favour with people. That was how she chose to move up in the world. But Dorson never knew it would come to dropping her friends into the grinder just to get a foot up.

Dorson remembered jumping at the chance to work with this newly designed team. This was the brainchild of Stanton. Which worked well initially ... until Brena showed up, and then it all went to hell. The people at the top gave this project two years to run. One and a half were already up. After which, they would decide to keep it or scrap it, which meant everyone would be reassigned. Dorson couldn't wait for it to flop, but at the same time, he felt terrible for the old man. If this whole operation went under, he went into retirement.

———

Dorson had spent a good hour checking and rechecking. Nothing. The people couldn't be more unlike or have so little contact with one another. The only thing they had in common was the sixteenth of September. On that day, they were all in New York or a nearby city. Which was a little odd, sure, but when Dorson rechecked, he found none of them was in the same area at the same time.

Dorson looked at the empty coffee mug on his desk and thought about moving. But the sudden appearance of Rachel at the refreshments table turned his stomach and made him lose the urge. He turned back to his work and decided to dissect each person's life, starting with the security guard.

Dorson noticed Rachel's reflection in the monitor, standing behind him, watching what he was doing. He didn't turn or acknowledge her presence. As far as he was concerned, she was just someone he had to work with, nothing more. Any trust had gone, along with any ideas of friendship. She was Brena's pet, and that meant to keep away, or you were going to get burnt.

Dorson looked back at the reflection; she had gone. He turned and saw she was again at her desk. He smiled and picked up his coffee mug. 'Now, I'll get that coffee,' he said to himself, hoping she'd stay at her desk and away from him.

'Find anything?' asked Brena, who suddenly appeared behind him.

Dorson jumped and spilt coffee onto his hand, causing him to cringe with pain; he placed down the cup and flicked the liquid from his hand.

'Jezus Brena,' Dorson cursed as he grabbed a paper towel and mopped up the coffee from the floor and table.

'Well?' Brena asked, grinning as he took particular pleasure in what he had just done.

'Not much. Any report on Trish yet?' Dorson asked, standing up straight and looking Brena in the eyes as he posed the question. Hoping to see something in the man's intense grey-blue eyes.

'Well, keep on it, and Trish is fine, I'm sure. Now, get back to work.' Brena's voice was raised, and his pupils dilated.

Brena was hiding something, and Dorson wanted to know what. But he knew he'd have to be careful; his trust issues were getting worse. However, there was *one* person he could trust, and he just walked through the door with Falkner in tow.

———

The Sentinel was glad that the British weather had turned for the worse. That meant wearing the hood didn't look out of place. It had been the second day of constant rain, but today was a light shower, a fine drizzle like powdered water in the air.

Red double-decker buses hurried down the street, past Parliament and Big Ben, heading both ways over the Westminster Bridge. Despite the rain, it was a bright day, with patches of blue breaking through stone-grey clouds as they drifted above. The Sentinel moved down Birdcage Walk and headed for Constitution Hill.

The Sentinel strolled along, head slightly down with the coat's hood pulled forwards, The Sentinel's face hidden in shadow. There was no hurry; The Sentinel had time. There was always time.

That was part of the game. Giving the hunter time to work out everything. The new player, Steel, was not a disappointment. The only one who took this seriously, the only one without an agenda. Agent Brena and Sabine Boese were in it for the glory, a step up in their evolutionary scale. But Steel was looking at the story, rescuing the targets, giving them a chance to fill in the blanks.

At each tourist trap, the streets began to swell with people. Worse still, people with cameras. Something The Sentinel had wanted to avoid. Even though nobody had any idea what The Sentinel looked like, why take the chance? Even though Steel was a worthy adversary, he was dangerous. Smart and experienced. If anyone could pick out The Sentinel from a crowd, it was him.

The Sentinel stopped and leant against the wall of a building. Looking around quickly, The Sentinel pulled out a cell phone and checked the feed coming from several cameras. This included a new one. This time a woman came into the frame.

She was a tall thin woman in her late forties. Her long mousey-coloured hair was unstyled but fell about the shoulders of her white blouse, which was matched with a light grey skirt.

The clothes hugged her figure enough to compliment her form, making her appear to be all business.

The Sentinel noticed she had an air of someone in charge.

The room was spacious, with rosewood furniture, white walls, and a wooden floor. The view from the window was obscured, but The Sentinel wasn't interested in that. The only necessary view was of the next target.

Tucking the cell back into the jacket pocket, The Sentinel continued down the street. There was still some way to walk before reaching the next safe house, but The Sentinel didn't mind. It was a beautiful day for a walk, and the fresh air helped The Sentinel think. Judging by Steel's rate of finding the targets, it wouldn't be long before he was in London once the next clue had been delivered.

The Sentinel had the decision to make. The next postcard hadn't been sent yet; it was too early. But Steel had already secured Graaf. So no, the postcard must be posted on time, at eleven that evening, or all the timings and preparation would have been for nothing.

The Sentinel hadn't anticipated Steel would be this good. But no matter. The extra time would give Steel time to dig into the targets' lives. Finally, somebody was paying attention. It would soon be over, but there was still much to be done. Two more targets to go. The Sentinel would have revenge, and those responsible would pay. One way or the other.

# CHAPTER TWENTY-SEVEN

STEEL HAD GONE BACK TO THE ROOM AND SHOWERED before putting some fresh clothes on; INTERPOL's little surprise visit had prevented him from doing so earlier. He packed and was ready to check out of the hotel, but not yet. He would be leaving for the ferry in a few hours and meeting up with Pat and Graaf in Hoek van Holland.

He had already booked passage on the ship with two rooms because he figured Graaf wouldn't want to share with a man who had violent nightmares. Besides, once Pat had told Graaf what was going on, the man wouldn't want to leave Steel's protection. No, Graaf would want to be as close to Steel as possible. If he was smart, that was.

Once Steel had all the information he needed, Graaf was useless. As far as Steel was concerned, Graaf could stay on the ship afterwards. He didn't care. Graaf was scum, and someone wanted him dead. No big deal, but until Steel knew why Graaf was significant, he was useful.

Steel set up his laptop in the dining area. It was a larger space to work in, and the coffee machine was just behind him.

Steel had ordered a mushroom and pepper omelette from room service. The protein would do him good, and he was starving from the chase, not to mention the few hours before with Sarah. Before sitting, Steel placed down an A4 legal pad and a fresh cup of coffee, then logged into the Hotels WI-FI and began his search. He wanted to know everything about the victims. And to do that, he needed help from a friend.

Steel contacted The Tailor. He gave the man all the details he needed for the search. Meanwhile, he would do some digging using his computer. He started with Alison Kline. There was something that tied them all together. They all had postcards warning what would happen, all except the security guard.

Steel looked at his watch and smiled. He knew Simms would have landed about now and was in Langley with Falkner.

Steel wished he could have been there just to see the angry look on Brena's smug face. But now Falkner was Stanton's problem; Steel had enough of his own. Sabine's little welcome had not been a surprise; in fact, he would have been disappointed if she hadn't shown up. But Brena had tipped her off and lied to her about Falkner. To Steel, that was unacceptable. Wrong information could get people hurt or killed. Steel had no love for the man before; now, Steel wanted to rip out his spine and beat him to death with it.

He sipped coffee and looked through his notes. There was something in those notations, a silent clue. He flipped back and forth through the pages, but there was nothing that stood out.

Frustrated, Steel tossed the pad onto the table's polished surface, and it skidded off and onto the floor. For a second, he found it amusing. But the feeling subsided, and he forced himself from his chair and walked to the other side of the table to retrieve the notepad. The pages had landed awkwardly, displaying the different locations and dates. Steel's hand froze just above the pad, taking in this new perspective.

'How the hell do you move about so quickly, Mr Watcher?' Steel said with a smile as he picked up the pad and raced back to his computer.

Finally, at last, something he could work with. Now, they had something in common: the killer wanted them to tell a story. A story they all played a part in. All of the targets had done something or had been a part of an incident. A cover-up or just in the wrong place at the wrong time. Either way, they knew something, and The Sentinel wanted the world to know.

Steel took a blank sheet and started to write down the dates, locations, and names of the people.

Mark Trent - New York Nov 7st

Alison Klien - New York Nov 9th

Karl Falkner - Berlin Nov 16th

Thomas Graaf - Amsterdam 18th

Steel looked at the list with puzzled eyes. To start with, there had been a constant week break between the postcards and attempts. But then everything started to move quicker, with only a few days between The Sentinel's deadlines.

Why the change?

What had happened to make The Sentinel move up his schedule?

*Steel had.*

Since Steel's integration into the case, The Sentinel had started to pick up the pace.

He shook his head, dispensing with the notion of his involvement enhancing the killer's time frame. No, this killer had everything planned, even down to the weather. The Sentinel would have anticipated Steel's movements.

Steel smiled as a thought crossed his mind. 'That's why you brought INTERPOL into this. You wanted to know exactly where they were and who the players would be.' Steel nodded at the brilliance of the plan. The Sentinel probably brought in Steel because Brena was too volatile and unpredictable. Not that Steel was, apart from one flaw.

His needed to find the truth and bring the correct people to justice. Brena didn't care about that; he just wanted his name on the front page and a larger office.

Steel took another sip of coffee. There was something else. The Sentinel had observed these people, possibly for some time. That meant a base of operations near the target's home, plus travel and funding. Steel stood up and grabbed his jacket. He needed to see Graaf's apartment.

# CHAPTER TWENTY-EIGHT

FALKNER SAT IN A TINY GREY ROOM. IT WAS FURNISHED with a metal table, two chairs, and a two-way mirror. Microphones and cameras were in the corners of the room to pick up every twitch and every whisper.

Falkner was starting to sweat. He rubbed his clammy hands on his trousers and wiped his brow on his sleeve.

They had thrown him in there an hour ago with only a cup of water and a simple order. 'Sit down, shut up, and don't move.' Falkner obeyed, but he needed the bathroom and was afraid to ask. He'd been in situations before and had just laughed them off, but this was serious. He couldn't call a lawyer because he was not under arrest for his protection, yet they treated him like a criminal.

Falkner looked at the empty clear plastic cup from the water cooler. He thought about using it to piss in, but they'd probably throw it at him. Falkner rocked back and forth. Then, finally, he couldn't take the silence or the need for the bathroom anymore.

'Hello, is anyone there?' Falkner yelled, not expecting a

reply anytime soon. 'Hello, I need to go the bathroom,' he yelled once more.

'What?' shouted a massive man who was guarding the room.

'I need the can,' Falkner said, trying to sound authoritative.

The guard growled, showed his teeth, and then gave Falkner a disgruntled wave, beckoning for him to follow.

———

Simms stood outside Stanton's office like a pupil waiting to go to see the headmaster. He could hear Brena inside, yelling at Stanton about his displeasure at the whole situation. First, Stanton had misled him into thinking Steel was off the case, and then Simms turned up with Falkner alone because Kitty had been killed following Steel's orders.

Simms could catch every word, almost as if Brena was shouting extra hard so everyone could hear. But the only voice Simms could make out was Brena's. Had the old man gone soft? Was he just sitting there, taking this abuse from a subordinate?

And that was when he heard it. Stanton's roar almost broke the glass of the office window. He had merely been biding his time, letting Brena vent before he bit back, and he was going to take a big bite.

'Agent Brena, who the fuck do you are talking to? The last time I looked, it said Section Chief on *my* door, not yours. How I choose to run my operations is *my* business, not yours; you just do as you are told. As for the unfortunate matter of Agent West, it was the killer who was responsible, not any of *my* agents.'

Simms could only imagine the look of fear on Brena's face, and Simms loved it.

For too long, the old man had let things go by like he knew he was due to go to pasture, so why bother?

'Now, Agent Brena, we have a witness downstairs who is ready for questioning. Do you think you can do that, or shall I get someone else to do it?' Stanton growled like a vicious beast.

Brena nodded, then turned to leave.

'Oh, one more thing, Agent Brena,' Stanton barked.

'Yes, sir,' Brena said, his words slight and boyish, like a scolded child.

'I'm not going anywhere,' Stanton said, standing up straight and folding his arms, showing his full height and powerful frame.

Brena didn't speak. There was nothing more to say. He stormed out and glared at Simms as they passed in the corridor.

Simms just smiled and walked through the open door.

'Simms, get your ass in here now,' Stanton roared with a smile, enjoying his revitalisation.

Simms walked in with a sheepish look.

'Shut the goddamn door and sit down,' Stanton said, crushing himself into his leather armchair.

Simms did as ordered. His mouth was nailed shut, fearful of speaking after what he had just witnessed.

'So, you brought Falkner back with you?' Stanton asked, his voice having dropped a million decibels.

'Yes, sir,' Simms replied.

'And Steel?' Stanton asked, picking up a glass of sparkling water from his desk.

'Amsterdam. He thought I should go with Falkner, make sure he gets here safely,' Simms answered.

'But that is what the team is there for. So the question is: why did Steel take them out?' Stanton asked, almost not wanting to hear the answer.

'They were a kill team, sir, not an escort. Steel recognised one of the men. He said he was the man who had replaced him,' Simms explained.

Stanton had a sudden look of panic on his face.

'Sir, who arranged the transport and pick up?' Simms stood.

Stanton rushed for the door, and Simms followed.

'Brenda, get hold of the interrogation wing; get them to close it off, nobody in or out,' Stanton ordered as he and Simms rushed for the elevators.

'Sir, who was it?' Simms asked again as they jumped into the elevator just as the doors began to close.

'Keep your mouth shut and follow me,' Stanton ordered, patting his side as though he was checking that his gun was still there.

As the elevator doors slid shut, Simms swallowed hard. Who were they after, and why did they want Falkner silenced?

———

Steel arrived at Graaf's apartment. Pat had texted Steel the address and the alarm code and then requested an update. Finally, Steel could say, 'All was well, and the dogs were no longer hunting.'

The building was pre-war 1930s, possibly older. The exterior had had a significant facelift, but the character of the place was restored rather than ruined. Graaf had the suite on the upper level. White walls and a red carpet greeted Steel as he entered the main entrance. He'd gotten in through the main door just as a stunning blonde was on her way out. Steel had held the door open as she exited, and he casually entered as though he lived there, then used the stairs to avoid anyone seeing him.

Steel moved with casual urgency, trying not to draw attention to himself. Then, when he reached the top floor, he took out his lock picks and worked the lock. A gentle click sounded, and he was in. Steel moved quickly, closing the door and typing in the deactivation code on the keypad next to the door. A small green LED blinked on, and he was safe.

Steel looked around at the spacious pad and smiled.

The man had a taste for sure. The decor was laid out in a Victorian style, with matte white walls and decorative ceilings and borders. Rosewood furniture sat upon bare wood floors and held Turkish rugs. Works of art hung in gilded frames. Chesterfield accent chairs and couches broke up the centre of the sitting room, and cast-iron and marble fireplace were situated in the centre of the right-hand wall.

Steel walked around; his eyes scanned the room, taking in the splendour. He moved up to a large globe and pulled back the top half to reveal an impressive drinks cabinet. He picked up a limited-edition Johnnie Walker Gold and cracked the seal. The scent of the golden liquid was intoxicating.

Steel went to pour himself a glass, but something stopped him. The Sentinel was trying to kill Graaf. The others had been by explosive devices, but nothing suggested The Sentinel had a particular method. Only the outcome remained the same: be found or be killed. Quickly, Steel screwed the cap back on and put the bottle back.

He turned and faced the room, scanning it for anything that might hold an explosive device. Steel figured that The Sentinel had everything planned, so he knew their routines and habits. For this to happen, you needed solid intelligence. This meant reconnaissance, cameras, microphones, and wiretaps. Steel walked up to a statue of a woman, a water jug held on her left shoulder as if she was pouring water from it; only a toga concealed her half-naked form. Steel looked inside the water jug.

Inside, a micro-camera lens winked as the light from the

chandelier above reflected in it. Steel smashed the statue against the fireplace and searched through the debris for the camera.

The device was no smaller than the nail on his little finger but efficient. He searched the rest of the apartment, knowing full well there would be more.

Graaf's office was the place that held the most devices. Steel assumed this was where Graaf did most of his business rather than an office somewhere. It made sense; no utilities for a place you hardly used.

He walked over to the window and stared across the view. It was a fantastic sight and well worth every penny of the blood money. But Steel was looking for a perfect place for a good observation site.

He searched for the residence that The Sentinel had used for his data collecting. Steel's eyes stopped at a building directly opposite. All the other tenants were starting to put on their lights, except one, which lay in direct line of sight with Graaf's apartment. It was a long shot, but Steel had a feeling about the place.

Leaving Graaf's apartment, Steel hurried across the street to the building he had observed. He knew roughly the position of the apartment, which made checking the names off easier. There was only one resident on the top floor; the other was empty. So Steel knew it would be the one that was occupied. It made sense; if any lights went on, people would put it down to someone being home or one of those security timers to make it look as if someone was home.

He ran his finger down the call buttons to the apartments in the hope someone would buzz him in. There was an electronic buzz, and the door latch was released. Steel rushed in before the bolt could reactivate. Knowing a second time would cause suspicion.

The main entrance was polished wood floors, bannister rails, and picture frames. All are complemented by coloured walls and brass fittings. Steel made his way up the wooden stairwell and towards the top floor. He bumped into a man in a blue boiler suit and brown-rimmed glasses on the way there. The man was in his early fifties but had a good build and long hair tied into a ponytail. Flashes of silver highlights gave his hair a distinguished look.

'Can I help you?' asked the man, startled and suspicious of this strange man in his building.

'Are you the *Hausmeister*?' Steel asked, somewhat hopeful but at the same time reluctant to ask.

'*Ja*, and you are?'

'My name is John Steel; I'm working with INTERPOL. The room at the top, do you know if the occupants are at home?' Steel flashed an ID badge he had stolen from one of the INTERPOL agents in Berlin.

The man looked at the badge and shook his head.

'No, they are on vacation ... have been for the last three weeks. Why?' the man asked, suddenly panicked.

'I need to see inside their apartment,' Steel insisted, beckoning the man forwards with an open flat palm towards the stairwell.

The man nodded, and they hurried towards the top floor.

'Are they in trouble?' asked the man, having sudden terrible thoughts about the couple who lived there.

'No, but I believe someone has been staying there while they have been away,' Steel said, trying to make a case for the unfortunate occupants.

They stopped at the door, and the *Hausmeister* took out his master key and opened the door.

'Could you wait here and, please, don't come in,' Steel insisted, knowing the man would mess up any potential evidence by touching things. He moved in and used a handkerchief to close the door behind him.

There was still enough light coming through the windows to illuminate the apartment without needing to switch on the torch he had or turn on the lights. The apartment was primarily open-plan with plenty of modern furnishings. Pictures of the couple hung on walls and sat on shelves. Fresh-faced and happy.

Steel walked around carefully, heel-to-toe, in a straight line and, most importantly, avoided touching anything. He knew the place would be clean. There wouldn't be any fingerprints or fibres. Nothing. The Sentinel was careful. But Steel could now see a profile coming together on The Sentinel. Even cautious people left something. A type of cleaning agent, how they cleaned, and where they cleaned. When something was removed, it then created a pattern.

Steel checked the rooms and found nothing. That was until he entered the owner's office. Steel stood open-mouthed at the array of rigged-up computer monitors and computer systems. The screens showed all the live feeds at Graaf's home and several unknown locations Graaf frequented.

Steel pulled out his cell and pressed the speed-dial. As he did so, he backed out of the apartment using the same line he'd come in on. The sound of ringing was cut short, and a female voice answered.

'Yes, Steel, what do you want?' Sabine answered.

'Sabine, you still want in on The Sentinel case?' Steel asked.

'Yes, why, what you got?' She suddenly sounded interested.

'Well, you'll need a warrant to search an apartment, and

your word you'll keep me in the loop,' Steel said, closing the front door.

'Where are you?' Sabine asked, struggling to find a pen that worked. Her heart was racing in anticipation.

Steel gave her the address and the name of the occupants.

If she couldn't get the warrant, asking permission from the owners would work just as well. Steel had passed his cell phone over to the *Hausmiester*, who gave all the relevant information to Sabine.

'That's great, thank you, sir,' she said. 'Now, can you give me back to Agent Steel?'

The *Hausmiester* looked around, and first, a blank expression came over his face, then one of confusion. 'I'm sorry he has gone.'

The phone went dead, and the *Hausmeister* stood for a second, looking around. As if waiting for the man in black to reappear. But he stood alone. The man smiled fleetingly, shrugged, and put the expensive cell phone into his pocket.

———

Sabine had hung up on the man. He was no more use to her, not over the phone anyway. She'd gotten the occupants' names and where they had gone. They were on a trip to New York to see the lighting of the Christmas tree at the Rockafeller Center and do some Christmas shopping. She looked up the hotel they were staying in on the internet for the phone number.

It would be around eleven o'clock in New York, so there would be little chance the apartment owners would be at the hotel. Sabine only hoped to leave a message and hoped the hotel would pass it on in time.

She knew she wouldn't get a warrant to search the apartment; what would she say? 'Oh, an NYPD detective broke in and told me there was evidence.' She would be laughed out of the courthouse or arrested for aiding with a crime. No, the owners were the only hope. Even then, that conversation would be awkward, but she could handle people better than lawyers or judges.

Sabine found the number for the hotel and began to dial. The phone rang for several seconds before being answered by George. Sabine explained who she was and the situation back at their home. George took down the message and assured her he would pass it on.

They exchanged thank yous and farewells before hanging up. Sabine didn't seem hopeful of hearing back anytime soon. After all, the couple was in New York; they could be out for hours.

Sabine rocked in her chair. The frustration was unbearable for her. She was close to getting some evidence but still too far away from it. She wondered about Steel's next move. If Steel had been alone in the hotel, where was Falkner? Then she remembered the two agents from Berlin. Had they gone back to the States with Falkner? If so, where was the new target Graaf? He wasn't at the hotel?

Sabine looked at the phone on her desk and contemplated talking to Brena. After all, he had tipped her off as to where Steel had been. But then he had also lied about Falkner. The man had proven to be an untrustworthy source. He had burned Steel to get him out of the way, possibly worse. The man was dangerous; Steel had told her as much.

Sabine's fingers danced above the device as if it was too far for her to reach. Finally, she growled and lost the battle with herself. She pressed a number in the dial history when she picked up the phone. It rang for a while and then went to voicemail.

'Hi, it's Sabine Boese from INTERPOL. We spoke the

other day. I believe Steel has the next target and is leaving Amsterdam, possibly returning to the States. Can you call me back? You've got my number.'

As she placed down the phone and sat back, a sudden terrible feeling ran down her spine. The feeling she hadn't accomplished anything apart from making things worse.

———

Steel headed back to the hotel using a flagged taxi outside Graaf's place. Visiting the apartment had given Steel some clarity on a few things.

One of them was that The Sentinel had planned this for some time. This wasn't just a spur-of-the-moment thing. Using the taxi gave Steel time to think. They weren't just looking for someone with a vendetta against these people but someone who had the funds and skills to carry it out.

The taxi pulled up outside the hotel, but Steel was too busy thinking to notice.

'Hey, Englander, we are here,' said the cabby impatiently.

Steel said nothing; he just gave the man a cold stare. But even with his sunglasses on, Steel's glare gave the man a cold shiver down his spine.

Steel looked at the meter. 10.00 was lit up on the digital display of the meter. Steel passed over fifteen and got out without a word. The man thanked Steel nervously and went to make change, but Steel had already jumped out of the taxi and was heading into the hotel.

The cabby took off, mumbling to himself while wiping the sweat from his brow, almost as if he'd had the Grim Reaper himself in the back seat of his taxi.

Steel took the elevator up to the room and grabbed his bag. It was time to leave. He was meeting Pat at the ferry port for the six-hour trip home. Steel would leave the investigation into the borrowed apartment to Sabine. It was the least he could do, for old times' sake. Besides, he had gotten all he needed for the moment; the rest would be made clear by Sabine's report.

Steel entered, walked to the couch, and grabbed the canvas travel bag, unlocking the door. He had to go now. Hit the road and get Graaf. Steel hoped the man was in a chatty mood because Steel had lots of questions.

He closed the door to the suite and made his way downstairs to the lobby to check out, then got on the road.

According to his cell phone route planner, the trip would take just over an hour, but Steel knew to add a few minutes for traffic. It was now six-thirty.

The check-out was swift, with no sign of Sarah. Steel thought she wouldn't be there, possibly for the best.

'Oh, a letter came for you while you were out,' said the pretty blonde behind the desk. She handed a small white envelope over to Steel with a smile and watched him open it.

Steel frowned as he pulled the postcard from the envelope.

'Did you see who delivered this?' Steel asked calmly.

The woman shook her head. 'Sorry, it was in with the mail,' she replied.

Steel turned it over and looked at the front. His name was typed out in Times Roman font, but no stamp crowned the corner. This was hand-delivered and snuck into the regular post. A bold move. The timing had to be perfect unless, of course, the killer was dressed like the mail courier.

Steel smiled at the thought but shrugged off the idea. It was more than likely that the killer had snuck the card in there after a misdirection. He had probably used the old trick of bumping into someone and helping them pick their items off the floor. An old method, but it is effective.

Steel made his way out the main entrance and around the

parking lot. Moving to the BMW, he pulled out his phone and checked for missed calls or messages. There was nothing of importance, so he tucked the phone back into his pocket and unlocked the car. He opened the trunk and placed the bag inside.

He started the engine and let it tick over for a while, letting the engine warm up. The fuel gauge read half-full. He'd have a chance to fill up before the ferry port; there was a gas station near the German-Dutch border he had used when he was stationed in Germany.

Steel set the satellite navigation for the port and set off. The car was quiet. No music or broadcast from the radio. Steel needed silence to think, to plan. Sure, he could have handed Graaf over to Sabine, but Graaf had answers, and he wasn't about to spill them to INTERPOL, but he might tell his story to the man who just saved his life. Besides, if Graaf didn't give anything useful, Steel would just throw the man overboard and do the world a favour.

# CHAPTER TWENTY-NINE

Stanton and Simms stood at the door of the men's restroom, looking down at Falkner, who lay in a pool of his own blood. Deep red filled the gaps in the floor tiles like small canals in a white landscape. By the bloody marks on the third sink in a row of six, Falkner smashed the mirror, then offed himself by cutting his throat. The ghastly signs of arterial spray started at the broken mirror and traversed up the wall and onto parts of the ceiling.

The whole place looked more like a slaughterhouse than a men's bathroom.

The agent who had found him stood outside, shivering. He was a new guy fresh out of the farm. It was his first week there, and he'd had his first look at a dead body.

'Why the hell wasn't someone watching him?' Stanton growled at another agent. His face was almost purple, and the veins in his forehead began to throb. 'I want to know who brought him here.' Stanton wasn't happy a witness had died on his watch and even less so, the fact it was in the building.

The new agent nodded and hurried away.

Simms stood next to Stanton, and they just looked at the bloody mess before them.

'What did he know?' Stanton asked.

'Well, whatever it was, he was scared to open his mouth about it,' Simms replied, shaking his head in disbelief.

'He must have said something on the flight?' Stanton asked, hopeful of a piece of information that could string the case altogether.

'Nah, the man didn't say much about anything.' Simms told him that the man was too full of himself to talk to anyone, remembering Falkner's incessant whining about how his apartment had been blown up. Simms had slipped Falkner a couple of sleeping pills and spent the rest of the flight in sweet silence. Something he'd dare not share with Stanton, not now.

No one was allowed in the men's room; it was now a crime scene, as though Stanton didn't have enough on his plate. Steel had gone silent, INTERPOL was asking questions, and now this.

'I want this place sealed and two guards on this door at all times. Only people in are the investigation team, no one else,' Stanton explained to two agents.

The men nodded and took their posts on either side of the door.

Simms looked up at the security cameras in the corners of the corridor. 'I'll check the feed, see who brought our man here.'

Stanton shook his head and put a sturdy hand on Simms's arm. 'No, that's for the investigation team to do. We have a case of our own. Go upstairs and find out where the hell Steel is,' he ordered.

Simms nodded and hurried towards the elevators.

Stanton stood for a moment with his clenched fists resting on his hips. He didn't believe for a second that Falkner had taken his own life. He needed to speak to the person who had arranged for the pick-up in Amsterdam. Also, he wanted to know why there was a kill team and not an extraction team at the airport—but most of all, he wanted to know why Trish had arranged for those things and on whose orders.

———

Brena stood over a group of monitors that showed the corridor was now a crime scene. His motionless body stood as straight and as still as a statue. He said nothing as he watched the events unfold. The forensics team turned up along with the agency's medical examiner. All the while, Stanton stood close by, taking everything in.

A buzzing sound from Brena's pocket alerted him to a new message on his cell. He took the device from his pocket and checked the text: Steel has left the hotel alone. No new target in sight. Location is unknown.

Brena ground his teeth and closed down the cell phone before placing it back in his jacket. So far, Steel had proven to be more resourceful than he'd expected. But he was still a threat to Brena's plans.

The men's room incident was only the start of Stanton's downfall, and Brena would be there to pick up the pieces and sit in his rightful place.

So far, everything was proceeding to plan.

Brena looked down at another monitor and saw Simms heading for the war room. He, too, was becoming tiresome. Another bug that needed treading on.

———

The sound of traffic woke The Sentinel from a troubled sleep. The Sentinel checked the time on the cell phone display, then stood and headed for the kitchen.

Unfortunately, the McDonalds hadn't stocked the refrigerator before their trip, but then they weren't expecting house guests. The interior was lit by fading sunlight through the thin fabric of the white curtains. It was six in the evening, and the sun had begun to set.

The street outside was quiet, a long stretch of houses full of expensive cars.

The Sentinel picked up the electric kettle and tested the weight, ensuring there was enough water for a coffee. Next to the kettle was a pricy-looking coffee machine, but using it would mean cleaning it afterwards. That meant leaving evidence someone had been in the apartment, and that would mean cops. The Sentinel prepared the hot drink. Coffee, milk, no sugar. Then waited for the water to boil. Eyes glued to the feed displayed on a monitor in a small office.

The sound of water boiling drew The Sentinel away from the screens and into the kitchen. The Sentinel poured water into the mug and headed back to the office. There wasn't much happening. Not yet. But The Sentinel was patient. Sitting down, The Sentinel grabbed the notepad and eased back into the chair. Making notes, sketches, and plans.

All The Sentinel needed was a how; when would follow that.

The image on the laptop that sat next to the monitor showed the man in his 1900s office. His feet were up on the desk. The man sat back and watched the latest news report, this time from Amsterdam.

The reporter stood in front of a hotel and talked about a unified anti-terrorist exercise involving the Dutch police and INTERPOL.

The man drank his whiskey and rocked back and forth in the chair. Finally, the man pulled himself forwards and put his glass down before dialling a number on his cell.

'Yes, it's me. Look, this whole thing is going sideways. I need a meet. How quickly can you get here?'

There was a pause as the person on the other end checked their diary.

'Two days' time? OK, OK, I understand,' the man said, tapping his fingers nervously. The Sentinel wrote 'two days' and circled it twice. This was the time frame. Now all The Sentinel required was the when.

———

Steel thought back to the new postcard and how it had been slipped into the mail. Sure, a sleight of hand or even the helping-to-pick-up-items trick. But it had been hand-delivered, just like Berlin. The picture on the card was of the Marble Arch in Hyde Park, London. Again it was a nighttime scene. Steel felt uncomfortable bringing Graaf to Britain; now, he knew that The Sentinel was there.

Earlier, Steel had spoken to someone in his agency and arranged for Graaf to be picked up at the port. At least he'd be safe with the Secret Service.

Steel was driving at a steady seventy kilometres an hour, the most the Dutch would allow in that region. But the roads were almost empty, leaving him space to keep the speed constant, giving him time to think.

It had been years since Steel had been to the Arch. Years since, he had watched his friend get gunned down.

Steel felt his grip on the steering wheel tighten at the thought of that night. But this was just a meeting point, like the rest of them. He looked up in time to see a sign for the Euro-ferry. He was early, but that made no difference.

That gave him more time with Graaf. Steel followed the route the satnav was showing him. Steel sighed heavily. He was nearly at the port.

He was nearly home.

# CHAPTER THIRTY

Simms walked into the elevator and pressed the call button, then wiped his sweaty palms on the legs of his trousers. He was starting to get nervous. Ever since he'd started this case, he'd been on edge. But this wasn't like the other times; there was something more deadly. A hidden enemy—and worst of all, one who wasn't just playing them, but using them as puppets.

The elevator stopped on two, and the doors slid open. Simms looked up to see Dorson with a panicked expression on his face.

'Hey man, you OK?' Simms asked, concerned about his colleague.

'Meet me at the smoker's corner, ten minutes, tell no one,' Dorson said quickly before stepping back and letting the doors close.

Simms stood there for a moment, open-mouthed and confused. What the hell was going on? First, the guys at the airport, then Falkner got killed, and now Dorson acting all mysterious. Simms waited until the elevator stopped on the third floor, then pressed the button for the lobby. Something was going on, and Simms hoped that Dorson had the answers.

---

Simms found Dorson at the arranged place. A quiet spot where the agents liked to come to smoke and forget about their jobs for five minutes. Dorson looked nervous, on edge, a man holding on to too many secrets, and it was eating him up inside.

'Hey, Dorson, what's up, man? I got to find Trish, find out what she knows about the death of my witness,' Simms grumbled. He didn't have time for this man's problems.

'Simms, Trish is missing. I tried looking for her earlier, but she wasn't home,' Dorson said quietly.

'Maybe she had something on today, a doctor's appointment or something?' Simms said.

'Yeah, that's what Brena told me, just before he told me to stop looking for her,' Dorson replied flatly.

Simms shot Dorson a puzzled look but said nothing.

'Look, man, something's going on here; something ain't right. I need your help to figure out what,' Dorson said, grabbing Simms's shoulder.

Simms shot Dorson an uneasy look. 'Why me, man?'

'Because you have been out of the country while these things have been going on. Because Steel trusts you, and most of all, you have no love for Brena,' Dorson whispered.

Simms stared with a distrustful scowl. 'What the hell are you talking about, man? We saw who sent that kill team for Falkner and me. I saw who gave authorisation for the jet that picked us up. Trish, that's who. So, you're tellin' me someone used her name to do all this. Why?' Simms growled. He was getting pissed off about not knowing what was going on.

'To throw us off, make us look one way when we should be looking in another, who knows? All I *do* know is Trish is missing, her car was on the driveway, but the house was empty. Someone isn't just killing your witnesses. They are killing our agents as well,' Dorson said, a tremor in his voice. The man was scared, not just for his life, but because he might have an idea who it was.

'So, who we lookin at?' Simms asked, looking around to make sure they were alone.

'No ... not yet. I need proof first. But I'm glad you're looking for Trish. Brena can't stop your investigation into her,' Dorson said with a strange smile.

'What is it?' Simms asked, sensing a sudden conflict of emotion.

'Why stop me from finding her? Then kill your witness, knowing full well the investigation will come back to her? It makes no sense,' Dorson said, puzzled.

'I need to find Trish ... if she is alive. She has some questions to answer.' Simms said, glancing at the main building.

'And if she's dead, that leads to a whole lot of different questions,' Dorson nodded. He wished he could help Simms, but he needed to carry on as if nothing had happened and do Brena's bidding. Besides, if Brena knew Dorson was helping, it could hinder the investigation. No, Dorson knew he had to carry on as usual and hoped he could find the proof he was looking for. 'Look, I got to go. Brena will be wondering where I got to. Check out Trish's place; try and find out what happened to her,' Dorson suggested.

Simms thought for a moment, then nodded.

'Oh, Simms, one more thing,'

'What?'

'Watch your ass. There is someone out there who *doesn't* want us to find out what these witnesses know,' Dorson warned him as he started to head back to the main entrance. 'No phone contact, only face-to-face like this,' he insisted.

'Roger that, and watch your six as well, Dorson,' Simms said, then watched him hurry away before heading to his car. He pulled out his cell and pressed the speed-dial on his phone for Stanton.

The phone rang for a couple of rings before Stanton's voice boomed over the speaker.

'You found Agent Edwards yet?' Stanton growled.

'Not yet, sir. I'm just about to check her place, see if she left anything for us,' Simms answered as he moved towards his car.

'OK, but watch your back. She's already a suspect in the murder of Falkner—don't need a dead agent as well.' Stanton's voice was filled with anger, and who could blame him?

'Copy that, sir; I'll call you later with updates.' Simms closed down the cell, then put the phone into his jacket pocket and took out his car keys.

———

The drive to Trish's house would take a good hour with traffic, but Simms didn't mind. It got him away from the chaos. Stanton had handed over the investigation into Falkner's death to the investigation team. Simms knew that must have stung Stanton to have done that, but it was regulations.

Simms got into his car; the sun had warmed it through the windshield, making touching the steering wheel virtually impossible. He let the engine tick over and opened the windows, allowing the cold air in, hoping to bring down the temperature. As he sat there, Simms thought about Steel. He had no idea whether their efforts to bring Falkner back were in vain. That Kitty had died for nothing, which hurt the most.

Simms slammed his palms against the steering wheel and silently cried out in anger. Why had he sent her? Sure, the plan was to snoop around, see if she could have found something, anything to incriminate Falkner, hoping to use that to make him talk. A good plan, but the wrong agent went. She was new and inexperienced. But that wasn't what got her killed.

Nobody could have foreseen a bomb in the laptop. Nobody but Steel. They were right. He was good, but now Simms saw why Steel preferred to work alone. Any mistakes, and it was your ass and nobody else's. Some might say that was the easy way, a cowardly way. The method of a person who didn't want to take responsibility. But it was also the smart way. No one to worry about when the shit hit the fan, no one that could be used against you if things went wrong.

Kitty had died because Simms hadn't wanted to be left out of what was going on. They could have both gone to pick up Falkner at the café, but Simms was impatient. He wanted to take Falkner in, and he wanted the evidence.

'Sorry Kitty, I let you down,' Simms murmured, almost as a prayer, just in case she was listening. He tested the warmth of the leather on the steering wheel before putting the shift into drive and taking off.

———

Simms pulled up outside Trish's house and sat for a moment. He stared out the side window of the Dodge Challenger, taking in the surroundings and parked cars. Dorson had said that everything looked normal, and her car was in the driveway when he got there earlier that day. Nothing had changed as far as Simms could see, but then he wasn't a white-picket-fence kind of guy.

The street was clear, apart from a delivery van and a couple of parked cars further down the street. Simms looked over at the house on the other side. A man stood slowly, raking the leaves on his front lawn. Simms gave the neighbour a quick nod, forcing the man to look the other way. Simms smiled and got out of his car. At least he knew who to talk to when he needed information.

He walked over to Trish's car and looked inside. The interior was empty, less for a jacket on the backseat. And after trying the door handle and finding it locked, Simms headed to the house. The front showed no signs of a struggle or anything that would indicate she had been abducted, but Simms couldn't rule anything out. He knew there were more ways to take someone away without the old chloroform-on-a-rag trick. Besides, chloroform took a while to take effect, unlike in movies, where it took seconds. Enough time to make a mess, anyway. If someone had taken her, it had likely been quick, possibly with the use of a taser.

Simms walked around the property, ensuring to check the windows and backdoor for signs of tampering. The house looked secure, and the view through the windows revealed nothing untoward. A confused look crossed Simms's face. Trish's car was there, but she was nowhere to be seen.

He made his way back to the front and stared over at the neighbour in the garden. If anyone had seen something, he had. As Simms approached the man, he scanned the house for security-system cameras. In the window was a sticker that read, 'Protected by the neighbourhood watch.' A black sticker with red writing, about A4 size.

Simms knew straight away this man had hidden cameras and possibly footage from when Trish came home.

'Hello there,' he said, giving a friendly wave with the greeting.

'You with the agency too?' the man asked, leaning on the handle of the rake.

'Yes, sir,' Simms said, showing the man his ID.

The man looked at it and nodded as if confirming he believed the credentials were real.

'You here about the woman from over the road?' the man asked, nodding towards Trish's place.

'Yes, sir. Have you seen her recently?' Simms asked, slipping his ID back into his pocket.

'She came back last night, kinda later. Didn't see anybody until this mornin'. Another fella was tryin' her door just like you,' he explained.

'White guy, six-feet, black hair, Italian looking?' Simms asked, knowing the man was going to confirm Dorson's description.

'Nah, that guy came later. The other man was kinda stiff, lookin' like he had a giant stick up his ass. Kinda unfriendly fucka. He musta got here around two in the mornin', just after she'd got home, in fact,' the man said, looking up into the air as if he remembered the situation.

'So, you saw this man?' Simms asked with interest.

'Only on TV, son,' the man laughed, pointing to a twelve-inch panda statue on his front porch. 'But he must have a key or somethin'. Probably snuck in a back way so nobody would see. Stop the neighbour's natterin'. Figured they done the old tango, and then it was time to leave while everyone was sleep.' The man smiled and winked.

'You know you're not supposed to film other people's properties?' Simms returned the smile.

The man raised his hands in a stop motion. 'Hey, slow down there; the lady asked me to. She'd come and get the CDs off of me once a week. Got twenty bucks for it,' the man told him with a shrewd look.

'Twenty, you say? Seems kinda steep?' Simms said, pulling a crisp note from his wallet.

'Hey, she set the price ... take it up with her when he brings her back, that is,' the man said, plucking the note from Simms's fingers.

'So she left with him, the man at two?' Simms asked angrily.

The man looked shocked at Simms's outburst.

'I ... I don't know. I just, uh, saw them with someone ... with him in a long coat or somethin',' the man replied, stumbling over his words.

'Get me those CDs now before I arrest you for obstruction,' Simms barked. So Trish was in trouble, and this asshole was trying to make a buck out of spying on people.

The man rushed inside his house, hoping that Simms wouldn't take him in.

Simms rushed over to Trish's house and tried the front door. It was locked and secured. But the man, the neighbour, had described that someone had gotten into the house, some-how, after Trish had arrived?

Simms checked the lock for signs of it having been picked, but the Yale lock was clean. He headed over to the garage but found that also secured. Simms was stumped. The only other choice would be that the guy had a key—but she lived alone.

The sheepish-looking neighbour came back holding several CDs in cases. Simms regarded him, noting the man's laboured breathing.

'Here you go, that's all of them,' the man said, stepping back an arm's length, just in case.

Simms took the disks, his mind searching for answers.

'So, how long have you been in the surveillance business?' Simms asked casually, not really expecting a reply.

'Oh, I'm not. Trish set all this up; she's a genius with

hidden cameras and stuff,' the man said, backing off and heading back home as quickly as he could.

Simms watched him cross the road, his mouth wide open. Had they been looking at this all wrong? Was she indeed involved in the death of Falkner?

Then another thought crept in. Was *she* The Sentinel?

# CHAPTER THIRTY-ONE

SABINE HAD WAITED OVER AN HOUR FOR AN ANSWER FROM the apartment owners. Another half an hour to convince them and another half hour to get the CSU teams in. Finally, Sabine had a call from her boss; this took only five minutes and a lot of shouting. The teams needed to find something that proved her intel, or she would be manning an office in the Alps, or worse.

She sat in her car and sipped the coffee she had gotten from a fast-food restaurant down the road. She knew better than to go in and contaminate the scene. But she needed clear/clean evidence. Ever since she'd gotten that postcard, she had been like a pit bull.

She had never suspected the CIA would be part of the investigation or that they would bring in Steel. However, that was the game that The Sentinel was playing. The big question: what were the rules?

The Sentinel was leaving clues, as Steel had told her, but why bring her in on this? If this individual wanted these people found, why not offer clear signs and less of the cat-and-mouse game? Or maybe it had to be this way? It was one sure way of sparking interest; plus, it had the added bonus of scaring the hell out of the targets.

Steel was on a ferry heading back to Britain, and he'd probably hand Graaf over to his agency. It made perfect sense. Graaf would be secure, and that agency did have a way of getting people to talk.

Sabine Boese looked over the street at the building opposite her. It was a tall building, built in the 1800s, and wore a recent paint job.

Her mind wandered to thoughts of how much an apartment like that would cost. Then, a sudden tap on the car window made her jump, and she praised her decision to go with the carry-out top for her cup.

'You can come up now,' said one of the techs when Sabine wound down her window.

She nodded and raised the window before getting out and locking her car. She walked up to the top floor, taking in the view at every level, walking in the footsteps of a killer, as she would call it. She knew The Sentinel wouldn't use the elevator —too much risk in being seen. No, the stairs were safer. Her gloved hand swept over the wood of the balustrade and bannister, the latex of the surgical glove gently rubbing over her fingers.

When Sabine reached the doorway, she saw the CSU techs busy at work, dusting for prints and taking photographs.

'Got anything?' Sabine asked, hopeful of something.

'Nothing, the place is clean,' said one tech with a smile and an excited look.

'Well, I'm glad *you* are happy. I have no idea what I'm going to tell the chief,' Sabine sighed.

'No, Agent Boese, the place is clean. No prints, fibres, nothing. Someone has wholly sterilised the apartment. They even emptied the hoover and took the bag with them,' the tech said, his smile even wider.

'I'm so glad you are enjoying this, but we have nothing.' Sabine hoped the man would stop smiling before she shot him.

'Agent, they took the evidence with them. That means they knew we would check the garbage for any signs of vacuumed trash. The person who did this knows our playbook.'

Sabine regarded the tech as he rushed off to another man who had called him over. Her eyes were wide with excitement. She didn't know whether to be happy or distraught about the news.

Was the killer a cop? Or had it been one?

She strolled to the balcony. Her face began to tingle from the cold breeze which was brushing against her. She closed her eyes and let the wind brush against her, hoping it would clear away her troubles.

Sabine opened her eyes and looked directly across the apartment across the street. Unfortunately, she couldn't see much due to the lack of light within. Nevertheless, her imagination took flight as she dreamed of what the place looked like within.

She let out a sigh and went to turn, but something stopped her. The rail was sticky as if some kind of adhesive tape had been used to hold something onto it. She called over one of the techs to take a closer look. It could have been for decorations, but there was only one patch.

Sabine looked over the street. She had wondered why Steel had sent her to that particular apartment. A chill ran down her spine as an idea sprung to her mind. She raced down the stairs and headed for the opposite building.

Reaching the front door, Sabine started to check the names of the tenants. And one name stuck out: Thomas Graaf.

'Steel, you tricky bastard. No wonder The Sentinel likes

you,' she said, shaking her head. Sabine pulled out her cell and pressed the speed-dial. She needed to talk to Stanton and fast.

———

Stanton answered on the sixth ring. Sabine didn't presume to ask what had kept him; after all, the man probably had enough on his plate as it was. Stanton sounded tired but, at the same time, alive. There was a ring to his tone that Sabine had remembered from years ago, before his wife's passing. Back when he gave a shit. Now, that sound was there again. Sabine smiled as she heard him ... a smile that soon faded.

'Avery, has Steel contacted you?' she asked, hoping that he had.

'No, I haven't heard from him since the fuck up in Amsterdam. Why?' His tone was deep. He paused before the question as if he was afraid to ask but knew he had to.

'Steel is heading back home with Thomas Graaf; he also led me to Graaf's place and...' Sabine stopped. Suddenly remembering what Steel had warned her about: Brena.

'And?' Stanton asked, hoping she wouldn't give lousy news about Steel. That Steel had blown something up or crashed something, or Graaf was dead.

Stanton somehow knew it wouldn't be her reporting Steel's death. The man had more lives than a room full of cats. He had once said that Steel was only hard to kill because he'd cause trouble in Hell.

'And, well, we are waiting for a warrant to search it,' she lied. She listened; the pregnant pause of Stanton's was unusually long.

'Thanks for letting me know, Sabine; I'll get some people on it,' he finally said softly, as if the news was painful to hear.

'I'm sure Steel has everything under control. You know

Steel, Mr Organised?' Sabine joked, hoping to hear a laugh at the other end of the phone. But her words were just met with a grunt, and then the call ended. She looked at the cell and wondered what was wrong, what had happened to change Stanton's mood.

Sabine understood she had that effect on people, but this was different. Something had happened at Langley; what she didn't know, but it was enough to piss off Stanton.

Sabine tucked the cell back into her pocket and looked up at the building. She knew she had no grounds to go into Graaf's apartment, and asking him would be out of the question as she had no contact with Steel.

She knew she had to get inside, and the threat of an explosive device inside would be grounds enough. So, Sabine took out her cell and called the police tactical squad. They would have to make the entry, and EOD would take care of finding the bomb.

The only grounds she had to base her hunch on was that Graaf was on The Sentinel's list. Nobody wanted a recurrence of what happened in Berlin. So, she spoke with the operations commander, a man called Joseph Wolf.

'We'll be there in fifteen minutes. In the meantime, get everyone out of the building,' Wolf ordered.

As Sabine ended the call, she looked back at the policemen guarding the other building.

'Hey, you two,' she shouted, 'I need this building emptied and a cordon set up. Nobody in until the EOD and tactical teams get here.'

The two officers nodded and ran over, one of them relaying the orders to the others inside the building. Sabine stood and watched, directing the officers where they should go. But, first, the other building would have to wait.

Then, naturally, two cops would have to make sure nobody

entered the apartment after CSU had finished. Still, the primary objective now was securing Graaf's apartment and ensuring the block was safe for the other tenants. Sabine looked at her watch; it was twenty-one-thirty, and Steel would be soon on his way with Graaf. She cursed Steel under her breath. He had left her with a ton of crap to sort out, and he had the only witness.

She began to regret her decision to help him, wishing she had locked him up until he gave up Graaf. Still, he didn't trust anyone, especially Brena.

What was it about the man that got Steel all riled up? Well, one thing was sure; if Steel didn't trust him, there *must* be something, and she should be careful what information she gave him or Stanton.

As another cold wind swept past her, Sabine shivered, pulling her coat tightly around her.

# CHAPTER THIRTY-TWO

Arriving at the port, Steel found Pat and Graaf sitting in a car park near the entrance to the terminal and pulled up close to Pat's car and got out, leaving the Bimmer's engine idling.

'Any problems?' Steel asked, knowing there wouldn't have been. If there were, Graaf would have been in the trunk.

'Nah, the man might be a monster, but he's alright,' Pat said with a grin.

Steel didn't even want to know what they had chosen to discuss on the journey down to the port, but whatever it was probably wasn't legal.

'Come on, Graaf; we've got a ferry to catch,' Steel said, leaning on the open window of Pat's car.

Graaf grumbled, got out, and walked towards Steel's BMW.

'Thanks, Pat; I'll catch you around. And stay out of trouble,' Steel said with a laugh, shaking his friend's hand.

'Hey, Johnny, try not to kill him. We've got some business

to discuss when this is all over.' Pat laughed out loud, and, with a rev of the engine and a spit of gravel, he was gone.

Steel watched Pat's car disappear into the distance, then turned his attention to Graaf, standing next to the passenger door.

'OK, come on, let's go,' Steel insisted, getting into the driver's side and making himself comfortable.

Graaf got in and turned to Steel. 'Just so you know, I'm not saying a word,' Graaf said sternly.

Steel just smiled and put his foot down on the accelerator.

––––––

After boarding, Steel hurried Graaf along to the cabins, searching for their rooms. Steel looked at the ticket for the room numbers and followed the plan on the wall but made sure he was walking behind Graaf, giving him instructions on which way to go.

'So, here we are,' Graaf said, pointing to the room number Steel had told him to look for.

Steel opened the door, and the two men walked in.

Graaf's eyes widened as he saw only one double bed in the middle of the cabin.

'I like to cuddle in the mornings. How about you?' Steel joked, causing Graaf to shake his head. 'Don't worry, this is your room. Mine is next door, just in case you get scared.' Steel laughed, slamming Graaf's boarding pass against his chest. 'We have reservations for the buffet at half-nine, don't be late.' Steel shut the door behind him.

Graaf sighed with relief at not sharing the room. But the thought of ferry buffet food turned his stomach.

––––––

Steel had showered and headed for the restaurant, where he found Graaf wearing a glum expression.

'Oh, good ... you made it,' Steel said with disappointment.

'I can stay in my room if you wish. After all, I am your prisoner.' Graaf spoke with discomfort at the thought of the cabin and possibly catching something from the food.

'Oh, my dear Graaf, and miss that charming smile of yours? Besides, we have so much to discuss.' Steel's smile changed to a sneer.

Graaf stepped back slightly, a shiver running down his spine.

As the restaurant line moved forward, a man at a small desk asked to see their tickets.

Steel smiled and showed him, and Graaf followed suit.

Steel and Graaf were ushered towards a table near the window. All the tables had white cotton tablecloths and sparkling cutlery. They finished with wine and water glasses, which made Graaf raise an eyebrow.

'What were you expecting? A burger and fries joint?' Steel smiled, ensuring his seat faced the doorway.

As Graaf sat, they were greeted by another waiter who was ready to take their drinks order. Steel chose a glass of Merlot and Graaf went for Chardonnay.

As they waited for the wine, Steel leant back and sized up Graaf. The man wore a tweed suit and dark-rimmed glasses. He held himself like a position man, possibly taking his name too literary.

'And what now, Mr Steel?' Graaf tried to appear unnerved.

'Well, once we get the wine, I was thinking of going for a side salad and possibly some curry I saw when we walked past the buffet,' Steel joked, knowing precisely what Graaf meant. Still, he wanted to get some alcohol into the man before they started.

When the waiter returned with their orders, he thought about the best truth serum ever made: alcohol.

———

Steel and Graaf had dinner in silence. He didn't want to jump straight in with the questions; he wanted Graaf to sweat for a bit. Besides, he didn't want to ruin his appetite. So Steel was on his third helping while Graaf played around with the roast beef he'd gotten from the carvery on his second time around.

The two men agreed the meal was over by nudging their plates away. After settling the bill for the wine, Steel headed for the exit and then for the bar. Graaf followed like a punished child.

Graaf wasn't happy about being abducted and shoved on a ferry to Britain, but the alternative seemed less appealing. He'd heard about the two killings in New York and the bombing in Berlin.

If Pat had been correct, he was better off with Steel. Pat had explained he wasn't under arrest, more under protection. However, he had to give something in return to get that protection: answer any questions Steel asked.

Steel found a seat next to a window away from the bar and stage. Steel didn't want to yell over a live band or loud chatter from the bar if they were to talk.

A steward came over to get their drinks order. Steel asked for a classic vodka martini with two shots of gin and a lime wedge on the side. Graaf opted for a beer.

Steel looked around at people who wandered by. Some headed for the duty-free shops, and others for the games and slot machines. The ferry was an hour out of port and cruising along steadily. As he looked out of the window, he could only see the reflection of the lounge. Outside was pitch black, with the lights from the port far behind.

The drinks arrived, and Steel paid straight away and tipped the man.

'Do you realise how difficult it is for some people to make this? A simple martini with gin? They have the same ingredients, but somehow, the drink has a different taste each place I go. Weird,' Steel said, causing Graaf to shoot him a puzzled look. 'And that's the puzzler. The same things in it, but each time something new. It's a bit like this case. We get postcards, each one a clue to the person and the place, but always people who have no connection to one another. So, a different taste, a different spin.' Steel leant forwards and placed down his drink.

'But you know what I think?' he asked with a crooked smile.

'No, Mr Steel, what?'

'I don't think they're that different after all; there are merely different ways of mixing them, just like these people who are connected. We just haven't found the right mix yet,' Steel smiled.

Graaf did not.

Steel stared into Graaf's eyes. Graaf's left eye twitched, and immediately he knew Graaf knew something.

'Oh, my dear Thomas, I hope you don't play poker because you have a lousy poker face,' Steel grinned as he took another sip. 'So, what do you know, Thomas? Why is this person after you?'

———

Steel listened to Graaf tell his life story. Three beers and six shots of whiskey were all it took to get Graaf in a talkative mood. Steel had gone to the bar to get the drinks rather than have Graaf overhear what he was ordering; he himself had been on apple juice most of the night. In Graaf's state, he'd have no idea which suited Steel fine.

'So, when were you in New York last?' Steel asked bluntly.

'New York ... a fantasy city. Love New York,' Graaf said before bursting into his Sinatra impression.

'Graaf, why were you in New York six months ago?' Steel plucked a random time out of the blue, hoping for a response.

'Wow, how do you know I was there ... here.' Graaf peered around, all confused, 'Where are we?'

'Graaf, New York, six months ago?' Steel asked again, urging him to stay on track.

'Yes,' Graaf said with a smile.

'New York, you, why?' Steel growled, thinking the drinking thing wasn't proving such a great idea. It was obvious Graaf's thoughts were elsewhere.

'Meeting with someone ... yes, that's right. I was smuggling some diamonds for someone from South Africa, but don't tell anyone.' Graaf laughed and put an index finger to his lips, and whispered, 'Shh-hoosh.'

'With who? Who was the buyer?' Steel asked insistently.

'It was ...' Graaf stopped and put a hand over his mouth.

Steel rolled his eyes and grabbed him, pulling him towards the toilets.

'Graaf, I swear, you throw up over this suit, and I'm chucking you overboard,' Steel declared, unhappy with Graaf's weak constitution. He dragged him into one of the stalls and left him leaning over the bowl while waiting outside.

As Steel stepped out, a man smaller than Steel moved out of the way, allowing Steel to pass. 'Thanks,' Steel smiled.

'No problem,' said the man as they passed each other. Then, as the door closed, Steel leant against the wall and contemplated how long he would give Graaf before he checked on him.

He let out a sigh of disappointment. Getting Graaf to talk hadn't been the hard part. Getting him to talk about what Steel *wanted* him to was the hard part.

Suddenly, Steel turned to face the door. There was something familiar about the man he had just passed, but he couldn't put his finger on it. He had seen the man recently, but where? His eyes turned into thin slits displaying anger as it came to him.

The man had been a member of the kill squad, the man from the magazine store.

Steel burst into the men's room just in time to see the man trying to drown Graaf in the toilet. He grabbed the man and pulled him out of the stall, smashing his back on the sink behind him.

The man yelped in pain as he arched his back from the impact.

Steel swept his legs, causing him to fall and smash the back of his head on a porcelain bowl. The man immediately recovered and stood up straight and ready to fight. The assassin threw a punch with his right and then his left. Each blow was dodged or deflected, then countered with quick jabs to the man's torso. The man grunted with every hit he received but kept on attacking.

The man was good, but Steel was better.

Graaf went to get up but was knocked back down as the man fell on top of him with Steel's hands around his throat.

Graaf fought desperately to hold his breath as the two men struggled on top of him, his head partially submerged in toilet water.

Steel dragged the assassin out of the stall and smashed his face against the tiled wall of the restroom. The man kicked back, almost catching Steel off guard, but it was enough for the man to break free and take flight. Steel followed the man out and up the stairwell; the man was heading outside.

Graaf crawled out of the stall, covered in water and looking battered, as two British students walked in and saw him.

'Bloody hell, I'd lay off the booze, mate. It looks like it tried to kill ya,' joked one of the young men and headed for the urinals.

Graaf sat for a moment, catching his breath and nodding in agreement. 'No more drinks, no more ships, and hopefully, no more Steel.'

————

The assassin slid open the door to the outer deck. Wind and seawater slapped him in the face, forcing him to close his eyes for a second.

A second distraction was all Steel needed.

He launched himself at the man, sending both of them out into the cold wind of the night. The man slammed against the safety rails and let out a lungful of air.

The man sent an elbow backwards, which contacted with the side of Steel's head, sending him back. Steel came back with a kidney punch and smack to the back of the head. The man yelped as his head contacted the lighting pole in front of him.

Punches and kicks were exchanged as the two men fought on the side deck. The passengers within were oblivious to the fight.

The man used a mix of jiu-jitsu and aikido, while Steel favoured Krav Maga for this situation.

The wind howled like a wounded beast. The waves crashed against the side of the ship, muffling the sounds of combat. But Steel was oblivious to the noise or the foamy spray; he was fixed on the man sent to silence Graaf. Steel would have preferred to keep him alive and get answers to questions, but this guy was a professional. He would rather die than give up anything.

The man's face was bloody, his nose broken, and a nasty gash ran along his forehead. But he still kept coming. Finally, the man lets loose a volley of kicks and punches. Even though both men had lost some energy, Steel was faster and countered every one of his foe's moves, followed by several hits of his own.

———

Thomas Graaf had gone back to his room and changed clothes, thankful that Pat had allowed him the pleasure of packing a bag, then returned to his seat in the lounge to wait for Steel.

As Graaf sat quietly, sipping old sparkling water he'd just ordered, he looked out the window, hoping to see something other than darkness. Instead, tiny lights in the distance danced about in the blackness like fireflies following each other.

Graaf reckoned it must be a fishing vessel or small boat. As he put his face against the glass to get a better look, another face met his before sliding into the night. Graaf stumbled backwards and fell onto the floor just as the two Brits walked past.

'Seriously, mate, have something to eat and lay off the booze,' laughed the young men as they walked towards the games room.

Graaf stumbled back to his chair and sat, his hands shaking with fear at what he had just seen ... or thought he had seen.

'I'll tell you one thing, that weather out there is an absolute killer,' joked Steel as he suddenly appeared from nowhere.

Graaf jumped and hugged his water glass for comfort.

'You OK?' Steel asked, spotting Graaf's strange demeanour.

'I don't know about you, but I'm famished.' Steel looked around to see if they made bar snacks.

———

Steel dragged a hysterical Graaf to a café that sold sandwiches and strong coffee and stuck him in a corner while he got refreshments.

He returned with two large coffees and two lunches. He figured Graaf needed something to soak up the alcohol, and a BLT seemed about right.

'What happened to the other man?' Graaf asked, sipping the black coffee.

'Possibly the same thing he had intended for you, but more dignified,' Steel replied as he ripped open the packaging on the sandwich and inspected the contents.

'Who was he?' Graaf asked, looking around to see if there were more.

'Who can say? But I've seen him before, in the airport in Amsterdam.'

'Was he ... ?'

'The Sentinel? No, more likely a guy on a payroll. Which clears one thing up,' Steel said, biting into the BLT on white bread.

'Clears what up?' Graaf asked, taking another sip.

'How The Sentinel can move about so quickly,' Steel said with a crooked smile.

'So, he was the one who was planting all the bombs?' Graaf asked, leaning forwards.

Steel thought for a second and then shook his head.

'No, I think that was The Sentinel, but you can bet whoever sent this guy was someone who doesn't want you breathing.' Steel paused as if going through things in his head before speaking. 'The Sentinel is all about seeing what unfolds, even if he's not there. The Sentinel is responsible for making the devices; chances are The Sentinel was in those countries days before I was to set up everything. The pleasant chap we just met was there to make sure things happened.'

Thomas Graaf looked into space while he sipped, his brain working out the information. It all made sense, apart from who wanted him dead. Sure the list was long, but none of those people would go to these lengths. Graaf's ordeal had sobered him up in more ways than one.

Steel needed answers, and he hoped Graaf could give them to him. Falkner had given him nothing, but hopefully, Simms had had more luck. Steel checked his watch; it was ten-past-ten local time, which meant it was four in the afternoon in Langley.

Stanton probably had Falkner in a six-by-six by now and was sweating the truth out of him. The thought made Steel smile, unaware that Falkner was dead and had said nothing to Simms or Stanton.

'So, what happened in New York?' Steel asked bluntly, hoping to catch Graaf off guard.

'When?' Graaf seemed confused at the question.

'Cut the crap, Graaf, you know when,' Steel growled, his patience wearing thin.

'OK, I was there but not six months ago. It was more like a year ago,' Graaf said, remembering the man's face at the window.

'Doing what? I swear if you say sightseeing, you'll be swimming after your friend,' Steel stated grimly.

'I was meeting a buyer, a man called Falkner. He was getting diamonds off of me,' Graaf admitted.

Steel sat back, a confused look on his face.

'But Falkner was an arms dealer. So, what was he doing

buying diamonds off you?' Steel asked, then took a bite of his sandwich.

'He wasn't so much buying as collecting, a down payment if you will.' Graaf's words were a whisper as if he didn't want to be overheard.

'Down payment for what ... or rather for who?' Steel sat back in his chair, realising this was a trade-off; nobody knew who the goods were for. All the players knew each other, but the brains of the operation would be invisible.

'More for who, and before you ask, I have no idea. My policy is discretion, Detective Steel, no questions asked or answered.'

Steel had heard that about Graaf. He found that plausible; deniability was more like a safety net for all concerned. 'Where was the meet and when?' He hoped for something he could check on later.

'Central Park, by the statue of Alice in Wonderland, midday, I believe,' Graaf answered with a smile, knowing full well Steel wouldn't be able to check on it.

'How much are we talking?'

'One million in uncut blood diamonds,' Graaf said, still smiling as he knew Steel wasn't getting the answers he wanted.

However, Steel was getting more than he had expected, and, in truth, he was surprised Graaf was still breathing. 'So, if the diamonds were payment for something, who footed the bill, and don't say you don't know,' Steel warned.

'I get a job through a sight on the dark web, a dropbox if you will. One million in diamonds, untraceable, and for my trouble, I get a painting.' Graaf offered a broad smile.

'Don't tell me that was your Renoir that went on auction two days ago?' Steel asked, looking through the scam.

'Payment by cash is dead; some use these Bitcoins, but I

find that vulgar. I appreciate art much more. Besides, it only goes up in value with art,' Graaf said smugly.

Steel had to admit it was a brilliant way of moving money without it being traced. However, even art left traces, especially an expensive paintings.

'When did you get the job?' Steel asked.

'Uhm, a year ago. Whoever it was called themselves Mr Nuntius.'

'Nuntius ... that's Latin for messenger,' Steel said, puzzled.

'Excellent, Mr Steel; nice to see the Army didn't beat every-thing out of you.' Graaf grinned before taking a bite of his sandwich.

Steel searched his memory for anyone who had called themselves that but came up empty. 'And *after* the exchange?' Steel pressed further.

'We went our separate ways, first time and last time I ever met the man,' Graaf explained. 'But he did speak with someone on his cell as he was leaving, telling them the job was done.' Graaf shrugged as if it meant nothing, but to Steel, it could mean everything. At last, Graaf had said something worthwhile.

'Who was the wire transfer from?' Steel leant forward intently.

'I can't remember,' Graaf shrugged, his expression showing he hadn't thought about it or cared to think about it.

'Try,' Steel growled.

'Look, it was some time ago, OK. I have all that stuff in files, so I wouldn't have to remember,' Graaf explained as he leaned back in his chair. 'It's in a draw on my desk.'

Steel pulled out his cell and hoped he had enough bars to make a call back to Sabine. It was a lead or possible dead end, but it was something.

Steel listened as the electronic ring came from the speaker.

He let it ring until it went to voicemail. Suddenly, he had that bad-feeling sensation again, and the hairs on his neck stood up.

Steel quickly searched for a new number on his speed-dial. It was Stanton's. After several rings, a familiar voice picked up.

'Chief of Operations, Stanton's office, Agent Brena speaking.' Brena's voice was smug and had a sickly tone to it as if he had been practising that answer for a long time, but with his name at the end, not Stanton's.

Steel hung up and tapped the cell phone on the metal table. His gaze swept the room, but he saw nothing except the faces of those he could call. He stopped tapping and searched his call logs again. Finally ... *finally*, there was one other person he could speak to.

Steel just hoped Pat wasn't drunk yet.

# CHAPTER THIRTY-THREE

ON THE SECOND RETRY, PAT PICKED UP. THE MAN WAS tipsy but not entirely juiced. 'Steel, what's up?' Pat laughed, thoughts of the two men on the same ship bringing all sorts of images. 'Oh, you didn't kill the little bastard, did ya?' he asked, panic in his voice.

'No, he's fine. But look, can you do me a favour and go to Graaf's apartment and speak to Agent Sabine Boese? She's with INTERPOL. I need to get in contact with her. It's urgent,' Steel said, his voice solemn.

'Graaf's place, ya say? Oh, sorry, Johnny boy. That place is ashes. That bomber ya after, he just took out Graaf's apart-ment. Nice job, too. Could have used the bloke back in the day,' Pat said, forgetting Steel had been on the other side of the wire at the time. 'Oh, sorry,' he apologised, then took another swig of Irish whiskey.

'Pat, you need to get down there. I need to know she's OK,' Steel said with some urgency. He hung up and hoped Pat could still walk, never mind, drive. A feeling of guilt shot through his veins. He had led Sabine to the apartment; if anything had happened to her, it was because of him. Now Steel knew how Simms felt after Kitty's death.

He stuck the cell phone hastily back in his pocket before he hurled it at the wall. He took a deep breath, hoping to suppress his anger. The Sentinel was setting up devices and not disarming them; innocent people were getting hurt, which didn't wash with Steel.

Graaf looked over at Steel, gritting his teeth and trying not to put his fist through something. 'What is it?' A sudden feeling of terror ran through his spine.

'The Sentinel just blew up your place,' Steel said grimly.

'Was anyone inside?' Graaf asked, genuinely concerned, but Steel figured it was more for his apartment than possible casualties.

'I don't know yet ... waiting on Pat to find out.' Steel picked up the coffee cup and looked at his reflection in the black liquid.

Steel gazed at himself for several seconds. His thoughts started to wander. He thought about his wife and family, about the day the kill team came and took everything from him. Then, the images in Steel's head changed. He was standing in the mall, and everything was still. The people were frozen in place as if someone had pressed the pause button. Steel looked around and saw King holding the kill switch wrapped tightly around his hand with the bandage. There was a small explosion from behind him, and the window shattered. Then a flash from the device, followed by the shockwave. Everything was in slow motion, everything but him. Steel shouted to the people to get out, but everyone stared at him with blank expressions. He yelled louder, but no words came out. His feet could not move; it was as if he were glued to the marble floor.

Steel looked up in time to see the blast wave lift everyone off their feet, then watched them burst into flame. He tried to move, but his legs were like stone. He watched in horror as the people were blown apart, but he was untouched.

A little girl walked up to him; she was around six years old. The flesh on her face was blackened and burnt, her piercing blue eyes wide but somehow calm. She took Steel's hand and smiled.

'Why are you sad? It's OK. Someone will always clean up the mess,' the child said before letting his hand go and stepping into the flames.

Steel's screams were muted by the blast wave, which lifted him off his feet and sent him crashing through the window.

With a start, Steel woke from the daymare. The crashing sound he had heard was the coffee mug smashing on the floor. He looked around to see people looking over at him but then turning back as if nothing exciting was going on.

Steel turned to Graaf, who was glued to his seat, his eyes wide with fear.

'Wow, no more coffee for you,' he said, shuddering.

Steel had never had an audience for his dreams before; he usually woke up with a broken whisky glass on the floor. 'Sorry, my mind wandered off for a second,' Steel said, kneeling down and picking up a broken piece of the porcelain mug. 'We need to get some rest. Got a long day tomorrow,' Steel lied.

In truth, Steel needed time alone to think, and he couldn't do that with Graaf hanging around. But Graaf had agreed; it was late, and after the day he'd had, hitting the sack sounded like a good idea. A good night's rest and a full breakfast the next day were just what they both needed. Besides, Graaf thought he'd be safer in his cabin with a locked door between him and the world.

Thomas Graaf headed to his cabin, leaving Steel to grab a bottle for someone from the duty-free shop. Steel had no intention of turning in just yet. He had too much to do; besides, he was waiting for a call from Pat.

Steel returned to the lounge with a bottle of Johnnie Walker Green and waited for a steward to take his drink order. It was now quarter to eleven, and the place was filling up. The live entertainment was already in full swing, but nobody was drunk enough to be singing along.

Steel sat in a corner booth and waited to be served. Stewards rushed here and there serving the many new arrivals, but Steel had time. The steward who had served him and Graaf before spotted Steel and headed for him with a broad smile.

'Large Johnnie Walker Green, no ice or water.'

The steward nodded and hurried away. Steel had no intention of sleeping, not yet. He had too much on his mind, like what had become of Sabine. That was at the top of the list.

———

Simms went to Trish's home to review the footage on the disk. It was too dangerous to take back to the agency. Not with Brena about.

If Dorson was right, Trish had been taken; why, however, was unclear. But one thing *was* clear: Simms didn't know who he could trust, not even Dorson.

Simms wished he had stayed with Steel, but he had to make sure Falkner arrived safely, which he had done.

However, he was now stuck finding Falkner's killer and tracking down Trish. Simms started by checking her computer for any unusual activity or files. Then, reviewing the web history and any hard drives or data sticks she had. He waded through her data and saved documents, hoping to find something that would explain her disappearance, but found nothing of interest. Trish's emails were spam or messages from her family back home, as well as a load of reminders of posts she had on social media. The hard drives held pictures from holidays that she had been on with her girlfriend, but nothing racy enough to copy, not that he would have.

A gentle buzz emanated from his jacket pocket. Pulling the cell from his jacket, he checked the new message. It was Dorson. 'The explosion in Amsterdam, Thomas Graaf's apartment. Police are investigating a couple of casualties, including Agent Sabine Boese of INTERPOL. No word on the condition. Brena is asking where you are. Watch your ass and silence your phone.'

Simms knew what that meant straight away and grabbed a paperclip from Trish's desk. He had to get the sim card out, toss it, and then get rid of the phone. A few years ago, it would have been simple, take out the sim card and drop the cell down the toilet; let the water fuse the electronics. But he had to be flash and get one of those damned waterproof jobs. Good for thirty meters. Usually a great idea, but not this time.

Simms looked outside and saw a removals van parked a few doors down, four burly men with sweaty, red faces and an apparent liking for fast-food loading the truck. The idea came to him in a blink; toss the phone in the back and walk away.

It would be a brilliant plan if he didn't get caught.

Simms headed out the front door, ensuring he didn't close it completely. As he moved closer, he noticed the men were all inside. Simms smiled at his good fortune and went to hurl the device in the back. Suddenly, another man appeared from behind a wardrobe, causing Simms to pull his arm down quickly and rethink the plan.

'Howdy,' the man said, wiping the sweat from his brow with a white and blue striped handkerchief. The man was six feet each way, but mainly around the middle. His round head held strands of brown hair that he probably couldn't bring himself to get rid of.

'Hi there,' Simms replied, waving a greeting with his empty hand. 'Had no idea the neighbours were moving.'

'Yeah, last-minute thing, apparently. Poor bastard's off to Alaska,' the man laughed but then stopped and looked around to see if he'd been seen.

'Alaska, wow, who did he piss off?'

The two men laughed, making the man cough like a horse and reach for the couch to steady himself.

'You OK?' Simms asked, feeling bad about nearly killing the man.

'Yeah, doctors say I should quit smoking, but what do they know?' The man sparked up a cigarette and inhaled a lung full of nicotine.

Simms watched the man have another cough attack, but he lost the contents of his top pocket this time. A pack of cigarettes hit the tailgate along with his wallet and a stainless-steel Zippo lighter.

Simms helped the man retrieve his items and waved the phone in his face. 'Hey, don't forget your phone.' Simms hoped he'd take the bait.

'Oh, yeah, thanks.' The man gave a broken smile and tucked the items away, including Simms's phone.

'Well, safe journey,' Simms said, giving the man a friendly wave before making his way back to Trish's house.

The man waved back and called Simms a 'sucker' under his breath as Simms disappeared into the house.

Simms would have felt bad for the man, but he caught the insult on the downwind. The man would have some explaining to do, but hey, he took the phone.

He was hoping they wouldn't catch up to him until the Alaskan border, but then Simms wasn't that lucky. He figured he had around thirty minutes tops until the other agents would be knocking on the door, asking questions. Questions he probably didn't have the answer for. And if Brena had sent them, he might have filled their heads with the thought that Simms had done something with Trish; after all, he was in her house, and she wasn't there.

Simms grabbed Trish's laptop and the hard drives he hadn't checked and hurried out of the door. As he was leaving, he saw the old man, who was back in his garden, this time watching the removal men. Simms walked over and waved a quick hello.

'You got what you need, son?' the old man asked.

Simms tapped the laptop and nodded.

'Look, some other men will be coming soon. These men will be pretending to be agents; chances are they're the ones who hurt Trish. So, I need you to stay inside and keep away from the windows. Can you do that, sir?' Simms asked with a look of concern for the man's safety.

'Don't worry, son, I'll keep out of their way, don't you fret,' said the old-timer.

Simms shook the man's hand and walked back to his car. He unlocked the car and got in, but as he shut the door, he looked over at the old man, and the more Simms stared, the more he had the feeling that was the last time he was going to see the fellow alive.

———

Big Ben chimed twelve. Alerting the people of London Town of a new day. The rain had stopped hours ago and was replaced by a blanket of stars that winked down at the world from a clear sky. The Sentinel had been woken by a passing police car. Sirens wailed as they headed down the street, followed by intermittent flashes of blue that filled the room.

The Sentinel sat up and stretched off before heading to the kitchen to make coffee. It had been a long day and an even longer night.

The Sentinel knew Steel had Thomas Graaf and had travelled back to Britain.

Everything was going to plan. Soon, the truth would be revealed. Soon, they would all pay. Soon, The Sentinel would have revenge.

Walking into the kitchen, The Sentinel poured coffee from the glass pot, then placed it back into the machine. The aroma of hour-old coffee filled the air, but The Sentinel didn't mind. Coffee was coffee.

Taking the brew back to the couch, where The Sentinel had crashed hours before, The Sentinel looked over at the one monitor that was still covering Graaf's apartment. The small screen showed only static snow as the feed had been cut or the camera had malfunctioned. The Sentinel sat up.

Something was wrong.

Perhaps the police had found the camera and taken it out?

Quickly, The Sentinel rewound the recording to the point the transmission had failed. Then, leaning forward, The Sentinel observed the feed.

A police tactical team smashed through the door and began their room-to-room search but found nothing. Then an EOD sweeper team followed with a small military robot. The tracked device wheeled in and started the search, starting with Graaf's computer, but found it safe.

After an hour of searching, the teams called the all-clear. Then Sabine Boese and the cops came into view. The scene was now cleared for them to start investigating.

On the way up the stairs, a phone began to ring. Sabine stopped the cops behind her as the sound of the call made her nervous somehow. The chimes started once, twice ... before the answering machine kicked in. Then, Sabine launched herself at the officers, knocking them back down the stairs.

There was a massive explosion that shook the building.

Then the camera went dead.

The Sentinel stood up in shock. A device had gone off, but it wasn't the one The Sentinel had put in. In fact, The Sentinel's explosive wasn't even in the building; it was somewhere else, and a disarm code had been sent.

Someone else had done this, just like at Falkner's place. Someone was silencing the witnesses. They were covering their tracks and making sure The Sentinel got the blame.

The Sentinel began to pace up and down. The new target had to be found and secured; Steel already had two, so the third was as good as safe. That just left the real killer.

The Sentinel stopped pacing. A new plan had come to mind. A risky and irrational plan. The Sentinel *had* to work with Agent John Steel.

# CHAPTER THIRTY-FOUR

IT TOOK ABOUT AN HOUR FOR THE AGENTS TO FIND THE truck and stop it outside Warfordsburg. They tracked the cell to a diner but only found the removal men instead of Simms. The lead agent phoned Brena to update him on the situation. A phone call that didn't go well. Brena had hung up the phone, and the agents left the diner with Simms's cell phone, leaving the three men shaken.

The three Yukon SUVs pulled up outside Trish's house, and twelve agents scatted information. Six went to the front, six to the back and waited for the order to breach.

The command came over the earpiece of each team leader, followed by a loud crash as both doors were kicked in. The teams moved in close, single file; this was followed by cries of 'room clear' as they searched for any signs of Simms or Trish.

Minutes later, the teams filed out; the lead agent pulled out his cell once more to make a call to Brena. As he stood on the front lawn, he held the cell phone up, so the glare of the sun didn't reflect on the gorilla glass screen. Suddenly, something caught his eye. A curtain had moved from the house over the road. They were being watched. The agent smiled and tucked the cell back into his pocket.

He left orders for the men to search the house for anything that may lead to Simms or Trish. The agent then called one of his men over, a giant of a man with a stern face and hands like bulldozer shovels, and they walked over to the house.

'Let's see if the neighbours saw anything,' said the agent as he pulled on his leather gloves.

———

Steel woke up around five with a bad taste in his mouth and the need for coffee. The bed had been comfortable, but then he could sleep on a razor blade if he had to. Steel showered and pulled on a black suit. He imagined Graaf had slept with one eye open; that was, if he had slept at all, given the attempt on his life the night before. He pulled on his jacket and slipped on his sunglasses even though he had put on his blue contacts ... just in case border control asked for the glasses to be removed while they checked passports.

———

Steel left his cabin to check on Graaf, if only to annoy the man and than be concerned about him.

'Graaf, are you up? Time for breakfast and then departure,' Steel said after giving three quick knocks on the door.

There was a thumping sound, as if something had fallen on the floor. Steel looked around anxiously. Was there someone in there with him, possibly another assassin?

He hammered on the door again while trying to find a way to pick the lock. But there was no way in that he could see, not with the equipment he had. Which led to the question: how did the assassin get in?

Finally, the door sprung open, and a dazed and confused Graaf stood before him; his hair was a mess, and he looked as if he'd had a rough night.

'Seasickness?' Steel asked with a sympathetic smile.

Graaf nodded while holding his stomach.

'Oh, well, never mind, breakfast is on,' Steel smiled.

Graaf slammed the door and ran to the toilet.

'I'll meet you at the restaurant; I'll get you a full English that will settle your stomach,' Steel grinned as he heard Graaf retch in the bathroom.

———

Graaf appeared at the restaurant looking pale and dehydrated. Steel was already on his second helping of a fried breakfast and his third coffee. Graaf sat hard in the chair opposite Steel. He sneered at the sight of the food in front of him.

'You feeling better?' Steel asked as he stood.

Graaf said nothing, just shook his head and turned his head away from the sight of Steel's breakfast.

Steel wandered off, leaving Graaf to drink the coffee Steel had gotten for him half an hour ago. It was lukewarm but wet. Steel returned and placed down a plate of English breakfast in front of Graaf and a glass of milk.

'I can't eat this,' Graaf complained, pushing the plate away.

'Get it down your throat, Graaf; it will line your stomach, which is now empty,' Steel explained.

Graaf looked at the glass of milk and shot Steel a look. 'What, I am I? six years old? They have no orange juice?' he complained.

'Yes, you've been a big baby. Look, the milk is better for

you; OJ is mainly acid; you drink that on an empty stomach, yeah, then you're gonna be poorly,' Steel explained. A lesson he'd learned in the Army after going on an all-nighter. When you got back to your bunk, they taught you to drink lots of water; that way, you wouldn't dehydrate and were likely to wake up without a headache. What they didn't tell you was when you'd been throwing up all night, how to get rid of that bad feeling.

The sergeant had taught him a lot. Everything except how to deal with your family's loss to a bunch of mercenaries.

Graaf pushed the plate away, and Steel pushed it back.

'I know to you it looks like a dog's dinner, but trust me, you'll feel better,' Steel insisted.

Graaf nodded reluctantly before slowly tucking into the bacon, sausage, and mushroom feast. Steel sat back and enjoyed his coffee while he watched the Dutchman eat and smiled to himself. Not because he was nearing home but because Pat had finally called. He told Steel that Sabine was fine, with only a few cuts and bruises; she'd probably have ringing in her ears for a while, but she was safe. She had saved the life of the other officers and would probably get a commendation for her actions, or so his contact had said.

Sabine was a good agent, a pain in the ass, but a good agent. Even though people thought it, she and Steel had never slept together, even though they had chemistry. No, Steel made it a rule never to get close to a partner; in fact, the rule applied to anyone. He had lost someone before, and he didn't want to go through that pain again. It was simpler not to feel that than to let people become distractions.

Steel sipped coffee and looked out through the windows to the side. The weather looked grey and uninviting, but he was sure it would brighten up later.

———

The call for the passengers to their vehicles disturbed Graaf and his third helping of breakfast. Steel was almost impressed at the Dutchman's recuperation; he just hoped he wouldn't get car sick after all the food.

A rendezvous with an MI8 agent had been set up, and a place and time arranged. Eight o'clock at an inn at a place called Horsley Cross. There would be four SUVs; after the pickup, each would take a different route to throw off any tails. Steel knew how this worked; he'd done it plenty of times with the agency. A simple tactic that dated back centuries, the art of misdirection was an agent's best friend in sticky situations.

Steel and Graaf finished their breakfasts and collected their belongings before heading to the car. At the docks, another vehicle would be waiting for them, and the BMW would be disposed of, just in case, someone was looking for it. If someone were following Steel and Graaf, the agency would make it as difficult as possible for the trackers. Finally, Graaf would be heading to London and Steel back to the family estate in Buckinghamshire.

The two men got into the car and waited for the vehicles in front to move. It had been a long couple of days for both of them, more so for Steel, but Graaf's ordeal was almost at an end. Steel's was to continue. The Sentinel was still out there, and the next target had been identified as being in Britain. Steel was glad to be going home; he missed it, even though it brought back bad memories.

He made a point to spend as much time back at the estate as possible or as work would allow. He had also inherited the family business, a multi-billion dollar company that made everything from children's toys to military equipment. His great-grandfather had created a company and was now a legacy along with the title.

Steel had joined the Army Cadets at sixteen, then later joined the regulars at seventeen and a half. Finally, at twenty, he had been picked to go on an exercise to play enemy against the special forces. He was spotted and poached by the SAS for his skills and attitude.

At thirty-two, his life changed, and his world fell apart. Steel had come home after a tour of Bosnia. But instead of a welcome-home party, Steel found a massacre. Mercenaries had invaded his home and had killed most of his family and friends —the grass was painted red with the blood of those he knew. Suddenly, the soldier kicked in, and he went hunting for those responsible. Taking them down one by one, leaving none alive.

The last thing Steel remembered from that terrible day was the laughter of the shooter and the footsteps that crept away. Then, as he began to lose consciousness, he was aware of someone else in the room. The man grabbed Steel and pulled him out of danger. The man was the family gardener, a Japanese guy who had worked for Steel's father for years, or so he had thought.

The man had nursed Steel back to health using old medicine. Steel knew the people would have done this would be after him, so he needed to hide; he had hidden at his family's cabin in Alaska. Unfortunately, his plan to stay out of sight hit a snag when a tour plane crashed. Aboard was his new boss, the head of the SEAL teams.

'They're going,' Graaf said, waking Steel from his dream-like memory.

Steel said nothing, just grumbled and put it into gear and moved forwards towards the ramp.

'So, what were you thinking about?' Graaf asked, interested in what nightmares this guy was haunted by.

'When?' Steel shrugged, hoping Graaf would shut up and let him drive in peace.

'Just then, you kind of looked into space and fazed out. Whoever pissed you off, I hope they had a big enough hole,' Graaf laughed.

The look on Steel's face almost made him wet his pants. This guy was broken and hurting, and worst of all, deadly. A great combination, just as long as you were on his side.

'Just stuff ... memories,' Steel said quietly.

'Like what?' Graaf asked, insistently curious.

'Graaf.'

'Yeah?'

'Shut up, or I'll put you in the trunk,' Steel said without looking at the man.

Graaf nodded as they drove in silence.

Finally, Steel headed for the motorway and the meeting point.

———

In the morning, Simms headed for a motel not far from his apartment in Arlington. He decided not to head home. If the agents were looking for him, they would look in the first place. It was a cheap place, twenty dollars a night, but it had a bed and a shower and a diner not too far away.

Simms wanted to go back to the agency and tell what he had found, but so far, he had only snippets of information and nothing solid. All he did know was Brena was a threat, Falkner was dead, and Trish was missing. He'd gotten a burner cell from a store and had slipped in a new sim card. Luckily, he had a head for numbers and put Steel's cell number into the memory, along with Stanton's.

Simms sat on the bed, looked at the cell, and then turned

his gaze out of the window. He felt alone and lost in his pursuits. Men were after him, *his* men. Like Stanton would do, Brena probably gave the agents as little information as possible. 'Bring me, Agent Simms, at any cost,' was probably all they got, as well as the added news of Falkner's death and Trish's disappearance. As far as the agents were concerned, by the time Brena had finished briefing them, Simms was a fugitive, without Brena actually saying that. That way, if Simms wound up dead, Brena had full plausible deniability and would put it down to misinterpretation.

Simms had to find who had killed Falkner and Trish. He prayed that she was alive, pain in the ass or not; she was one of the good ones. Simms headed over to a small desk in a corner and started the laptop. As he waited for it to boot up, he arranged the hard drives and the disks that he had gotten from the house and from the old man. If the old guy had been filming Trish's home for her, she might have transferred the data from a disk to one of the hard drives. Something had spooked her for her to take such measures.

As the home screen opened, it asked for a password. Simms growled at the screen and sat back. Trish was careful, so her password wouldn't be 'Password' or '12345.' Simms tried her birthday and came up with nothing, then tried her girlfriend's name, which also came up short. He closed down the computer and lay back on the bed. What he needed was a hacker ... or at least a computer genius.

Simms smiled. He had just the man: Dorson.

––––––

Graaf slept in the backseat of the new car as Steel drove to the inn. Just outside the port was a filling station for those who needed to fill up before their long drive. Steel had met with two other agents to drop off the new vehicle and get rid of the BMW.

He looked at the blacked-out Jaguar F-PACE SUV and smiled. 'That will do' Steel brushed his fingers over the polished paintwork.

Graaf just yawned and climbed into the back as if it was a car from the airport rental service.

'Oh, don't mind him; someone tried to kill him,' Steel explained to the two bruisers. 'And someone still might if you get the seats dirty,' he yelled through the window so Graaf could hear him.

A gentle tap on the smoked privacy glass let Steel know he understood.

Steel shook hands with the men and made his way to the driver's side while the men got into the BMW. As the two cars got underway, Graaf curled up and closed his eyes. They were safe for now; all Steel hoped was that the handoff went well.

It was still some way before they got there, and Steel was enjoying the silence. He thought about putting the radio on, but he didn't want to disturb Graaf, not because he was being kind, he just didn't want to talk to the man just now. Once the agency had Graaf, someone would interview him to get more out of him than what Steel already had. Any bit of information would be crucial in trying to figure out who was doing this and why. But Steel was on the clock; he had to get to the Marble Arch at Hyde Park that evening. The journey would take two hours if the traffic were terrible.

Steel smiled to himself as he enjoyed watching the scenery blur past. The green roaming fields, trees, and wall-like bushes were fence lines. Steel couldn't wait to see the old place again, even for a short while. He had business there and also needed to pick up a few things. He had called ahead, so the head butler knew of his arrival. He still found it amusing that he had a butler, but then Jamerson also looked after the estate while he was away.

Steel had allowed it to be open to the public and permitted it to be used by film companies. All the revenue made went back into the house and gave a bonus to the staff. Steel preferred it that way; at least it was used and not left to fall into decline like some other places he had heard about that had been bought and turned into hotels or golf resorts.

The estate was still his home, and despite everything, he would never give it up. But it was more than a home; it was somewhere he could talk to his family. Although most chose to do this at a graveside, his family were still part of the Hall for him.

———

The built-in navigation system alerted Steel of the turnoff he had to take to get to the inn. He saw a huge roundabout upfront and turned to his right-hand side. He followed the satnav's instructions and pulled into the car park, following the round-about. The inn was a quaint place in the middle of nowhere, with food, drink, and accommodation signs.

Steel parked the car but left the motor running. Looking around, he saw the parking lot was virtually empty, less for a couple of cars and a motorcycle. He checked the time on the vehicle head-up display. He was ten minutes early, but then the roads had been kind.

Steel switched off the motor and got out. The fresh British air smelled of the countryside. Grass, cows, and car fumes. He sucked in a lungful of air and closed his eyes. The inn looked tempting. One quick pint of the best British beer, but he needed his wits about him if something were to go wrong.

A blacked-out Land Rover Discovery pulled up, and a man got out. Dressed all in black, with a shaven head and a goatee.

'What's the password?' asked the man.

'Doesn't matter; you would have forgotten it anyway,' Steel replied.

The two men laughed out loud and embraced like brothers.

'I hear you're causing trouble again,' said the agent.

Steel shrugged and moved his hand in a rocking motion.

'Where is he?' asked the agent, looking around. 'He's not in the trunk. But Steel, you know you can't keep doing that,' laughed the man.

'Relax, he's in the back seat. And believe me, once he starts talking, I bet you'll think about it.' Steel nodded to the rear of his vehicle.

The man nodded, then spoke softly as if to himself. Suddenly, three other cars drove up, each one identical to the other, including the same licence plates.

'Showtime,' the man announced, making sure the cars lined up with their tails to the wall, then all four opened their rear passenger doors.

Steel went to Graaf's sleeping body and opened the door, completing the wall.

'Graaf,' Steel said, shaking the man to wake him up.

Graaf woke with a start. But Steel's hand muffled the cry out for help.

'Shut up and listen. You are going with these agents. You need to cross over from one vehicle to the other without touching the floor. You follow their instructions to the letter. Nod if you understand,' Steel said with a quiet but firm voice.

Graaf nodded, more out of fear than anything.

'Do it now, and do it slowly,' Steel ordered.

Graaf turned around and inched himself over until his feet were just inside the door of the other vehicle before dragging himself over. The driver inside the first vehicle told Graaf to keep going until he was in the third car. Again, Graaf said nothing, only obeyed. Steel watched as each car shut its doors and took off in different directions before getting in the Jaguar and, with a smile, putting the radio on.

# CHAPTER THIRTY-FIVE

AFTER A TWO-HOUR DRIVE, STEEL PULLED UP TO THE gated entrance of his home. The sound of the tyres crunching the in a gravel driveway as he approached the hall. The grounds looked empty, less for Jamerson, who stood at the main entrance. Jamerson was a tall, stocky man with greased-back grey hair and a proud look about him. Steel switched off the engine and got out, wearing a broad smile.

'Good morning, sir; I hope you had a sound journey without further incidents,' Jamerson said in a deep baritone voice.

'Morning Jamerson, yes, it turned out alright in the end, and how have you been?' Steel asked, moving towards the man and shaking his hand.

'As well as can be expected, sir. Thank you for asking.' Jamerson's mouth curled into a crooked smile.

'Your leg again?' Steel asked, shrugging slightly as if to say it was nothing. 'Maybe this will help?' He took his canvas bag out of the trunk.

'Oh, sir, you shouldn't have,' Jamerson jibbed, holding the bag.

'Ha-ha, very droll. The bottle and cigars are inside,' Steel said with a grin.

'And will sir be joining me in a nightcap?' Jamerson asked with a curious look.

'I'm afraid not. Got a killer to catch,' Steel said, looking at his watch and thinking about what he had to do. 'Cup of tea and a bacon sandwich would be great, though,' Steel grinned.

Jamerson smiled and shook his head. Even though Steel carried a title, he was foremost a soldier, like himself, and nobody could take that away from him.

———

Steel had taken a long shower while he loaded the updates on his new phone, watch, and unique sunglasses. The water was like tiny balls bombarding his skin. The steam filled the vast bathroom, fogging up the mirrors. Steel leant forwards, his hands resting on the polished sandstone walls, and let the boiling water wash over him.

He had lost track of time and hurried out of the shower, wrapping a towel around him and stepping into his bedroom. Jamerson sat in one of the two Chesterfield armchairs and sipped tea. He looked up at Steel and gasped. Steel's body was taut with muscle as though he had overdone his training.

'I see you've put on weight,' joked Jamerson.

Steel laughed and dropped down and pushed out a hundred push-ups.

'I remember when you couldn't do one of those bloody things without crying about it,' Jamerson winked, taking a bite of his sandwich.

'Practice makes perfect,' Steel replied, sending the mockery back.

'Touché,' Jamerson replied, raising his china teacup.

Steel finished his exercise and stood. The smell of the turkey-bacon sandwich was more than a reward for his effort.

'So, what is it this time, and how can I help?' Jamerson asked, filling Steel's cup with the fresh brew.

'You heard about the postcard killer?'

'The Sentinel, I believe he calls himself, yes. Nasty bugger,' Jamerson said, handing over the teacup and saucer.

'Well, he has been sending me clues to find the targets,' Steel explained before taking a sip.

'That's a new one, a killer who wants you to find the victims.' Jamerson shook his head, unable to fathom the reasoning.

'I think The Sentinel wants them found; he wants them to talk. Why I don't know yet, but someone *else* doesn't want them to.'

'Did you find any ... alive, that is?' Jamerson asked, remembering the blast in Berlin that was all over the news.

'Two so far. I'm off to get the next one tonight,' Steel said before he dug his teeth into the thick fluffy white bread and closed his eyes before giving a moan of appreciation. 'Oh God, that's heaven.'

Jamerson laughed and refilled his cup. 'So, where is this little meet and greet?'

'Marble Arch, Hyde Park, midnight,' Steel answered, his voice low as if just saying the name brought him pain.

'You're joking?' Jamerson sat back. ' Have you been back since—'

'Since they killed Thomas at Speakers' Corner? No, I've tried to avoid it,' Steel admitted. Nevertheless, the thought of that night sprang back into his memory. How he had been too late to save his friend.

'So, what are we going to do?' Jamerson smiled.

'*We?*' Steel asked, surprised at the presumption of helping.

'You don't think you're getting all the fun to yourself this time, do you?' Jamerson stood.

'No, Sarge, I guess I'm not.' Steel stood, and the two men shook hands.

Now, all they needed was a plan that wouldn't get anyone killed, especially themselves.

———

Simms woke and turned to face the alarm clock. The red digital display read five-past-five. Simms sat up and rubbed his eyes with his palms while letting out a yawn. He'd only gotten a few hours of sleep, but it had been deep, and he felt better for it. The bed was comfortable, possibly too much, as he fought to roll out from between the sheets and head to the bathroom to take a leak.

Simms had no plan; he just knew he had to somehow get in touch with Dorson. He could call, but Simms knew as soon as the man had told him to ditch his phone, he'd probably done the same. He flushed and headed for the shower. His usual routine was to take a long run, but that was out of the question. Instead, he would shower, change, and head for breakfast at the diner. Not much of a plan, but it was a start.

Dorson lived on the other side of Arlington from Simms's apartment, a five-minute drive at most. But the chances of Brena having agents watching Dorson's place were high. Moreover, Brena knew that Dorson had been looking for Trish earlier and that Brena was a red flag. So, Simms had to get a message to Dorson somehow. Sure, they were trained in this kind of stuff, but so were the people looking for him. Simms almost wished Steel was there; he would have found a way to do it. But he wasn't there; Simms was alone.

After a hearty breakfast and a lot of coffee, he drove close to Dorson's street but avoided the turn. Instead, he took the next road, parked between two parked cars, and waited. It was quarter-to-six and still dark. The one thing Simms had in his favour.

Simms gave it five minutes before getting out and walking to the house that sat opposite Dorson's. Trees lined the streets, and ever-green bushes acted as fences.

Simms had to admit Dorson had done well for himself. But he knew that Dorson had inherited it after the death of his parents six months ago when they had been killed in an accident while on a trip to New York.

Simms wore stuff from a thrift store he had found: jeans, a red and blue chequered shirt, and a baseball cap. Not much of a disguise, but then he was on a budget. He walked with his hands in his pockets and his shirt hanging out. The sunglasses were a nice touch, along with the dog he had offered to take for a walk. The hotel owner was sceptical at first, but then, she knew where he lived. Room 12.

Simms walked down a side road that split the block into two, more of a dirt track used as a shortcut, but it had one quality: it ran along the back of Dorson's house.

Simms knew that Dorson would have left hours ago; he was conscientious like that, so knocking on the back door was out. So, instead, Simms wrote out a note on a paper napkin earlier at the diner. 'We need to talk; I have something, Trish's computer. So urgent.' That was all it said, besides his new cell phone number. He hoped those few words would be enough to get Dorson's attention. The idea was to slip it into the mailbox, but then it would look suspicious; some guy walking up and dropping something in someone's mailbox. And breaking in would be out. Dorson was a gadget freak and security nut; the chances were he had cameras all over the house and garden. And that was what Simms was counting on.

Simms had also bought a dog's squeezy ball and slit it so that he could place the napkin inside with enough of it sticking out for Dorson to notice. If he were right, the moment the ball went near the house, a silent alarm would go off, and Dorson would return home to check. Simms had to admit it wasn't the best plan, but he was working against the clock with no other way to communicate with Dorson. So, Simms held up the pink toy, causing the chihuahua to look at the thing and tilt its tiny head.

'Oh well, here goes nothing,' Simms said, tossing the toy.

The dog let out a displeased 'woof' as the toy sailed over the fence and hit one of the windows. Simms hurried off, making sure he wasn't seen. Stage one was complete. Now for the hard part: setting up a meeting.

―――――

A text message from the lead agent informed Steel that Graaf had gotten to the HQ in one piece. Steel nodded as if to reassure himself he could now breathe easy.

Two targets had been secured.

Steel wondered about Falkner and what he had told them. Stanton was a good interrogator. He'd done it as a young Lieutenant in Vietnam and in Gulf conflicts and Bosnia again.

Steel placed down the cell and looked over to the three murder boards he had re-created in the study. It was still early, and there was no point rushing into London just to sit about. The picture of the Arch had been another nighttime scene, and the address had been '2359 Precinct.' Steel perched himself against the edge of the desk and crossed his arms as he stared at the boards. Finally, there was the other board, but this held information that Graaf had told him, along with names and dates.

Steel knew that something or someone connected them all but couldn't see how. However, there was one thing for sure: they were all in New York at the same time for one reason or another. Steel rubbed his unshaded eyes and rolled his neck and shoulders. He was beginning to feel the effects of not training for a while.

There was a gym in the house, however, and the distraction might be good for him. Steel pushed himself off the polished oak desk and headed back to his room to change. He needed to train until his body hurt, hoping the rush of blood would kick-start his brain.

—————

Steel's rigorous workout involved running ten miles with weights and finishing with a sparring session. All of which took around two hours. The time he didn't have time to waste but thought it necessary; after all, he hadn't done anything for the two weeks he'd been off.

Sweaty but refreshed, Steel returned to the study with a large smoothie he'd made with vegetables and fruit he'd found in the kitchen. Steel sipped the healthy drink as he returned his attention to the boards. The information was still blotchy, and he hoped that Stanton's interview with Falkner would fill in some of the gaps. He looked at the ornate Victorian metal clock; it was eleven in the morning, which meant it was around six in the morning in Langley.

Steel pressed the speed dial on his phone, knowing Stanton would be at the office, that is if he'd actually left since this whole thing started.

He listened to the rings while he continued to drink the tasty sludge from the plastic sports cup, his eyes scanning the boards to make sense of it all.

'Morning, John,' said a tired Stanton.

'Morning, Avery,' Steel replied, his eyes locked on the one board.

'Now the pleasantries are over; where the fuck are you?' Stanton barked.

'Nice to hear your voice too,' Steel said, nearly losing a mouthful of the drink from the shock of Stanton's outburst. 'I take it things are not well at your end?'

'You could say that. Falkner is dead; they are calling it suicide,'Stanton told him.

'But you're not?'

'Hell no. Doesn't make sense. Him offing himself. He was safe here, or so we thought.' Stanton's voice calmed the more he spoke, but there was something in the tone that had Steel wondering.

'And, what else? Come on, Avery, I can hear it in your voice.'

'Trish is missing, and Simms has gone to ground after I sent him to try and find out what had happened to Falkner. So, something is happening in my own backyard, and I don't know what.' There was a brief pause from both sides as they took in the information. 'Tell me Graaf is OK?'

'He's in London at the head office; they are speaking with him now,' Steel reassured his friend and, puzzled, asked, 'So, why would Simms leave the building if he was looking for someone on the inside?'

'Beats me. I guess he got a lead that took him outside. Besides, I have Brena looking for them both; they'll turn up. Hell, we'll probably find out that they were shaggin' each other,' Stanton laughed.

'Doubtful. Trish was gay,' Steel said, sipping.

'What, Trish? Nahhhhh,' Stanton declared, unconvinced at Steel's theory. 'What makes you come up with that?'

'I could see it in the way she carried herself, how she looked at women and men,' Steel said with an almost patronizing tone.

'You came on to her, and she shot you down, didn't she?' Stanton chuckled.

'The pictures of her girlfriend pretty much sealed it ... nice looking couple.' Steel laughed.

'So, where are you?' Stanton asked.

'I'm back home and off to London tonight.' Steel explained that the latest postcard showed Marble Arch in Hyde Park, a nighttime scene.

'Yes, we got it from a courier from the embassy. It arrived a couple of minutes ago. The lab is running it now,' Stanton said, looking at a photocopy on his desk. '2359, midnight.'

'The Sentinel wants these people found, Avery. He doesn't want to kill them.' He placed down the cup and walked over to the boards. 'He wants these people to talk, not die.'

'So, why kill them? Two apartments were destroyed because of this lunatic, and two good agents were injured or killed in the process. As far as I can see, this loon will stop at nothing to get rid of these people, not make them talk,' Stanton argued.

'So, how do you explain Falkner?' Steel asked, not convinced by Stanton's mindset.

'The Sentinel probably had something on one of my agents, threatened their family. We are dealing with a highly skilled person that uses surveillance on people. Hell, the nut job probably had this in a contingency plan if things went wrong. Bastard probably had this whole thing planned for months,' Stanton said, his tone suggesting respect for the killer's tenacity.

Suddenly, Steel's eyes widened. Something Stanton had

said had filled one of the missing pieces. 'Avery, something has come up. I'll call you later.' He hung up before Stanton had time to respond.

Steel realized something, a clue he had overlooked that was there all this time. He had been looking at the wrong timeline. He had been so focused on when the targets had been in New York that he had forgotten one thing: *when* The Sentinel had started.

The first killing was of the security guard a week ago. However, how did The Sentinel get everything on him? The surveillance took weeks, maybe months. Steel could feel a theory on the tip of his tongue, but there was still something eluding him. The houses in Berlin, Amsterdam, and now London. These nests didn't just happen overnight; they took severe planning to arrange ... movement of equipment and time schedules. The Sentinel knew when these people would be away and for how long.

Steel raced over to the computer and started to look into any records of investigations into Graaf and Falkner, precisely where the surveillance on them was carried out. Steel rocked in the chair while the agency database compiled the information.

Jamerson stood in the doorway with a tray of coffee, but he dared not enter. He could see the look on Steel's face. He had seen it before. And it always ended one way, with someone paying for what they had done.

———

The nightmare he'd just had seemed real, too real. It had been hours since Simms had returned from Dorson's place. He figured that he would get more research done while he was awake.

Unfortunately, the lack of sleep the night before had

caught up with him, and he woke up in his hotel room with a start, his head against the keyboard of his laptop. Simms stretched off and wiped the drool from his mouth.

With blurry eyes, he checked the time. It was ten minutes to ten.

He grumbled at the thought of the lost time, but then he did feel better for the nap, less for the markings on his face and the millions of zzzzzzzs written on the screen. He found it curious the only key he'd hit was the 'z', which was basically the letter associated with sleeping. Simms smiled and stretched off again. His mouth was dry, and his stomach empty.

The early breakfast had been burnt off hours ago, and now, like an angry beast, his belly was reminding him of it.

Simms agreed there wasn't much he could do until he heard back from Dorson. He needed to know what was on that computer. The hard drives were mainly work-related, and he hadn't had time to go through them all. One file was about some rich guy in New York that the cops and the agencies had been after. Apparently, she had been on a task force before being assigned to Langley and Brena's team, or that was what he liked to call it. The truth was that he was the same as the rest, apart from getting chosen to take on this case. Before that, Trish was in charge. They all took turns. That was how Stanton liked it. But Brena had visions of grandeur and a stick up his ass.

Each team member had been picked from different offices around the country. Still, only Brena, Trish, Dutton, and Kitty had been to New York and Boston. Everyone else had been from Washington, Chicago, and other cities in various states. Kitty had been there six months; the others nearly a year.

Simms had left a contact number on the back of the napkin, so Dorson had a way of reaching him. However, he had no idea if Dorson had gotten the message or had even been back to his place to check the alarm. The worst case was that Brena hadn't let Dorson go but had sent one of his goons instead. If that were the case, this whole thing could be over in no time, and Simms would be in front of Stanton or the director.

Simms had disappeared, and it looked bad, especially considering he was supposed to be looking for Falkner's killer. It had 'guilty' written all over it. Plus, Trish was missing. Simms couldn't go back until he had proof that Trish had been taken, and hopefully, that was the same person who had killed Falkner.

Simms's belly growled once more, this time with more vigour. He was hungry and tired and had no leads for either of his assignments. He looked at the other hard drives that sat next to his laptop. There was still plenty more to look through, including the rest of the files on the three-terabyte drive. Simms packed the drives and the computer into his sports bag and walked over to the air vent near the floor.

Taking out his knife, Simms flicked open the blade and undid the screws that were holding the vent cover in place. A perfect hiding place, he thought. Better than under the bed or stuck in a draw for any snooper to find. Simms was careful not the make any scratches or marks that would indicate the cover had been taken off.

Simms stood and headed for the door.

He slipped the 'do not disturb' sign on the handle and headed for the stairs as he closed it behind him. His stomach growled yet again as the stairwell door closed behind him. He was hungry, thirsty, and sick of being kept in the dark.

# CHAPTER THIRTY-SIX

STANTON SAT IN HIS OFFICE AND STARED OUT OF THE panoramic window that overlooked the grassy area and the other buildings on the grounds. The sun was high, but passing clouds blocked out the brightness and the warmth.

He watched people walking here and there, coming and going, oblivious of the chaos that was unfolding in Stanton's world. He would turn and look at his desk phone every so often, waiting for it to ring. He was expecting two calls. One was from Steel, and the other was from upstairs. No matter how this played out, Stanton knew his career was over, had been for some time. He was just treading water until it happened. He was a dinosaur, a remnant from the old ways, the Cold War days. They were looking for someone new in this modern age, someone like Brena.

A knock on his door caused Stanton to turn and face the door. It was Brena, and he was wearing the look of a lost child.

'What is it?' Stanton asked, expecting more bad news.

'The investigation team has finished. Although they are calling it suicide, there were no markings on Falkner that would indicate he had been in a fight or subdued, and no chemicals in his system. The only marks were on his fists, telling us he punched the mirror several times before it broke,' Brena said, almost disappointed at the finding.

'So, we are not looking for a killer. So, why have you got your dogs hunting Simms like he'd done it himself?' Stanton growled, angry at Brena's heavy-handed approach to his own people. 'I thought I told you to tell him to come in, not track him like mass murder. Fix it, now,' Stanton barked before turning around and returning to his view of the grounds.

Brena went to speak but decided it was best to keep silent and just walk away. He knew that Stanton was right, but he enjoyed the chase too much, regardless of who it was on the other end. Of course, Steel remained the best query he'd had and possibly ever would.

Brena stood by the elevator and pressed the button for the second floor. A flurry of thoughts raced through his mind while he waited. Like how had it gone so wrong?

Kitty was dead, Trish was missing, and Simms had gone to ground. This, for him, was a career disaster. He was the lead agent on this, and somehow it had all fallen apart. Of course, he wanted to blame Steel, but the man had a reputation that couldn't even be scratched.

The doors opened, and the button illuminated the second floor.

Brena stepped out and headed for the war room. He still had five agents, including Dorson, when he got back from checking his house alarm, that was. Brena had only let him go because he was sick of looking at the man's angry expression every five minutes.

Brena had grounded him for looking into Trish's disappearance. But little did Brena know that Dorson had been right. Trish had gone, and nobody had any idea how or where she had gone too.

Brena's agents had spoken to a neighbour, but that had proved fruitless, apart from scaring the man half to death and landing him in hospital.

Nobody looked up as Brena entered the room. They were too busy checking for a pattern between Graaf, Falkner and the two victims. They knew that New York was a significant piece of the puzzle, but the rest was a mystery. There, one lead was in the morgue, and the other was in London. The new postcard Steel had sent was clean, just like the others. They were at a dead end, with the clock ticking. Their only hope was that Steel could get the next target before The Sentinel.

Brena walked past each desk, checking on their progress but ensuring he didn't disturb their trail of thought. Each had a different task to research. One had the New York angle, and another had background checks on all the targets. Another was to determine anything The Sentinel may have done previously, just in case this wasn't a singular occurrence. The last was tracking Steel or the best he could. Somehow, Steel had the knack of disappearing, almost as if he had vanished entirely. Stanton had told Brena that Steel was good, but he hadn't appreciated just how good, until now.

Brena walked over to Kitty's desk and sat down. His fingers danced over the keys with a light touch, but not enough to activate them. Her desk was pristine. Everything had a place and purpose. Brena leant back in the chair and swivelled it side to side, his thoughts a million miles away. He started to open drawers and look inside, more out of boredom than actual interest in the contents.

Brena picked up a notebook and flicked through the pages. He knew there wouldn't be anything interesting or prudent to this case, but he wanted to know the thoughts of one of his agents. Most of the notes were of things to do or other equally nonwork-related stuff. Finally, Brena came across a woman and a man with a baby photograph. The couple couldn't have been more than twenty-seven, and the baby was just an infant.

Brena figured it was a picture of her birth parents that she had lost at an early age, but he found it curious there were no pictures of her adopted parents.

Brena shrugged it off. He wasn't interested enough to care about her way of dealing with personal things, only how she reacted in the field. She had done OK; she wasn't the best or the worst. His only regret was she wouldn't have the chance to grow or experience life, which had been taken from her. Brena put the notebook and photographs back and closed the drawer.

'Do you want to send some agents to London?' asked Rachel.

Brena smiled and shook his head. 'No, it's OK. We have someone already there,' he replied. 'From the London office.'

Rachel smiled and nodded as if accepting the explanation.

———

Jamerson had insisted Steel shower and change, almost as if he was afraid the smell of sweat would seep into the furniture and would never come out. Steel had seen his point and done just that. He found the water soothing and good stimulation for the grey cells.

He used his parent's old shower because the one in his room held too many memories. A distraction he couldn't afford to have at that moment. His mind was focused on the problem at hand. How did The Sentinel research all those properties so fast?

—————

Steel returned to the study with fresh clothes and smelling clean but no new ideas. There was a pot of fresh coffee on a silver tray, along with his favourite mug with the SAS insignia on it. Jamerson had left Steel to it; he understood that he should be left alone when Steel was in the zone.

Steel checked the progress of the database and found what he needed. The apartment opposite Graaf's had once been empty, and INTERPOL had a surveillance team watching Graaf from there. When they came up empty, the place was sold off. It was also the same for Falkner's apartment. The place across the street had the same history.

He checked with London to see if there had been any agency surveillance on anyone in the area. One name popped up: Christian Dollman.

He was the worst kind of human being, a 'fixer' to Steel. Predominantly juries, not that it could be proved. If you have enough money, this man could make sure a jury swung in your favour.

Steel rocked back and forth in his chair, pondering whether he should track down and save him or leave the bastard to The Sentinel. Finally, Steel stood up, walked over to the coffee table next to the two Chesterfield armchairs, and poured himself a black coffee. The smell of the Jamaican Blue Mountain coffee was intoxicating.

Steel took a sip and walked back to the desk. Still not entirely convinced he should save Dollman, Steel had questions, and Dollman had the answers. On the way to the desk, Steel passed the boards. He stopped for a moment and took another look at the fourth board. It was still full of gaps, but there was still some useful information. Taking another sip, he headed for the desk. He had work to do. He had to find Dollman's location before midnight tonight before the next postcard came. He opened up the database once more; he needed an address, if not Dollman's, then that of the nest, knowing Dollman's place would be right opposite.

Steel soon found the nest's address, an apartment near the US Embassy in Mayfair. He knew the area, possibly all too well. He thought back to the Christmas market they had in Hyde Park, the sounds of people, the smells from the food vendors, and the bright lights.

True, it was a fantastic sight to behold, but he had not returned to the park since his friend's murder, not even for the market.

Dollman was a smug son-of-a-bitch who needed to be taken off of the planet. He had used his influence to get some real scum from doing time, and he didn't care as long as the paycheck was right. Steel knew plenty of detectives who had their perps dead to rights, but somehow they walked free. He started to take another sip of his coffee but stopped. Suddenly, he stood up and looked at the fourth board.

'Dollman got them all off. They all walked free,' Steel said to himself, or so he thought.

'Who walked free?' asked Jamerson, who stood in the doorway.

Steel didn't answer; he put down his coffee mug and ran out of the door past a confused Jamerson.

'God, I hate it when he does that,' Jamerson said to himself, hearing the front door slam.

Steel had jumped into the Jaguar and drove to Dollman's apartment. He didn't have time to mess about it, he had an address, and he would get him and bring him in. Steel pressed the button with the telephone icon and scrolled down to the contact that read 'Office.' Steel clicked on it and waited for the ringing to start.

'Yes, Steel?' came a woman's voice over the surround-sound speakers.

'I'm on the way to Mayfair. The next target is a man named Dollman, Christian Dollman,' Steel said as he took corners like a rally driver.

'Are you sure?' said the voice, alarmed at the news.

'Positive, why?' Steel asked, suddenly having one of those bad-feeling moments.

'Because he isn't in Mayfair; he's having lunch with Charles Benetton at The Connaught.'

'The billionaire?' Steel asked.

'Yes, the very one.'

'Can't you send a team to secure him? say he is a threat to Benetton because he's got a killer after him?' Steel requested, throwing the car across the road, past vehicles and avoiding oncoming traffic.

'I don't think he would see it that way. Besides, what proof do we have?' the woman asked.

'I guess gut feelings don't wash,' Steel laughed. Not expecting an answer. 'Right, I'm off to The Connaught then,' he said before disconnecting the call. A cold smile crossed Steel's face as he gripped the steering wheel and pressed down the gas pedal.

———

Steel parked his car in front of the restaurant and got out. A chilly wind brushed against his face, making the skin tingle at nature's touch. Steel straightened his suit jacket and entered the building.

There was a gentle buzz of conversation and the soft clatter of silverware against bone china. Steel stood at the greeting point and looked around but saw no sign of Dollman.

'Can I help you, sir?' asked a smartly dressed man in his late fifties. The *matre d'* smiled and waved a waiter across to show Steel to a table.

'Is Mr Dollman here?' Steel asked, hoping for a quick answer and no fuss.

'I'm sorry, sir, I'm unable to answer—'

'Never mind, I've got him,' Steel had already spotted him in a corner, next to a window. Grinning, he walked on to the dismay of the man.

Steel found Dollman and Benetton in a discussion about something; their whispers and glances around the room made them look guilty of something, which they probably were.

'Christian, my goodness, good to see you. Well, actually, I'm not, but then I'm just being nice for the moment,' Steel said, grabbing a chair from another table and joining the two men.

'Sorry, whoever you are, this is a private meeting, so I'll kindly ask you to leave,' Bennetton said, nodding at a man in the corner. The bruiser walked over, his Armani suit adding to his size.

'Don't worry, David, this is Detective Steel of the NYPD. He's probably come all this way for nothing,' Dollman laughed.

The bruiser placed a massive hand on Steel's shoulder as a first warning.

'Friend, move it or lose it,' Steel warned the goon.

Dollman sat back and waited. There was a quick movement from Steel, and the man dropped to the floor in pain, holding his hand.

'I'm here to bring you in, Christian, I'm afraid,' Steel said, hiding the real reason for his appearance.

'You've got nothing on me, so scurry back to your hole in

New York,' Dollman said, picking up a half-filled champagne flute and sipping.

'Unfortunately, it's not like that; I'm here to save your life. It appears someone is out to get certain people. You heard about the bombs in Berlin and Amsterdam?' Steel asked as he poured himself a glass of the Bollinger '75 and took a sip.

Dollman nodded as though he had little interest. After all, that was there; he was far away from that trouble.

'Well, it appears you are on that list. Now, believe me, I would much prefer to let the killer do his thing where you are concerned, but unfortunately, you have the information I need, so ...' Steel stood, raising an arm as if ushering Dollman to the door.

'Your concern is touching. However, I must decline your kind offer. I think I will be fine,' Dollman said smugly.

'Oh, I'm sorry, you misunderstood. I wasn't asking,' Steel said sternly.

Suddenly, the beast of a man came up behind Steel and locked his massive arms around him in a bearhug.

Steel bared his teeth in anger and scraped the side of his shoe down the man's shin bone, then shot his head backwards, catching the man full in the face. He whirled and jabbed the man in the throat with a quick jab.

The bodyguard released his grip. Unable to breathe, he stumbled back, straight into a couple's table, then fell through it.

Steel turned to Dollman, who sat with a smug look.

He turned to see two more men quickly approach. Both attacked simultaneously, but Steel was quick and countered many of the blows, giving as good as he got.

One of the men threw a punch towards Steel's head, but he caught the fist, twisted the man's arm, and sent the man crashing into the other, just in time to stop the man from reaching for a knife from the table. Both men fell backwards, collapsing on top of two empty tables.

'Dollman, call off your dogs before they get hurt,' Steel said, preparing himself for the next volley of punches.

Dollman sat sipping his champagne while he enjoyed the show.

The guerrilla returned, rushing at Steel like a quarterback. But Steel moved quickly, tripping the man as he shot past. There was a loud crash when the big man sailed through the window. The sound of glass echoed through the building, and people ran for cover.

The other two men also rushed at Steel, hoping at least one of them would catch him off balance so the other could finish the job. Steel's movements were fluid, almost like a dance, as he countered and landed several strategic hits to the men's bodies. Each let out muffled cries of pain as straight-hand punches landed on specific pressure points.

The men went down, unconscious. And that was when Steel heard the click. The sound of a pistol hammer being drawn back, ready to fire. Steel spun around and jabbed Dollman in the side of both upper thighs, causing him to crouch forwards.

Steel landed an uppercut to the man's jaw as he leant down, sending Dollman into the air and out the window. Steel caught the revolver, put the hammer back, and spun out of the chamber before emptying the cartridges into his hand and tossing the weapon onto the table.

Steel leapt out the window and landed with a roll. As he stood up, he grabbed Dollman by the scruff of the neck and dragged him to the Jaguar.

'Quick, someone calls the police,' a man yelled.

'Don't worry, I *am* the police. He didn't pay for parking,'

Steel said as he watched partons scrabble to get change for the parking meters.

Benetton stared out the broken window and watched Steel drive away. As he did, he took out his cell and made a call. 'Yes, it's me. We have a problem.'

# CHAPTER THIRTY-SEVEN

It was twelve-twenty when Simms got the call from Dorson. No idle chit-chat, only a one-way conversation. 'Your hotel room, 13:00 hours.'

The call was brief, but at least he got hold of his only ally.

Simms had gotten fresh coffee and some sandwiches. He figured if they were going to be there for some time, they might as well be comfortable. He hoped that Dorson would crack the password on Trish's computer. The three terabytes were useless, just lots of work, nonsense related to an old case in New York, which had been months back. The others he hadn't had time to check.

After his second breakfast, Simms used the time to check up on Graaf's file, which, oddly enough, Trish had on one of her drives.

He had to admit Graaf was a scumbag of enormous proportions, and he had no problems trying to figure out why someone would want to kill him.

A knock at the door made him jump. Slowly, he calmed

himself down, headed to the door, and looked through the peephole.

There stood Dorson, dressed in a black hooded jogging outfit. He opened the door, greeted Dorson with a hearty handshake, and let him in.

'I got your message. It sounded important,' Dorson said with a serious face.

'You were right. Something did happen to Trish,' Simms said, leading him over to the desk that also held the small flatscreen television.

'I knew it. So, what did you find?' Dorson waited as Simms poured two cups of coffee.

'I got her laptop and a couple of hard drives.' Simms pointed to the devices that lay next to Dorson.

'Anything on them?'

'I haven't checked all of the drives because her password is proving to be a bitch to crack,' Simms admitted.

Dorson took hold of the coffee mug that Simms offered him and took a sip.

'The neighbour was filming her place and kept the disks,' Simms explained, causing Dorson to raise an eyebrow.

'So, the neighbour is a perv, stalker, or something?' he smiled.

'No, get this. Trish *asked* him to do it. She was nervous about something ... or someone.' Simms sat down on the bed and cradled his coffee mug in both hands.

'And you got the footage?' Dorson asked with interest.

'I don't know. The drive she was using was encrypted. It can only be played using her laptop, I think.' Simms shrugged.

Dorson nodded. If Trish were that concerned about her security, he could understand she would have done just that. Like him, Trish was a computer whiz and gadget freak. That was why she was good at surveillance, wiretaps, and hidden cameras.

Dorson spun, lifted the lid on the laptop, and got to work. Simms watched patiently as he got to work. All the while, his mind went back to Falkner and his mistake of not questioning him on the flight over.

'This may take a while, so if you have something else to do, now is the time,' Dorson told Simms.

'I got nothing but this for the moment. I'm betting whoever grabbed Trish killed Falkner.' Simms rested his back against the headboard.

Dorson smiled and nodded once as if to say he understood, then returned to the computer. Simms sat and watched. Feeling useless as he sipped his coffee and let his mind wander, trying to piece everything together in his head.

———

Steel drove like he stole the Jaguar. The muffled sounds of Dollman whining and sliding around in the trunk. Steel ignored him and continued his journey, hoping the uncomfortable travel arrangements would loosen Dollman's tongue for their little chat later. Steel was heading home, which was a good hour away. He had informed the agency that he had Dollman and where he would take him, which gave him roughly half an hour before they came, and his talk with Dollman would be interrupted.

Steel hoped that they wouldn't be complete arses and send a helicopter, which would be there to greet them.

He threw the car about on the road, even when there was no traffic to be overtaken. He wore a broad, satisfied grin as he did so, enjoying every bang, bump, and groan from behind him.

———

It was two o'clock when Steel returned home with his guest. Jamerson waited at the front door with his hands behind his back, his chin raised, and his chest out. Steel pulled up the entrance and switched off the car before getting out.

'Can you see our guest to the library?' Steel rushed inside to make a quick phone call.

Jamerson shot Steel a puzzled look. 'But there's nobody ... oh, you didn't?' A series of thumps from the trunk made Jamerson look up and shake his head. 'Of course you did.' He opened the trunk and looked down at a bruised and frightened Dollman.

'Good afternoon, sir. May I offer you some assistance?' Jamerson asked, offering a hand.

'Wh-what?' Dollman asked, confused.

Jamerson rephrased the question. 'Can I help you get your fat arse out of the car ... sir?'

Dollman looked at the massive butler with a blank expression.

Jamerson mumbled something and ripped Dollman from the trunk as if he were nothing and showed him into the library, a large room with two floors of books shelved on oak shelving. Stained-glass windows and a high ceiling and archways gave the place an aesthetic look and feel.

Jamerson ushered him to two red leather Chesterfield armchairs and beckoned him to sit. Dollman sat and looked around, marvelling at the room, which had to be at least two hundred years old.

As Dollman sat there with his mouth open, Jamerson went to pour him a large brandy from the drinks globe. 'I believe this should settle your nerves, sir,' he said, offering a drink on a silver salver.

Dollman took the brandy bowl and downed the eighteen-year-old brandy in one loud gulp, to Jamerson's annoyance.

Steel returned holding an electronic tablet and a large brown file.

'My lawyers are going to have a field day with you, and all this will be gone,' Dollman laughed, gesturing the room.

Steel just smiled, sat down in the other chair, and waited for Jamerson to bring the second round of drinks.

'Dollman, shut up and pin your ears back. Someone is out to get you. Now, personally, I don't give a damn, but you have information that this killer wants to suppress,' Steel explained. 'So, tell me about New York. Why were you there about six months ago?'

'Six months ago?' Dollman looked into space while he searched his memory for specific appointments that would warrant someone trying to kill him. After a while, he shook his head. 'Nah, nothing comes to mind. I was in New York a lot during that period ... lots of clients.' He laughed. But Steel didn't.

Steel handed the tablet to Dollman and told him to press the file icon. As Dollman watched, he saw pictures of the crime scenes.

'So, what's this?' Dollman asked, raising the tablet.

'Crime scene photos from The Sentinel file.'

'The Sentinel? Is that meant to mean anything?' Dollman asked quizzically.

'No, not really, he's just the bloke who wants to kill you. These are the other people who were on his list,' Steel said, cracking a smile.

Dollman's eyes widened as the severity of his situation kicked in.

'Now, like I said, I'm here to protect you, but if you don't need protection, then be my guest and go. In fact, I will drive you back myself. But be assured you will not see tomorrow.' He sat back in his chair and sipped his brandy.

Dollman looked at the pictures as they automatically swept through via a slideshow setting.

'Charles King. I got Charles King acquitted,' Dollman said, shaking with fear.

A new set of pictures appeared at a different crime scene.

'What's this?' Dollman asked, holding up the tablet so Steel could see.

'King's handy work, courtesy of you,' he growled, fighting the urge to smash the man's head against the marble fireplace.

'You knew?'

'I suspected. I just needed you to admit it,' Steel replied coolly.

'It won't stand up in court,' Dollman said smugly.

'And neither will you,' Steel grinned.

Dollman began to sweat, afraid of what he meant.

'A recording of this conversation will be sent to the press; everyone will know who you are and what you've done. You're finished, Dollman.' Steel stood just as two men in dark suits appeared in the doorway.

'Are you done?' asked one of the agents.

Steel nodded and turned his back. As the agents began to drag the dazed Dollman away, he turned. 'Dollman, how much did King give you for getting him off?'

'It wasn't Charles who retained my services. It was Edward, his father,' Dollman answered as he was quickly pulled through the door.

Steel shot Jamerson a look of desperation.

'The next target will be New York. After that, The Sentinel will be going after Edward King next,' Steel said, running full pelt to the study to call Stanton.

———

Simms was woken by the sound of the bathroom door closing. He opened his eyes and looked around for any sign of Dorson but found the chair he had been working at empty. He sat up and rubbed his eyes. He couldn't believe that he had fallen asleep. Still, the monotony of just sitting there, especially on a bed, could inspire slumber.

He figured Dorson had gone to take a leak; after all, he had put away a lot of coffee before Simms had crashed into a deep sleep. He looked over at his coffee cup sitting on the nightstand and let out a disappointed groan at the empty vessel. Dragging himself to his feet. He headed to the coffee machine. The strong scent of the coffee was helping him wake up as he filled his mug with the steaming liquid.

Simms walked back to the bed via the desk. He was curious about Dorson's progress and whether he had been able to crack Trish's password. As he neared, he saw the computer was unlocked, and he was staring at an image from the old man's garden camera. He rubbed the sleep out of his eyes and sat down, wondering how long ago Dorson had cracked the code and why he hadn't woken him after he had. But then, he knew he'd probably have let his colleague sleep as well if the roles had been reversed.

The image was of Trish's house at night. The front was clear, and the driveway was empty. Simms leant forwards and checked the time stamp. It was ten o'clock the evening before. Simms went to press the play icon but snatched his hand back. Dorson had cracked the code; he should be here to watch it as well. After all, they were in this together.

He felt a rush of excitement at the prospect of bringing this all to an end or being able to go back to Stanton and say 'it was him' or 'her', respectively. The cursor hovered over the play button. He felt selfish, but then what would it hurt? After all, they could play it again, and he had earned it.

Simms nodded and pressed the button. The video played out. First, Trish's car arrived and parked in her driveway. Then, after a few moments, she got out and headed for her front door. He was impressed with how clear the image was, even though it was night. Simms sat and watched as it played through, with no other vehicle stopping but several driving past. A couple of strollers and dog walkers walked by, but none of them stopped.

As Simms took a sip, he was beginning to feel bad about bringing Dorson all that way; the footage showed nothing.

Suddenly, as the clock on the screen showed ten past ten, a dark-coloured SUV pulled up, and a man got out.

Intrigued by this new development, Simms leant forward to better view the screen. Unfortunately, all he could see was that the fellow was tall and dressed all in black with a hoodie. Simms was engrossed in the footage like it was a gripping movie on TV. Trish suddenly came into view with the man behind her. She seemed scared, but she followed whatever instructions he was giving her. Finally, Trish got into the car; the man opened the door and looked around. Simms's mouth fell open as the man's face was revealed; it was Brena.

Simms never heard Dorson step out of the bathroom. The man was as quiet as a mouse in a room full of sleeping cats. But Simms caught Dorson's reflection in the laptop's display. He went to say something, but that was when he saw the gun pointing at his head. The silenced GLOCK SF 30 was Trish's favourite backup weapon. It was a 45 Auto calibre. A favourite for undercover law enforcement members or special forces groups. It was a perfect choice with a ten-shot magazine and a weight of 745 grammes.

Dorson probably used his time in the bathroom to place the suppressor on.

'You know, if you'd stayed asleep, I could have just wiped the drive, and nobody would have been the wiser, but of course, you had to wake up and start watching,' Dorson said angrily.

Simms looked confused. Why the hell did Dorson have a gun pointing at him if Brena was the one they were after? But then, as the video played on, he saw why—when a dark van pulled up around midnight, and several men got out and broke into Trish's place. After ten minutes, they returned, angry at the house's emptiness. As two of the men came into view, Simms's eyes widened. One of them was the man from the Amsterdam airport, and the other was Dorson.

Simms felt a burning rage well up from deep inside of him. All of this time, he had been played, lied to by his colleagues, and made to think everyone else was the enemy.

'Why?' Simms demanded.

'Because the pay is so good,' Dorson replied with a smirk.

Simms caught his reflection again; he was looking at his watch. That was never a good sign. Not even in the movies.

'Wait,' Simms said, hoping to buy time.

'Uhm ... no.' Dorson chose the back of Simms' head as a point of aim. There was a gentle thud, and blood splattered over the screen of the laptop and the wall behind it. Pieces of brain matter and skull clung to the wallpaper in small lumps and fragments. Then, a noise like a sack of potatoes hitting the floor resounded through the room. Followed by the sound of a door opening and a set of footsteps.

# CHAPTER THIRTY-EIGHT

STEEL HAD CAUGHT STANTON IN THE MIDDLE OF HIS lunch, a roast beef sandwich on wholemeal bread from the cantine. He had explained the situation and who he believed the next target to be. Stanton had rushed out of his office and headed down to the war room with Steel still explaining on the cell phone.

'Get your shit together; we know who the next target is,' Stanton said, bashing through the war room doors.

Brena looked up excitedly. At last, progress.

'I want Edward King secured. The Sentinel is going after him next,' Stanton ordered, and the agents grabbed their gear and hurried out.

Brena stayed behind for a moment, curious at the new development. There wasn't due to be a postcard for hours yet, but Stanton seemed to have the information now.

Then it clicked.

Stanton was on the phone with someone.

Steel. Of course, it could only be that interfering Brit.

Stanton looked at Brena, who stood before him, wearing a confused look, and hung up the phone.

'Yes, Martin?' Stanton asked, 'Ah, you want to know how we got it. Steel managed to get hold of the next target in London, a man called Dollman. He gave us King. Dollman got King's son off that bombing charge by influencing the jury,' Stanton explained.

'King, as in Charles King ... of the mall bombings six months ago?' Brena's eyes opened wide with surprise as the pieces began to fit into place. The Sentinel was seeking revenge for the mall bombing. 'And he figures Edward King is the last target?' Brena asked with a hopeful look.

'It looks like it. Now, go and bring King in. He's got some explaining to do,' Stanton ordered.

Brena nodded and raced out after his team.

———

Steel watched as the helicopter carrying Dollman and the agents took off and headed south. Even though he'd gotten the information, He still felt something was wrong, missing even. For him, the puzzle still didn't fit together.

'I take it now that Dollman is secured, you'll be heading off to New York?' Jamerson asked as he stood next to Steel, watching the black AgustaWestland AW139 disappear over the tree line.

'No, I still have a meeting to attend at midnight,' Steel said with a low, gruff voice. Then he walked away, heading back to the study. He had plans to make.

'Right then, better get the coffee on,' Jamerson said with a shrug and proceeded to the kitchen.

Steel went back to the boards. There was still something bothering him besides the unknown identity of The Sentinel.

He couldn't figure out why the killer set off the devices, knowing that the people had been taken into custody. It was likely that the devices didn't have a remote safety switch; they had to be disarmed at the source. But that made no sense. The Sentinel was thorough, so a device without an off switch went against Steel's profile of The Sentinel.

The Sentinel only wanted to hurt the targets, not innocent persons. So, why was Kitty killed and Sabine Boese injured?

Steel hoped his next theory would be correct. He would soon find out at midnight.

———

The Sentinel had seen the footage of Steel at the restaurant, which Dollman often frequented, as it was only around the corner from where he lived. After Steel had left with Dollman, The Sentinel continued observing.

Charles Benetton had made a call, and he didn't seem happy that Steel had snatched up Dollman.

The Sentinel cursed the small surveillance camera for not having audio, but it didn't matter. The Sentinel typed a few keys on a laptop, and the lipreading software kicked in. The electronic voice sounded almost human as it repeated what Benetton had said.

'We have a problem; some damned policeman just grabbed Dollman. His name? He called himself Steel if that means anything to you.' There was a pause as if Benetton was receiving instructions. 'Yes, I'll get right on it, certainly, Mr Williams.' Benetton's voice seemed to tremble at the very utterance of this man's name.

The Sentinel turned and took notice of the other monitors. One of them showed a man in his early sixties. He wore a thousand-dollar suit and sat with a Manhattan skyline in his office.

It was Edward King. Next to the image of King was another: the judge that had let Charles King go free. In The Sentinel's eyes, the judge was just as guilty and needed to be 'judged'.

The Sentinel picked up a postcard that had been specially made as a clue for King: a picture of George Washington coming off Mount Vernon. As The Sentinel was starting to fill out the address for Steel, the image of King's office caught The Sentinel's eye. Several agents moved in and snatched up King, telling him he was in danger and he had to come with them. The Sentinel laughed and clapped. Amused at how resourceful Steel had been. Steel had exceeded all of The Sentinel's expectations. He was the best and could understand why Stanton liked him, and why Brena hated him.

The Sentinel finished filling out the card, but the address was different this time: Christ Church Spitalfields 0100. Come alone.

The Sentinel knew it was time. Eventually, Steel would work it all out, but now, The Sentinel needed Steel's help reel in one more fish.

---

Steel sat in the study at the computer. He wanted to know every detail of Charles King's life before his death. Associates, friends, and girlfriends, with whom he had breakfast and even when he changed his underwear. The bombing at the mall was the key to this whole thing. The Sentinel wanted payback, revenge. The question: who had The Sentinel lost in the bombing? Steel had his old notes on King on a hard drive. Nearly five hundred gigabytes on the bastard. Photos, documents, files. All of which proved that man was a psycho nut case and a self-absorbed dick.

Charles King was in trouble from day one, probably

because of Daddy's money. The rich always seemed to get off doing stuff they shouldn't. So, at fifteen, he was arrested for being drunk and disorderly, and at seventeen, he got a DUI. Twenty-one, he got off on a hit-and-run charge due to a lack of witnesses or evidence.

At twenty-eight, he got pinched for beating up a hooker, which again disappeared, including the witness. Finally, at thirty, King got MI8's and Steel's attention.

The bombings happened all around the city, mostly in isolated places. The FBI was investigating because bomb nuts were their domain. That was until seven homeless people got a building dropped on them, and then that became NYPD's problem, so Steel made it his problem.

It took months of investigative work and months more to build a case. Steel remembered the look on King's face when the judge said he was a free man. But Steel knew he'd do it again; he couldn't help it.

He liked it too much.

Steel pulled up the file on the bombing. There were crime scene photograph

statements from the witnesses. One even mentioned the homeless guy who had saved their life. Steel smiled, always amused by how his costumes fooled people, but that was the idea.

Steel found the list of casualties and the dead. Thirty-two in total; thirty-two too many for Steel's liking. Steel saw his name on the list, and it made him scowl. He didn't deserve to be on the list; he most certainly didn't deserve the medal they wanted to give him, the Medal of Honour. Steel had refused it, but Captain Brant and the Mayor had other thoughts on the matter.

Jamerson walked in with a silver tray supporting coffee and Marmite on toast. Most people hated the brown paste, but

Steel had learned to appreciate the stuff. After a cold march on a night-nav exercise, a cup of hot water and a spoon of the thing were welcome. It tasted like crap, but it had all the nutrients and minerals to keep your body going for a while.

Steel smiled and nodded a thank you to his old sergeant.

Jamerson wasn't a butler to Steel. He was a comrade in arms.

A man who had been failed by the system after he had left the forces. So, Steel offered him a position as head of the house when Steel was away. The butler thing was more Jamerson's idea of blending in. Besides, he had a thing for the cook, and she thought the uniform was sexy. Steel found the cover amusing; who would argue with a butler that was ex-special forces?

———

The list was hard to read, as each name came with age. But as Steel read each name, he could swear he could see a face to go with the name. That was when he got to a name of a little girl, the girl from his nightmares. She had perished with her grandparents. Steel's eyes froze at the names. If she was the daughter and they were the grandparents, where were the parents? Henry and Alice Siar and Lilly Marks.

Steel went into the database and looked up Henry Siar.

Henry Siar was Irish, born in Dublin in '68, moved over to the States after leaving the Irish Rangers, and served with NYPD for twelve years. He opened an Irish bar on 35 street. He was married to Alice for thirty-five years and had two daughters, Mary and Cara, and a son, Patrick.

The little girl, Lilly, was eight years old; her parents were Cara and Martin Marks. Martin was a Forces Recon Sergeant, but he was killed by an IED attack in Kabul two years before.

Cara was also Forces Recon, but she was back home teaching recruits.

The son, Patrick, had gone into the US Army Rangers, and the other daughter Mary joined the Boston Police Department and was in HRT.

The family were all specialists and had enough training to be The Sentinel. Still, Steel was sure that only one of them was the person they were tracking. So, he rechecked the database for real-time locations on the two girls and the son but came up empty on the son and one of the daughters; the other was laid up in bed, six months pregnant.

A good alibi if ever he heard one.

Could The Sentinel be both of them? It would make sense; they were both qualified, but he shook off the idea. Not as being improbable, but more as unlikely. The Sentinel was a loner, someone who wasn't just hurting but wanted justice. Steel had already ascertained that The Sentinel was intelligent, thorough, and well-trained. Most people would have done something rash, but everything The Sentinel did was meticulous.

Steel bit into the cold toast and sipped the coffee while he absorbed all the new data, and Jamerson sat nearby and played Candy Crush on his cell phone.

Steel studied the boards. Each of the targets had something to do with King; each played a part in his bombing scheme without knowing. Graaf paid off Falkner with imported diamonds to pay for the explosives he had smuggled in from Berlin. Dollman had gotten the jury to vote not guilty, and Alison Klien was the lawyer for the prosecution. She must have taken a bribe to do as little as possible but not enough, so it looked like she was taking a dive.

But that left the security guard. What the hell did he have to do with it? Steel checked the files to see where Mark Trent was working. His eyes widened as he went to bite into another piece of toast. Mark Trent was in charge of the security cameras at the mall at the bombing. So, that would explain why there was no footage of King up until he had been caught by security. After that point, Trent went on a break, a very long break.

Steel sat back in his chair and began to rock back and forth. The more he looked at it, the easier it became to understand. He eyed the boards again and nodded; he was happy with his investigation. But when he looked again, his smile faded away.

'What about the judge?' Steel suddenly straightened, scaring Jamerson enough for him to lose his game.

'Oh, bollocks,' Jamerson said, shooting Steel a look of irritation.

'Quite,' Steel replied, picking up the phone and pressing the redial number.

Jamerson's looked confused.

'Avery, do you have King? Good, don't forget about the judge who presided over the King case. I think she will be next,' Steel explained before putting down the phone.

Steel looked up at the time. It was nine o'clock. He had around an hour and a half trip, and he could probably do it in less, but he definitely had time.

———

Stanton sat in his office. He'd had a long day, and it was only four o'clock. He'd informed Brena to swing past the courthouse and pull in the judge. He'd told him of Steel's theory. Surprisingly, Brena had agreed Steel was on to something. In fact, Stanton was so shocked he'd choked on his coffee.

He got up and headed to the war room, which was virtually empty, less for a few agents who were finishing background checks. Another was checking the data Steel had sent them via email. This was more of a report, divulging his theories and the evidence to back them. How everything fits together around King, the bombings and his father.

Stanton walked over to the young agent, busy checking and rechecking Steel's theory. 'What you working on, son?' Stanton asked, looking over the man's shoulder.

'Oh, just the report from Agent ... sorry, Detective Steel.'

'Very well. Make sure I get this as soon as you are done.'

The agent just nodded and got back to work.

Stanton put his hands behind his back and headed back to his office. They were all a good team and didn't need him looking over their shoulders. Besides, there were other things to take care of.

# CHAPTER THIRTY-NINE

Steel had arrived at Hyde Park with plenty of time to spare. His military-style watch said it was ten-fifteen. Steel found a fast-food restaurant that was still open and ordered coffee. The place was full of teenagers and people who had just finished work and needed a quick fix before heading home. The server was a spotty teenager called Tom; his jet-black hair stuck out from under his cap, and his black-rimmed glasses kept sliding off of his nose due to sweat.

Steel paid for the coffee and put the change into the staff tips box. He found a seat that faced the door. An old habit he had picked up in the Army; that way so he could see what was coming so he could react to it. The coffee was strong, way too strong as if they had emptied a week's worth of coffee packets into the machine. The smell of greasy burgers and body odour filled the air, reminding Steel why he didn't frequent these places unless he had to.

The door sign had said the place was open until twelve. Perfect, at least he would be in the warm and dry, with plenty of people around if something happened.

Steel had no idea if the next postcard would be delivered. After all, The Sentinel would have seen that both Dollman and King had been picked up. But he was curious to see what was going to happen next.

Of course, by now, the CIA had picked up the judge as well. Steel smiled at the thought of Stanton sitting in his office, fending off phone calls from lawyers and people in high places. But then, they were there for their protection, not under arrest, not yet anyway. All it would take was one of them to crack to bring down the whole circus.

Steel sipped the coffee but tried to avoid smelling it if he could ... failed on many occasions, causing him to push the cup away.

———

At twelve-fifty, the staff closed up after Steel had been the only customer for an hour, and he still had the same cup of coffee. Steel thanked them and said goodnight before stepping into the bitter chill of the night. The small park area where the Arch stood seemed deserted.

A couple of cars passed every few minutes; commuters and taxis headed to or from home. Steel was fifteen minutes early, but there was nowhere else to wait at that hour. So, he strolled over to a bench that wasn't too far from the Arch and sat it out. He figured, rather than stand around looking suspicious, he could do that sitting down.

Steel pulled back the sleeve of his jacket and looked at the luminous dials of his watch. It was five-to.

As he rolled the sleeve back, he spotted kids heading his way. Each one must have been nineteen and was badly dressed. Two of them had trousers that hung around their waists as if the garments were too big for them; the others had named jackets and baseball caps, along with gold chains and big watches.

'Nice watch, pops. Can I have a look?' asked a tall, thin kid whose sunglasses were stuck on top of the brim of his cap.

'Sure, you can tell the time?' Steel responded, knowing what was coming next.

Four against one. Each kid had long arms, meaning a long reach, which was only good if you knew what you were doing.

Steel was easily an inch taller than the tallest of the crew, and he had more muscle and experience. These were street punks after their next payday. But today, all they would get was a good thrashing and sent home whimpering to their mothers.

'Watch, wallet, and cell phone,' said another. This kid was shorter than the others but stockier; he was probably the muscle. He figured his size would intimidate. To Steel, he was just sport.

'Look, the guy's pissed off; I've had a long day, and I'm waiting for someone,' Steel said flatly, unwilling to move, especially for them.

'I said watch, wallet and cell phone, mother fucka,' said another one, who was getting brave while he stood behind the other two.

Steel just looked at them and shot a look that said one thing: get lost, or I'm going to hurt you.

'I said *now*,' said the stocky guy and reached for Steel's jacket.

Wrong move, number one. There was a crack, and a scream as Steel grabbed the kid's hand, then twisted, popping his shoulder out of its socket. He stood and caught the foot of the next brave soul who thought he knew kung fu. Mistake number two sent the boy to the ground with a swift kick to the groan and one to the other kneecap, resulting in him yelping on a higher note than he thought possible. The leader pushed the other kid into the ring and told him to mess up Steel.

The kid got brave and angry. He yelled out a war cry and charged. Steel sidestepped him and kicked him in the small of the back; the force hurled him forwards into the two screaming accomplices. Steel looked at the leader, the "big man", who'd just turned tail and headed in several directions before focusing on one.

Steel thought he looked like a scared rabbit ... but a rabbit knew from the start when to quit.

He reached down to the one with the popped shoulder and grabbed his arm to check the time. The kid let out a shriek of pain, making Steel smile.

'Thanks, brother,' Steel said mockingly.

It was twelve o'clock; he had been distracted. Steel stopped after taking a few steps in the direction of the Arch and looked at the three men.

'Did someone pay you to rob me?' Steel yelled.

He got nothing but moans and groans.

'If I come over there, I won't be asking nicely,' Steel said in a fake angry voice.

'Yes, yes ... just chill, man,' begged the big kid.

'Who?' Steel asked.

'Don't know ... some dude in a long black coat with a hood ... looked kinda cool,' the kid replied.

Steel thought for a moment, then worked on a hunch. 'This dude, did he give you something for me?'

'Yeah, how'd you know?' said the other kid holding his balls with one hand and his knee with the other.

'I'm psychic,' Steel snarled, walking over to them.

'Really?' replied one of the kids.

'Yes, I foresee if you don't give me the postcard, I'm going to rip an arm off and beat you to death with it.' Steel rolled his eyes at the stupidity of the question.

'Wow, how did you know it was a postcard?' asked another kid, handing over the newest clue.

'It's what they teach us at the police school, numbnuts; I'm a cop,' Steel showed his ID. Leaving the kids to 'wow' at being beaten up by an NYPD cop.

———

Steel took the card, headed back to his car, climbed into the driver's seat, and shut the door. He started the engine, pulled out the postcard, and read the note.

'Christ Church Spitalfields 01:00. Come alone.'

He looked at his watch. It was five past twelve, and it was a thirty-minute drive, depending on the traffic lights.

Steel put the car into drive, took off down the street towards Glouster Place, and then right onto the A501 towards Whitechapel. It had been a while since he had been down that part of town, but he was confident he would find it without the satnav sending him all over the place.

Steel drove in silence. There wasn't much on the radio that interested him at that time in the morning. Even the Radio 2 programmes he liked weren't on yet.

The streets were relatively clear, and the traffic lights seemed in his favour. The only sound was from the three-litre engine, which growled like its namesake. Steel had always been a fan of British cars. The Aston Martin, the old Rovers, Jaguar, and not forgetting the beasts, Land Rover and Range Rover. The British automotive system had reached a peak until the VW group brought out the Golf. After that, the thing went downhill from there. Some would argue it happened earlier.

Steel was concerned that if they were made in Britain, they were British regardless of who paid the bills.

Soon, he found a parking space down the road from a church next to a clothing store. Over the way was a traditional-looking pub, with an old painted sign above the door and decorative iron surrounding the door. The only things that spoilt the traditional aesthetic look were the large glass windows and the overhangs advertising cocktails.

Steel walked towards the church. Its white stone walls and impressive two-hundred-and-twenty-five-foot steeple loomed over Steel as he stood at the gates. It had stood there since the 1700s and had stood the tests of time.

Steel looked at his watch. It was nearly one; he'd made good time. But unfortunately, the temperature change had brought a mist that didn't help with where he was standing.

Steel felt a chill run down his spine, more of a primaeval fear than anything. One of those feelings you get after years of horror movies and novels. He was standing outside an ancient church with a crypt, and it was foggy. Sure, he felt something— his imagination kicking in.

He smiled at his childish foolishness, but he felt happy he could still feel that fear.

Steel pulled up the collar of his jacket but left his hands out of his pockets. It would take too long to react, seconds pulling his hands out instead of being raised up. Seconds that could make all the difference. Steel wondered about the meeting. Had The Sentinel decided to give himself up now that everyone had been taken in ... or most at any rate?

But Steel had the feeling there was more to this than just a meeting. The Sentinel wanted something. He was desperate; something had not gone to plan, and he was stuck. It was a hell of a risk, asking the person chasing you for a favour. It was that, or Steel was the next one and the last on the list. He had, after all, caused the bomb to go off. If he hadn't been there, King might have just walked out and blown something else up. Steel shook his head. No, there was only one person responsible for the bomb going off: King.

Steel cupped his hands and blew warm air on them before rubbing them together. His long black coat reached down to the back of his ankles, but the wind had carried it up, so it flapped in the wind. Then, taking out his gloves from his pocket, Steel slipped his hands inside and pulled them tight; warm lining met with flesh without a gap.

The sudden chimes of the church signalled it was one o'clock, but Steel stood alone. He would wait five minutes before heading off.

At ten past, he gave up after waiting for an extra five, just in case. Steel walked towards the car, all the while thinking he had been played or distracted from something happening somewhere else.

Steel froze.

The hairs on the back of his neck stood to attention like he'd just been electrocuted. He turned to see a hooded figure standing by the church entrance in a long black coat.

So, naturally, The Sentinel had waited and done what The Sentinel did best ... observe.

———

Steel had walked up to the gate, then up the stone steps that led to the church.

The Sentinel was standing at the main entrance with crossed arms and leaning on the entrance wall.

He made his way by jumping around one of the walls next to a pillar. He found it strange that he didn't fear for his life, no feeling of concern or the need to watch his back. A situation he had never found himself in before.

'I take it you want something?' Steel asked as he approached the hooded figure.

But The Sentinel remained silent, as if unsure whether speaking wouldn't give away the hidden identity.

'Well, you're not here to kill me, that's for sure. If you were, I think I'd be dead,' Steel added.

The Sentinel's hooded head rocked from side to side as if to say, 'Pretty much.'

'And you're definitely not here to talk me to death,' Steel joked.

The Sentinel remained still this time, possibly not finding the pun amusing.

'So, tell me, what is it you want? All the targets are either caught or dead, thanks to you, including some agents, I may add ... sorry agent,' Steel said, correcting himself.

The Sentinel straightened as if displaying an act of defiance against the allegation.

Steel smiled and turned to face the building in front.

'You know, there used to be a street down there, Dorset Street it was called, back in the 1800s. A woman was murdered there, Mary Jane Kelly,' Steel said. 'The last victim of the Ripper, or Jack as he had come to be known. One of the greatest crimes ever committed because, even to this day, the killer is unknown. Sure, people have speculated, but no one has come forward with actual proof.' Steel turned to face The Sentinel.

'But that is what you've been after all this time, proof. Proof of a crime that was committed that went unpunished. A crime against you,' Steel said with a sympathetic tone.

'So, what is it you are after now, I wonder. There is nobody left. Even the judge has been picked up. So, who have we missed?' Steel asked, not just The Sentinel but himself.

He waited a few seconds, then growled, 'I swear if you don't start talking, Kitty, I'm out of here.'

Kitty drew back the hood and wore an impressed look. 'How long have you known?' she asked, walking over to him.

'I suspected, but it didn't hit home until I checked out the list of victims. Siar, it's Irish for West. Nice touch. So, I take it you are Cara because you don't look six months pregnant,' Steel said.

She clapped as if to congratulate him on his deduction, 'I prefer Kitty, but either will do.'

'But how did you get into the CIA, past all the vetting paperwork?' Steel asked, 'They don't just grab people off of the street, plus you would have had to have done the farm, so how'd you do it?' Steel was impressed at the infiltration by Kitty. But he had gotten help getting into the SEALs, so Steel believed she also got a boost. Someone was helping her.

Steel thought back to the list of victims. But the only family who stuck out were the Siar's. He smiled. He remembered reading that Cara, or Kitty, had a brother who was supposed to be killed in action, or KIA. So what if the CIA recruited them for their skills? After all, Forces Recon would be the perfect skillset for the CIA Black Ops programmes.

Steel stopped as a thought came to him.

Something was wrong; suddenly, the math didn't add up. So, how was it that they had both been recruited before the bombings, just in time for The Sentinel to appear?

Steel smiled again, 'The Sentinel, it's not a nickname; it's a call sign, a programme. You and your brother are part of it,' He thought hard again. 'A programme like this would have to have a mission set; they wouldn't just be a rogue call sign setting their missions. Please don't tell me your brother is Brena?' Steel asked, the identity of the second member suddenly coming into his head.

'No, my brother is dead, killed by an IED, but it wasn't one of theirs. It was one of ours. Someone killed him because of an operation he'd been involved in out there. One someone wanted to keep quiet,' Kitty explained. 'But I believe you know my sister, Trish. And no, she's not pregnant. She lost the baby through complications after the bombing that killed our parents. You see, we were also meant to be at the mall that day, but something had come up at the agency. The bomb was intended for us, Mr Steel,' Kitty said with a tearful look on her face.

'After our brother was killed, we were approached by a man in the agency. He explained The Sentinel programme, entirely off the books so nobody would know our real names or what we're doing. We could be inserted anywhere. We were brought into Stanton's section because of you, John Steel; your investigation into King brought more to the surface than what you thought,' she continued solemnly. 'But you failed to see the big picture because you were too focused on Charles King.'

Kitty moved up to Steel and looked into his blue contact lenses.

Her scent was intoxicating, a sweet perfume he only noticed when he was up close to her. Steel's eyes widened. He knew that scent; it was the same as what he had smelt before going into the hotel. It had been her that had made the drop-off in Berlin.

'So, what *is* the bigger picture?' Steel said calmly as he stared at her.

Her eyes were large and sultry. Her cheeks had a faint tint of red as the wind brushed against her bare flesh.

'Charles King was blowing up properties, but they were empty, so nobody really took that much notice apart from you.

You didn't see that the buildings were all owned by the banks. However, that was on paper; the real owner was Edward King. The buildings were worthless, but ....'

'The land, it was the land that was worth a fortune,' Steel said, looking away for a second, realising his mistake was in not digging deeper into the owner and just concentrating on bringing King down.

'Correct. However, Edward was just a pawn in this; a bigger brain had organised everything. You don't think that Edward King was the sort of person who ran in the circles of smugglers and arms dealers, do you? No, there was someone higher up in the food chain,' Kitty said, pulling the coat tighter around her as a howling breeze shot past them.

'Let's talk in the car, out of the wind,' Steel said, knowing that Kitty had walked there and not driven.

She nodded in agreement as she began to shiver from the last blast of cold air.

'Nice to see you still keep up appearances,' she said, climbing into the passenger side of the Jaguar.

'I borrowed it from ... a friend,' Steel said, pausing midsentence as if trying to find the right words.

'Nice friend. You must introduce me sometime,' Kitty laughed.

Steel smiled and nodded as he started the engine. The beast roared as he touched the gas pedal slightly. 'We'll see,' he replied, putting it into gear and pulling away from the curb.

'Where are we going?' Kitty asked with a sudden look of panic.

'Well, we could talk on the street all night, or we could talk at my place; besides, I'm hungry,' Steel answered as he put his foot down and raced through the empty streets.

'So, this house of yours, is it far?' She wriggled about on the leather seat like a cat trying to find a comfortable spot to relax in.

'About an hour, just a little place in the country; it's not much, but it's home,' Steel replied, trying to look humble. 'Try and get some sleep; you're safe ....'

Steel stopped; she had already succumbed to the warmth and comfort of the car and was fast asleep. Steel smiled as he watched the sleeping 'Cara', but to him, she would always be Kitty, the shy and innocent agent.

He turned his gaze back to the road, and the smile faded. Kitty was investigating a big fish, as she called it. But it wasn't a fish; it was a shark, a shark that apparently worked in the CIA.

That was why she and Trish were there. They were looking for someone in their own department, and Steel had an idea who it was. His gut would say it was Brena—or not so much gut feeling as a need for him to be the one. If Kitty was right, this wasn't just some guy in an office; this was top brass.

Steel looked over at the sleeping woman again and smiled. He was glad she had made it, glad she was in his car. He searched the telephone list on the car's media centre; he thought about calling Stanton to let him know Kitty was alive but would leave out The Sentinel details. The highlighted box with Avery's name flashed, but Stanton scrolled up to Jamerson's number.

After a couple of rings, he picked up. 'Yes, John?' the gruff-sounding man asked.

'We have a guest. Can you get the cook to rustle something up? Nothing too fancy,' Steel requested, knowing the cook would probably go overboard with the food.

'I'm sure she would be delighted to make something other than steak and chips,' Jamerson said mockingly.

Steel smiled and shook his head, and tried to keep his voice even. 'Oh, one other thing, I need to speak to HQ; we have a problem.'

Jamerson replied, 'Right you are, boss.' And hung up. Leaving Steel to power on down the street until he hit the A1 and followed that until the M1 Northbound.

As he drove in silence, his mind sorted through facts, trying to leave personal feelings out of it, considering they could always cloud a detective's judgment.

Someone in the CIA had been helping Edward King and making money, and a lot of it. The only questions now were, who was it and were the new targets in CIA custody safe?

# CHAPTER FORTY

SIMMS LOOKED UP AS HE LAY ON THE FLOOR. HE WAS covered in blood and brain matter, but it was Dorson's. The shot had come from the doorway; someone had come in at the last second and taken out Dorson. Simms tried to wipe the blood from his eyes, but his hands were also covered. The round had hit the right spot, taking most of Dorson's head off and making a mess of anything in front of him. Suddenly, Simms felt a tug on his arm, and he was being led somewhere in the room. Then the sound of running water.

Was it a shower in the bathroom?

The other person said nothing; they just shoved him into the stall and under the running water. Simms raised his hands as if to shield himself from any bullets, even though he knew it was pointless. The shot had been silent, which meant a suppressor. Dorson never heard them come in; that said, military training, possible black ops and special forces.

As the water ran over his face, it washed away the caked blood from his eyes. Simms blinked several times, allowing his eyes to adjust to their freedom. He leaned back and looked up. His face changed from a look of fear to one of relief.

'I was wondering when you were going to get here; bastard nearly had me,' Simms said, trying not to show he had nearly pissed his pants.

'Sorry, traffic,' replied a voice from outside the bathroom.

'What traffic? The route was clear,' Simms yelled back, feeling the shooter was playing with him.

'You're alive; he's dead. What's the problem?'

Simms struggled out and headed back into the main room.

'What now?' Simms asked, looking at Dorson's body. The entry wound was around three millimetres in diameter, and the exit was the size of a quarter. The bullet had entered through the right side of the back of his head. It exited through the left front, just above the eye, before finally embedding itself into the brick wall.

'We hang up a "do not disturb" sign on the door and come back later; in the meantime, grab your shit.'

Simms looked over at the bed. There sat Trish, unscrewing the six-inch suppressor from the pistol. Simms looked at the weapon. The sleek black polymer weapon looked more space-age than the conventional armaments he used. Even the bullets were special. 5.7x28mm 40gr armour-piercing rounds resembled miniature rifle rounds more than the standard 9mm bullets he was used to. The clip was a twenty-round mag. It was a nice little number that made a lot of mess.

Simms walked over to Trish and watched as she tucked the pistol into the holster at the small of her back. She stood and smoothed her tight blue jeans and rearranged her quarter-length leather jacket; her white blouse complemented the look, along with the ankle-high boots.

'Come on, let's get you cleaned up. Don't worry about the computer and stuff; the team will take it back to the lab,' Trish explained, but Simms wasn't worried. It was nearly over, and he could get his life back again, or at least the new one the agency would have for him when the case was over.

———

Kitty woke suddenly. The sound of the beach crept into her dreams. She looked around, confused and disorientated. There was no beach, only a gravel path which led to a massive turn-of-the-century stately home. Kitty rubbed her eyes and tried to read her watch, but she hadn't fully awoken yet, and everything close was a blur.

'Where the hell are we?' Kitty complained as she took in the view before her.

The path was lined with tiny lights guiding the way like a landing strip. The hall was a three-story wonder that she had only seen the likes of on TV. Spotlights from the gardens illuminated the outside, giving it a mysterious look. Four stone pillars marked the entrance, and a statue fountain to the front acted as a turning circle for visitors.

'Home,' Steel said with a smile.

Her eyes widened as they drew near. She had seen big houses and mansions in the States, but nothing like this. 'Wow, whose house is it anyway, and do they know we're coming?' Kitty asked, her mouth agape.

Steel laughed to himself. 'They have a fair idea,' he said with a childish grin. As he brought the Jaguar to a gentle halt, Jamerson opened Kitty's door and stepped to the side to allow her room to exit the vehicle.

'Good morning, miss; I hope you had a pleasant journey?' Offering his most Oxford accent, Jamerson bowed slightly.

Kitty swung out her legs and pulled herself out, all the while her gaze captured by the front of the hall. She had to admit it was the grandest place she had seen, less for hotels, but an actual stately home; she had never had the pleasure.

'Chef has laid on a small snack for you and the lady in the dining room, sir,' Jamerson said, trying to seem pompous.

'Thanks, Sarge, and you can drop the act; we're working,' Steel said, racing around the front of the car towards the entrance.

Kitty's eyes widened as she looked at Steel, realising his Lord status wasn't a cover at all; it was real.

'Are you really—'

'Hungry, thirsty, in need of a stiff martini with gin, yes.' Steel grabbed her by the arm and dragged her inside. There was no time for sightseeing or explanations; they had work to do. 'Can you ...?' Steel asked with a desperate look at Jamerson.

'Certainly can, boss,' Jamerson said with his broad London accent.

They passed through the dining room first to grab a snack before getting to work. Steel opened the double doors and stood there for a few seconds.

'I see Chef has gone slightly overboard again,' he said at the sight of the banquet before them. Steel turned to apologise, but Kitty had already rushed forward and filled her plate.

'I guess it beats MRE meals?' Steel strolled past the stack of plates and started to fill one with roast chicken, salads, and miniature sausage rolls. Chef had indeed surpassed herself, but Steel suspected she knew he would send the remaining food to the shelters and soup kitchens. But he didn't mind; most of the folks at the shelters were ex-servicemen who had fallen on hard times. He sometimes employed street people as informants and infiltrators, as he liked to call them. He would pay them well, but most of all, he was giving them a purpose and not charity.

'Kitty ... Cara,' Steel said, shooting her an apologetic look.

She just smiled and shrugged as if to say either name would do, unable to speak due to the lobster claw in her mouth.

'We need to come up with a plan before we go back to New York.'

She shot him a puzzled look. 'New York? Don't you mean Langley?' Kitty asked after swallowing.

'King and the judge will be in New York; that is where they will have their accidents. Whoever this is can't afford another death on the grounds. Falkner looked like a suicide, another two, and you have a killer on base ... no, they are there, and my guess is whoever is running the show will be there to watch or do it themselves,' Steel explained.

Kitty thought for a moment and nodded in agreement. Steel had a point; the question was, did he have a *fast plane*?

Steel knew they had very little time before they had to leave.

Kitty followed Steel into the study and watched him exchange his contact lenses for a pair of sunglasses that had been plugged into a special loading station. He grabbed a laptop and a cell phone and then hurried back towards the door. Kitty watched with interest and a moderate amount of confusion at what he was doing.

Steel darted here and there, gathering items she didn't quite see before they disappeared into a black military-style canvas carrier.

'Come on,' Steel ordered, and they headed back to the car.

'Where to? We just got here, and ...' Kitty held up her plate.

Steel lifted his arms in a show of annoyance at her display.

'Right, bring it with you; I'm driving anyway,' Steel tossed the bag onto the back seat and then opened the driver's side and climbed behind the wheel.

Kitty hurried into the car; her plate and mouth were still

full. She hadn't had real food for days, and this was definitely making up for it.

'Where we goin'?' Kitty asked before popping another sausage roll into her mouth.

'The airport. We have to try and get to New York before your targets get a visit,' Steel said, pulling over his seat belt and fasting it. He knew it would be close, but he had to try. Jamerson would be phoning the pilot to tell him to get the plane ready. The aircraft would be ready in minutes as the pilot always did regular pre-checks when Steel was in the country for just such reasons.

Steel pressed the starter button, put it first, and raced down the driveway towards the gated entrance. It would be a thirty-minute drive to the airport. Enough time for Kitty to finish her banquet on a plate. All Steel could hope for was good weather, them being on time, or better still, something stalling the agents who would be leaving for New York.

––––––

The London Oxford Airport was an old airfield established in 1935. By 1968, it had flourished to become one of the busiest in Britain. It was primarily used by smaller aircraft such as Seneca and Gulfstreams and, of course, Steel's Cessna Citation X private jet.

He pulled onto the small airfield and found a parking space near the Aviation Academy. He and Kitty ran from the lot and headed for the jet that Steel had indicated they were using with an outstretched arm.

There was a low whir as the turbines warmed up and a stream of light from the cabin showed the open doorway, ready to receive them.

'Hope this is a fast plane,' Kitty yelled over the noise.

Steel didn't reply; he just urged her to hurry up. A young woman greeted them and helped them aboard when they reached the steps. As Steel got on, the woman pulled the doorsteps up, sealing the aircraft. The co-pilot looked around at her, and she gave the thumbs up. Steel strapped in, and Kitty did the same. It was all done with perfection, almost with military precision. They were in the air and en route to New York minutes after parking on the tarmac.

Kitty had to admit; she was impressed. The house, the jet. Whomever Steel was working for was connected.

'So, I take it you're not really NYPD, not with a pad like that for a cover,' Kitty said as she finished off the last of the food. 'You British Secret Service or something ... you know, the whole Bond thing?' The question had only just popped into her head, but the more she thought about it, the more sense it made. It would explain the house and the company jet. The great hall was probably the headquarters.

She thought back to Steel's file, and Kitty couldn't remember reading anything about his childhood. Just that he went to Oxford; his father was a minister in British Intelligence and a businessman who owned a massive family company. Steel's mother had been a nurse before getting pregnant with him. But then, his whole past was vague. He'd joined the Army at a young age, where he had joined the Royal Tactical Combat Engineers as a private, not an officer. Later, after his third year and first stripe, he was picked by the regiment for selection with the SAS; he passed with flying colours and served with them for several years.

The subsequent note stated that he had joined the US Navy SEAL team. Why was it a mystery, but some army guys just like a challenge? She had heard a tale about one British soldier who went through every special forces selection. But on completion, he turned down the chance to join because he just wanted to do a selection to see if he could pass it.

'Who else have you got inside, apart from your sister?' Steel asked as he swivelled the cream leather chair to face Kitty.

Kitty tried to look shocked at the insinuation, but Steel just shot her a come-on look.

'Just two more people, and that is all you need to know,' Kitty said sternly.

Steel smiled and nodded. He could understand she wanted to keep the other person's identity secret, but Steel needed to know whom he could trust. Then Steel thought for a moment; there was only one possible choice out of all the people he had met. Steel cracked a smile and sat back in the chair.

'So, how long have you and your sister worked with Dutton and Simms undercover?' Steel questioned, causing Kitty to stare at him with a look of surprise.

'What gave them away?' Kitty asked with a smile.

Steel looked behind him as the young stewardess brought two glasses of champagne on a silver salver.

Kitty took hers first after Steel beckoned her, then he took the remaining glass and thanked the woman before she returned to the back of the plane.

'It was the way you all acted around each other,' Steel said. 'As if you had been through a lot together, even though you had just started. I've seen it before, back in the Army. People learn to know each others' moves and thoughts. This takes time and experience, which neither of you has had with each other,' Steel explained.

He didn't want to admit that it had been a complete fluke— that he had just guessed, given the way the others treated her, Dutton and Simms seemed the most likely of candidates to have worked with her.

Trish had been harder to read. He had only seen her a

couple of times, and then it was for a few minutes, so he couldn't get an accurate reading of her.

'It makes sense, really; you needed Simms to cover for you in Berlin. I thought it strange he would have sent you to a target's apartment alone,' Steel said with a smile as if it were all coming together. 'So, when did you leave for Amsterdam? The minute I went to the meeting at the cafè with my contact, or later?' It was the one piece of the puzzle he couldn't get.

'After you left, sure, it was a big risk, but as you said, Simms was there to cover for me.' Kitty smiled as if to congratulate him on his deduction.

The flight would take around four hours at the present speed. The Cessna Citation X had been voted the fastest private jet in the world, which was probably why Steel wanted one. The flight would land around midnight at JFK Airport. It would be close, to be sure. Steel had arranged for a delay of the team's departure from Langley by having another postcard sent; this, of course, had a double effect. The first would, of course, have the team running over themselves to try and break it; on the other hand, the person they were after would know it was a fake and would try and get out of wasting time. Steel figured whoever made it to New York had to be part of the cleanup operation.

It was just over an hour's flight from Washington to New York. Steel would have preferred they drive; however, flying was quicker, and they were running out of time. Steel had no doubt that word had gotten out he was on his way.

He sipped his drink and looked out the window. It was a seemingly pointless act due to the lack of visibility in the dark of the night, but he found it comforting. Next, he needed to gather his thoughts to formulate a plan. If they were going up against someone in the agency, that meant they had to get it right, or they could be classed as the enemy.

. . .

The flight was smooth and without incident or turbulence, almost like driving down a street when you were late for work and hitting nothing but green lights. Kitty had fallen asleep on the couch at the rear, leaving Steel to think in peace. He had come up with a plan, but it would be complicated, and they would only have one shot at it.

Steel pulled out his phone and started to make calls to people back in New York. They would land in two hours, which gave his people plenty of time to get the ball rolling.

# CHAPTER FORTY-ONE

AVERY STANTON SAT IN HIS OFFICE CHAIR WITH A BROAD smile on his face. He'd just had a phone call; Steel was on the way back to the US, specifically New York. For Stanton, this meant one thing: it was almost over, his boy was coming back, and they had most of the targets safe and sound. The London office would be flying the others over early in the morning. Stanton had made it clear to the top brass that he didn't feel comfortable with them all meeting in New York. Still, Director Headly thought it best, considering the loss of Falkner.

Stanton had voiced his reservations; he didn't know anyone in the New York office. Sure, he had met a few at conferences but didn't know any of them. The ones he had been friends with had all retired or moved to greener pastures.

———

The new postcard had come in around eight o'clock that evening, and it had gotten everyone giddy but not Stanton. In fact, he was getting bored of it all, bored of playing this killer's game. All he wanted was to go home, eat a TV dinner, and watch sports.

He'd left Brena with the postcard while he flew to New York, even though Stanton still felt something amiss about Brena, but then there were no other agents he could call on. Trish, Simms, and now Dorson were missing. Someone he had definitely gotten their ass chewed for from upstairs because the word came down that Headly wanted results and fast. Stanton remembered how much Headly had opposed bringing Steel in on the case—called Steel a loose cannon. Stanton had smiled at the description; of course, he was, and that was why Stanton needed him.

He went to a small safe and took out his passport, a long brown leather wallet, and an HK SFP9 pistol with a polished steel top slide and placed them into a metal briefcase. Stanton closed the case and headed for the door. He stopped and smiled at his secretary as he walked out but said nothing. She smiled back and nodded slightly. Stanton returned the gesture and headed for the elevator. As Brenda watched him leave, a solitary tear rolled down her face as if to say goodbye.

———

Brena moved about frantically, yelling orders and trying to get ahead of the task. Find out who the latest target was going to be. He didn't want to be there; he wanted to be on the plane with Stanton, but Headly had insisted someone should stay and oversee the investigation regarding the latest clue. Usually, Brena would have been proud to have been chosen for such a task of leadership, but to him, this was just a numbers game. He was the only one left. All the agents with him were either new or too inexperienced to carry out the task.

Brena was annoyed he wasn't heading up the investigation

into the disappearance of the three agents, but that was another department's baby. He was just tidying up an almost-finished case. To Brena's disappointment, they had all of the Sentinel's targets, and Steel had broken the case wide open.

They had King and were building a case against him with the help of the 11<sup>th</sup> Precinct and Captain Brant's homicide division; after all, it was they who had tried to indict King's son. So, with the fixer being out of the way, King was going down for a long time, his co-conspirators along with him.

Brena felt his throat grow raw from the shouting and picked up his coffee mug. A disappointed look crossed his face as he stared at the empty vessel. He walked past the busy agents and went to get a refill. It was nearly twenty-two hundred, and this wasn't the thing he was hoping to be doing at ten o'clock on a Friday night. Nevertheless, the thought of Steel returning late in the afternoon the next day amused Brena. Sure, Steel would have solved the case, but it would be Brena's face on the front page of the newspapers for being the agent in charge.

He topped up the blue mug with the CIA badge on both sides. He preferred it black, with no sugar. A proper cup of coffee, or so he would say. Brena walked back to check on the team's progress.

One agent was doing background on King, tying up loose ends for the NYPD and the DA. Another was finding anything to reference the picture on the postcard. It was of a wild bird, a goose or swan of some kind, with a background of an aerial photograph of an ancient hill site for a castle or village.

The female agent was busy with location software that would identify the site. But Brena didn't seem hopeful; in fact, he was confused about why there was another card. Undoubtedly, there wasn't anyone else left to catch, was there?

Brena sipped his coffee and paced about impatiently, like a child waiting for Christmas presents. To him, this was torcher.

He had to be on a plane to New York; it was, if anything, imperative. But Stanton was taking the company jet; if Brena were to go, it would be by a civilian airline. He thought about helicopters, but he'd never get clearance, not from Headly anyway. Brena sat down at Trish's terminal and looked up flights to New York using an airline site. There was a Delta flight leaving Ronald Reagan Airport in the next hour. Brena stood up and walked over to the female agent.

'I've just got to go off base for a while, something I have to check out to reference the case,' Brena lied, but he was her superior, so she didn't need to know the ins and outs. She nodded and went back to work. Brena smiled and looked at his watch. The airport wasn't that far. Time enough to get there, get a ticket, and check in. He didn't need much, just his ID and his gun.

---

The Cessna Citation X landed at JFK. A storm had just hit, bringing a rain of biblical proportions. Steel and Kitty hurried off the plane and into a waiting vehicle a friend had sent to pick them up. As soon as the rear passenger doors had closed, the blacked-out Yukon SUV powered off the tarmac and headed for the exit. Traffic on the Brooklyn Bridge was backed up halfway down the Brooklyn-Queens Expressway.

'Nick, who arrived from the Langley office?' Steel asked the driver.

Nick was a big man, with around two hundred pounds of muscle from too much time in a prison gym. His tattoos were barely visible on his dark skin. He was of Jamaican descent and had a nose for sniffing out information.

Nick stroked his goatee and looked around at the traffic to

see if there was any sign of moving forward. 'Nobody yet, but I got feelers out.'

'Are they secure?' Steel asked, looking at the time ticking away.

'Yes, they separated them and put them into safe houses, as you suggested. I think the knowledge about what happened in Langley had convinced them to agree with you,' Nick said, pulling into an open space and then waiting for the next gap to appear.

The traffic was slow and was beginning to annoy Steel. His plan was perfect, but it would be for nothing if they couldn't get to the meeting point in time.

'Are they OK with the second phase?' Steel asked, leaning forward, so his head was almost through the gap between the two front seats.

'They were not happy, but after your friends convinced them it was you who was taking the blame if it went wrong, they agreed,' Nick said with a chuckle in his voice.

'Oh, lovely. No pressure then,' Steel said, raising an eyebrow.

'Phase two? What was phase one?' Kitty asked, puzzled at what they were heading into.

'Well, phase one was getting everyone together. Step two— oh, you are going to love phase two,' Steel said with excitement.

He spent the next half hour breaking it down for her and requesting her assistance and that of her colleagues.

Kitty took out her cell and pressed the speed-dial icon for Trish.

'You're out of your mind; you know that, don't you?' Kitty said to Steel while she waited for Trish to pick up.

Steel just shrugged and checked the time on his watch again. The meeting was at two o'clock; it was now midnight.

Steel looked over to Kitty and began to speak with the cell on loudspeaker, so Steel could hear.

Trish had picked up and explained what had happened with Dorson and Simms.

Kitty shook her head in disbelief; she never figured Dorson was capable of that, not him. She could have imagined most of the others in the team but not him.

'Where are you now?' Steel interjected.

'We're heading to New York; we are just outside the Philadelphia border crossing,' Trish replied with a curious tone.

'Where is Dorson's body?' Steel pulled out his cell and prepared to send a text.

'The Fairway Hotel, Arlington, Room 213,' Simms said with a regretful tone.

Steel sent a quick text to someone and placed the cell back into his pocket. Kitty gave Steel a curious look. 'Why do you have a cleaning crew on speed dial?' Kitty asked, stopping Trish from speaking.

'The question is, why don't *you*?' Steel replied with a straight face.

Nick laughed out loud and shook his head.

'When you get to New York, head for this address,' Steel ordered Dutton and Trish. He gave them the time and place and what they were meant to do when they got there.

Dutton and Trish said they understood and hung up, leaving an awkward silence in the car.

Kitty stared at Steel, trying to make him out. 'So, why do this? I have my reasons, but what have you got against this guy, whoever he is? Is it a justice thing that you want to bring him in?'

'You brought me in, giving me clues to prove what you had already discovered. But you couldn't do anything, not without proof or indeed blowing your cover. So, you needed someone to investigate,' Steel explained.

Kitty raised her eyebrows in astonishment at his investigative mind.

'But you never counted on a killer cleaning up his mess. Okay, you built devices that would cause damage, but those were meant to go off when the people weren't there, hence the minimum of destruction. But someone cottoned on to your plan and decided to use that to hang you; sure, if you were caught and nobody got hurt, you might be able to sway the jury. But if people died, that would be a different story. So, you go to jail, and the killer goes free,' Steel continued as he looked out the smoked glass.

'What drives me, you asked. At first, it was a challenge, but now it's for whole other reasons ... that day, I saved over thirty people by securing the device. Someone else set off the bomb. I watched as those people were engulfed in flames or ripped to pieces. Yes, I want justice, but this time the bastard isn't going to walk; I'll make sure of that,' Steel promised grimly.

'Fine words, Mr Steel, but until you have lost someone, I'll take the whole justice speech with a pinch of salt,' Kitty said angrily.

Suddenly, she caught a look that Nick shot her, a look of contempt over something she had said. As he went to speak, Steel interrupted. 'You are right, of course; I can't imagine what you are going through; I apologise,' Steel said humbly.

Kitty smiled softly, feeling she had been too harsh. After all, he was helping her, and as he said, he had witnessed everything, including those being injured.

'We need to get out of this,' Steel said, looking around at the stationary traffic. 'We need to run.' He got up and headed to the trunk to retrieve a long canvas bag. 'Nick, meet us when you get there; you know what to do.' He caught his friend's reflection in the rearview.

As he slammed the trunk shut, Kitty stepped out and followed Steel as they weaved in between vehicles until they reached the bridge's footpath. Nick leant back into the seat of the SUV and rubbed his face with his massive hands out of frustration. He knew he would be there for hours and he would miss the party.

———

It was a fifteen-minute walk to Brookfield Place and around eight minutes to run there. For Steel, this was where it all began, and he would make sure that was where it would come to an end. The plan was in motion; Steel just hoped everyone played their part, or this could go south real fast.

As they approached the mall, Steel stopped on Vesey Street and looked across at the renovated structure. To Steel's annoyance, they found that the front was cordoned off by fencing while continuing the construction, meaning they would have to go to the underground parking structure. In addition, the blast from King's bomb had done significant structural damage. Still, the architects thought it was also a good time to iron out issues they had discovered while it was open.

Steel gave the structure another once-over before rushing forwards and over the street with Kitty close behind. All the while, she was hoping his plan would work and they would flush out the real killer.

Brookfield Place wasn't just a building; it was several different structures combined over a shopping mall; this meant many entrances, but they just needed one. Steel pulled out his phone and went to a city map, notably over the mall. He needed to know alternative entry points. Steel smiled, tucked the cell back into his pocket, and started down West Street towards Liberty Street and Pumphouse Park.

There was an entrance out of sight from the street, with trees and bushes in the park giving perfect cover. All he had to do was break in.

The park was quiet and shrouded in darkness. It was half one in the morning, with a biting chill in the air. As Steel worked on the lock, Kitty kept a lookout.

'Why are we breaking in if they are expecting us?' Kitty asked, confused and cold.

'They are expecting me, not you, and they definitely aren't expecting me so soon. Don't forget; we just travelled from the UK; that was an eight-hour flight,' Steel said with a grin.

Kitty stared at him as he finished the final tumbler. 'So, why set the meeting for now?'

'A, it gives everyone time to get here. B, it allows the agencies to set up their men that they think they will need,' Steel explained as he inched open the door, allowing Kitty through first and then himself.

'What do you mean they think they will need?' Kitty asked, confused as ever. Sure, Steel had explained his plan, but by the sounds of what he was now saying, he'd left out some details. Steel said nothing; he just gave a quick smile before racing down the expansive ground floor of the mall's south side. Empty glass window fronts reflected their images as they moved quickly to the spot that Steel had chosen to be the meeting place. However, they weren't going there; they were going to the first floor above.

They used the motionless escalators to reach the level above. All the while, Steel shifted his gaze to pick up any movement or anything that might cause him concern but found the way clear. There were blank spaces where the 360-degree view security would eventually go. This was both a good and a bad thing. It was great that nobody could see their approach, but on the other hand, if something were to happen, it wasn't captured on tape.

Kitty followed Steel, keeping low but moving quickly across the dusty stone floor. Seeing the empty stores saddened Kitty as she remembered what it used to look like. She had visited the scene sometime after the explosion. Her CIA credentials had seen her pass security without too many questions. That and a friendly smile could always open doors for her.

'How do you know they will all show?' Kitty asked with a look of doubt.

'Simple, I told them I knew who the real killer was,' Steel said with conviction.

'And *do* you?' Kitty asked, grabbing Steel's arm and holding him fast in place.

Steel stopped, looked down at her hand on his arm, and then noticed her tearful blue eyes.

'In truth, I won't know until we get to the meeting. I know you want your revenge, and I know you also want to be the one who brings him down; just be patient,' Steel said, resting a large hand on hers.

Kitty smiled and nodded. She knew if anyone could find the real killer, it would be Steel.

Smiling, he nodded over to the balcony that overlooked the ground floor, the exact place where he had been months ago. Kitty looked over to the glass railings and then let go of his arm. 'Shall we?' Kitty asked calmly.

'*I* shall. I need you to do something else,' Steel said solemnly.

'Do what?' she asked sternly, having the feeling he was trying to keep her out of the way.

'I need you to find a bomb,' Steel said with an expressionless face. His mood had suddenly changed. He had cut off all feelings and had slipped back into the mindset of his old cold agent self.

'Where should I start?' Kitty's voice held a hint of fear. She had never seen anything like him before, not like this. It was as if he were a completely different person.

'My guess is the parking garage. Pack a van with explosives, and you would bring the whole building down,' Steel replied, looking back at the balcony. Flashes from the past blurred with the present like two films overlapping each other on the same screen. Thoughts started to run through his head ... and questions.

'What was the bomb for?'

Kitty looked over at Steel, who wore a puzzled look.

'Probably to level the building and kill us all, I suppose. Who cares? I'll find it and stop it,' Kitty asked, perplexed.

'No, not the one now ... if there is one, and I'm quite certain there is. I mean the one King had. It was a single device meant to cause devastation but not big enough to "level" this place, as you colourfully put it. He wasn't here to kill anyone because that wasn't his MO. By all accounts, he was a coward who hid behind his father and his money, but a killer he wasn't; he didn't have the balls for it. So, what was it for?'

'Who knows, and who cares? The sick bastard is dead, and now we have the chance to get rid of another killer and stop his bomb,' Kitty stated, looking confident.

Steel nodded, and his expression changed again as he put on his cold, game face. 'Let's go,' he said coolly.

Kitty turned and headed towards the lower levels.

'Kitty?' Steel called out suddenly, forcing her to turn around.

'What?' She hoped for something inspirational from him.

'You're going the wrong way; it's over there,' Steel said, pointing over to the north.

Kitty quietly scratched her nose with an extended middle finger. Steel smiled as he got the message, and they went their separate ways.

———

Steel moved to the spot where he had observed King on the day of the explosion. Not much had changed as if they were rebuilding using the same reference to the former building.

Below, the targets had gathered along with the agents from the justice department playing babysitters. The targets looked worried, the agents on edge. Both with the same idea: had they just walked into a trap? Steel would give it a few minutes and wait for the rest of the party to show up. He did not doubt that Graaf and Dollman would not be too far away, and neither would whoever was coming from Langley.

Steel checked his watch as two more agents arrived, along with Dollman and Graaf in tow.

'So, what's this all about anyway?' Dollman yelled as if to make himself seem superior to the rest of them.

'It's about all of you,' Steel said, his voice echoing around the empty building. 'It's about all of you being part of a plan to bomb the city.'

All the targets started to talk at once, and the volume of voices grew louder as they started to compete with one another.

Steel yelled, causing them to become silent and look at him as he walked down the stationary escalator. 'Most of all, it's about you all being loose ends.' Steel had a stern, displeased look on his face. 'Now, personally, I don't care if someone is taking you guys out; they're doing the world a favour by all accounts.

But I do care about the innocent people who died in this very spot to cover up what you people helped do all those years ago. So, now I was wondering what all of you had in common—yes, you all did things to help dear little Charles get off of death row, but there was something more, something I couldn't put my finger on at first.' Steel moved about the massive mall lobby.

'You all had one specific thing in common on one particular day. Now, agents back in Langley had been researching your movements before the bombing to try and put you and Charles King together. And at a stretch, they had, but all these meetings happened separately, weeks apart. But then I got to thinking about the bomb that went off here. It wasn't large enough to bring down a building, but it would cause some serious damage if it were in, say ... a parking garage. I bet that all of you were downstairs waiting for a meeting that was never going to happen; in fact, I bet the killer even went as far as to tell you all where to park?'

Looks of realisation washed over their faces as they understood they had been set up that day, that the bomb was meant for them.

'Well, if it was meant for us, why was it up here and not down there?' Graaf asked, wiping the sweat from his brow with his handkerchief.

'When I saw King leave his building, he didn't have a bag; the next time I saw him here, he had a long heavy-looking canvas bag. King had gotten the bomb from in here, and he was probably told to drop it off in a certain location, namely where you were all parked,' Steel stated, taking note of all their expressions.

'But he set it off up here, not downstairs,' Dollman said, his arms flapping about.

'King was on his way downstairs when he saw security; he

thought they were after him when they were after a homeless man,' Steel explained.

'A homeless guy?' Graaf repeated, his brow furrowed.

'Well, actually, it was me in disguise. But the point is Charles King panicked. He had a bomb. The cops were coming, so he did the only thing a spineless sod would do; he dropped the bag and made a hostage situation,' Steel said, looking over at Edward King.

He was saying nothing or making eye contact.

'Someone sent Charles there, not just to set up the bomb, but to die with it also. A great plan by all accounts. The killer got rid of all loose ends simultaneously. With what was in the device, the corner of CSU wouldn't be able to get anything to identify the bodies,' Steel said, walking up and down, his gaze fixed on the targets. 'But Charles had to go; whether it was downstairs or right here, he had to go. He knew too much. He had already dodged the bombing bullet, but what if someone found something else? No, he was a liability, so they killed him along with thirty other people.' Steel's voice was calm.

'But in your report, you said you had secured the kill switch by wrapping a bandage around his hand, so what happened?' asked a familiar voice.

Steel looked behind the line of people and saw Brena standing there with his agents.

'Just before the explosion, I remembered the window being broken in one specific place,' Steel answered. Walking over to the replacement pane of glass, he touched it where the small spiderweb shape had appeared in his memories.

'A gunshot?' Brena asked.

'A sniper, to be more precise, from over there,' Steel said, pointing at the river.

'So, what are we thinking, Mermaid or Sponge Bob?' said one of the agents from justice.

'I'd say boat. The shot is too far away to come from over the other side unless it was a highly trained sniper. It's too high for it to be shot from the grounds,' Steel answered as he pointed back at the view.

'They shot the bag?' Brena was unconvinced. 'Sure, you're not saying that to cover your ass?' S

Steel didn't move; he just continued to stare out of the window. 'You are right, of course; I could be lying or mistaken.' Steel said, causing Brena to smile and the others to gasp. Steel reached out a congratulatory hand.

Brena smirked and took the handshake to mean he had won. Brena was on the floor in seconds. Steel had grabbed his hand, put him into a lock, and rapidly handwrapped a bandage around his hand. Steel stood up, and Brena clambered to his feet.

'So, Brena, did I drop the ball?' Steel asked after proving his point.

Brena sulked in defeat and struggled with the bandage around his hand.

'I believe the sniper was a contingency plan in case something screwed up. All of you could go later, but he had to go then. With Charles dead with a bomb in his possession, the business could continue, and every past deed would be forgotten,' Steel added.

'Business, what business?' Dollman asked, a look of concern on his face.

'Edward King was making money from the bombings. The buildings would be damaged beyond repair. His firm would be contracted to clear the site and build whatever monstrosity was on the drawing board,' Steel explained. 'Clearly, when Charles was arrested for being the bomber, your business took a dive; people were adding things together. But after he had been cleared, there was a doubt, but business was coming back,'

Steel moved about as he spoke. ' So, what to do? Well, it would be simple, if your son was killed in a bomb attack, you would get the sympathy vote, and business would boom again. Unfortunately, someone had left the bomb in the public lockers for him to pick up. Leaving the bag downstairs was too risky; someone might see it. So, all he had to do was pick it up and drop it off,' Steel stared at Edward King, his expression condemning.

'And he couldn't get that right,' King said, rolling his eyes and crossing his arms.

'You sent your own son on a suicide mission?' Graaf asked a look of disgust on his face. 'And they call me an evil bastard?'

'OK, so where is your proof?' King said with a knowing grin.

'In truth, it's all theory. In time, we will fit it all together, but for now, we have nothing,' Steel said with a broad smile and raised his arms as though he were tossing something in the air, making King's smile grow. 'But I don't need any; you are all dead anyway. The killer is after you, and I've no doubt he will find you.'

'What, this Sentinel person?' King continued wearing his smug look.

'No, The Sentinel wanted you found so you could tell the truth; someone else wants you guys dead,' Steel explained with a strange sense of enjoyment.

'Who then?' Brena asked, confused at where Steel was going with this.

'Good question,' Steel said, looking in Brena's direction.

# CHAPTER FORTY-TWO

KITTY CREPT DOWN TO THE PARKING LOT, STICKING TO THE shadows and avoiding anything that could give off light. She had no idea what she was looking for, but she knew it had to be big to bring the building down on top of them.

As Kitty exited the stairwell and stepped onto the lot, she found nothing unusual at first. A few parked cars were there, but she put that down to the justice department and the Feds. She walked further in, but nothing stuck out, no big trucks or vans. Eighteen-wheelers would have to go elsewhere as the ceiling was too low for them to enter.

Kitty turned to walk back and report Steel's theory was wrong.

That was when she stopped and looked around again. Besides the typical blacked-out Yukon SU's, there were twelve cars parked at irregular intervals, some of which was next to the roof supports. Carefully, Kitty walked over to one of the cars and looked inside. The whole interior had been stripped, and it was filled with explosives. If one of these went off, it would be devastating; if all went off, it would be catastrophic.

Kitty backed off slowly but then picked up speed. She
began running for her life and those upstairs.

———

Kitty pulled out her phone and pressed the speed dial for
Steel's cell. She needed to tell him, warn him.

'Yes, what's up?' Steel asked, shocked she was calling so
soon.

'You were wrong about the bomb,' Kitty said, trying to
sprint and talk simultaneously.

'Really, that's odd; I'm usually quite good at things like
that,' Steel said arrogantly.

'There's not one! There are at least twelve! And they are all
car bombs, and I do mean *car bombs*,' Kitty declared.

'Kitty, I want you to get out and find a cop as soon as you
can. Let him know, but I want you away from this building, do
you understand?' Steel growled.

'Yes, but what about you?' Kitty asked, heading for the
nearest exit.

'We'll be fine; you just get yourself away,' Steel said before
hanging up and pocketing his phone. Steel turned to the others.
An unsurprised look crossed his face. 'So, who told someone
where we were meeting?'

Everyone looked around, surprised at the question.

'No one, why?' Dollman spoke up, pushing his chest out as
if taking the question as an insult.

'Well, unless someone just left twelve cars packed with
explosives here overnight before they took them further, I
would say we were blown. So, who talked?' Steel asked again.

The men in front of him began to panic. Agents got onto
their radios and cell phones to call for backup, but all the while,
Steel just stood and stared at the chaos before him.

'Aren't you going to do anything?' Dollman turned to Brena.

'Like what? There are twelve devices, and I'm not trained for that shit,' Brena said with a tone of alarm in his voice.

'Well, I suggest we leave, possibly through the north entrance,' Steel put forth.

'Why? Is it further from the blast?' asked Graaf.

'Yes, and there is a coffee shop with fantastic pastries just outside,' Steel said with a surprised tone in his voice.

———

Steel made his way to the north entrance on Vesey Street. The targets and their keepers followed. The team leaders talking on their wrist mics, giving HQ updates.

'I don't understand why we don't just go back to the vehicles,' Graaf said, his voice filled with fear.

'Be my guest, but can you make sure I'm out of the building first? I've been blown up here once before; I don't want a repeat performance,' Steel said as he scanned the area for anything out of place. As he walked, he had that feeling that something wasn't quite right.

Steel stopped and raised a clenched fist; for him, it was second nature to give the military sign for stop and don't move, something the others weren't aware of.

'What is it?' asked one of the agents, grabbing Graaf's collar to stop him from moving.

'You know when something is too easy?' Steel asked as he crouched down and looked across the open floor.

'What are you thinking, Steel?' asked the agent as he followed suit.

'I was thinking about the bombs downstairs; if nobody said anything about the meet, that means they had been here for some time. If that is the case, for what?' Steel's gaze fixed on the floor as if he were expecting something to appear.

'Mr King, when was this meant to open?' Steel asked without moving from his position.

'Around two days from now, why?' King answered, confused by the question.

'Anyone special meant to be here?'

'Myself, the governor, the mayor, a couple of investors,' King answered, still failing to see a point.

'And no one else? A top name you are hiding so you don't ruin the surprise?' Steel pressed, feeling King wasn't entirely forthcoming with his answer.

'OK, the Vice President was asked to come and cut the ribbon,' King said with a disappointed tone.

Steel and the agent turned around slowly and stared at King with raised eyebrows.

'And you didn't think that was important enough to tell us?' the agent asked, suddenly getting onto his sleeve microphone.

Steel walked up to King, grabbing him by the epaulettes of his thousand-dollar suit and lifting him off the floor before slamming his back against one of the store windows. The glass shook but held. 'What's the connection between all this and the Vice President?' Steel growled.

King looked around, hoping someone would help him, but the rest held the look of people who would enjoy watching Steel tear him apart.

'Nothing, he has nothing to do with this,' King cried out.

Steel snarled, spun around, and launched King at the opposite window. There was a massive crash of glass as King flew through the display window and lay in broken glass and blood from the scratches he'd just endured.

Steel reached down and grabbed King again. 'Talk,' Steel ordered with bared teeth.

'I don't know anything,' King said between gasps of breath.

'That's OK; it's a big mall with lots of windows. Starting with this one,' Steel said, tossing King through the window he had just been forced against. The sound of breaking glass and yelps from King filled the walkway.

The other targets looked on with worried looks as if they knew they would be next if King died.

Steel walked over to King, dragged him out of the store, and tossed his bloodied body to the ground. King crouched on all fours, gasping to take in air like a runner after a marathon.

'No more, please, no more,' King begged, raising a hand to halt Steel's advance.

'So, what is the connection?' Steel asked again.

'Before he got where he is, he was a senator in New York, in charge of housing and refurbishment plans. You know what goes where, how much, and who gets the contract,' King started to explain as he lay on his side. 'He was doing OK, lots of work for the city, but then things started to dry up. The economy was taking a dive; fewer buildings were commissioned to local firms because they cost too much. So, we needed an edge.'

A look of anger crossed Steel's face as he figured out what was going on. 'So, if there were a crazy bomber, it would push out the competition, and your firm could move in, and the senator would get a cut,' Steel said, nodding as everything started to make sense.

'But, what's with the bombs downstairs?' asked the agent with a bemused look.

'If this place goes up, they could say that the police were wrong all of this time and that the bomber was still at large. And there would be the added bonus of getting rid of the senator, who I have no doubt was asking for more money, or he would blow the whistle,' Steel said with a smile. 'You wanted to shut up shop, but he wanted to keep going, knowing there was no trail to himself?'

'Pretty much,' King replied with a grim laugh. 'The greedy bastard said he had kept proof of everything; he would send it to the police and media if we didn't give him more money. A contribution to his run for President, he called it.'

'But that doesn't explain who was clearing house, why The Sentinel was after us,' Graaf said, shrugging.

'The Sentinel wanted revenge, The bombing here robbed The Sentinel of family, mom, dad, sister; you get the idea. So, The Sentinel tried to frighten you into giving up the details of all of your connections with Charles King, how he got the bomb used, and how he got off going to prison. The Sentinel wants you to talk, not to die. But yes, that does leave the question of who is trying to keep you silent.' Steel looked down at King, who simply shook his head as if to say he had no idea.

Steel turned back to the floor leading to their exit.

'So, why don't we just go?' Graaf said, pointing to the glass doors.

'I think this whole place is wired. When we broke in, it activated something,' Steel said, kneeling down again and grabbing a handful of dust and dirt from the floor. Steel looked at the secret service agent who had rejoined him.

'Do it,' said the agent, switching his gaze from Steel to the ground in front. Steel tossed the dust into the air as far as it would go and waited for it to float gently down. Thin green beams of light stretched from one side to the other.

Steel and the agent stood up and looked at each other.

'I believe the term you are looking for is "oh bugger,"' Steel said with a dry smile.

'I was going for something a little stronger, but yep, that sums it up,' replied the agent.

'What is it?' Dollman asked, unsure of what they had seen.

'Laser tripwire, probably one on each exit as well,' explained the agent before walking to the side and giving HQ an update.

'So, in other words, we are trapped here?' Graaf asked with a note of hysteria as he began to wander around in a circle.

'Someone wants you dead ... *all of you*. One of you knows who it is,' Steel said, looking at his watch.

All eyes fell on King, who was nursemaiding his wounds, until he felt everyone's staring eyes on him.

'Hey, don't look at me! I told you all I got,' King bleated, waving a bloody hand.

Steel looked around at the group of people, agents and targets together in a shitty situation. But there was something else bothering Steel as he looked closer at the crowd. Suddenly, his gaze landed on Brena.

'Why are you here, Brena?' he asked cautiously.

'We got the word about the meeting, and I thought I should be here because it's my case, remember?' Brena barked.

It was true, someone from the section was expected, but it wasn't Brena he was waiting for.

'So, where is Stanton?' Steel asked, his tone monotone and unfeeling, as though he was preparing himself for the bad news.

'What you asking about him for? He's probably back in his office, drinking himself to death.' Brena shrugged.

'Because I sent a message to Stanton to let him know about this. I told him to tell no one but leave the address written down somewhere on his desk; it's funny you should show, though,' Steel admitted in a disappointed tone.

'Why is that then?' Brena asked as he began to nudge his jacket to the side, feeling the walkway walls starting to close in as all eyes began to stare at him.

'Because you are here. If you had anything to do with all

this, you would have stayed away; I'm sorry to say I was wrong about you, Brena. I thought it was you,' Steel said with an angry look.

'Happy to disappoint you,' Brena said, taking Steel's look as a sign of defeat. A broad smile crossed his face.

'I'm disappointed, but it's not because of you; it's Stanton. So, either it's him we are looking for or ...' Frowning, Steel paused as if he could not complete the sentence for fear of it being true.

'The killer got to him,' Brena said, filling in the missing words. Brena had had suspicions that something was amiss when he'd arrived, and Stanton was a no-show.

Steel looked over at Brena, his anger still welling inside of him like a volcano ready to erupt.

'Get some people over to Stanton's place, check all flights out of Ronald Reagan, and make sure Stanton doesn't leave the state,' Steel ordered.

Brena nodded and complied; he didn't wasn't to get on Steel's bad side while he was still volatile.

Suddenly, Steel's phone let out three electronic beeps, signalling an incoming text. Yanking the cell from his pocket, he opened the message and read it. His look of anger seemed to double as he tucked the cell into his pocket.

'Bad news, I take it?' Brena asked, hoping to get more information than Steel's usual evasive shrug.

'The worst,' Steel answered before he started to walk down the walkway towards the door; everyone looked at him with confusion and fear.

'What are you doing—the tripwire, the bombs!' yelled Graaf as he grabbed King and hid behind him.

King shrugged off Graaf's weak grip, stood, and joined the others.

As Steel approached where the laser had been seen, he

knelt down and picked up a laser pointer and stuck it into his pocket. The others watched with anger at the deception.

'And the bombs?' Brena asked, walking towards Steel.

'Ah, that would be our doing, but it's his fault,' said the secret service agent with a half-cocked smile. 'Steel asked us to place stripped-out vehicles in the parking lot, dress them up like there were bombs inside. He said we would get a confession, and oh boy, was he right,' he explained, grabbing King and slapping handcuffs onto his wrists.

'So, this was all an elaborate setup; who else was part of this?' Brena asked.

'We were,' said familiar voices in unison. Brena turned to see Trish, Dutton, Simms, and Kitty standing before him. His mouth fell open from shock.

'You're—'

'Alive, very much so,' Kitty finished his sentence with a cat-like smile.

'Gentlemen, I'd like you to meet the team who was responsible for saving your worthless hides from The Sentinel and the killer.' Steel lied, knowing telling their actual involvement would jeopardise what they had been working on for so long.

'You were in on this?' Brena asked, shocked and angered nobody had told him.

'Yeah, sorry about that. They need to know that what they were doing was way past your pay grade. They had to act as they did to make the killer seem comfortable and make mistakes, and he did,' Steel continued matter-of-factly.

Brena shot him a confused look. 'How?' Brena asked as they stood on the walkway.

'He sent his assassin to take me out; as you can see, the mother failed, and he got his,' Dutton said with a grin.

Trish looked over at Dutton and gave him a look. Dutton's smile faded, and he stood cross-armed and moody.

'Assassin?' Brena asked, still trying to take it all in.

'Dorson ... real name Derick Abbot, ex-special forces Delta,' Steel answered.

Brena leant a hand against the concrete wall and tried to digest the information he had been thrown.

'And all this was Stanton's doing?' Brena asked slowly, 'He was this brains of the operation you were talking about?'

Steel smiled and shrugged before walking away, followed by Kitty and the rest of The Sentinel group. Brena watched them leave while the agents arrested the targets and led them downstairs. Brena stood up and put his hands on his hips as he looked around at the empty mall. Confusion and the fear of not knowing what he was supposed to do next swept over him. Finally, he let out a massive yell, kicked a wall, and ran after Steel and the team.

# CHAPTER FORTY-THREE

A FULL MOON HUNG IN A BLANKET OF A BILLION STARS. The midnight air was warm, with an occasional cool breeze that swept away the heat for a few seconds. The Cuban Hotel was lit up, giving it a grand appearance. The sound of crashing waves was dulled by the traditional music playing in the bar.

The door opened to room 120, and the drunken silhouette stumbled into the suite and headed for the bathroom. Brief grumbles and groans came from the unlit bathroom. The guest hadn't placed the room card into the slot to turn on the power. But he was too drunk to notice or care. The sound of him relieving himself echoed from the marble-fitted bathroom. Followed by another groan and mumble as he stumbled out and made his way to the bed.

There was a loud crash as the man's colossal body hit the bed like a dead weight. Then silence. The only sound was the muffled music downstairs and couples walking along the corridor. The man scratched himself and rubbed his gut, forcing the short-armed shirt bottom to come up over his navel. The drink and heavy meal had taken their toll and made the man tired and weak ... or possibly it was the cocktail of drugs that a quick hand had slipped into his drink at the bar.

As the man lay there, a figure slipped out of the shadows and moved carefully up to the man. A gloved hand went over his mouth to prevent any crying out. If the drugs had taken effect, the man would be unable to move, which would make the assassin's life easier. But, instead, the man's eyes opened as the gloved hand slipped over his mouth.

Director Frank Headly froze in place. Mostly out of fear, as well as the cocktail starting to take effect. He looked up at the masked figure. The suit was of a strange neoprene composition and a full-headed mask with two dark glass eyelets. Headly went to scream, but his vocal cords were frozen by the drug.

The assassin stood over Headly and took a syringe from a leg pouch. Headly began to sweat and tried to cry out. The drug had entirely kicked in, and the assassin would only have a short window before it wore off and disappeared from Headly's system.

The assassin took the safety cap off the needle and knelt over Headly but didn't tap the syringe to remove air bubbles. After all, Headly was going to die anyway.

The assassin moved the needle over Headly's navel and found a perfect spot in a crease of skin where a mosquito had gotten there before him. The assassin struck the needle in slowly but didn't inject the contents, not yet. The assassin wanted to look Headly in the eyes, to watch the life drain out of him before slipping away into the shadows.

The assassin pressed the plunger and watched. At first, there was nothing. Then, after several seconds, Headly started to convulse.

The assassin stood and moved back, knowing exactly what would occur. Vomit spewed from Headly's mouth, but he was powerless to do anything. Then the gurgling came as the vomit began to seep back into the trachea. It wouldn't be long now. The assassin could have left but decided to stay and watch the man who had ruined so many lives for profit choke.

The assassin didn't check to see if Headly was dead; if he weren't now, he would be later. Instead, the assassin headed to the balcony window and slipped out into the night.

———

The hotel bar was packed with tourists. The music was loud, but the roar of conversation was even louder. Kitty leant on the bar and ordered a drink ... six glasses of tequila. She smiled at the handsome young barkeep, then took the drinks that he had placed on a small tablet for her.

Kitty spotted a table in a quiet corner and made her way there. Her short black dress hugged her curves and complemented the black high heels. She placed the tray down, took a glass, and raised it as if to make a toast.

'To those, we have lost, and to those, we have gained,' Kitty said. There was a noise from behind her, but she didn't look.

'A bit selfish, starting without us,' Dutton said, sitting down beside her.

'She always was a little selfish, keeping all that stuff to herself about Steel,' Trish said, moving in close and giving her sister a loving peck on the cheek.

'What now, now it's all over, I mean?' Dutton asked, picking up his glass and raising it to salute the toast before downing it and sucking on the lime wedge.

Kitty and Trish stared at each other, almost as if hoping the other had the answer.

'Well, we are still active, so we can still do missions for the agency,' Kitty admitted.

Trish shrugged and nodded as though agreeing with the

plan.

'I'll drink to that,' Dutton said, picking up another glass and raising it up above his head. He looked around, puzzled for a moment as the glass was picked from his hand.

'Not if that's my drink, you're not,' said Steel, appearing from nowhere. He raised the glass and downed the liquid in one swallow before taking his seat.

Kitty looked at Steel and smiled.

'So, why are we all here?' she asked, puzzled but also happy at the location.

'Well, I figured you could all do with a vacation and possibly a new prospect,' Steel said, leaning back in his chair.

'What do you mean, prospect?' Dutton asked.

Steel looked up as a tall, thin man in his late fifties approached. He looked out of place in his white suit, but the white straw fedora made it work.

'Whose that? The guy from the 70s Bond movie?' Dutton asked.

Steel smiled and stood and said, 'He's your new employer. Meet Staff.'

The others looked at Steel, shocked.

'But we have an employer,' Kitty declared.

'Not anymore, you are still dead, and your two counterparts will be found in a burnt-out building; I'm afraid you were both killed on the last mission,' said Staff as he took Steel's seat.

'Right, Staff, I'll let you get acquainted,' Steel said, nodded at him and gave a strange smile before walking away slowly without so much as a goodbye.

'Wait! What happened to Headly and Stanton?' Kitty asked while Steel was in earshot.

'Stanton ... I'm afraid ... was found at the bottom of Potomac River. His car had come off the road. Well, that's the official story; he is actually head of our Bermuda office,' Staff smiled. 'As for Headly, who knows? Maybe he finally choked on his own greed.'

Steel smiled at the thought that justice had been served, but he couldn't shake the feeling that something still needed to be done.

Kitty excused herself from the table and ran after him. 'Hey, wait!'

Steel turned. 'What is it?' he asked with that cold stare he gave when detached from his feelings.

'You can't just go without saying goodbye,' Kitty said.

A thought slipped into Steel's head. He knew now what it was that he had to do. He reached forwards and cupped Kitty's face in his hands before placing a gentle kiss on her forehead.

'You'll be fine, all of you,' Steel said with a warm smile.

'And you?' Kitty asked with a concerned look.

Steel looked into the horizon and shrugged. 'I have to go. I'm wanted back in London; they have a new assignment for me.'

Kitty nodded. 'Until next time, then.'

'I can't wait' Steel smiled. He turned and walked away.

Kitty watched him disappear into a crowd of people. She sighed and turned towards the table and the group waiting for her. She whirled, taking one last glance at where Steel had been standing in time to see the police rushing into the hotel and a hysterical maid being led downstairs.

'What happened?' she asked one of the waiters taking fresh drinks to her table.

'Oh, some guy in one of the suites was found dead, choked on his own vomit they said. He was American, some guy named Hatley or something,' the waiter said before heading to the table.

'Headly. His name was Headly,' Kitty said with a satisfied smile.

## OTHER NOVELS IN THE JOHN STEEL SERIES:

# ABOUT THE AUTHOR

 Stuart Field is the author of the John Steel thriller series.

He's born in the West Midlands, Great Britain. Later, he joined the armed forces where after 22 years of fun and adventure, he left to start as a writer. Married with a daughter, he still hasn't grown up, which helps with the imagination. He loves to travel and experience other cultures. He loves to love life.

———

To learn more about Stuart Field and discover more Next Chapter authors, visit our website at www.nextchapter.pub.

Running Steel
ISBN: 978-4-82415-471-2

Published by
Next Chapter
2-5-6 SANNO
SANNO BRIDGE
143-0023 Ota-Ku, Tokyo
+818035793528

26th October 2022

CPSIA information can be obtained
at www.ICGtesting.com
Printed in the USA
LVHW101140191122
733278LV00024B/1392